The ties that bind
bring peril and
pleasure . . .

One last time . . .

I want to make love to you, Sophie."

With lowered eyes, she nodded even as guilt speared through her chest. Tristan seemed to sense it, and he pulled her more tightly against him. "You're my wife," he murmured. "Still mine."

He was right. She was lost in his arms, in his touch. There was no denying him. She was his and she wanted him.

His palm drifted down her back, curved over her bottom. She raised her mouth to his, anticipating the soft touch of his lips.

The door swung open so forcefully it banged against the inside wall. Tristan's arms fell. As if a bucket of cold water had been dumped over her head, Sophie jumped to her feet. Her heart pounding, she smoothed out the wrinkles in her skirt before looking up.

Garrett.

A Hint of Wicked

JENNIFER HAYMORE

FOREVER

NEW YORK   BOSTON

Copyright © 2009 by Jennifer Haymore
Excerpt from *A Touch of Scandal* copyright © 2009 by Jennifer Haymore
All rights reserved. Except as permitted under the U.S. Copyright Act of 1976, no part of this publication may be reproduced, distributed, or transmitted in any form or by any means, or stored in a database or retrieval system, without the prior written permission of the publisher.

Cover design by Claire Brown
Book design by Giorgetta Bell McRee

Forever
Hachette Book Group
237 Park Avenue
New York, NY 10017
Visit our Web site at www.HachetteBookGroup.com

Forever is an imprint of Grand Central Publishing.
The Forever name and logo is a trademark of Hachette Book Group, Inc.

Printed in the United States of America

First printing: June 2009

10 9 8 7 6 5 4 3 2

*To my husband. My partner and best friend,
and the sole human being responsible for my belief
in happily ever afters.*

Acknowledgments

My heartfelt gratitude goes to my incredible editor, Selina McLemore, who has helped me see the light again and again. If this book makes any sense at all, it is due to her skillful guidance. Also, to everyone at Grand Central Publishing, thank you so much.

To my brilliant agent, Barbara Poelle . . . I could go on and on about how fantastic she is, but I doubt the publisher will allow me ten pages of acknowledgments! To have Barbara in my corner feels like winning the lottery—it really does.

To my patient, understanding, and supportive family and friends, especially Alex, Nicholas, and Natasha, the most incredible kids in the world.

To all the ladies and gentlemen of The Beau Monde, who helped me with travel times and information about the British Army, and who are founts of information when it comes to anything to do with the Regency. Along the same lines, thanks to Courtney Milan, who took time away from busy and exciting events in her life to answer my legal questions, and to Tam D'Lyt, equestrienne extraordinaire, who taught me all about sidesaddles and what it's like to fall off a horse.

Heaps of thanks to Christine Wells—the gifted author who inspired me to write romance. And finally to all the people who helped shape *A Hint of Wicked* into the book it is today: Evie Byrne, Moira McTark, Maya Banks, Kate McKinley, Anya Delvay, and the talented writers at ERCC.

A Hint of Wicked

Prologue

London, June 1815

Sophie perched on the edge of the sofa cushion, her head tilted in concentration, her embroidery forgotten in her lap. Outside the drawing room's window, propped open by a servant to allow fresh air to waft into the otherwise stuffy room, the clomping of a horse's hooves came to an abrupt halt on the paving stones.

She glanced at Tristan, her dearest friend, who sat beside her on the silk palm-print sofa, his posture relaxed and his black hair extending in soft curls down his nape. He and his wife, Nancy, called on Sophie daily to rescue her from the incessant loneliness that had plagued her since her husband left for war. Nancy had recently gone to visit her ailing mother in Somerset, so this week Tristan had come alone.

Sensing Sophie's inability to speak, Tristan smiled at her, showing his dimple—a deep impression at the edge of his lips. He curled his fingers over hers and squeezed gently. "Should I see who it is, Soph?"

Sophie looked back at the window. The curtains fluttered in the breeze, the satiny material shimmering like a sunlit forest, as if welcoming someone to part them and peer into the gathering dusk. She nodded stiffly and blinked hard against the sting in her eyes.

It had been like this for days, ever since they'd heard the battle of Waterloo was over. Each time a carriage rolled down the drive or she heard horseshoes clattering over the paving stones, a tumultuous mixture of excitement and fear boiled through her. Was it Garrett coming home to her? News of his whereabouts? News of his death on the field of battle?

Tristan released her hand and unfolded his tall, graceful body from the sofa. As always, he was dressed smartly, in an expertly tailored black tailcoat with a striped waistcoat and matching buff trousers. As Tristan strode over to the window, Sophie's heart constricted, for she knew he feared for Garrett as much as she did. Tristan was Garrett's closest companion, his heir and cousin. Since Garrett had left them, Tristan had been the one to offer her support and strength, but subtle signs of strain had appeared in him during the past month: the lines around his expressive brown eyes, the tightening of his features, and seriousness replacing his usual debonair approach to life.

Parting the curtains, he stood with his back to her, his body framed by the green fabric as he bent his dark head and surveyed the activity on the drive below. Sophie watched him mutely, her hand resting atop the rounded curve of her belly.

It must be something to do with Garrett, otherwise

Tristan would have comforted her the instant he glanced outside.

She prayed Tristan had seen Garrett dismounting and entering the house at a near run, eager to see her. Perhaps her husband was on his way upstairs right now. Sophie closed her eyes, picturing him throwing open the door with a grin spread over his rugged, handsome face. Her frozen limbs would melt, and she'd cry out with joy and leap into his arms.

Finally, Tristan spoke. "It's Sir Thomas," he said raggedly. "Alone."

Sophie pried her eyes open, but she couldn't look at Tristan. Sir Thomas was Garrett's aide. To see him anywhere but at Garrett's side was simply . . . *wrong*. She stared across at the dying embers of the fire, at the flickering golden light glancing through the room's shadows. Suddenly her London drawing room felt oppressive. She wanted to be outside, but not in the city. At Calton House in the north, where she and Garrett and Tristan had played together as children, young and carefree, all of them believing they could live forever.

The baby fluttered against her ribs, and she soothed her fingers over the soft blue muslin of her dress. Likely the poor babe sensed her anxiety. She took deep breaths and willed herself to be calm. She'd do anything to keep this miracle child from harm.

She felt Tristan's gaze resting on her. His footsteps echoed hollowly on the wood floor as he came to stand beside the sofa.

The wait seemed an eternity, but in fact it was just a few moments before a soft knock sounded at the door.

When she didn't answer, Tristan said, "Come in," his voice gruff.

Connor opened the door, and Sophie's eyes riveted to him. "Lieutenant Sir Thomas Johnson is here to see you, Your Grace." The butler took a deep breath, but managed to keep his expression professionally blank. "He says it is a matter of some urgency."

Still Sophie couldn't find her voice. Beside her, Tristan nodded at Connor, who left, returning a few moments later in the company of the red-haired officer. She had met Sir Thomas before, and she had known him to be a jovial sort of man. Today his lips were drawn tight and curved down at their edges, and deep grooves furrowed his forehead.

Tristan's palm rested on her shoulder blade, gentle, lending her strength. She pushed the embroidery off her lap and rose to her feet on wobbly legs.

Connor closed the door behind the lieutenant, leaving the three of them alone. Sir Thomas bowed stiffly. Her gaze roamed over him, taking in his stiff posture and dress, the letter clutched in his left hand, his curly red hair combed sternly back from his face, his heavy auburn side whiskers. His somber expression and sorrowful eyes. The pungent smell of perfumed soap wafted from his body, making her lightheaded.

"No," she whispered. Tristan's arm tightened round her waist, the only thing keeping her upright.

Sir Thomas's Adam's apple moved up and down as he swallowed. He blinked several times, then seemed to find the power of speech. "Your Grace, I've come with news of your husband."

He paused.

"Out with it," Tristan growled.

"The colonel, ah . . . the duke . . ."

"No," Sophie murmured again, shaking her head violently.

Sir Thomas licked his lips. When he spoke, the words came in rapid fire, each as painful as a dart stabbing into her chest. "I'm sorry, ma'am. But the Duke of Calton fell at the battle of Waterloo. He was injured, but we do not yet know if he perished, as we have not been able to locate his body. However, we retain little hope that he survived."

"No, no, no . . ." Hot tears streaming down her face, Sophie turned to Tristan. He wrapped his arms around her and consoled her while she wept, stroking her back and muttering soothing words into her ear. Sir Thomas stood silently, awkwardly, to the side, his gaze fastened on a potted palm in the corner of the room.

When her sobs had abated and only the tears remained, rolling down her face like drops of rain against a windowpane, Sir Thomas spoke again. "I've a letter from His Grace the Duke of Wellington, madam. He told me personally that it commends your husband's valiant and honorable deeds on the battlefield. Also, be assured that the British Army is determined to find the colonel, and that we will bring his . . . him home."

She clung to Tristan. Was her life over? How could she go on without Garrett? How could she possibly survive this?

"He might still be alive," Tristan said into her hair, his voice low and echoing her own grief. "Until we find him, we must believe that he lives."

"No," she whispered between her sobs. "No, no. Don't

you see?" If Garrett lived, he'd have already come home to her. He'd promised her it would be so. Colonel Garrett James, Third Duke of Calton, never broke a promise.

"We will find him, Sophie. We will go to the Continent and we will find him."

But they never did.

Chapter One

London, April 1823—Eight Years Later

Sophie slowed her chestnut mare to a walk. Beside her, tall and handsome in the saddle of his dapple gray, Tristan mimicked her command, and their horses fell in step side by side. Holding the reins in one hand, Sophie flattened her gloved palm against her mount's warm neck and took a deep, refreshing breath of the crisp morning air. The tree-lined track was quiet and serene this morning, likely due to the impending foul weather. The atmosphere was cool and heavy with the promise of rain, so she and Tristan had left home early hoping for a brisk outing before the heavens opened. A heavy frost glistened on the branches. Drops coalesced beneath the budding leaves and slipped to the ground, shimmering like tiny diamonds.

She slid a glance at Tristan, smiling at the way the dampness made his satiny black hair curl beneath the rim of his hat. "Are you ready for tonight?"

It was to be their first dinner party in London since they'd arrived in February for the opening of Parliament.

Their first dinner party as husband and wife. They'd wed last July, but they'd spent the short nine months of their married life in the relative quiet of Calton House in Yorkshire. Tonight was to be the first of many parties to come—in a few weeks' time, Garrett's young sister would be joining them for her first London Season.

Tristan gave Sophie a cocky, boyish grin that reached all the way to his sparkling chocolate-colored eyes. "I'm more than ready for tonight. What about you?"

She urged her horse into a gallop, and before he could respond, she threw a smile over her shoulder. "Of course I am," she called back.

Tristan's eyes narrowed, and he flicked the reins. Giddy with the prospect of a little competition, Sophie turned forward, tightened her knee around the pommel, and leaned close to the horse's sleek neck, whispering encouragement for more speed.

Hooves churned the earth, splattering wet clumps of dirt in their wake. Cold wind whipped through Sophie's hair as she crouched low, the rhythm of the gallop singing through her body. The skirts of her riding habit whipped against the mare's flanks, and she squealed in glee. They were winning.

She saw the patch of ice a moment too late. The horse slid on the white surface, her legs thrashing with the effort to stay upright. Sophie struggled to stay balanced. She hauled backward on the reins to keep the mare's head up, but the poor animal's body flailed beneath her. They were going down. The horse was going to fall on her.

Sophie wrenched her right leg from the sidesaddle pommel and kicked her left foot free of the stirrup. She launched herself from the horse just as the animal's legs buckled.

Sophie slammed to the ground in a puddle of icy water. The jolt speared pain from her hip through her body. With a thud that seemed to shake the earth, the horse hit the ground, her girth missing Sophie's legs by mere inches.

Sweet relief coursed through her, only to be replaced by renewed panic as the struggling mare scrambled for footing and jerked Sophie through soft mud toward her kicking legs.

Oh, no. Oh, Lord. The train of her riding habit had caught on one of the pommels.

As the mare heaved her body upright, Sophie grabbed handfuls of dark wool and yanked on her skirts with all her might.

The fabric came free with a screeching tear just as the horse found her feet, a flailing hoof pummeling Sophie on the thigh.

She lay there in the frigid puddle, stunned, straining for air, her skirts tangled around her legs and heavy with mud. Her leg throbbed. Her lungs had closed. She couldn't breathe.

Tristan came to a sliding stop on his knees in the mud beside her. He gathered her into his arms, combing the hair out of her face with his fingers. She dimly registered that she must've lost her hat.

"Sophie! Are you all right? Are you all right, love?"

Her lungs opened slightly and she gasped in a deep breath. "Yes. I—I think so."

Tristan's dark eyes glimmered. His body was like steel, strong all around her, but the slightest tremble in his movements betrayed his fear.

Clutching her husband's arms and taking great gulps of air, Sophie assessed herself. Her thigh throbbed, but she could move her leg, so it was probably only badly bruised. She was wet, bogged down with water and muck. It was quite embarrassing, really. "I—I'm all right, Tristan."

He gripped her closer and pressed his lips to her hair. She held on to him for several minutes, sitting on his lap with his large body curled around her smaller one. Buried within the cocoon of his warmth and comfort, she began to breathe normally again.

The sound of scuffing dirt made her pull her face away from Tristan. She raised her head to see a man had taken hold of her horse's reins and was leading her back to them. The animal walked normally and seemed fine. Thank goodness she hadn't been hurt.

Conscious of her disheveled appearance, Sophie tensed. Tristan tucked the skirt of her riding habit down so it covered her calves, and adjusting her to a comfortable position against him, he rose, easily lifting her.

"Oh goodness, Tristan. I can walk. I can ride, too."

He looked down at her, his brow creased. "Are you sure?"

"Quite sure."

Gently, he eased her to her feet. Pain radiated down her leg, and she tightened her hand over his arm. He held on to her, his strength keeping her steady. "All right?"

Sophie grimaced. The fall itself was humiliating, and she had no wish to make a dramatic production of it. She'd been kicked in the leg, but that was a minor injury, and she didn't need coddling. She smiled reassuringly at him. "Absolutely all right."

He released his hold and gave her a quick, jerky nod

before striding over to thank the man who'd returned with her horse. She saw that he was just as disheveled as she—maybe even more so. Tristan was usually fastidious in the extreme, but he didn't pay any attention to the mud drenching him from the waist down.

After exchanging a few polite words with the Good Samaritan, Tristan took his leave and led the mare over to her.

"How is she?" Sophie tried not to limp as she stepped toward them. She stroked the horse's silky brown muzzle, murmuring apologies. Her pocket had remained miraculously dry, and scooping out a crushed lump of sugar, she offered it to the mare.

"Uninjured and surprisingly calm." Tristan's big, warm hand curled over her upper arm and squeezed. "Can you ride, love?"

"Of course." She smiled up at him. "It is my own fault—a foolish mistake. I should have paid more attention."

Tristan nodded grimly, but he didn't argue with her. "We're going straight home." Without asking her if she needed help—he knew she did—he lifted her and set her upon the saddle. He held on to her longer than necessary as she slid her muddy foot into the stirrup and adjusted the torn and muddy skirts modestly around her. When he did let her go, it was with hesitation. "Straight home," he repeated firmly, meeting her eyes with an expression that brooked no argument.

She watched his lithe, muscular body move with grace as he mounted his horse and rode beside her. His dark gaze bore into her. "Ready?"

His eyes glimmered with worry. His shoulders were tight with frustration, and she knew he had wanted to hold her longer, to comfort her, to carry her home rather than let her risk riding. But he'd respected her wishes and let her show her independence and save her pride.

She could hardly tear her eyes from him. Even half drenched in mud, he was so magnificent, it made her blood heat and her pulse quicken just to look at him.

With a secret inner smile, she turned her horse toward Mayfair. "Yes, I'm ready, Tristan. Let's go home."

The patterned red silk of Sophie's dressing robe whispered over her skin, light and cool after the warm, heavy brocade she had worn to the party. She'd gone to check on the children, and finding them fast asleep, had kissed them goodnight, returned to her dressing room, and called her maid to undress her. Now she sat, finally alone at her table, drawing the pins from her coiffure one by one, watching in the oval gilded mirror as the tendrils of honey-brown hair fell away from her tight chignon.

She paused in midaction as a sudden memory assailed her. Garrett standing behind her, removing her hairpins in the same methodical order, using his fingers to fan her hair over her shoulders. He watched her in the mirror with that stormy look in his blue eyes. The look that reminded her of crashing ocean waves in a storm. The look that said he wanted her.

Sophie curled her toes into the lush ivory strands of the carpet. Dropping the final hairpin on the glossy surface of the mahogany table, she clutched its edge and stared into the mirror, taking deep breaths to regain her composure.

The unbidden memories came less frequently now. She supposed that was natural after so many years.

She didn't want to forget Garrett. At times, she welcomed the memories, coveted them. But not tonight. Tonight she wished to think only of Tristan, of his long, lean body, his disarming smile, his caresses. The way he'd slid into the mud today to hold her body against his, tight and comforting. The sheer desperation in his expression before he'd realized she was all right.

As if her thoughts had summoned him, the door separating her dressing room from their bedchamber swung open. Swiping the back of her hand over her damp eyes, Sophie reached for her hairbrush. She watched in the mirror as Tristan closed the distance between them, sharp as ever in his snug gray trousers and embroidered waistcoat, the gold thread matching the color of his cravat. He'd untied the cravat, and it hung loose about his neck.

"That didn't take long," she murmured, smiling at him.

"I came as quickly as I could, love." He grinned at her, revealing straight white teeth and the single dimple that always had the ability to melt her heart. "Got rid of Billingsly. Even tales of his Egyptian travels can't entice me when I know you're in our bedchamber . . ." a hint of wickedness quirked his lips and sparkled in his eyes in an expression he reserved for her alone, ". . . waiting."

As she dragged the brush through her hair, Tristan rested his hands on her shoulders. Long-fingered and elegant, with blunt, clean fingernails, his hands weren't the only part of him that hinted at his position in society. His face was aristocratic, with clean lines, sharp angles, and shrewd, dark eyes. But his refined mannerisms and famed control proved he was of the higher orders. Though he may not have coveted Garrett's legacy, he suited his new role as the Duke of Calton.

"How's your leg?"

She forced a smile. A nasty bruise had bloomed on her thigh, but she was thankful. It could have been so much worse. "It's all right. I scarcely feel it anymore."

His smile faded as they locked gazes in the mirror. "Ah, Soph . . ." His voice trailed off, and he must have seen the residual grief in her expression, because the pain in his eyes suddenly reflected her own.

He squeezed her shoulders. "I miss him, too, love. Every day."

Tilting her head to glance up at him, she smiled sadly. Tristan was the one person in the world who understood her loss. He, too, had lost a spouse. Nancy had died giving birth to their son two years after Waterloo. Though Sophie knew he'd loved her, Tristan rarely spoke of Nancy.

Yet the loss of Garrett was different. Garrett had been gone longer, but he remained a solid presence in their lives— perhaps because they had retained hope for so long.

Tristan was patient with her melancholy. Most men would have despised her for continuing to love a dead man. Most men would have been jealous of her unwilling- ness to let go of her affection for Garrett. But not Tristan. He knew how much she had loved Garrett, and he never tried to take that away from her.

"It's just—nights like tonight—" Struggling to order her thoughts, she shrugged helplessly.

She never intended to make Tristan feel inferior, be- cause he wasn't. He was simply different. When she fell in love with Tristan, it seemed her heart swelled to twice its previous capacity to make room for him.

Still, more than anything, she feared hurting Tristan by clinging so desperately to her feelings for Garrett. If she lost him as she had lost Garrett . . . The thought was intolerable. If that happened, she wouldn't be able to endure it.

"I know," he murmured, as if reading her mind. His lips brushed against her hair. "I understand. I do."

"I'm sorry."

He rose to his full height. "Don't be sorry, Soph."

She set the brush on the table and stood, twining her arms around his neck. The linen of his cravat brushed against her skin as she pressed her cheek to his solid chest. He smelled like exotic spice, like the Eastern countries he was so fond of. "I adore you," she said. "You mean everything to me."

His fingers sifted through her hair as he tilted her head to face him. He laughed, but the sound was ragged. "I can't force you to forget him, Sophie. Hell, I can't forget him. You know how strongly I cared for him. He was more than a brother to me."

"Yes." She tightened her arms around him. "Thank you."

He nuzzled his face in her hair, his breath hot against her scalp. "We've come far, wouldn't you say?"

Sophie nodded. "Yes."

They'd come much farther than she ever would have imagined. Their wedding night had been difficult. She'd been shy and awkward, and she couldn't shake the feeling that she was betraying Garrett's memory. It was the first time for her since the day Garrett left with his regiment to fight at Waterloo.

But Garrett was gone. Tristan was her husband now, and in the past months, he'd earned her complete trust. In his arms, she'd exposed everything to him, from her life's desires to her deepest and darkest fantasies. They shared a level of openness and communication she'd never thought to have with anyone.

"There was no need to rush up," she said in order to change the subject, her voice muffled against his chest. "I would not have begrudged your talking with Mr. Billingsly. I know how you crave news of Egypt."

"Not as much as I used to. I find myself perfectly content wherever you and the children are. Egypt seems more of a youthful fancy these days."

His admission stole the breath from her lungs. Tristan was an adventurer, a traveler. His wanderlust had always been a mystery to her. She felt most comfortable at home, either here in Mayfair or at Calton House in the north. While she'd waited patiently for Garrett's infrequent trips home, Tristan had explored half the globe. China, India, Madagascar. Jamaica, Ireland, Italy, and America. When he married Nancy, he didn't stop. Nancy always said good-naturedly that it was a miracle he'd managed to get her with child, he was gone so often.

He'd never visited Egypt, though. When they were children, an Egyptian adventure had been his dream.

She rubbed her cheek against his chest and sighed. "Perhaps I have domesticated you after all."

A soft murmur of contentment was his only response. His body pressed against her in all the right places, hinting at the pleasure he could give. She slipped her hands from his neck to his shoulders. Muscles rippled beneath her fingertips, and keeping her fingers light, she skimmed lower, down his back to curve over his behind.

He stroked the slippery fabric of her robe and pulled her tight against him so his erection prodded her belly. When he spoke, his voice was husky in her ear. "Billingsly's travels couldn't hold my attention tonight. I kept thinking of you alone up here. Everything pales beside the promise of having you, love. Seeing you, touching you . . . taking you . . ."

The way he spoke to her, the way he felt against her . . . there was nothing like it in the world. The blood ran heavy and slow through Sophie's veins, warming her, making her muscles languid. Her breaths came in shallow little pants. As hard as pebbles, her nipples pushed against the silk of her dressing gown. She sensed the change inside her body as it heated and opened, eager for his invasion.

Sophie reached between them and untied the belt of her robe. The silk slipped off her shoulders and pooled on the floor, leaving her bare. Cool air brushed over her sensitive skin, raising gooseflesh on her legs and arms.

She ran her lips along his jaw, speaking softly. "Make love to me, Tristan."

Cupping her face in his hands, he brought his lips down over hers. "You taste so good, Sophie," he murmured against her mouth. "I can't get enough of you."

He knelt lower, his lips drifting over her shoulder. "I thought I might lose you this morning." His hands dropped to her waist and tugged her even closer, pressing her against him from top to bottom, and a deep shudder resonated through his body.

Sophie reached up to caress the masculine planes of his face. "I was scared, too," she admitted. She slid the cravat from his neck and kissed him. She loved his lips. So soft and firm at the same time. Delicious.

The wool of his trousers was in the way, and she fumbled at the buttons of his falls, but he stopped her by capturing her wrists in his hand.

She pulled away from their kiss. "No?"

"No, love. Not yet."

Soft material slid over her skin and she glanced downward to see he'd caught his cravat and looped it around her wrists.

Her heart pounding, she looked up at him, running her tongue nervously over her bottom lip. His expression was serious when he met her gaze. But she knew him well enough to see the glint of anticipation lurking in the depths of his eyes.

"I'm going to tie you to the bed."

Her lips parted as she stared at him. It was a secret desire of hers to be bound while he ravished her. She had told him of it once, late in the night when they had shared their most intimate fantasies, but he had remained silent. Later, she dismissed it, thinking her easygoing husband would never desire such a thing. Then again, in the past months she had learned that his nighttime personality differed from his daytime façade. With the shift between his public and private existence, Tristan transformed from respectable and personable to dark and mysterious.

Her throat was so dry, she could scarcely speak. "Why?"

He held her wrists loosely in his hand, unmoving, studying her with eyes that bored into her soul. "It will please me."

She released a shallow breath.

"I want you tied down. Helplessly bound." His voice grew rough. "I want you focused on me alone."

Sophie closed her eyes. In her daily life, she was a mother, a leader, a *duchess*. An upright model of society. She made important decisions quickly and with aplomb. She avoided showing weakness.

At night, though, Tristan relished exposing the secret fragile part of her. For whatever the reason, she gloried in it. When he exercised his power over her, it made her feel feminine and beautiful, cherished and protected. It was the ultimate release.

Nonetheless, if she told him no, he would stop. Instantly.

With her heart pounding against her breastbone, she looked up at him and made a small movement of her head. A nod.

The corners of his lips quirked upward, then he tugged her hands. "Hold them out for me."

Biting her lower lip, she did as he instructed. She felt so vulnerable like this, with him still fully clothed and her naked and standing before him, offering herself to him to do with as he pleased. Yet it felt right.

She shivered from heat rather than cold as he wrapped the neckcloth around her wrists, twisted and looped, deftly creating an intricate knot.

"It's a French bowline. Should keep you nicely bound," he murmured with one final tug. "Now go lie on the bed and wait for me there."

She walked through the door into their bedchamber and to their high, ornately carved antique bed, feeling his gaze on her bottom as she mounted the step and crawled between the rust damask bed curtains. The gold tassel brushed against her hip as she climbed onto the mattress. A chambermaid had turned down the heavy counterpane earlier, and the bed linens cooled Sophie's heated skin as she settled over them. Her cheeks burned, whether with embarrassment or arousal, she wasn't certain. Probably both.

On her knees with her hands clasped together in front

of her, she paused to look over her shoulder. Tristan stood at the threshold between the rooms, watching.

"Good. I'll be right back." Turning away, he vanished into her dressing room.

She wondered why he had left her, but she knew he wouldn't keep her alone for long. Relishing each scrape of the sheets on her sensitive skin, she settled onto her back. A puff of warm air washed over her as the fire hissed and crackled. By the time she'd situated herself, Tristan had reentered the bedroom with a pair of her silk stockings dangling from his fingertips.

"For your ankles." He arched a questioning brow at her.

Pressing her lips together, her heart beating wild with anticipation, she nodded again. She would do anything he asked—anything for him to touch her, satisfy her. Focused solely on the man she loved, she had nearly forgotten her melancholy. How had Tristan known how much she wanted this—*needed it*—tonight?

Silently and with exquisite slowness, he bound her hands to a bedpost, then followed suit with her ankles, using a stocking to tie each one to an opposing post. He paused to brush soothing fingers near the lurid bruise on her thigh, his face darkening at the memory of her fall.

Finally he stepped back to survey his handiwork. The ties dug into the flesh of her wrists and ankles enough to make her very aware of them but not enough to cut off the flow of blood. She lay with her arms overhead and her hands clasped, her legs spread and her center pulsing hot. Her breasts were heavy and tender, her nipples flushed dark. From her toes to her fingertips, her skin prickled with sensitivity and ached for his soothing touch.

He walked around the high bed, scrutinizing her body.

He cupped her mound in his palm and pressed gently. She fought against the urge to wiggle, to beg him for more. "It's what you want, isn't it?" he said in a low voice. "To be bound to my bed, subjected to my will?"

"Yes," she breathed.

His dark gaze snapped to her mouth. "What was that?"

"Yes, Tristan. It's what I need. What I want."

His lips curled into a predatory smile.

Never breaking his focus from her body, he removed his waistcoat, taking time with each cloth-covered button, and finally pulled off his shirt, exposing his lean torso. If she'd been free, nothing could have stopped Sophie from touching him, from running her hands up and down his body, over the smooth, taut skin of his chest.

He doused the two lamps—one on a round table by the hearth and the other near the doorway. Now, the fire and a single burning candle on the bedside table provided the faint, flickering light in the room.

He climbed onto the step. She turned her head toward him, at eye level with his falls, watching as he slid the buttons through their holes and pushed the trousers down his narrow hips.

Just then, a crashing noise sounded from below. From the entry hall, perhaps. Sophie froze, and Tristan did as well, but he relaxed when there was no further sound. "The servants must've dropped something."

"I should make sure everything is all right."

He frowned, and his eyes sparked. "Now?"

"Well . . ." She hesitated, unsure, her desire to please him warring with her need for control in her household.

"No," he said flatly. "You're mine now, you know that."

He paused. "You're not to worry about anything else, not until morning. Do you understand?"

His words sent a thrill of pleasure through her, and any lingering desire for control fled. She shuddered, warm and wet and wanting. His fingers tightened over her jaw, hard enough to leave pink imprints on her cheek. She didn't care about the crash downstairs. She needed only him.

"I understand."

His fingers loosened, and he ran them down her cheek, light as a feather. He skimmed her jawline, then moved downward. She arched her neck to welcome his touch as he found her pulse point and murmured, "Your heart beats so fast, Soph."

He focused intently on the path of his hand as it traced her collarbone and then smoothed down the center of her chest before curling around the breast closest to him, squeezing gently. Sophie strained toward him. A muscle moved in his jaw. His lips, even pressed together in concentration, were full and soft. If she were free, she would pull his head down to her so she could kiss him. She would tug his body over hers and feel him everywhere she could, reveling in the contact of their skin in all the possible places it could touch. But she couldn't. She couldn't kiss him, couldn't touch him. She could only be patient and wait for him to give her more.

He rubbed his thumb over her nipple, and Sophie drew in a sharp breath. She was so needy, so sensitive.

Light flickered over his torso, capturing her focus as shades of bronze spattered across his olive-toned skin. Tristan was not a bulky man, but he was an active one, and taut muscles enhanced the shape of his body from his wide shoulders to his flat stomach and narrow hips. His chest expanded as he took a deep breath and stroked her nipple again.

"Tristan . . ." Her eyes fluttered shut as his touch rebounded through her. When she opened them, she let her gaze roam lower.

His waist tapered into his hips, the edges of his buttocks hollowed. Rising from its nest of dark curls, his erection strained upward. Gooseflesh broke out on her arms and legs. She was hot and cold and achy . . . and she wanted him.

He squeezed her breast, and she squirmed against the resulting vibration between her legs. "Don't do that again, Sophie."

"Don't . . . what?"

"Scare me like you did this morning." His eyes narrowed at her, his jaw tight, his posture stiff. He was dead serious.

"I'll . . . try," she breathed as he palmed her breast.

"I can't lose you," he said from between gritted teeth. "Do you understand?"

"Yes . . . Tristan . . . I need . . ." But she couldn't finish the thought, because his hand left her breast and slipped between her parted legs.

"I know what you need, love." He groaned as he slid two fingers deep inside her. "You're so wet for me."

She tilted her hips, angling for him to press his fingers deeper.

He pulled out until his fingertips feathered over her sensitive folds. "Do you want me, Sophie?"

"Yes."

He rewarded her with a thrust of his fingers so deep it made her toes curl.

"Over you?"

"Yes."

Another thrust. She moaned, squeezing her eyes shut.

"Do you want me inside you?"

"Yes, Tristan. Yes, please."

In seconds, he was looming over her, his muscles flexing as he supported himself on his arms. Spread and trussed as she was, she couldn't wrap her legs around him—she could only take whatever he chose to give. But she didn't care. Tristan on top was her favorite position. She loved watching the raw, intense need on his face as he moved inside her.

She looked into his eyes as he arranged himself at her entrance. He didn't need to say he loved her. Words were unnecessary. Love poured from his expression, from his actions, from his pores. Her love for him, she knew, was equally evident. In every movement, every blink, every gasp she made for him, she loved him. How he made her feel, the sublime intensity of his caresses, could only be explained by the depth of their affection for each another.

He inched into her, making her whimper with every slight movement that pushed his sex deeper inside. Her channel was slick and tight around him, and so sensitive.

Finally he was fully seated. They throbbed together, their bodies held immobile by the sensation. Whose heartbeat was beating so deeply between her legs? Hers or his? Both, perhaps, joined as they themselves were joined, in body, heart, and spirit.

Holding his hips still, he bent to flick his tongue over her nipples. When she was reduced to gasping and squirming with need, impatient for him to let go, he rose to face her. Bracing his elbows on either side of her head, he slanted his lips over hers as he moved inside her, deep enough to make her pant uncontrollably at the end of each thrust as the tip of his shaft nudged against her womb.

His lips slid softly against hers, gentle in contrast to the hot, slick hardness between her legs. She sucked his bottom lip between her teeth and nipped. He deepened the kiss, strengthening his penetration, exploring her mouth with his tongue until the thrusts of his tongue matched the thrusts of his body.

He pushed into her again and again, brushing her inside, stroking her most sensitive spot. The pleasure spread through her, hot and piercing, building until her every muscle tightened and trembled from the tension.

Until, all at once, she shattered.

Her eyes squeezed shut, she gasped as waves of pleasure crashed through her body, making it undulate so fiercely, the silk and linen binding her strained against the bedposts. Some part of her pleasure-drenched consciousness heard a second crash and registered that it was much closer than the first.

And then Tristan shouted, but it was a cry of surprise rather than fulfillment. His body was ripped away from hers. Cold air washed over her skin, and with her limbs still shuddering from the aftereffects of the orgasm, she opened her eyes, squinting against a harsh light.

A shadowy male figure held her naked husband by the neck. The man's fists flew, pummeling Tristan as he cursed at him in a low, hate-filled, growling voice, calling him a bastard, a perverse bloody rapist. Light came from the doorway and haloed both men, making them appear as black figures silhouetted by the stark brightness behind them.

One big fist clipped Tristan in the jaw, snapping his

head back. Tristan grunted in surprise, and Sophie yanked against her bonds with all her might. "No!" she cried. "Stop! Stop at once!"

She had to break free, save Tristan, separate him from the intruder, the lunatic was trying to kill him . . .

A crack resonated through the room as another fist smashed against bone.

Not Tristan. Please . . . She writhed, her skin burning where the twisted fabric dug into it, the knots unforgiving.

More muffled curses and the thump of connecting blows made her struggle harder—she had to get loose, if it meant tearing the bed apart, ripping the fabric . . . But Tristan had bound her expertly, and no matter how desperately she fought, she couldn't free herself.

A group of figures huddled at the threshold beyond the fighting men. The servants, she realized, most of them holding lanterns. Watching the scene, mouths agape—her naked and tied to the bed, the stranger attempting to kill their master.

Oh, Lord, no. This couldn't be happening. Her shouts faded, the fight in her body drained away. With effort, she focused on Tristan. He had wrenched himself free from the man and was defending himself, now striking at the man's ribs . . . his head.

His face.

Sophie froze. His face swam in her vision as her eyes adjusted to the light, blurring and then snapping into focus.

She knew that man. She knew the way he moved, knew the shape of him. She knew the broad cheekbones and the stormy look in his blue eyes.

It was her dead husband.

It was Garrett.

Chapter Two

Somewhere deep in Tristan's consciousness it registered that a dead man had dragged him away from his wife and was attempting to beat the hell out of him.

The intensity of the shock and surprise sweeping through him didn't seem to matter, though. Fighting Garrett came as naturally as it always had.

Light flooded the room and Sophie's protests faded into the background. Tristan squinted at his assailant. Garrett looked somewhat the worse for wear, but he was as wide and imposing as ever. A cracking jolt speared through Tristan's knuckles and up his arm as one of his jabs glanced off Garrett's ribs, and something nudged at the edge of his mind. Why hadn't Sophie broken them up? Whenever they fought, she came between them, and in her calming way, always made them stop.

Then he remembered why she didn't intervene. And . . . *oh, hell* . . .

He took a precious moment to glance at his wife,

confirming the worst. Still bound to their bed, her exposed body shimmered in the lamplight, the dark bruise on her thigh a stark contrast to her pale skin. She lay limp and unmoving, her glazed eyes fixed upon Garrett.

In the instant it took for Tristan to process that information, Garrett's fist slammed against his cheek. Tristan went reeling, pain ripping through his face. The hit propelled him toward Sophie, and he lunged for the bed.

"Sophie!" He wrenched the twisted counterpane from beneath her legs and tossed it over her body.

Garrett grabbed his shoulder and yanked him around, his blue eyes swirling with violence. "Bastard."

Sophie's voice, calm and clear, cut through the battle haze. "Stop it."

He blinked and watched Garrett do the same. But Garrett shook it off, raised a bunched fist, and aimed for Tristan's nose.

As the punch shot forward, Tristan ducked and leveled two quick strikes at Garrett's abdomen. It was like connecting with steel, though he was mollified to hear Garrett release his breath in pained gasps as the blows connected.

The big man's jabs came in rapid fire, but Tristan, always the faster, ducked away. As he leveled another solid blow at Garrett's gut, Sophie gave a desperate shout. "Tom, please restrain my husband!"

The burly groom rushed toward them. He yanked Garrett's arms behind him, dragging him backward over the carpet. Garrett twisted from Tom's grip, but another man, a dark-haired gentleman Tristan had never seen before, joined Tom, and together they managed to restrain him.

Her husband. Garrett was her husband.

Tristan ground his teeth so hard his jaw hurt. His heart tightened in his chest, balling into a heavy lump as the gravity of the situation barreled through him.

Good God.

"Garrett . . ." Sophie whispered.

Garrett finally tore his focus from Tristan. He stopped struggling the instant his gaze met hers. "Sophie?"

The way he looked at her, as if she were his only hope for salvation in a world of madness, made Tristan tense and ready for battle all over again. Sophie returned that look, her expression full of all the pain of the past years. Overwhelming all the other emotions was joy. Tears pooled in her eyes, and she smiled, mouthing, *Garrett, Garrett, Garrett.*

As a cloud of dread settled over him, Tristan caught a glimpse of a wool throw on the edge of the bed. He grabbed it and wrapped it around his naked waist.

"What are you—why is he here?" Garrett's tone was deeper and more gravelly than Tristan remembered. He stood frozen in place, looking from Sophie to Tristan and back again. "What are you doing, Sophie? Did he hurt you? You're bruised—" Despite the low timbre of Garrett's voice, Tristan recognized a hint of uncertainty on its fringes.

With a little toss of her head, Sophie seemed to fling away the cobwebs and regain some composure. "Of course he didn't hurt me." Still staring at Garrett, she took in a shaky gulp of a breath. Her gaze flickered to the servants, then to Tristan. "Untie me, please."

Tristan glanced at the crowd standing on the threshold. Several maidservants, Sophie's lady's maid, Delia, the housekeeper, Mrs. Krum, and the butler, Connor, were gathered there, still as death, gawking at the drama unfolding before them.

Tristan gave the butler a pointed look. "I do not doubt your discretion, Connor. Please remind the others of theirs. We'll discuss this in the morning."

Connor snapped to attention. "Of course, Your Grace." With a firm nod, he bustled the servants out. Only Tom, Garrett, and the stranger remained. Ignoring them, Tristan climbed to the edge of the bed to release his wife's wrists. When her hands were free, she sat up, pulled the heavy counterpane to her chin, and quietly worked on one ankle while he focused on the other.

Everyone seemed frozen in place, watching in silence. Their presence was unnerving. Overwhelming. Panic threatened to consume Tristan as thoughts jumped around in his head like cricket balls bouncing against his skull.

Sophie would leave him now. He was going to lose her. She had always belonged to Garrett.

Taking Sophie's lead, he focused on untying the knot and regulating his breaths. As he did so, a grim determination overtook him. He wouldn't let her go. Not this time.

When she was loose, Sophie glanced at Garrett, her expression seemingly normal—cool and duchesslike. "Tristan and I will dress and meet you in the drawing room."

"No," Garrett said, his voice flat. "I'm not leaving you alone with him."

Tristan started to tell Garrett to go to the devil, but his wife's gentle hand on his arm restrained him.

"Very well. Garrett, you may stay. Tom, you'll escort

Mr. . . . ?" Sophie raised an eyebrow at the stranger, who bowed, his youthful round face unreadable.

"William Fisk. At your service, Your Grace."

Sophie nodded. "A pleasure, Mr. Fisk. However, under the circumstances . . ."

"Of course." Fisk nodded gravely, his doelike brown eyes solemn.

Hysterical laughter bubbled up from Tristan's gut. Under the circumstances, indeed. The pleasantries of society had long since been dispensed with tonight, and yet Sophie retained her practical demeanor. She hardly wavered, despite having just been discovered tied to a bed being taken savagely by her husband. Despite discovering her deceased first husband was, in fact, alive. By now, any other woman would require resuscitation.

Tristan tamped down the mad desire to laugh and distracted himself by gathering clothing from the floor.

"Tom will escort you to the drawing room, Mr. Fisk," Sophie said politely, but the command in her tone was unmistakable.

Fisk bowed again, his manners impeccable and at odds with this ridiculous situation. "Thank you, Your Grace."

When the door closed behind them, Sophie turned to Garrett. He focused on her, fixated, his jaw ticking as if he were on the verge of exploding again.

It was just the three of them, Tristan realized. As it had been when they were children. The three of them against the world. Garrett, the eldest and strongest, whom Tristan and Sophie looked to for protection. Tristan, adventurous and impetuous, always using charm to wheedle them out of trouble. Sophie, quiet and wise, though she was younger than Tristan by over a year and four years younger than Garrett. She was the capable one, the peace-keeper, but she was also the idealist. The dreamer. The little girl who'd taught two motherless, unloved boys how to be happy and carefree.

Things had changed. Tristan and Sophie had learned to get by without Garrett's protection. They'd developed strength of their own. He had abandoned them to their own devices, and they had survived . . . and ultimately prospered. *Together.*

Now, instead of the three of them against the world, it was the three of them against one another. When Garrett looked at Tristan, his eyes weren't filled with protective affection or brotherly love. Instead they were replete with disgust. Anger. Hatred so strong, it dug like a knife into Tristan's chest.

Now that the servants and Fisk had gone, vulnerability flooded Sophie's expression, and Tristan felt her emotions as strongly as if he were experiencing them himself. He could see the questions swimming in her hazel eyes, which had taken on the bronze quality of the light of a lantern left by the servants. *Where were you? Why did you come back? Why did you leave us for so long?*

"Garrett . . ." Her lower lip trembled. The blanket slipped, baring a perfect, white shoulder, and Tristan stepped between them to cover her. He'd be damned if Garrett would see any more of her bare skin. She didn't even look at Tristan. Her shining gaze focused solely on Garrett.

Keeping her covered, Tristan helped her out of the bed, feeling her legs tremble as they brushed against him.

She wanted to go to Garrett. Her desire to touch him was nearly palpable. Yet she didn't. She didn't move. Perhaps because Tristan was standing between the two of them.

Perhaps he should move aside and see what happened. But no way in hell would he give either of them the opportunity.

He looked over his shoulder, eyes narrowed. "Allow us to dress, if you please."

Garrett gave a jerk of a nod, crossed his arms over his chest, and turned to stare broodingly at the fire.

Tristan met Sophie's gaze briefly before she pulled away. Blood roared through his veins at her expression of confusion.

She pulled the blanket tightly around her, took the candle from the bedside table, and headed for the door to the adjoining room. As she passed the fire, she stopped and turned. For a long moment, she stared at Garrett, simply stared at him, her lips parted. He stared back at her, his gaze stormy, hot, intense. Tristan felt like an intruder, an outsider to the private, personal moment shared between lovers.

Finally Sophie turned and padded on bare feet across the carpet, her pale feet and calves flashing beneath the dark blanket. Irrationally, Tristan glanced around in search of shoes, or anything to cover the alluring turn of her ankle. Garrett studied her every move, looking away only when the door to her dressing room snapped shut.

Tristan yanked on his now-wrinkled trousers and shirt, making no attempt to smooth them. Garrett didn't glance in his direction but stood as stiff and impenetrable as an iceberg, staring at the hearth. The coals had grown cold along with Garrett's arctic presence, and a chill settled deep in Tristan's bones.

He found his waistcoat on the floor on the far side of the bed near the foot post where the gold trim of the bed curtains skimmed the burgundy carpet. Pushing his arms through the openings, he glanced at his cravat lying in disarray on the sheet but decided against wearing it. Instead he thrust his feet into his shoes, crossed his arms, and stood on guard by Sophie's dressing room door.

He studied Garrett, who stared at the fire as if by his gaze alone he could force the coals to explode into flame. Beneath his heavy black overcoat, the man's broad shoulders were tense—clearly he felt Tristan's eyes on him. Still, he didn't say a word.

A large scar blazed red above the old hairline scar through his left eyebrow. Tristan couldn't have been over six years old when Garrett injured himself that first time, but he remembered it vividly. His parents had just died and his uncle, Garrett's father, had brought him to live at Calton House, where he and Garrett had become fast friends and close companions. On that particular spring day, they were racing in the meadows. Garrett was winning, but then he'd tripped on a branch and fallen headfirst into a pile of rocks. Garrett's head had gushed bright red blood, and Tristan had panicked, certain he was dead. He remembered the intense relief that flooded through him when Garrett had cracked open his eyes. The fall had left a permanent white line running from just over the bridge of Garrett's nose through his eyebrow.

The new scar was different—bigger, twisted, a glaring knot on his forehead. It drew attention to itself as the older wound never had. In conjunction with Garrett's tangled shoulder-length blond hair, it made him look wild and feral, more like a savage lion than the well-bred Colonel Garrett James, Duke of Calton.

How was this possible? How could Garrett be alive, after all the effort they had made to find him? Where had he been all this time? Above all, why the hell had he come back now?

Just as he opened his mouth to voice the questions, Sophie entered from her dressing room, and Garrett's attention riveted to her. Without the help of a maid, she had dressed herself in a white muslin gown, combed her honey-colored hair, and twisted it at her nape. She wore a soft pink Pashmina shawl over her shoulders. Pride swelled in Tristan's chest. She looked every bit the Duchess of Calton.

Sophie's gaze moved slowly from one man to the other. "Garrett . . . ?"

The man stiffened further, then turned away. "We will adjourn to the drawing room."

She took a step toward him and reached out her hand to stop him. "Please. Tell me what—why—how—?"

Garrett bowed stiffly and motioned toward the door. "After you, Your Grace."

Sophie blinked away some strong emotion, straightened her shoulders, and inclined her head. "We thought you were never coming home. We were certain you were dead. How is it that you're here?"

Garrett's lips tightened. "In the drawing room. If you please." The words came out in a low growl through his clenched jaw.

"You will not speak to Sophie in that tone of voice." Tristan took a menacing step toward Garrett, but he swiveled away and stomped toward the door.

Sophie's hand closed over Tristan's sleeve. "It's all right."

Grinding his teeth, Tristan stared down at her.

She nodded in Garrett's direction, then followed him out the door. With conflicting emotions swirling in his chest, Tristan kept by her side as they walked to the drawing room.

Tom had lit the chandelier and the candles set in the gold-plated wall sconces, and the room was blazing. Light danced off the polished green leaves of the potted palms in the corners, and glistened along the gold trim of the wainscoting. As Garrett entered, followed by Sophie and Tristan, the young groom stirred the coals in the fireplace. Fisk stepped forward and bowed as they filed in.

"Your Graces."

Tristan quickly masked the falter in his step. As Garrett's trustee and heir, he had been responsible for all of Garrett's affairs after his disappearance. He'd officially assumed the title and the duties of the Duke of Calton less than a year ago.

Now he would be forced to give it all up. Nobody would deny Garrett was the legal Duke of Calton. Not that it mattered, ultimately. Tristan had never lusted after anything of Garrett's.

Except his wife.

Tristan had loved Sophie since they were children. He'd kept his secret longing to himself since his school days at Eton when Garrett had told him of his intention to marry her. Out of loyalty to his friend, Tristan had valiantly buried his desire for her and married Nancy, a cheerful lady whose disposition seemed compatible with his. She was a good woman, and he'd even loved her. But she wasn't Sophie.

Finally, six years after Garrett disappeared from the field and four years after Nancy's death, Tristan revealed his feelings to Sophie. And she reciprocated.

This time would be different. He wouldn't give her up so easily—hell, he wouldn't give her up at all. He'd be damned if he'd martyr himself for his cousin again. Garrett had abandoned them both, and Tristan no longer owed him anything, least of all his heart.

Now Sophie stood before him, the small tremors running down her spine invisible to the untrained eye. Tristan wanted nothing more than to hold her, to comfort her. To protect her. But he restrained himself. She wouldn't want him to coddle her.

Sophie passed Garrett and went to sit on one of the palm-print sofas. Garrett lowered himself beside her. She kept her eyes cast downward, but her skin was as pale as Tristan had ever seen it. Her hands clenched and relaxed over and over in her lap, belying her attempt to appear calm.

Tristan flicked his gaze back to Garrett, who stared at Sophie hungrily. The brazenness of his expression made Tristan's gut twist with possessive fury, but he refused to allow the emotion to consume him. Instead, keeping his face blank, he sat on the chair facing them. It was said that when he wasn't busy charming the opposition, he possessed the most impassive expression in all of Parliament. He intended to make use of that expression tonight.

Seeing all of them settled without any blood shed, Fisk smiled, his cherubic cheeks glowing pink. He lowered himself into the adjacent silk-covered armchair. Tristan

nodded to Tom, who slipped out the door, shutting it
softly behind him. Tristan trusted him to stay close in the
event of any further trouble.

He glanced at Fisk. "I wish to offer my thanks for
your assistance earlier. However, this is a private matter
between—"

"Fisk stays," Garrett growled.

A muscle spasmed in Tristan's jaw, but he kept his face
and voice blank. He'd humor the man. For now. Tristan
met Garrett's gaze evenly, absorbing the vitriol in his expression and reflecting no visible effect in his own. "Very
well. Explain yourself. If you please."

Garrett didn't respond. Instead his lip curled in a snarl.
"What were you doing in my bedchamber, Westcliff?"

Garrett had always called him by his Christian name,
so the use of his old title was unsettling. Tristan's father had been granted the viscountcy for services to the
crown, and orphaned as a young boy, Tristan had been
known by acquaintances as Lord Westcliff for the greater
part of his life. Until he'd become the Duke of Calton ten
months ago.

Through his tight jaw, Tristan spoke the truth, not caring that he goaded the other man. "What do you think I
was doing in your bedchamber? I was making love to my
wife."

Garrett shot up, hands clenched, ready to brawl again,
but Sophie was just as fast. She took his balled hand in her
own. Her delicate fingers didn't cover his big fist, but her
will was strong. "Please don't. Not again."

She stroked his knuckles, and Tristan's lip curled at the
intimacy of the gesture. This was the first time Sophie
had touched Garrett, and by the expression on her face

as she stared up at him, it was clear she didn't want to let him go.

Garrett's arms relaxed, but he didn't sit down. Tristan wasn't about to be cowed. Rage threatened to boil up through his chest, but he fiercely tamped it down. He remained in his seat, keeping his unflinching gaze on Garrett. "In the event you haven't heard, we married last year. Really, man. Do you think you can barrel back into our lives after nearly eight years and expect to find everything as you left it?"

Garrett's breath came out in a hiss. "You're not married. It's impossible. And illegal. You're already married." He looked from Tristan to Sophie. "*Both* of you."

For a long moment, Tristan stared at him in shock. *Hell.* Garrett still wanted her. Tristan's pulse ratcheted upward, and his heart thudded against his ribcage.

Sophie shook her head. "No, Garrett. Nancy died five years ago. And you . . ."

". . . were officially confirmed dead a year ago," Tristan finished, pushing the words through his dry throat. "Your estate has been distributed according to your will. Sophie was a widow when I married her." He forced a smile. "I could provide proof, if you wish."

Fisk coughed behind his hand, and his eyebrows drew together in distress. "I'm so sorry, Cal—" this was directed to Garrett, "—I have been on the Continent this past year. You know how I feel about London gossip—I avoid it like the plague. I didn't know. Last I heard, evidence of your death on the field was inadequate, and you were still legally alive."

"The courts came to a decision." Tristan kept his focus on Garrett, taking deep, even breaths to stay calm. "You were officially declared dead six and a half years after the battle of Waterloo."

"*No.*" Expressions of shock and rage streamed over Garrett's face. His lips twisted and his forehead creased, causing the big scar to appear even more lumpy and mottled. His pupils dilated, making his eyes look black rather than their normal light blue. "God, it can't be true." He raked his hand through his long hair and turned on Sophie. "Sophie . . . ?"

Tristan watched them both, fighting the impression that the solid walls of the life he'd built with Sophie and their children was crumbling into dust, and there was nothing he could do to stop it.

How was she feeling? He knew she'd always loved Garrett, and he understood her fond memories of what they'd shared. He'd been beside her through her mourning, the birth of her daughter, the subsequent years of struggle. He'd missed Garrett nearly as much as she did.

Despite her continuing affection for Garrett, she'd fallen madly in love with Tristan. They shared a connection he doubted she'd ever felt with Garrett. Her love for Garrett centered on sweet memories of them together, of gentle love, of mutual discovery. From childhood, she had hero-worshiped Garrett. But she loved Tristan passionately, unconditionally, in bed and out. They shared more than he'd thought possible between a man and a woman. Their love was mature, and their souls were irrevocably connected.

All of that wouldn't just disappear because Garrett had reappeared. Would it?

"I'm sorry," she whispered to Garrett, her expression filled with pain. "You were gone so long. We went to the

Continent, and we searched for you everywhere . . . we were certain you'd been lost to us forever." She blinked hard. "Where have you been, Garrett?"

He ignored the question and turned back to Tristan, speaking through bared teeth. "Why?"

Tristan knew the strength of Garrett's feelings for Sophie—he had grown up with both of them and served as Garrett's best man on their wedding day. Since they were children, Garrett's love for her had run deep. That was why Tristan hadn't fought for her then. Garrett claimed her first. He was older. He had much more to offer her. It was clear to all that she loved him in return.

But that was many years ago, before Garrett had abandoned her, abandoned them both. It took Tristan five years after Waterloo to realize how wrong he was to have given her up. Sophie was his life.

Tristan took a deep breath before answering. "I love her. You were long gone. I did what I've always wanted to do—I made her mine."

Garrett shook his head as if to clear it. When he spoke, his voice was staccato, filled with emotion. "You were like a brother to me. I come home . . . for my wife . . ." His fingers curled at his sides. "For the people who once brought me happiness . . . to regain the happiness I once possessed, to reclaim my life . . . only to discover you have . . ." Again he pushed his hand through his tangled hair. ". . . betrayed me."

As suddenly as it appeared, the emotion bled from his eyes, leaving them as stark as blue steel when they refocused on Tristan. His tone hardened, and he threw Sophie's hand from his own. "No. I won't let you do this.

I won't let you take everything from me. Not after—" He shook his head and snapped his mouth shut.

Tristan stared at him. How dare he? After leaving them alone for so long, condemning them to live with the grief of losing him, forcing them to rebuild their lives? The way his "death" had affected Sophie, the way she'd suffered for him. Only in the past year had Tristan witnessed the gradual reemergence of the bright, joyful smiles of her youth. Only recently had they both begun to heal.

Tristan released a tempered breath and reined in his anger. "Of course you will have your title and lands, *Your Grace*. Nobody can take those from you as long as you are alive. But Sophie is mine now."

Sophie let out a little gasp, but Tristan ignored it, thinking quickly. "We are legally wed. Nothing can tear that asunder." He lied. He could only hope Garrett had never paid attention to the law regarding marital matters. "We will gather our belongings and leave London."

Garrett merely snorted. "Like hell."

"Try to stop us," Tristan said calmly.

Fisk cleared his throat, directing his words to Tristan and Sophie. "I'm certain you have many questions, Your Graces."

Tristan swung his head toward Fisk. *I'm not a "Your Grace" anymore*, he wanted to say. From the corner of his eye, he saw Sophie studying the gentleman curiously, a hint of a flush adding color to her pale cheeks.

"I do have questions. Hundreds of damn questions," he pushed out. God, this was a fine mess. "First and foremost, who the hell are you?"

His demand didn't seem to ruffle Fisk in the least. "I was a young lieutenant of eighteen in His Grace's regiment of guards. I saw the duke fall on the field at Waterloo," he said pleasantly. "I wasn't one of the closest to the scene, which is why I assumed they never called me to testify in any of the hearings regarding the colonel's . . . status. Suffice it to say I saw him wounded, and I saw him fall. I was among the search parties scouring the field for him in the days following. As you know, we never found a trace of the colonel. It turns out last month I was on the Continent, and . . . well, I went back to the area, to revisit the scene for the first time in so many years . . ." His voice faded as he seemed to fall into a memory.

"And?" Sophie sank onto the sofa, clutching its arm so hard her knuckles whitened.

Fisk gave her a sad smile. "Well, I found Cal—His Grace—hearty and hale."

Tristan glanced at Garrett, who watched Sophie. Sophie's lips parted, mirroring Tristan's amazement. Seven years in Belgium? So close to France? What on God's green earth could Garrett have been doing there for seven years? And why hadn't they found him when they'd scoured every inch within a hundred-mile radius of the battlefield?

And why didn't the blasted man talk? Garrett had never been a man of many words, but it was about time he explained himself.

Sophie pressed her trembling hand to her breast.

Garrett's voice was hollow. "I'd forgotten you, Sophie."

"Well, that much is clear." Her voice shook as much as her hand. She blinked hard, visibly struggling to contain her emotions.

Damn Garrett to hell. Tristan flexed his fingers. Had he abandoned Sophie only to return to renew her suffering?

"Why did you come back then?" he ground out.

"This is my home," Garrett muttered, looking around the room frowning, as if it were the first time he'd ever seen it.

"After all the grief you have caused, you come back now? To what end?" Tristan asked. "To cause us more pain?"

Garrett looked away. "You don't understand pain."

Sophie gasped, her eyes wide with shock. "How could you say such a thing?"

"Christ. You married *Tristan*."

Tristan couldn't stop the primal sound that emerged from his throat, but Garrett paid no attention to him. His voice sounded as if it was being raked over hot coals. "Do you know what it feels like to see your wife tied to your bed, being—hell, there's no other appropriate word—being *tupped* by your closest friend? Hell, Sophie, do you know what that feels like? He was raping you, hurting you—"

"He wasn't," she said shortly. She faced forward, her posture rigid, her hands clasped in her lap. She flicked a glance at Fisk, then said in a low voice, "I wanted it."

A long, thick silence blanketed the room. Fisk lowered his head and fidgeted with the carved wooden armrest of his chair. The fire crackled. Wax popped in one of the candles, casting a flickering shadow over one of the walls. Tristan had to push each shallow, tight breath from his lungs. His gut clenched for his wife. Forced to discuss such a personal topic in front of a stranger. How dare Garrett humiliate her like this?

Finally Garrett spoke, his voice glacial. "You wanted

it, did you?" His lips thinned. "Well. I don't know if that makes it better or worse."

After all she had suffered for the man. Tristan could kill him now. In cold blood. "So," he said flatly, "after abandoning her for nearly eight years, you would not wish her happiness."

Garrett's eyes snapped to his, his blue gaze as frosty as his voice. "Before I left for Waterloo, she said she loved me. That she'd love me forever, no matter what. If that were true, she would have waited. *Forever*, if necessary. Since I came home to find her playing the part of your whore, I can only assume she lied."

Tristan jumped to his feet and lunged at Garrett. If he'd had a sword, he would have run the bastard through right then and there. Sophie didn't move—she gaped at Garrett, too shocked to react. Next thing Tristan knew, Fisk had grabbed his arms and pulled him back. Tom must have heard the scuffle, because he leaped into the room and already had one burly arm locked over Garrett's chest.

"Let me go, goddamn it." Garrett threw Tom off, his expression like stone, as if he had gone past rage, past the urge to kill, and was now in a far more dangerous place. The coldness in his voice prickled the hair on the back of Tristan's neck. "You will be out of my home by the end of the week, Westcliff."

"Gladly," Tristan shot back. "But Sophie is coming with me."

Garrett snorted. "We'll see about that."

Chapter Three

Garrett barreled out of the room, nearly knocking Tom over in his haste, leaving Tristan, Sophie, and Fisk staring after him in shock. After a long moment of silence, Fisk cleared his throat.

"Perhaps we all ought to go to bed."

Tristan and Sophie swung round to face him, blinking in surprise. He met their gazes evenly. "I think it would be best—for all of us—if you were to sleep in separate rooms tonight, Your Graces."

Tristan bared his teeth and was about to say Fisk and Garrett could both rot in hell, because nobody was going to forcefully separate him from his wife, when Sophie nodded. "It is probably for the best," she agreed. "I'll sleep in the duchess's chambers." She glanced at Tristan, then swiftly away. "Tristan, will you sleep in the Tulip Room?"

Tristan's jaw dropped in shock. Downgraded so swiftly to a guest bedchamber?

"He *is* the duke now," she murmured. As if he required a reminder of that fact.

He couldn't argue with her. And yet . . . "Sophie—" he began, but stopped himself when he studied her face. Her skin had lost all color, leaving her pale and sallow, and her lips were thin and blanched.

"Please, Tristan . . . I can't—" She shook her head. "Please."

She'd reached the end of her endurance, and it would be brutal of him to push her. He reached out and drew her against him. Pressing his lips to her hair, he whispered, "It's going to be all right, love," as he felt her body quake in his embrace.

She clung to him for a long moment then abruptly pulled away. Tristan's chest tightened, and he simply watched as she shuffled out of the drawing room, her head bowed.

God, she didn't even want to talk to him.

He resolved not to panic. Sophie was overwhelmed and overwrought. Maybe she was right—maybe it would be better if they addressed this in the morning.

Numbly, he walked to the room Sophie had assigned him, removed his clothes, slid under the lace-fringed quilt, and dropped into a fitful sleep.

Sophie.

Tristan awoke with a jolt to a bleak daylight filtering in through a crack in the lacy yellow curtains.

He tossed off the blankets and strode across the cold wooden floor planks to the door. He turned the knob and pulled, but the door didn't budge. It was locked from the outside. Tristan yanked harder, to no avail.

Tristan curled his fingers into a fist over the smooth

white paint of the door. Taking deep breaths to calm himself, he turned to stare at the portrait over the mantel. The Tulip Room was named for this likeness of the first duke's children frolicking in a field of red and yellow tulips.

Once upon a time, Tristan would have been cowed by Garrett's extreme methods. Not anymore. He'd suffered through the death of his closest friend and his wife. He'd fathered a child. He'd taken his seat in the House of Lords and had calmly won arguments that made lesser men recoil in fear. He would *not* be locked in his own house like a common criminal.

He had to get out of here. Once he did, he would find Sophie. And once he found her, he'd take her and the children somewhere safe.

Just as he turned back to study the lock, it turned and clicked, and Tristan stepped back as the door was flung open. Garrett loomed on the threshold, still dressed in the long, black overcoat, his face haggard, and dark circles ringed his eyes as if he hadn't slept a wink.

The two men glared at each another in silence, until finally Garrett spoke. "I insist you remain here until I return, Westcliff."

With effort, Tristan schooled his expression. "Why is that . . . Your Grace?"

Garrett's eyes flickered away briefly before returning to him. "I am to see Ansley."

Tristan lifted one shoulder in a shrug. "Of course. You will request that our solicitor clear up the matter of the titles and land as quickly as possible."

"No."

Tristan raised a questioning eyebrow.

"I don't care about the blasted lands or the damned title."

"Oh?" Tristan inquired politely. Funny, neither did he. "Then why are you so eager to see Ansley?"

"Ansley will go to Doctors' Commons with a suit to declare the nullity of your marriage to Sophie."

Garrett's words hit him like a blow burying into his lungs. For a long moment, he couldn't speak.

"I thought you should know," Garrett added.

Tristan stared at him. For once, words failed him. God, it was impossible—Sophie had married Garrett first, and if Garrett wanted her, nothing in the law said he couldn't have her. Tristan would lose.

No, he wouldn't accept that, damn it. He scrambled for a retort while his mind engaged, planning his counterattack. First of all, he would need a new solicitor. Together they'd find a loophole in the law, something that would prevent Garrett from dissolving his marriage.

"I insist you remain here until I return," Garrett said. "If all goes well, by the end of the day, we will have begun to clear up this matter."

As Garrett made to leave, Tristan spoke softly. "I'll fight you for her."

Garrett slowly turned around, his blue eyes narrow. "You will lose."

"No. I will use every resource at my disposal, and I *will* have her." Tristan had only a shaky legal leg to stand on—if that—but the first rule of defeating your opponent was to make him believe you had the stronger case.

"You may try, Westcliff. But she is mine. She always has been."

Tristan stared at him unflinchingly. "She won't leave me. Not willingly."

Garrett's lip curled. "Stay away from my wife, or I will kill you." With that, he strode out the door, pausing to speak in a low tone to a boy posted just outside. Tristan studied his guard—young, clearly from the lower orders, wearing street clothes, nodding up at Garrett as if it were God himself instructing him.

Tristan knew precisely how to control men like that.

After Garrett had gone, he watched the clock and waited. An hour later, he scratched on the door. When the boy came to see what was amiss, Tristan said, "May I speak with you a moment, sir?" and began his work.

Dust particles drifted in the beam of late afternoon sunlight streaming through the window. Sophie had never slept in this long, narrow second-story room before last night. When she was married to Garrett, she slept with him in his bedchamber, and she'd had no desire to move when she lost him. Then Tristan had joined her there.

Sophie had pushed aside the drab floral-print chintz curtain earlier to let in the light, but otherwise the room felt dank and oppressive, perhaps because of the low, sloped ceiling or perhaps due to its empty, disused atmosphere.

All day she had paced like a caged animal.

Last night, Garrett had left her and Tristan frustrated and confused, none of their questions answered. When Mr. Fisk had wisely suggested she and Tristan sleep apart, she couldn't disagree with him. It seemed the logical thing to do, given the awkwardness of the circumstances.

Beyond logic, however, she admitted to herself that she couldn't face Tristan. Not after seeing Garrett alive stirred up such confusing emotions. Now, imprisoned in this unfamiliar room, she wondered if she'd made the right decision.

Sophie despised nothing more than feeling impotent, and she had struggled against the sensation from the moment she awakened at dawn. She'd opened the door only to find a person she'd never seen looming at the threshold. The man, a dark, beady-eyed fellow, insisted none too politely that she remain inside the room. She demanded he let her pass, but he flatly refused to allow her to leave. When she attempted to push past him, he merely picked her up, deposited her on the bed, stepped back outside, and closed the door.

Why, why, why? Why had Garrett come back? Why had he stayed away so long? Why had he made her and Tristan suffer? Above all, why did he make her a prisoner in her own house?

The children, Tristan . . . and Garrett himself. Where were they all? Were they safe? Had Garrett seen his daughter? How many times Sophie had pictured that meeting in her mind, and now, trapped in this narrow prison, it was likely she'd missed it.

Where was Tristan? Why hadn't he come for her?

She had called for him through the door. She called for Garrett, for her lady's maid, Delia, for Connor and Mrs. Krum the housekeeper, for *anyone*, but nobody acknowledged her save a young chambermaid to bring her meals and help her dress in a serviceable day dress of white muslin with navy stripes. As the girl fastened the fabric-covered buttons up her back, Sophie had demanded information. Though the maid had been part of the ducal household for two years, her brown eyes had widened and she'd merely whispered, "I couldn't say, ma'am."

She'd finished the buttoning with shaking fingers and fled, leaving a bemused Sophie to fix her own hair. Clearly someone had put the fear of God into the poor girl before sending her.

Since she had no answers, Sophie spent the hours alternating between worrying for her family and inventing answers to her countless questions.

For years, she'd dreamed of Garrett returning to her. In her wildest imaginings, it had never happened quite like this. Seeing him again, even as angry and frightening as he was, made all her old feelings for him well to the surface, only to mingle with her resident feelings for Tristan. Her husband.

Good Lord, which of them was her husband? Garrett or Tristan?

Which one did she *want* to be her husband? She didn't know. The realization twisted her insides into a million knots.

Her chest constricting, Sophie strode to the window, yanked it up, and leaned out, sucking in lungfuls of fresh air. As always, London smelled of coal smoke and refuse, but the sweet fresh smell of spring tinged each breath she gulped in, soothing her tight chest.

She closed her eyes. Last night, she had fought not to throw herself into Garrett's arms. In the past, she had always felt so safe when he held her. Would it be the same now? Would there be peace in his embrace?

As much peace as she found in Tristan's embrace?

She feared she wouldn't find safety in Garrett's arms anymore. Even more, she feared she *would*—a disconcerting thought, considering his intolerable behavior. But last night Tristan was there, watching every move she made, his eyes dark with anguish. He was still her husband. She couldn't fall into another man's arms with him looking on. It would destroy him. It would destroy her.

She clutched the sleek wood of the windowsill and gazed across the mews toward the busy street where the people of Mayfair carried on their business as usual. Behind the row of trees bordering the property, carriages rattled by, horseshoes clomped rhythmically on the pavement, and even from this distance, indistinguishable voices of pedestrians carried to the window as they strolled by, flashes of color beyond the drab browns and blacks and emerging greens of early spring.

Tristan was everything to her.

If Garrett tried to keep them separated . . . No. She would die before she hurt Tristan, or allowed him to be hurt.

She fisted her hands on the windowsill. How could Garrett behave like such an arrogant ass? He was the one who'd burst in upon them. He was the one who'd been gone for so long. He was the one who'd abandoned them all. After all that, how dare he expect her to fall back into his arms?

She had suffered, and Tristan had suffered, and her daughter had never known a father. Garrett had allowed all that to happen. The man she remembered, the noble, honest, loving man whose soul was twined with hers— that man would never have countenanced any of it. What had happened to him to change him into someone who could desert his family? Was it the horror of war? She'd heard some men had gone mad from it. Could that have happened to Garrett?

Gooseflesh erupted over her skin, and she shut the window. The sounds of the outside faded away, cloaking her in stifling silence once again. Chafing her hands over her arms, she lowered herself on an old relic of an armchair with faded flower-patterned upholstery and frayed seams. The anger, the excitement and joy, the confusion, the worry for Garrett's sanity, the fear for her marriage to Tristan. All the emotions swirled in her mind, leaving her so overwhelmed there was nothing to do but be numb.

Taking a deep breath, she shook off the swarming confusion. If she let herself overthink the matter, it would only drive her to distraction. No, she had to escape from this room, talk to her husband—her *husbands*—to understand what Garrett wanted, what had happened to him, why he had come back.

And to form a plan for what they would all do next.

The door swung open, jolting her out of her reverie.

"Tristan!" She leaped out of the chair and flung herself at him.

Tristan enfolded her in his arms, stroking her back, his hands strong and comforting. "Are you all right, Soph?"

"Yes." She drew back a little to look at him, and flinched. His face was swollen, covered on one side by a mottled, colorful bruise. She reached a tentative finger to his skin. His jaw was rough and unshaven, an unheard-of state for her sleek and well-put-together husband. "You should have this looked at."

He shrugged. "It's nothing."

"Arnica would help. I shall ask Mrs. Krum to prepare you a poultice."

His dark eyes met hers. "A bruised face is the least of our worries."

Sophie's throat went dry, and the questions flowed from her. "Where is he? Have you spoken to him? What's happened? Where have you been all day? Are the children safe?"

"I don't think the children have crossed paths with Garrett, if that's what you mean." Tristan ran his fingers lightly up her back. "I don't even know whether he's aware they're here." He glanced back at the open door. The beady-eyed stranger glared at them from the threshold.

The expression on Tristan's face as he turned back to her caused a frisson of unease to run down Sophie's spine. "Garrett has gone, for now, but he'll return. He went to see Ansley."

This came as no surprise—Ansley was their solicitor. Nonetheless, a queasy feeling settled in her stomach, and she sent a quick prayer that his visit to Ansley had nothing to do with her. "Perhaps to settle the matter of his title and lands, though one would think the two of you should take care of the matter jointly." She looked at Tristan sharply. "You weren't thinking of challenging him for any of it, were you?"

"Of course not, Soph."

Of course not. Tristan had never craved Garrett's title or lands. Dread twisted at the knot in her stomach. "What is it?"

"He's hired a small army of men. They're armed and blocking every exit. One of them informed me their orders are to shoot to kill if anyone sets foot out of the house."

Sophie's jaw went slack with surprise, then she ground her teeth. This was her domain, and she managed it impeccably. To have Garrett storm in as if on a military engagement and allow strange, violent men to swarm her house made her blood boil.

Tristan lowered his voice. "It took me the better part of the day to convince the boy posted at my door to allow me to leave."

She wanted to ask him how he'd accomplished that, but the man posted at her own door was listening to their conversation. No doubt Tristan had used his endless charm on the poor boy. Or maybe he had simply ended up bribing him.

She slipped her arms around her husband's waist. "He's changed, Tristan."

It pained her to admit it, but Garrett was different. She'd seen the difference last night. Not him pulling Tristan off her and attempting to beat him to a pulp—that was something she would have expected from the old Garrett. Once she'd moved beyond the shock of seeing him again, she'd known exactly how to manage his anger. It was his aloof behavior afterward, his cruel words, and the blank expression on his face before he left the drawing room that scared her more. He had seemed calculating. Cruel and impenetrable. Truly dangerous.

Tristan nodded. "Yes. He's grown . . . cold."

Sophie closed her eyes. Perhaps Waterloo—and time itself—had indeed changed Garrett's soul. She must face the very real possibility that he wasn't the same man she had tearfully watched sail away so many years ago.

Tristan's arms tightened around her, and he bent his head to brush his lips against her ear. He angled their bodies so his back effectively hid her from the doorway, and his hands slid to her buttocks and tugged her more tightly against him.

Using his palms, he tilted her head up and touched his mouth to hers, brushing over her lips until she parted them. He scraped his teeth along her lower lip, then sucked it gently.

He never kissed her before the servants, and Sophie knew Garrett's sour-looking guard watched them. But after all that had happened, she couldn't bring herself to care. Her mind was a muddle, but her body knew what it wanted—what it needed—right now. The comfort and security of her husband's arms.

There was an edge to Tristan today—a desperation in his touch she'd never sensed before. He nipped at the edge of her mouth, and when she parted for him, he plundered her thoroughly, hot and hard and hungry, as if he thirsted for her mouth like the only oasis in the Sahara. He held her as if he was afraid to let her go. He kissed her as if he feared he'd never kiss her again. His clean, spicy taste flowed into her, strengthening her, and her eyelids sank as she lost herself in his erotic embrace.

"Ahem."

Sophie and Tristan jumped apart, then spun toward the doorway. Heat crawled over Sophie's face as she saw Mr. Fisk standing there, smiling graciously, as if he hadn't just seen what they were doing. She hoped that was the case. She had no doubt that if he had seen them kissing, he'd report that information to Garrett—a fact that made her insides squirm in discomfort.

Mr. Fisk bowed. "Good afternoon, Your Graces. I trust you are both well."

A muscle twitched in Tristan's jaw, but he held on to

his famed composure, choosing strained politeness over venting his anger to Mr. Fisk. "A matter of opinion, I suppose. Considering we have been locked in our rooms."

"Ah," Mr. Fisk said, "I didn't know you had been confined. My apologies. Yet I see you have been given your freedom?"

"In a manner of speaking."

"Very good." Mr. Fisk glanced at the guard, then back to them. "I was hoping you would spare me a few moments of your time, Your Graces."

Tristan glanced at Sophie, who nodded. "Of course," he said. "Shall we reconvene in a more appropriate place for conversation?"

The guard coughed and spoke in a low voice to Mr. Fisk. "I'm not to allow the duchess to leave the room, sir."

A furrow appeared between Mr. Fisk's eyebrows. "I see. Hm, well, I know this is most irregular, but would it be possible for us to speak here? Privately?"

Sophie released a breath. After what Mr. Fisk had witnessed last night, surely it was ridiculous to consider propriety. "Of course, Mr. Fisk." She motioned to the lone tattered armchair. "Please come in and sit down."

"Thank you, madam." He bowed politely then nodded at the guard before closing the door.

Tristan eyed him warily as he strode deeper into the room.

He looked from the chair to the bed, then at Sophie. "I shall remain standing, if it is all right."

"Whatever you like, Mr. Fisk."

"I'm so sorry to interrupt your . . . discussion."

Sophie's flush deepened. Perhaps he had seen the kiss after all.

"However," he continued, "I've just come from Regent Street. Cal was . . . ah . . . shopping, and asked me to come home to ascertain your welfare and comfort."

Tristan snorted. "I would have liked to witness him saying that. Please spare the embellishments, Fisk, and get to the point, if you don't mind."

"Of course." An odd look passed over Mr. Fisk's face, but he turned away before Sophie could decipher it. He clasped his hands behind his back, wandered to the window, and peered outside. "I just wanted to explain a bit more of Cal's . . . predicament to you."

"Predicament?" Sophie echoed. But he'd piqued her attention. Finally—an explanation.

"Predicament." Tristan's mouth twisted into a rare sneer. "He comes back after nigh on eight years, full of violence and rancor. What a *predicament*."

"But it is," Mr. Fisk said calmly.

"Hell," Tristan spat. "We've been locked in our own house all day. Separated. Not knowing what's become of each other or our children."

"Nobody has been harmed." Mr. Fisk's gaze flickered away from Tristan's swollen face.

"And then I learn he intends to tear apart my family, destroy all our lives. Goddamn it, I won't let him—"

Raising his hand, Mr. Fisk interrupted him. "When I found him in Belgium, the colonel had no recollection of his life before Waterloo." He took a deep breath. "He didn't have the first idea who he was or where he had come from."

"What?" Sophie gasped.

Mr. Fisk nodded gravely. "Yes, madam. Cal was afflicted with amnesia. The worst, most insidious kind of amnesia, I believe. He suffered a grave head wound at Waterloo, and the doctors believe that was what caused the severity of the memory loss. Imagine, all those years . . ." His voice petered out, and he stared out the window once again, seemingly at a loss how to continue.

Sophie stared at him, stunned. When Garrett said he'd forgotten her, amnesia hadn't crossed her mind. But of course it was the most obvious answer—he would never have left her of his own accord. Relief swept through her, clear and sweet, like an ocean breeze. For years she had dreamed that he lived, that there was some good reason he'd been kept away from her. And now she knew it was true. He was alive, and he hadn't abandoned her. Garrett had stayed away due to circumstances beyond his control.

Tristan frowned at Mr. Fisk. "How did he regain his memories?"

"Oh, he hasn't regained all of them, sir. The doctor told us that may take some time. He may never remember everything. But many of his memories returned after I found him. I think he remembers more every day. Quite possibly every hour."

"Did this all begin when you first saw him in Belgium, Mr. Fisk?" Sophie asked in a breathless voice.

Mr. Fisk nodded. "Yes. As soon as he laid eyes on me, he remembered me, though I was only a mere lieutenant in his regiment. I have helped him with the rest. Now he recalls most things on his own—just about everything he sees from his life before Waterloo sparks a fresh batch of memories. Some of them are twisted and confused. But others are as clear as day. Being here, in his old house— well, I believe he's being bombarded by recollections."

"Goodness," Sophie said softly.

"That is why, I believe, he may seem . . . distant at times. It has been difficult for him to assimilate all the information after having lost it for so long."

"Of course," Sophie murmured.

Rubbing his forehead, Tristan lowered himself into the chair. "So you're saying he didn't deliberately abandon Sophie."

"Not at all," Mr. Fisk confirmed.

Tristan's face went utterly blank. Sophie knew what it meant when this expressionless look came over him. He was squelching some strong emotion.

In the muddled workings of her mind, she couldn't fathom why Tristan should be distressed by this news. Knowing Garrett as they did, it made so much more sense.

Mr. Fisk turned to Sophie. "Rest assured, madam, if he had recalled anything about you during all those years, he would have come home to you as quickly as he possibly could. As it was, the moment he remembered you, he flew into action. We traveled directly to Calais and took the very next ship bound for England."

"Thank you, Mr. Fisk," she whispered. "Thank you so much for telling us this. I—*we*—had no idea."

"I realize you have been confused, and Cal has been rather tightlipped about how he's spent the past years. I think . . . well, I believe he is simply struggling to absorb it all."

"Of course," Sophie said.

Mr. Fisk stepped away from the window. "Thank you for your understanding, Your Grace. Now, I have some business to attend, so I will beg your indulgence."

"Certainly, Mr. Fisk."

"Also—" He lowered his voice. "—I have need of the man posted outside your door. Cal has required him to deliver some documents to his solicitor."

Sophie glanced at Tristan. Only the slightest twitch in his eye gave away his dismay.

"I trust everything will remain . . . calm, if I remove him from his post?"

Sophie hoped he was only referring to her possibly attempting to escape from her room, and not to any illicit relations he thought she and Tristan might indulge in. "I shall remain here until Garrett himself tells me I can go," she promised.

Mr. Fisk smiled, and she relaxed. "Thank you, Your Grace." He glanced at Tristan. "I'm sure the two of you have much to discuss, given this new information. But I do hope you will be patient with Cal—with the duke. As you can see, he is struggling . . . with everything."

"Yes, of course," she said. "I thank you again, Mr. Fisk."

At the door, Mr. Fisk bowed. Then he turned and stepped out, closing it softly behind him.

Chapter Four

"Come here, Soph."

Tristan leaned back in the armchair, reaching out to her. She approached him and took his hand. He tugged her down so she sat on his lap.

For several long minutes, she reclined against him, reveling in the hard feel of his body against hers as she slowly relaxed, her breaths evening and her heartbeat slowing. He held her pressed tightly to his side, stroking her hair, her back. She buried her face in his shoulder and breathed him in.

"He's ordering Ansley to take steps to have our marriage declared illegal," he murmured finally.

Instantly, all the tension returned to her body. A part of her wanted to pledge herself eternally to Tristan and say she'd forsake Garrett forever. A greater part of her knew she couldn't. She was bound to two men. It had seemed natural enough when she thought one of them gone forever. But now . . .

She looked up into Tristan's tense face and passed a fingertip over a line of strain at the edge of his mouth, avoiding the garish blue and purple marks of his bruises. Garrett had always loved Tristan. He wouldn't purposefully ruin him. This action was only pretense—a swift response to seeing Tristan in bed with her. It couldn't be real. "He cares for you, Tristan."

Tristan gave a grim laugh. "No. Perhaps once, but he hates me now."

"He only thinks he hates you. It was a visceral response to seeing us together. That will fade when he realizes how absurd it is. And then he will realize how he cares for you and doesn't want to destroy you."

"And when he does so, do you believe he will relinquish you to me, Soph?"

She hesitated, her breath stalling in her throat. Suddenly, she understood the look of anguish on Tristan's face. There was no way the three of them could be as close as they once were. Garrett wouldn't give her up, and Tristan would fight for her. The two men would become mortal enemies, and she'd have to choose between them.

She turned away from Tristan to calm her roiling stomach. The thought of losing him made her physically ill. She couldn't let him go. She *wouldn't*.

Tristan answered for her. "He won't relinquish you to me. And when he meets Miranda . . ."

When he meets Miranda . . . The rough man and the delicate little girl. How would they react to each other? And would Garrett use his daughter as a weapon to tear Sophie and Tristan apart?

"Tristan . . ." What could she say to allay his fears? It would hardly encourage him if she told him how torn she was. "We'll find a way. We'll survive this," she finally finished.

She reached up and brushed back a lock of dark hair that had fallen over his forehead. She slid her fingers over his temple and his high cheekbone, finally curving them around the uninjured side of his jaw and adding subtle pressure so he'd turn toward her. When he did, she kissed him softly on the lips. "I love you."

Tristan accepted her kisses, and his eyes drifted shut as she skimmed her lips over his, then over his unshaven jaw and down his neck. She couldn't ignore the voice inside her telling her it could be her last chance to kiss him. To caress him.

When her lips collided with the starch linen of his stock, she paused, then reached up to loosen it, suddenly desperate to see him free of clothing, to touch him skin against skin.

"They might return," Tristan murmured, catching her hand in his own.

She glanced at the door. The duchess's bedchamber had no bolt on it, either outside or in. If she undressed him, someone might very well interrupt. And she couldn't fathom what Garrett might do if he caught them making love again.

She slumped against Tristan. "I'm sorry. I—I just wanted to touch you."

"I know, love," Tristan said, stroking her back. "I want to touch you, too."

She couldn't say to the devil with whoever might walk in on them. As much as she wanted to, she couldn't. Instead, she simply nodded.

"I wasn't able to finish last night." Tristan twined his

finger in one of the curls at the side of her face and tugged gently. "I want to make love to you, Sophie."

One last time. The unspoken words hung in the silence between them.

"Tonight. I'll come to you."

With lowered eyes, she nodded even as guilt speared through her chest. Tristan seemed to sense it, and he pulled her more tightly against him. "You're my wife," he murmured. "Still mine."

He was right. She was lost in his arms, in his touch. There was no denying him. She *was* his, and, as always, she wanted him.

His palm drifted down her back, curved over her bottom. She raised her mouth to his, anticipating the soft touch of his lips.

The door swung open so forcefully it banged against the inside wall. Tristan's arms fell. As if a bucket of cold water had been dumped over her head, Sophie leaped to her feet. Her heart pounding, she smoothed out the wrinkles in her skirt before looking up.

Garrett. Of course. Guilt threatened to choke her when she saw the expression of pain on his face. She'd hurt him again.

Tristan jumped in front of her, shielding her body with his own. She peeked past his shoulder.

Garrett stood at the threshold, his blue eyes freezing into chips of ice. Once again he wore the long, dark overcoat. The only other visible items of his clothing were his well-worn muddied leather boots. His blond hair stood out from his scalp at odd angles, as if it hadn't been combed in weeks. The largest, most deadly-looking pistol Sophie had ever seen dangled from his fingers. The guard Mr. Fisk had taken away stood behind him, also holding a gun.

Sophie bit back a whimper. Her knees turned into jelly, threatening to collapse beneath her.

"Couldn't keep your hands off my wife, even when I asked you nicely, could you, Westcliff?" Garrett's voice was conversational, but it didn't fool Sophie. The look on his face had transformed from pained to murderous, and the scar on his forehead was fire red and twisted with rage.

"She's *my* wife," Tristan said evenly.

Garrett arched an eyebrow, making the scar bulge. He raised the pistol until it was level with Tristan's chest. "Sophie, please move away. The bullet in this weapon is capable of tearing a hole through three men, and I wouldn't want it to go straight through him and mar your pretty skin."

His awful words strengthened her, brought her back to her senses.

"What on earth are you doing?" She pushed her body in front of Tristan's. By God, if he intended to murder Tristan, he'd have to go through her first.

He ignored her, keeping his focus on the much taller figure behind her. "I did say I'd kill you if you went near her, did I not? And now I come home to see you not only in her bedchamber but pawing her like a goddamned animal."

Tristan set his hands on Sophie's shoulders and moved beside her, holding her securely to prevent her from shielding him.

"Why are you doing this?" she asked in desperation. "What do you want from us?"

A loud click echoed through the room as Garrett cocked the pistol.

"Garrett, please!" she cried.

"I want my life back," he said, still not looking at her. His eyes narrowed into slits as he took his aim.

"Don't be a fool," she said desperately. "Think of Tristan, of what an important part of your life he was before you went to the Continent. Don't you remember? If you kill him now, how could you ever expect to have your life back?"

"I won't allow him to touch you. You're already a bloody bigamist. I won't have him make you into an adulterer a second time before my eyes."

"She's not your wife," Tristan growled.

"We'll debate that in hell," Garrett retorted, his eyes as sharp as shards of blue-tinged glass.

She swallowed down her panic. "I don't know what's happening between all of us," she said softly. "Do you want me to be your wife again? Is that it? Do you want us to continue where we left off so many years ago?"

"Yes," he blurted out.

"Never," Tristan muttered. She sent him a hard glance. Garrett had a pistol trained at his chest, and he was being far too reckless.

Nonetheless, Tristan was ultimately right—things had changed too much. She was a mature woman now, different from the besotted girl Garrett had left eight years ago. She could never go back to being that girl.

Tristan had changed, too. And Garrett was so different that she felt she scarcely knew him.

And then there was Miranda . . . Eight years ago, Miranda had existed only as a secret promise in Sophie's womb.

"What of Miranda? Have you seen her?"

Finally his gaze slid toward Sophie. "Miranda? What the hell are you talking about?"

Emotion clogged her throat. How on earth could no one have told him about Miranda?

"Your daughter," she said gently. His eyes widened. "When you left for Waterloo, I was with child, though neither of us knew it at the time. I was waiting to tell you, to surprise you when you came home . . . but you never did." She swallowed against the flood of memories of that terrible time.

Garrett lowered the gun to his side, his features frozen in shock. "What?"

"Your daughter. You have a daughter. Her name is Miranda. She's seven years old."

He blinked hard at her, as if by doing so he'd certainly wake from this bizarre dream. "Where?"

"She's upstairs in the nursery, I imagine. Their governess usually takes them to the park in the afternoons, but—"

Garrett's lips pursed. Without another word, he turned, shoved the gun at the guard so hard it caused the man to stumble backward, and stomped away. Sophie and Tristan exchanged an alarmed glance, then she picked up her skirts and hurried down the corridor as Tristan closed in behind.

Garrett took the stairs two at a time. Sophie rushed behind him, nearly slamming into him when he came to an abrupt halt before the door at the landing. The nursery covered the entire third level of the house—Garrett, Tristan, and Sophie had always jested that the previous Dukes of Calton must have envisioned themselves prolific breeders. Garrett was well-acquainted with the nursery, having spent many hours there with Tristan when they were children and Garrett's father or aunt brought them to Town. The space was open, airy, and bright, always cheerful and pleasant.

After a long pause, Garrett took a deep breath and flung open the door.

The sound of childish chatter came to an abrupt halt as Miranda and Gary looked up with rounded eyes from the book of rhymes they'd been reading. Their governess, Miss Dalworthy, gasped and slapped her hand to her chest in shock.

After a moment of silence, Sophie brushed past Garrett to kneel by the children. Upon seeing her, Gary released a loud sigh of relief and Miranda asked in a low voice, "Who's that big man, Mama?"

There was no reason to beat about the bush. No one had ever accused Sophie of being indirect. "It's your papa, darling."

Miranda stared at Garrett. "It can't be," she said simply. "My papa's dead. He's with the angels."

"My papa's alive, though," Gary said, always one to jump in on a conversation whenever he could. "He's right there." He pointed a blunt finger at Tristan, who stood at Garrett's shoulder.

"We all thought he had gone to the angels, Miranda, but we were wrong. He's alive, and he's come back to us." Sophie glanced at Garrett. He still stood frozen at the door.

Miranda merely frowned and narrowed her blue eyes at him. Sophie's breath caught in her throat. She'd always thought how alike Garrett and Miranda were, so tawny and bright, but the similarities between the two, now that they stood in the same room so close together, stole the breath from her lungs.

Finding her voice, Sophie rose. "Miranda, come greet your father."

Miranda was obedient but hesitant as Sophie walked

her toward Garrett. Little Gary pranced ahead, holding his chubby five-year-old hand out to Garrett. "I am Garrett James, the Marquis of Newbury. Pleasure to meet you, sir."

Garrett sucked in a breath when the boy said his name. Looking bemused, he took the little hand in his much larger one and shook. He gazed at Sophie over Gary's head.

"Tristan and Nancy's son." She glanced at Tristan, who nodded. "Tristan named him to honor you."

Garrett's face hardened, but Gary didn't seem to notice. "My papa says my name comes from the bravest soldier who ever lived," he said blithely.

"Indeed, Gary," Tristan said in a low voice. "And that very soldier is standing before you right now."

Gary's jaw dropped. He gaped at the big man in front of him, his eyes widening as he stared at Garrett's scar. "You? You've been in a real battle?"

A muscle twitched in Garrett's jaw, and Sophie saw his attention had moved back to Miranda, who stared up at the tall stranger before her, clinging to Sophie as if she were a lifeline.

"Come now," Sophie urged.

With the help of a gentle prod to her back, Miranda stepped closer to her father and curtsied. With a dazed look on his face, Garrett looked from his daughter to Sophie.

"She looks like you," he murmured.

Sophie laughed, but it sounded more like a sob. "No, Garrett. She looks like you."

It was too much. He couldn't breathe. Couldn't face any of them. The pretty little girl in front of him, looking up at him with big blue eyes . . . his daughter? No. God, could it be?

Garrett growled an excuse and blindly made his way downstairs, locking himself in the study.

Surrounded by brimming bookshelves and the comforting smell of leather and old books, he slid into the chair behind the desk and sat there with his head in his hands. Minutes turned into hours. Shudders rippled through his shoulders. It hardly seemed real. He had a child. A *daughter*. It would take some time, months maybe, for that to fully register. He hadn't the first idea how to be a father.

Finally he pushed his hand through his hair and stared down at the polished mahogany surface of the desk—the grandest desk he had ever seen, but he remembered it. Remembered sitting here, working on accounts, talking to people who sat in the velvet-cushioned chairs on its other side. A claw-footed marble inkstand stood in one corner of the desk, bearing matching gilt inkpots, summoning bell, and pen holder. Adjacent to it sat a silver salver carrying a short stack of letters addressed to Sophie. A decidedly feminine perfume wafted from the stationery.

This morning, Garrett had ordered the butler to hand him all of Sophie's mail. He vaguely remembered that to read his wife's personal correspondence was a faux pas, a terrible breach of propriety. He hated to do it, but what choice did he have? Taking her letters was the only way he could learn more about her—the inner workings of her mind, who she kept as her friends, what they discussed. It also would keep him apprised of the gossip regarding his return and give him the ability to censor her communication if the need arose.

He took the pile of letters and flipped through them. The heavy scrawl on one of the thicker envelopes looked familiar, and he took it in hand to weigh it before turning it over and breaking the wafer sealing it shut. He unfolded it and discarded several sheets of drawings and scribbled notes to get to the meat of the letter.

It was a missive from his aunt, Lady Bertrice. In it, she discussed every possible aspect of "Becky's" Season in great detail.

Becky. Fisk had told him that he had a younger half sister who lived at Calton House with his aunt. Now he remembered. Rebecca was just a child of ten when he had last seen her, a small, thin, quiet creature who'd preferred to read and study over dancing and social events. Their father had died when she was just a toddler. Her mother, a lady Garrett had hardly known, died of consumption a few years later, leaving Rebecca in the care of their aunt.

Rebecca had always behaved as if she were afraid of him—Garrett had supposed it was because she never had much male influence beyond his own infrequent visits to Calton House when he was not otherwise engaged with his military duties. When he was in his early twenties and madly in love with Sophie, he was so focused on his wife whenever he returned home that he had never found much time to spend with his sister.

Sophie, however, had apparently spent a great deal of time with both Rebecca and his aunt, for they were planning to stay here when they arrived in London for the Season. Garrett quickly scanned the letter, skimming the many passages offering up excruciatingly detailed plans for shackling Becky to the most eligible bachelor in London.

But could this be correct? A Season? For his little waif of a sister? He scowled at the letter, calculating her age. By God . . . Rebecca was eighteen now.

He skimmed more of the letter—silks, muslins, bows,

and bonnets, a page of specifics on a pair of gloves with diamond buttons that made him want to pull his hair out, names of lords and ladies that sounded completely foreign to him—ah, there it was. Rebecca and Aunt Bertrice planned to arrive in London on the twenty-third of April.

"Christ." Garrett slammed the letter down. That was in just over two weeks. How could he be ready to face them by then?

A servant knocked on the door and murmured it was time for dinner. Garrett didn't even look up to acknowledge the man, just waved him away.

He took a long moment to muster his faltering courage before dragging himself to the dining room. He paused at the doorway to take in the scene. A crystal chandelier burned brightly overhead. Tristan and Fisk, both wearing black with white neckcloths, sat across from each other and Sophie sat at one end of the table, dressed in a satiny red evening gown festooned along the neckline and around the edges of the puffy short sleeves with tiny budding roses. Her hair was swept high, leaving curling locks to fall delicately about her ears, and complementing fresh rosebuds wreathed her head. Diamond earrings dangled from her ears, and a matching diamond necklace encircled her neck, glittering in the candlelight. She was elegant. Lovely. An unlikely match for Garrett, who was not only scarred beyond redemption, but wore muddied trousers, boots with holes in their soles, and a plain, yellowed shirt beneath his unfashionable coat.

Fortunately, Fisk had procured this bulky coat for him. He'd worn it to hide his real appearance, but the wool was beginning to scratch at his neck. Too busy facing more serious crises, he hadn't yet had enough time to use his newly discovered riches to buy proper clothes. Nevertheless, it was a problem he'd have to address soon. He couldn't very well pretend to lord over this place looking like a farm worker.

Grinding his teeth, he tore his gaze from Sophie and found the one unoccupied place setting at the head of the table.

Had Tristan sat at the head of the table for the past year? Was this a concession on his part?

He took the available chair, realizing belatedly that the table's centerpiece, a garish, twisted mass of metal that he was certain wasn't supposed to look like Medusa's locks encased in gold, obscured his view of his wife.

He debated commanding one of the hovering footmen to remove it, but he couldn't recall whether such a demand would be appropriate. Damn, but he wished he could remember more of the basics of living the life of a duke.

Dinner was a quiet, nearly morbid affair. The soft clink of silver on china made the only sound, and with a pang of something—longing?—Garrett remembered the cheerful, intimate dinner conversations he, Sophie, and Tristan used to have. He didn't really remember what they spoke of, only the image of their younger faces and the sense of utter contentment he'd felt in their presence then. They'd been so happy.

The spring soup was oversalted, the vegetables overcooked, and the roasted chicken tasted like cardboard. Garrett ate it all—he was accustomed to eating tasteless food. In the past years, he'd learned the true purpose of food was nourishment, not enjoyment. The only thing that slid over his tongue bursting with flavor was the wine, and

Garrett drank several glasses. It seemed everyone else partook generously as well.

He leaned to the side and, out of the corner of his eye, watched Sophie force a few bites and wash them down with wine. Adjusting himself to a more upright position, he took a bite of dark meat as a strange sensation of gratification poked at his hardened spirit. He and Sophie had a daughter.

When they were first married, she'd desperately prayed for a child to nurture, and he'd always thought she'd make a perfect mother. After four years, however, she still hadn't conceived and they'd all but given up, certain she was barren. Yet through some miracle, she'd conceived Miranda before he went to war. He'd been able to leave her the gift of their child.

He shoveled a bite of chicken into his mouth, thinking of the pretty little girl in the nursery who shared his blood. She was lovely, really, with a sweet heart-shaped face, wise large blue eyes, and light blonde hair. She had searched his face—his eyes—but hadn't given his scar a second glance. That pleased him more than he cared to contemplate.

He'd missed seven years of the joys of parenting he once ached for. Perhaps Sophie could teach him how to be an adequate father to their daughter. Perhaps . . . if the rift between him and his wife could be breached. At the moment, the prospects appeared grim.

Glancing at Tristan, whose eyes were firmly fixed on Sophie, Garrett set down his fork with a loud clink and took a generous swallow of wine. Whatever they thought about him didn't matter. He would hold on to Sophie even if she hated him for the rest of his life. She was his, just as much as his title and his lands. He'd lived far too long without the things that belonged to him by rights. He would take it all back, and this time, damn it, he'd hang on to it. To hell with the consequences.

He lowered his glass and stared at his wine. Light from the candles sparkled and danced through the pale liquid. Hell . . . he was fooling himself. As much as he wished to remain immune to Sophie, he couldn't deny that a part of him longed for the way she used to look at him, her hazel eyes brimming with love. Even his limited memory could recall that.

Her love was worth fighting for. Even if it meant fighting Tristan.

A figure materialized beside him, and Garrett went tense all over before realizing it was just a footman offering him more stewed celery. Waving the man away, he forced himself to relax. He still had not grown accustomed to the servants always milling about. His memories of them were elusive, as if they hadn't meant anything to him at all, so didn't warrant a single precious piece of his fractured mind. But how could that be the case, considering they were everywhere, always watching with silent attentiveness, like hovering phantoms? They made his skin crawl.

Finally Garrett finished his wine, set down his glass, and looked up at his melancholy companions. "We will take our port in the study," he announced. Everyone paused to glance at him, but he stared across the table, growing more annoyed at that damned centerpiece by the second. "Will you join us, Sophie?"

The order in his tone belied the polite nature of the question—though he remembered hazily that it was hardly polite to ask a lady to join with the gentlemen to drink port. Not that he cared.

She inclined her head. "Of course, Your Grace."

He tore his gaze away from her as another memory surfaced, this one of her whispering soft words into his ear as she soothed the lash marks on his back after his father had beaten him for some infraction.

He closed his eyes. Each time he looked at her, more memories assailed him. He recalled her chasing him and Tristan across the meadow behind Calton House, first on foot and then on ponies and finally on horses. He remembered bumping noses on their first awkward kiss, and he remembered making love to her for the first time, when she'd gasped as he'd breached her maidenhead.

There were so many memories of them making love. He remembered now what it had been like to sleep with Sophie . . . she had a hot sensuality to her like no woman he'd experienced since.

He couldn't believe he'd forgotten, but now he understood why he'd never felt quite right with any of the women he'd known in Belgium . . . not even Joelle, whom he'd considered taking to wife, though he'd had no prospects to entice her. He had unknowingly committed adultery. The man he was before Waterloo had never touched a woman outside of wedlock. Sophie was his first—the only woman he'd ever planned to make love to. Now they'd both strayed, both in innocence, unaware of the other's existence.

Drawing in a pained breath, Garrett rose from the table, and the rest of them followed suit. He didn't miss the wary glance Tristan exchanged with Sophie. Their silent, shared communication sent painful jealousy knifing through him, and he had to curl his fists to keep his hands from shaking. Once upon a time, he and Sophie had communicated that way.

Somberly, they filed out of the dining room and moved four doors down to the study. Rather like a funeral procession, he thought.

Since he'd left for dinner, someone had come to light the tall lamps in the corners and stoke the fire, which now crackled cheerfully behind the brass grate. Green velvet draperies were drawn tight over the tall windows facing the fireplace. Garrett passed his writing desk near the far wall and sank onto the leather chair behind it.

Looking grim, Tristan took a seat in the mint-green velvet armchair nearest the desk and beside the windows. A footman bustled about with a tray bearing glasses of port and claret, and Garrett took a glass of the dark red liquid. Waving off the servant, Fisk took a straight-backed chair close to the fire, and with a glass of claret in hand, Sophie lowered herself into a soft-looking armchair with roses embroidered on the arms.

Garrett blinked against a memory. They had made love here once. Sophie bent over the arm of that chair, him holding her, thrusting into her from behind. He bowed his head, fighting the onslaught. He couldn't control how the memories came back to him, and he craved them as a pauper covets gold. Yet three people faced him, all with expectant looks on their faces. He couldn't allow himself to be distracted by what happened in the deepest recesses of his mind. They wouldn't understand.

He placed both his hands flat on the desk and leaned forward, raising his head to meet Tristan's dark gaze. The man's presence threatened everything. Garrett couldn't rebuild his life when Tristan claimed to love Sophie and declared she belonged to him. No . . . Garrett would nip that delusion—a delusion both of them seemed to share—in the bud.

A very large part of him wished he'd pulled the pistol's trigger earlier, but an even larger part knew that he couldn't do it. Yes, he could kill men, and he had. But he wouldn't kill the man he'd once loved like a brother.

As with Sophie, every time he looked at Tristan, memories crowded his mind . . . Of tricking their tutor into believing they'd done more reading than they actually had. Of Garrett breaking another boy's nose for sneering at Tristan's gawky height during his first year at Eton. Of digging in the dirt on one of Tristan's famous "archaeological" expeditions at Calton House.

And yet this man had betrayed Garrett in the worst way imaginable. Today, Ansley had confirmed that in his greed, Tristan had stolen Garrett's title, his money, and his lands and then mismanaged them all. Worst of all, however, he'd stolen Sophie's affections.

Garrett would never forgive him. As long as he lived, he doubted he'd be able to look at Tristan without wanting to murder him in cold blood.

But he couldn't kill him. Christ, he didn't even want to hurt him. He just wanted—*needed*—the man out of his sight.

"I want you to leave, Westcliff." He tried to modulate his tone but inwardly flinched at the grating rage he heard on the fringes of his voice.

Tristan gave a slight nod, his expression unreadable. "Of course."

Sophie sucked in a breath, but Garrett ignored her. He couldn't look at her now and risk more memories assaulting him. Last night they had come so fast and hard he had barely possessed the ability to function when he sat beside her on the drawing room sofa. It was far safer to keep his gaze fixed on Tristan. "You will take your child with you, but you will not take mine."

Sophie gasped. Apparently it had not occurred to her that he'd want to keep his own child.

Tristan's eyes narrowed.

"Nor," Garrett continued through his teeth, "will you take my wife."

Tristan returned his stare levelly. "I will not leave this house without Sophie and Miranda."

Fisk rose, raising a calming hand at Garrett and taking a step toward the desk. Garrett sat back, happy to allow him to take the reins. Fisk could manage this with far more poise than he could.

Fisk turned to Tristan. "Your Grace, this is a simple legal matter."

"Fine," Tristan snapped. "Sophie is legally mine."

"But Miranda," Sophie whispered, clearly stricken by the thought of being separated from her daughter.

Fisk inclined his head at Sophie, his expression gentle. "No, Your Grace, you misunderstand. We were with Mr. Ansley today, sorting it all out in the proper legal fashion." He turned to Garrett. "Cal, I believe the best course of action will be for Lord Westcliff to remain in the house until everything is settled."

Garrett raised a brow. He wasn't so certain. On the other hand, if Tristan remained in the house, he could watch him, ascertain he did nothing subversive to try to undermine his attempts to win Sophie or his estates back. Perhaps Fisk was right.

Still, Garrett knew he couldn't control the violence that might ensue if he saw Tristan touching Sophie again.

"I'll not remain here as a prisoner," Tristan said.

Fisk let out a long sigh and gave Garrett a pointed look before returning his attention to Tristan. "Truly you are not a prisoner, sir. Please remember the matter we discussed earlier."

"What matter might that be?" Garrett asked.

"The matter of your amnesia," Sophie said softly. She rose and stepped toward the table, placing her small, perfect hand over his scarred and callused one. "Mr. Fisk told us everything, Garrett."

Unable to meet her eyes, Garrett stared down at the polished wood gleaming in the lamplight. Her hand looked so pale, so delicate over his. Her skin was soft and smooth. With her touch alone, she could melt his bitter insides like butter.

He glanced away. His gaze met Fisk's, and he hardened. Damn the man for revealing his weakness.

Releasing him, Sophie turned to Tristan. "Please stay, Tristan. We should all work this out together."

Garrett hated hearing the tone of voice she used to speak to his rival. Gentle. *Loving.*

Tristan hissed out a breath. "I will not be treated like a common prisoner. That technique might have proven successful when we were children, but it won't work with me now. I won't stand for it."

Garrett narrowed his eyes at the other man. "I need assurance that you won't touch her, won't speak to her, won't approach her—"

"You won't have it," Tristan shot back.

"Perhaps you might consider yourself a guest, then," Fisk said smoothly.

Tristan snorted. "Civilized Englishmen don't lock their guests in their bedchambers."

"I never claimed to be civilized," Garrett retorted.

"Surely we might come to some arrangement so you aren't limited to a single room," Fisk continued.

Garrett gave Fisk a hard look. He hoped the man knew what the hell he was doing, because he couldn't stand living in the same house with Tristan, watching the lovers casting longing glances at each other over their dinners. It would drive him mad.

Fisk caught his gaze and gave a subtle nod. His expression said, *trust me*.

God, he didn't know how this would turn out, but Fisk would think things through when his own raging emotions got in the way. Garrett released a breath. "Very well. You may have your freedom. I warn you, Westcliff—"

Tristan raised his hand. "Don't say it. I know. More threats of death and murder. I don't need to hear them again."

"The decision of the court will undoubtedly prove that your marriage is invalid and illegal," Garrett said. "Don't do anything stupid or there will be repercussions."

Tristan snorted. "You make ridiculous assumptions. Though it has now been proven you are alive, you abandoned her for more than seven years, left her alone when she was with child, and forced her into mourning—"

Garrett shot up from his chair. "Bastard," he growled. If the damned desk wasn't between them, he'd grab Tristan and throw him out by the scruff of his neck. How dare he accuse Garrett of abandoning Sophie as if his actions had been malicious and deliberate? "If Fisk told you anything of what happened, you damn well know I never abandoned her. Your accusations will never hold up in court."

Fisk flashed him a warning glance, and Garrett stood down, thankful his friend was here to keep him reasonable. God knew he couldn't manage any of this in an appropriately calm fashion.

Sophie clasped her hands together in front of her. She looked back and forth from Garrett to Tristan. "The three of us lived harmoniously for years before Waterloo," she said softly. "We were the best of friends, the closest companions one could ever imagine. Surely somehow we can rediscover that love for one another and regain something of our past."

Her gaze settled on Garrett, and her eyes shone bronze in the glimmering light of the chandelier. *Sophie.* Ever the optimist, the girl who lay between them on the grass and whispered grand dreams of future happiness for all three of them as they stared up at the stars.

Garrett glanced at Fisk, who nodded and beamed at Sophie, then at Tristan, who gave her a dubious look. Garrett shook his head hopelessly. This would never work. One of them would certainly be dead or mad before it was all over. He hoped it wouldn't be him.

Chapter Five

Every morning, surrounded by pens, ink, and paper, Sophie sat at a makeshift desk the servants had erected in her bedchamber. She'd sent word to her mother and all the cousins in Yorkshire while Miranda sat next to her, laboriously writing to her cousins using big words like "amazingly incredible" and "utterly unbelievable" to describe the reappearance of her long-lost papa.

Sophie wrote notes to their staff at Calton House and one to Tristan and Garrett's unmarried uncle. She'd dispatched letters to her friends at their estates scattered throughout the country. On this particular morning, Miranda was with her tutor, so Sophie sat alone as she penned missives to Tristan's Parliament friends, Garrett's old army companions, including the Duke of Wellington, and the aristocrats who had begun to filter into Town for the Season.

Signing her name on the final letter, she set her pen

down and held her wrist, rotating her hand and curling her cramping fingers.

Of course she hadn't addressed the marriage problem. The ladies and gentlemen of the *ton* weren't fools, and they'd recognize the dilemma right away. An ugly scandal loomed on the horizon, and there was nothing she could do to stop it. They'd likely call her *The Adulterous Duchess*; perhaps something as awful as *Her Grace the Bigamist*. They'd publish scathing caricatures of her, Tristan, and Garrett. Sophie and her two husbands would be watched carefully, their every public move scrutinized ad nauseam.

No matter what happened, Sophie resolved to maintain her dignity. Neither she nor Tristan had been the subject of a scandal before, but they had witnessed them from afar, and they knew how not to behave. They would keep their chins up and never falter.

Choosing a wafer from the box one of the servants had brought, Sophie sealed the letter she'd written to the Countess of Harpsford expressing her excitement over Garrett's return and subtly suggesting the countess and earl refrain from visiting until Garrett and his family had a chance to become reacquainted.

While the countess would likely respect Sophie's wishes, many others would not, and soon people would crowd their doorstep intending to welcome the Duke of Calton home. Sophie planned to fend off visitors for as long as possible. It fell on her to see to it that Garrett's re-emergence into the public eye went as seamlessly as possible, and he wasn't ready yet. He displayed no interest in reacquainting himself with his peers. From his behavior, Sophie began to wonder whether he'd interacted with polite society while in Belgium. In fact, he hardly seemed accustomed to interacting with anyone, and the servants seemed to discompose him most of all. She tapped the letter on the desk, thinking. Could it be possible he hadn't managed servants for so many years?

She frowned as she tried to imagine the Duke of Calton, the Garrett she had known, strong but accustomed to getting his way in all matters, dressing himself, shaving himself, preparing his own food. Even in the army, he had servants and Sir Thomas to wait upon him.

Perhaps he had forgotten his social standing. Perhaps he had forgotten he'd once depended on others to manage nearly all the mundane tasks associated with his well-being.

Troubled, she considered Garrett's sister Becky and his aunt, Lady Bertrice, who were due to arrive in London soon. Was he aware they were coming? Did he even remember them?

She straightened the desk, creating neat piles of letters and stationery, and resolved to seek Garrett out and ask him herself.

She rose, smoothing her hair and straightening the long sleeves and shaking out the pleated skirt of her red-trimmed ivory lawn day dress. She fussed with the fichu tucked into her neckline—she could never get the folds as perfect as Delia could, but Delia was nowhere to be found. Giving up on adjusting the gauzy material, she retrieved the batch of letters and stepped out of the duchess's chambers. At the bottom of the stairs, she handed a footman the letters to post and headed toward the study, certain that if Garrett was home, she'd find him there.

Garrett was hunched over the desk, his face in his

hands, wearing that same tattered black coat he never seemed to remove. He looked up when she entered, the exhaustion in his expression transforming to wariness.

"Sophie." His voice was completely flat, devoid of any emotion. "To what do I owe this pleasure, my love?"

The words were gentle, but the tone was as hard as granite. She paused just inside the doorway. The first time he'd called her "my love" was on their wedding night. They were both naked, and he was holding himself over her. She'd stroked the strong planes of his chest, awed by this man who now belonged to her. Smiling, he bent to run his lips over the shell of her ear. "Sophie," he whispered, and the timbre of his voice sent a shudder through her that she felt all the way to the tips of her toes, "my love." He placed the emphasis on "my"—a subtle claim of possession. And then he had slowly pushed inside her. It was the first time for both of them.

Perhaps he didn't recall that moment. His face was devoid of emotion except for a quizzical tilt to his brow.

Remembering he'd asked her a question, she stepped deeper into the room. Someone had opened the curtains, and hazy sunlight drifted in the two tall windows. She walked over and pretended to look out at the back garden, where she grew herbs and a few rosebushes. The roses, pruned into sticks a few months ago by the grounds-keeper, were covered with tiny new leaves and buds almost invisible to the eye.

"We've not had the opportunity to spend much time together." She ran her fingertips over the green velvet of the curtain. "I thought we ought to begin to reacquaint ourselves."

She watched him from the corner of her eye. His face

darkened as surely as if storm clouds had passed overhead before he dropped his gaze to a paper on his desk and casually dipped a pen in the inkpot.

"I have work to do."

Curling her fingers round the soft edge of the curtain, she turned to face him. "Garrett, are you aware that your sister and aunt will be here soon?"

He glanced at her, then back to his writing. "Yes."

She paused. It wasn't the answer she'd expected, but she shrugged it off. He must've heard about his family's impending visit from Connor or another one of the servants. Or, more likely, Mr. Fisk had heard and then told Garrett.

"I considered stopping them, or at least asking them to delay their visit while you and Tristan and I work through our . . . dilemma."

Garrett shrugged and dipped his pen into the ink.

"But we have very high expectations for Becky's Season," she continued.

At that, he paused, pen in midair. Looking up, he raised a brow at her. "Are you certain you want to go forward with a Season for her? I'm informed my shocking arrival is likely to cause a scandal of the first order."

She set her shoulders. "Canceling her Season will be akin to conceding defeat, admitting that there is legitimacy to whatever gossip people choose to bandy about. I won't do it."

"I am certain you will prevail," he said. "But Rebecca? What will her reaction be to the ladies twittering from behind their fans?"

"She will hold her head high, just as we all shall." Sophie released the curtain and lowered her hand to her side, facing Garrett head-on. "She is a duke's daughter, a duke's sister, a lady in her own right with a sizeable fortune to boot. No one will dare spurn her."

He smiled thinly. "Go forward with your plans, then. I am sure you won't disappoint."

"But what about you? Are you prepared to see her again?"

He shrugged. "It appears I don't have much choice in the matter."

"Just be civil with her, Garrett. Your sister . . ."

"What about her?"

Sophie took a deep breath. "She has become a lovely young woman. She's beautiful, but she is quite innocent. Rather soft-hearted and unused to shows of temper."

"I'll endeavor not to shout in her presence, then."

"You must disband your henchmen."

"No."

"I shouldn't like them gawking at her. They might frighten her."

He swallowed and seemed to deliberate before releasing a breath through pursed lips. "I'll take that into consideration."

"Thank you."

He inclined his head.

"There's so much to do. And when they arrive, I've no doubt things will become hectic."

"No doubt."

"And, Garrett, you will ultimately be the one responsible for approving her choice for a husband."

"I realize this." He plunged his pen into the ink again and began scribbling.

She took a step toward him. "Don't do this. Please."

"Do what, Sophie?" He kept writing, diligently keeping his gaze averted from hers.

"Avoid me. Cut yourself off from me. This isn't you—this isn't who you were before Waterloo. Surely there must be something of the old Garrett inside you. Remember how it was before? It was never like this between us. Why are you so cold?"

"Walking in on your wife in bed with someone else rather forces it, wouldn't you say?"

Garrett smacked the pen down and rose from his chair, ominous and large in his big black coat, a ferocious scowl painted across his face. Sophie faced him head-on, unwilling to be cowed.

"How could you stand beside him, even after he hurt you like that? He tied you to the bed, for Christ's sake. And I saw the bruises—" His lips thinned. "Hell. He beat you, too. I could kill him for that alone."

"No! Tristan would never hurt me."

He shook his head, disbelieving.

"We went riding that morning and I was kicked by my horse. He was frantic with worry."

Garrett's scowl deepened, and just as she opened her mouth to tell him more, a gentle knock sounded at the door. Mr. Fisk leaned in. "Forgive me for the interruption, Your Graces. Cal—they're here. I offered them some refreshment and told them you'd meet them in your bedchamber."

In his bedchamber? Who on earth would meet with Garrett there?

"Thank you, Fisk."

Smiling graciously, Mr. Fisk retreated, closing the door softly behind him.

She turned back to Garrett, and he gave her a small shrug. "As I said, Sophie. I've some matters I must attend to."

"In your bedchamber," she said dryly. "Very well, Your Grace."

Garrett lips curled into a smirk. "Never fear, *wife*. I have no intention of engaging in adulterous behavior, contrary to—"

"Don't be a fool, Garrett," she snapped. "Lord. I thought you were dead. Honestly! Would you rather I'd joined a nunnery than marry the man I loved most in the world? Would you rather I lived in purgatory than find happiness again?"

"Yes."

She gaped at him. Then she shook her head. "Did you never touch another woman during our years apart?"

He rose and took one menacing step toward her. Then another, and another, until he was hovering over her, close but not touching.

"I didn't recall that I was married."

"And I was a widow! I didn't touch another man for seven years. How long was it before you took a lover?"

He gritted his teeth. "That is of no consequence."

She laughed bitterly. "Less than a year? I wouldn't be shocked if it was before I gave birth to our daughter."

Garrett threw up his hands. "You're dwelling on the past."

"So are you."

"No, I'm not. You know I've returned, yet you're still in love with another man." His features tightened. "And of all the men in the world, you had to choose Tristan, didn't you? I might be able to accept it if it were any other man, but Tristan? Goddamn it, Sophie."

Clenching her fists at her sides, she met his narrowed eyes. "You can't expect me to douse my love for him as easily as I can douse a candle flame. We've lived the better part of a year as man and wife. I can't simply extinguish that."

"Why not?" Garrett asked. He raked a hand through his hair, causing it to stick up in clumps. "I could."

They stared at each other, so close she could feel the warmth of Garrett's powerful body. The air between them seemed to crackle. His lips were so close, she could almost taste them. She remembered their taste. So masculine. Firm and strong.

From the way he was gazing at her mouth, she knew he was remembering, too.

Slowly, he reached for her hand. His big fingers twined with hers.

"Sophie." His voice rasped over her, low and alluring, sending skitters down her spine.

The door's hinges creaked as it swung open. "Sophie, I—"

Her attention swung to the threshold. Tristan stood there, the look of shock on his face transforming to anger then dissolving into impassivity. Mr. Fisk hovered just behind him, his expression unreadable.

Tristan gave a short bow. "I'm sorry to interrupt. I was led to believe you were in here alone, Soph—Your Grace. Please forgive me."

Garrett didn't falter. Squeezing her hand, he dragged his gaze from her to glare at Tristan and Mr. Fisk. But he said nothing.

The tension in the room thickened to a muddling mist. Sophie wished Garrett would let her hand go, but he gripped it firmly, and she couldn't tug away without being obvious. She looked helplessly at Tristan, easily reading the anger and betrayal behind the blank expression on his face.

"I will thank you to unhand my wife," Tristan finally said, his voice as rigid as she'd ever heard it.

Garrett didn't flinch. "The conversation becomes tiring. We both know whose wife she is."

"Yes. She's mine."

"Do stop, both of you," Sophie said. Finding strength in exasperation, she wrenched her hand from Garrett's.

Garrett turned to Mr. Fisk and Tristan. "If you will excuse me—I have someone awaiting me in my bedchamber."

Brushing hard past Tristan, he exited the room. As soon as he disappeared, Mr. Fisk excused himself as well and left, shutting the door behind him.

Sophie released a pent-up breath as Tristan strode to her. Reaching out, he took hold of her shoulders and gripped tight. "What happened in here, Sophie?"

"Nothing. We were merely talking."

"I don't want him touching you."

"It was nothing, Tristan."

He was silent for a moment, then muttered, "Goddamn it," and strode to the window, thrusting his fingers through his dark hair in a frustrated move contrary to his normal calm and precise mannerisms.

Garrett had posted armed guards outside her room at all hours, so Tristan hadn't come to her that first night, nor any of the nights since. She missed him desperately.

It was so unnatural to live in the same house as him and yet be forced to maintain such distance.

"You are still legally my wife," he said through gritted teeth. "Do you think I will allow him to touch you, to worm his way back into your affections?"

She frowned. Tristan well knew Garrett had never left her affections to begin with.

"Nothing happened," she repeated.

"I will not stand by idly as another man makes love to my wife."

"He was merely holding my hand. He wasn't making love to me, Tristan."

Tristan spun to face her, his eyes wild. "But he will, Sophie. Don't you see? He will."

Soon afterward, a still-frustrated Tristan left to meet with a new solicitor, for he had determined it would be impossible to work with Mr. Ansley, who was first and foremost employed by the true Duke of Calton.

It was a fine spring day, and Sophie had been cooped up in the house for far too long. Every room was oppressive to her, and the duchess's bedchamber was intolerable. A walk would clear her mind of cobwebs and help her to think more clearly.

"Delia?" she called as she entered the narrow little room she'd slept in for the past several days.

Her lady's maid turned from the clothes press and peeked through the door to the tiny dressing room. "Yes ma'am?"

"We shall be going for a walk."

"Of course, Your Grace."

Delia donned a cloak and helped Sophie into a red

pelisse that matched the color of the satin ribbons shot through the hem and sleeves of her ivory dress. Her hat, piled high with feathers and red apples, provided a jaunty complement to the ensemble.

Tugging on her gloves, Sophie walked downstairs and through the back room toward the door opening on the path along the edge of the property that led to the street. Carrying her parasol, Delia followed close behind.

As Sophie stepped onto the path, a hand clamped around her wrist.

"I think not, milady."

Yet another of Garrett's henchmen. She stared from the dirty fingers clasped around her snow-white gloves to a man's sneering, pockmarked face, too surprised to inform him he had addressed her improperly.

After a long, silent moment of shock, she found her voice. "Please unhand me, sir."

"No, ma'am. You're not to leave the house. Master's orders."

Sophie's jaw dropped. "*What* did you say?"

She'd assumed Garrett had dispensed with the ridiculous notion of caging her inside the house when he'd granted Tristan his freedom. Apparently not.

The man laughed. His breath reeked of onions, and she staggered backward. Only his continued grip on her wrist prevented her from stumbling over a loose rock in the path. "The duke says you're not to leave the house, even if it's to walk the grounds. Under no circumstances are you to set foot outside." The man dropped her hand. "Now you'd best get back inside, ma'am."

Sophie hesitated. She could return to the house and cower in her cramped room for the remainder of the day.

The Sophie Garrett had married would have done so without a second thought.

She glanced at Delia, whose blue eyes were wide with shock. She stood frozen, as if waiting to see what her mistress would do.

This was impossible, intolerable, insufferable. Garrett could not imprison her in the house. He could *not*.

Sophie pinned the guard with a disdainful stare. "You will not dare to place your hand upon my person again," she said, her voice calm but laced with steel. "I am going for a walk. You may inform your master that I refused to be bullied and that I shall return home before dinner."

The man seemed to lose some of his bravado, but his hand wandered to the pistol at his waist. Sophie laughed tightly. "What do you plan to do? Shoot me? I should think that would be rather unwise."

"My orders are—"

"Your orders? Last I checked, I was the mistress of this house. Come along, Delia." Her back stiff, she turned to march down the path leading to the street. She didn't deign to look back at the guard, much as she wished to view the expression on his face. When she reached Curzon Street, she released a breath of relief, for a small part of her had wondered if he'd shoot her regardless. Or, more likely, toss her over his shoulder and carry her back into the house. But he had done neither, and she was free.

Delia didn't say a word, and for that she was grateful. Sophie glanced at her to see her eyes still large with shock. "Everything's all right," she soothed.

Delia gulped. "Yes, ma'am."

"Come. Let's walk."

With Delia hurrying after her, Sophie strode along

Curzon Street and turned past Berkeley Square, which was crowded with people on this fine spring afternoon. Hoping she wouldn't meet anyone she knew, she kept her gaze on the pavement as she marched down the far side of the street past the square and turned into Mount Street. By the time she reached the street that led back home, she was bristling.

How dare he set his henchman on her on the grounds of the house that had been her home for the past twelve years? With a gun, no less. What if Miranda or Gary had been with her?

Delia puffed behind her, nearly having to run to keep up. Taking pity on her maid, Sophie slowed to let her catch her breath.

Had he truly intended to lock her in the house? For what purpose? Was his level of distrust for her so severe that he thought such lengths were necessary?

When Delia seemed rested enough, she hurried back to the house, stormed through the gate, passed the now-sheepish guard without so much as a glance, and burst in the front door, ignoring Connor, who rushed toward her as she entered. She mounted the stairs, removing the pins from her hat with shaking hands. Breathing harshly, Delia scampered behind her, collecting the pins as Sophie passed them back. By the time she reached the top of the stairs, she'd yanked off the heavy hat, and she handed it along with her pelisse to Delia as she reached the door to the master bedchamber.

"Return these to my room, please," she said to Delia, whose cheeks were shiny with sweat and flushed pink. "And then you may have the remainder of the day off to rest." She plucked off her gloves and passed those to Delia as well.

"Yes, madam." Her mouth agape, the girl curtsied, then turned and scurried away.

As soon as her maid disappeared, Sophie turned back to the door and flung it open.

"I will never—"

But what she saw in Garrett's bedchamber cut her words off as sharply as if they'd been hacked with a knife.

Chapter Six

Garrett stood in the center of the room wearing a tattered shirt, yellowed with age, and mud-caked trousers, shoddily made, well used, and frayed at the ankles. His feet were bare, but they were nearly as dirty as the trousers.

Two men flanked him, one holding a measuring tape and the other with swaths of fabrics draped over his arm. One of the men had been speaking as she'd entered—the word "fashion" overlapped Sophie's abbreviated tirade as the door banged into the wall.

"Sophie." Garrett's voice was dry, but his eyes sparked with challenge.

After a long moment, she found her voice. "Garrett."

A long pause ensued as they stared at each other.

Finally, she asked, "Why are you wearing . . . those filthy garments?" Then she berated herself for asking such a foolish question.

He glanced down at himself. "They happen to be all I own."

The two other men, clearly uncomfortable, shifted from foot to foot. Garrett raised a blond eyebrow at her. "Do you require my assistance for some matter of importance? As you can see—" He motioned to the tailors. "—I am occupied."

He wouldn't give her an inch. Sophie straightened her spine. She was finished with allowing him to sidle away from confrontation.

She marched up to him, stopping just an arm's length away. "Yes, there's a matter of great importance I must discuss with you. I insist."

"Well, gentlemen, it seems we will have to continue at another time. You have enough to occupy you for now, I imagine."

Both men snapped to attention. "Yes, Your Grace, of course," said the tailor carrying the fabric samples. They bowed at Garrett and Sophie before scurrying about to collect their things and disappearing.

Garrett just stood there, staring at her, his gaze never wavering. When the door shut, he was silent for a long moment before speaking. "I fear it's true. I spent the last seven years a pauper. I imagine you will mock me for it. Or perhaps—" His lips twisted in a sneer. "—you will even pity me."

So many thoughts rampaged through Sophie's mind, she found it difficult to form them into something cohesive. Why had he kept this from her? And yet it explained so much.

She glanced around the room—her bedroom, with its familiar colors, textures, and smells. On the fringes, she could still sense Tristan. But Garrett's strong, masculine presence had begun to edge him out.

"Neither pity nor mockery, Garrett."

She reached up to touch his shirt. Her fingertips brushed over his chest. The fabric had grown stiff with a mixture of dirt and sweat.

"I haven't had time to wash it." He wasn't in the least apologetic.

"I'll order a bath for you, and the clothes to be washed."

"Don't you think it would be inappropriate for the servants to wash clothing for their master that is far inferior to their own?"

She shrugged. "It hardly matters."

Perhaps it was her imagination, but she thought she saw some of the tightness around his lips ease.

Sophie rang for a maid and ordered the bath. When the girl had gone, she returned her gaze to Garrett. "Did you plan to imprison me in the house forever? If so, I'd suggest you hire more adequate guards. It only took a few words for me to pass that scoundrel you hired to imprison me."

His lips thinned once more, and she almost regretted her words. Almost.

"I wish to keep you close. Until I'm certain you can be trusted."

"Trusted? Where would I go? What would I do?"

"When you are at home, you can be watched."

"Of course. After all, what reason have I given you to trust me? I hurt every single day. I longed for you, and I missed you. But you don't see that, do you? You saw one moment of my life, and from that singular incident, you judge my character and think you can interpret how I feel about you and what actions I'm likely to take. Do you think you know me, Garrett?"

"What will it be, Sophie? You would have me in your bed one night and him in your bed the next? You know neither of us could live with such an arrangement."

"I don't know. I only know I won't allow you to destroy everything Tristan and I have built together."

"And I won't allow him to destroy me."

They were at a stalemate. And, in truth, what had she expected? His generous approval of her keeping Tristan in her bed?

She huffed out a breath. "Nevertheless, neither of us will allow you to bully us. Do you think that is a way to reestablish our affection for you?"

"I have no wish to reestablish anything with Tristan James."

She ground her teeth to prevent herself from calling him a stubborn, stupid oaf. "You're blinded by your anger. Stop and think, Garrett. Don't be a fool."

"Think about what?"

"Your behavior. I won't be bullied, nor will I be ignored or treated like a child. I might have been a child when we married, but I'm not anymore. I'm a full-grown independent woman who has endured too much to be browbeaten by gun-wielding henchmen or blustering idiots who call themselves men. If you refuse to treat me with respect, then I have nothing more to say to you."

"I saw you—"

"I know what you saw!" she snapped. "I was there, too. That was a private moment, and you had no right to interfere. But it has nothing to do with what's happening now, or what's going to happen between the three of us."

"What's that, Sophie? What's going to happen?"

Her hands flew upward in frustration. "I don't know!

If you'd stop behaving like an overbearing ass, perhaps we could begin to work together to solve our problem. Shouldn't we be endeavoring to learn more about one another? Shouldn't we be attempting to rebuild our lives instead of tearing them apart?"

He studied her with crystalline eyes. "Tell me how," he said in a low voice. "Please, Sophie. Because I don't know."

He stood in the center of the room dressed in tatters, his body strong, his stance powerful, his expression fierce. The raw emotion in his voice alleviated her frustration, and the anguished look in his eyes told her that he spoke the truth.

"There's so much I want to know, Garrett. All about the years you were away. Please tell me what happened to you and how you found your way home. Surely I deserve that much. And I'll tell you anything you want to know about our lives since you left us."

She considered leading him into the adjoining sitting room, but she heard the servants moving to set up the bath there. In any case, he seemed more comfortable where he was. He still hadn't moved from the spot where he'd stood since she entered, but his fingers and shoulders had relaxed, and tension no longer radiated from him in waves.

"You were a . . . peasant?"

"A farm worker," he said shortly.

"Where?"

He looked away from her, his jaw tight. "I'd rather forget those years. Start anew."

"I understand that. It must have been difficult for you. But I still need to know, Garrett, because it was difficult for me, too. What were you doing when I lay alone in our bed missing you? Aching for you?"

He stared at her, lips pursed. But his expression softened, and she knew he was thawing.

She turned partly away and placed her hand flat against the back of one of the rust-colored damask armchairs near the fireplace. "I used to sit here and think of you. Think of us together. Laughing. Talking. Making love . . ."

He took a step toward her. His gaze seemed to spear right through her, stabbing deep into her soul. If he could see into her soul surely he wouldn't remain angry with her.

"I didn't awaken fully until three months after Waterloo," he said in a quiet voice. "Even then, it was . . . difficult. Many months passed before I was able to leave my bed."

"Who cared for you?"

"The farmer I later worked for hired a doctor and saw to my recovery. I lived with him and his family for . . . a few years." He cleared his throat, and his eyes skittered away. She knew there was so much he wasn't telling her. "He was a Papist," he continued, "I never understood why he endeavored to keep me alive."

In an abrupt, jerky motion, he lifted the shirt over his head. A ghastly, mangled scar marred his torso in the spot between his abdomen and his side.

Sophie's heart slammed into her throat. She sucked in a breath.

"Gunshot wound. It festered, I am told." He brushed a finger over the new scar above his eyebrow. "This bayonet wound wasn't so bad." He turned to the wall, and lifted his shoulder-length hair. Just above his ear was an angry red line—yet another scar. "But this—bayonet to the side of my skull." He showed her the other ear. An identical scar marred his scalp there. "Both sides. These were the worst. They didn't fester, but I think they took my memories."

Sheer relief that he stood before her, living and breathing, coursed through her. "Oh, Garrett. It's a miracle you're alive."

He turned back around. "So they told me. But somehow I did survive . . . though I didn't know who I was. I knew I was English." He frowned. "It wasn't only my accent that told me so, but the fact that I never felt completely at home there."

"Did you know you were a gentleman?"

"I'm told I was found naked—that they assumed I was a soldier, but they couldn't know my rank. I knew I sounded like a gentleman when I opened my mouth and spoke English. At night, when I searched in vain for a memory, I imagined I was, but I was never certain." He laughed mirthlessly. "And now I am no longer a gentleman, despite my esteemed title and blue blood. In fact, I think I lost it all on the battlefield. The blood I've regenerated is as base as the earth I nearly lost my life upon."

"Nonsense. You are the same man, just with different experiences. Your soul cannot change."

His lips twisted with cynicism. "Do you think so?"

"I do." She stared at him, realizing she hadn't seen a man other than Tristan shirtless for many years. Her flesh warmed. She recalled Garrett's unmarred, perfect body as if she had seen it only yesterday. Now he was large, imposing, still beautiful . . . but harsher and less innocent than the man she remembered. "Why didn't you come home? To try to learn more about who you were?"

"I tried. I saved as much as I could . . . but each time I was close to having enough, it seemed something came up preventing me from returning to England." His brow furrowed, making the scar on his forehead pucker at its edges. "Odd, silly things, really. In any case, it never happened, and eventually I came to believe I was meant to be there."

"Do you still think so?"

"No." But his gaze faltered, and he stared at a spot on the wall beyond her.

She stepped forward. "I don't think so, either. You belong here. In London and at Calton House. With your family." She reached out tentatively to touch his scarred side, but jumped away when her skin made contact with his. An electric sensation jolted through her body. Her heart beating erratically, she turned away to compose herself. Finally, she glanced back up at him. "Do they hurt?"

He took a ragged breath, and she wondered if her touch had affected him as much as it had her.

"Not anymore," he said. "Sometimes they itch."

Tears pricked her eyes. He'd survived all this, and she'd been so far away, ignorant of what he was going through. "I will find you a soothing salve. Mrs. Krum can—"

"It isn't necessary." His voice and posture were stiff. "I am accustomed to it."

Just then, a footman entered through the door to the adjoining sitting room. "The bath is ready, Your Grace."

When Garrett didn't answer, Sophie said, "Thank you. That will be all."

The footman disappeared, leaving Sophie and Garrett staring at each other.

Their discussion wasn't over, by any means. Now that she had him speaking to her, she wouldn't abandon the opportunity.

"Well come along, then." She turned brusquely, leading the way to the door connecting the rooms. She glanced over her shoulder to make certain he was following, and a little flush of victory spread through her chest when she saw he was.

Steam rose from the large tub placed in the center of the room. She had requested the water piping hot—she remembered Garrett liked it that way.

She busied herself with the soaps and washcloths set on a small table beside the bathtub. In truth, there was nothing to do with them. Making a show of choosing the right soap, she picked through the bowl over and over, keeping her back to Garrett to avoid watching him disrobe.

Memories flooded through her. Their first time together, on their wedding night. He'd been so gentle, so thorough, even though he'd been nearly as inexperienced as her. The joy they'd found in each other, how they'd experimented and learned everything about the joining of a man and a woman from each other.

All her senses on high alert, she heard the rustle of fabric brushing over his skin as he removed his trousers. The water splashed as he stepped into the tub, then he groaned as he lowered his big body down.

When she was certain he had immersed himself in the water, she chose an almond oil soap from the bowl and turned around to face him. Diligently keeping her focus on the parts of him showing above the waterline, she smiled. "How does it feel?"

His eyes closed, and he leaned back against the pillow attached to the top lip of the brass tub. "I haven't felt anything this good in . . . a long time."

"Just rest for a moment. I'm going to send your clothes to be washed."

He made an affirmative murmur, so she gathered his trousers and went into the bedchamber to collect his shirt. She found his stockings and boots, both caked with mud, in a corner of the room. She rang for a maid and shook her head in bemusement as the girl took the garments between her fingers and held them as far away as possible from her body, her nose wrinkled in disgust as she left to carry them downstairs.

Sophie found Garrett in the same position she had left him in, his eyes closed, his breathing deep. Quietly, she set a chair beside him and just watched, loath to awaken him.

The man was exhausted. Had his life been so full of turmoil that he hadn't found a moment's peace? Goodness, it had taken him nearly a week to be measured for proper clothing. To go from pauper to duke within a matter of days must be overwhelming.

He had gone through so much, so fast. When he behaved like a man about to lose his grip on sanity, how could she blame him? If she had experienced what he had, she would surely have gone mad long ago.

In slumber, the grooves of tension around Garrett's mouth and eyes relaxed. His lips parted, and his chest rose and fell with deep, regular breaths. The furrow between his eyebrows smoothed, and he once again became the man who'd been the center of her world. Except for the scar on his forehead, he looked like the boy she would have moved mountains for. The youth she'd offered her body to. The man she still loved.

His shoulders were above water, bulging with muscle, highlighted by the strong, straight lines of his collarbones.

A few days' growth of beard covered his jaw, hiding the tiny cleft in his chin. She remembered running her fingers over his firm skin, tracing his bones. She used to delight in touching him. Using her fingertips to explore him, memorizing every angle, every inch of his face. Lower, to his neck and shoulders. And still lower.

For a brief moment, she let her gaze wander down his torso, to his sex nestling in the light-colored hair at the apex of his large thighs. How she had once explored him there. As a virgin, she'd been curious and fascinated by this strange appendage, enthralled by the feel of it as it hardened in her hands, in her mouth . . . And Garrett had encouraged her curiosity.

She quickly averted her eyes, guilt squeezing at her chest.

When Garrett's eyes fluttered and finally opened, she watched as his focus settled on her. She forced herself to smile at him. "Would you like me to wash your hair?"

The tilt of his lips was hardly noticeable, but she remembered that look. It reminded her of the way he used to gaze at her, in the way that made her feel strong and invincible while at the same time causing a soft, warm buzz to spread through her.

"Thank you," he said, his voice still rough from sleep.

She dipped a ladle in the still-warm bathwater.

"Close your eyes."

He obeyed and leaned forward so the water wouldn't drip onto the floor. She poured slowly, watching the rivulets run down his cheeks. Afterward, she would send one of the footmen in to shave him. Or perhaps she'd do it herself.

Sophie lathered her hands, moved behind him, and plunged her hands into his thick blond hair. She sank into the task, rubbing his scalp with her fingertips, reveling in the feel of Garrett. Just touching him was almost recompense enough for the desperate confusion he had caused her in the past few days. Taking her time, she worked through every strand until it was soft and gleaming, stopping often to lather her hands with more soap.

His gruff voice startled her. "You bathed me once before. I remember."

Her fingers stilled, then started moving again with renewed vigor. "Do you?"

"Yes. There was a difference—you were in the bathtub with me at the time."

Heat prickled across her chest. After she had washed his hair, he'd washed hers. All the while, she touched him, and when it was over, she had crawled atop him and pushed herself down upon him. They'd made sweet, slow love in the bathtub, and afterward they had lain in each other's arms until the water had turned tepid. Then they'd dried each other off and retired to bed, where they'd made love again.

"I remember," she said in a low voice.

On edge, she continued washing his hair, terrified he would ask her to disrobe and join him in the bath, yet oddly disappointed when he didn't.

And then she was angry with herself for being disappointed. The clergymen didn't exaggerate when they spoke of how the flesh was weak. She'd vowed not to think of Garrett in a carnal way. But then again, how could she stop herself? This was the man she'd loved for most of her life. Ever since she was a young girl, she'd dreamed about taking off his clothes and touching him in secret places. This was the man who'd taken her the first time, when she married him at the age of eighteen, and countless times after. Until she was twenty-two and he left for Waterloo. Then when he was gone, he'd ruled her fantasies for years—until Tristan had taken over.

Finally, she nudged him forward and rinsed the soap from his hair and shoulders. She couldn't stay here. She had to go, to rebuild her strength against these erotic memories. "I'll leave you so you can—"

"No!" When she froze, he added, "Stay with me." And then as an afterthought, "Please."

She ran her tongue over her bottom lip. "All right."

She handed him the soap. The way his fingers lingered, touching hers, when he took it made her shudder all the way to her toes.

As he washed himself, she occupied herself with mundane tasks. She folded the towels and placed them close by so he could easily retrieve them as he stepped from the bath. Rummaging in the wardrobe, she found a green silk banyan she'd never seen Tristan wear and placed it beside the towels. Then she turned away once again to smooth a wrinkle from the lace tablecloth on one of the side tables.

Finally, as she repositioned the clock upon the mantel, she heard the water slosh as he stepped out. She counted the number of times she moved the clock, stepped back to observe the new placement, then stepped forward to move it again as if she sought the perfect place for it. Her senses were so attuned to Garrett that she knew his every move. He used brusque, military swipes to dry himself, then all was silent as he eyed the banyan, no doubt finding it too effeminate for his taste. Finally, he reached for it, and some wicked part of Sophie deep within her consciousness envied the silk sliding over his skin.

She had repositioned the clock ten times when his big hands closed over her shoulders. She dropped her arms at her sides, staring at the clock.

His hands were warm. They covered her shoulders completely, their warmth seeping through the fabric of her dress and the short sleeves of her petticoats and chemise.

It was quarter past three.

"Sophie."

Slowly, she turned, trembling all over as he closed his strong arms around her. She simply held on, pressing her cheek against his chest, and sank into the pleasure of being held by him.

"I missed you so much," she whispered. "So much."

After a long moment, he pulled away slightly but didn't let her go. He stared down at her, his eyes questioning. His arms slipped up her sides, running over the soft lawn and then down her bare forearms and shoulders. Then he cupped her cheeks in his warm, big hands.

She stared up at him, entranced, in awe, terrified, guilty, as he lowered his lips to hers.

Her fingers curled, gripping the silk of the banyan in her fists. His kiss was soft, hard, desperate, and gentle all at the same time.

Different from Tristan's kisses.

She wrenched away, gasping. Stumbling backward, she shook her head. "I can't . . . I can't do this."

She turned on her heel and fled.

Chapter Seven

"There is a scarcity of legal precedent in matters such as this." Griffiths rubbed at his temple. "Especially pertaining to the aristocracy."

The solicitor sat across from Tristan in a dark corner of the Talnut Tavern. They'd met here out on the fringes of Town due to Tristan's desire to remain inconspicuous until the bruises on his face had healed. There was no point in fueling the scandal. The streets were already abuzz with news of Garrett's return, and the lane outside the duke's London estate was crowded with twice as much traffic as normal—people driving by, no doubt, in hopes of catching a glimpse of the long-lost hero. It wouldn't help for anyone to know that Garrett had tried to kill him after discovering him in bed with Sophie.

Griffiths gazed at Tristan from round, pale brown eyes. His face was almost childlike, with no hint of a shadow of an afternoon beard—rare for a man who claimed to be halfway through his third decade. Yet Tristan's peers had claimed this man was ambitious and aggressive when it came to securing his clients' interests.

"Your marriage to the duchess was legal, by all accounts, but upon the return of the previous husband . . . well, according to the laws of the kingdom, your marriage is henceforth a nullity."

Tristan had already determined this news wasn't as devastating as Griffiths made it sound. If there was a precedent, the case would be more solidly set in stone. If no similar situation had ever beset a member of the aristocracy before, he had a greater hope of triumphing in the end. Tristan turned his ale in his hands, swiping his thumb over the condensation on the lip of the pewter cup. "We shall endeavor to create a new precedent."

"We can try, of course." Deep in thought, Griffiths drummed his fingers on the table. "His Grace has already brought a suit for the nullity of your marriage to the Consistory Court. The only way I see it, the court will uphold the legality of the duke's marriage to Her Grace, and the next step will be for the duchess to press a countersuit against the duke for a divorce. It is rare for ladies to succeed in such matters, but it might be our only hope. Is there any basis, besides desertion, upon which she might sue for divorce?"

"Such as?"

"Adultery, perhaps? If we combine it with the charge of desertion—"

Tristan held up his hand. "No."

Even if Garrett had dallied in Belgium, Tristan suspected Sophie wouldn't pursue an adultery charge, and if she did, no doubt Parliament would forgive him en masse due to the amnesia.

"In any case," Tristan continued, "I would like to keep the duchess out of this completely."

Griffiths raised a pale eyebrow. "It will make it more difficult, my lord."

"You don't know my wife. She won't take sides."

"I see."

But by the doubtful look on his face, clearly Griffiths didn't see. It was impossible for Tristan to explain that her inability to choose a side had little to do with weakness and everything to do with her innate strength of character and her unwillingness to cause pain to those she loved. She was struggling, because no matter what happened, either he or Garrett would lose her.

Tristan tilted his head back and finished his ale.

"Would you be caring for more, sir?"

Tristan glanced up at the barmaid and nodded. She was a slip of a girl, no more than fifteen, with dirty smudges on her cheeks and wispy reddish-brown hair that crowned her head like a halo of twigs. Beyond her, Tristan could scarcely make out the shapes of the couple sitting at a table tucked into the near corner, the smoke swirled so thickly in this place. When the barmaid finished pouring, he passed her a crown. Flushing, she bobbed a curtsy and disappeared.

Tristan returned his attention to Griffiths. "I wish to respond to the duke's allegation of nullity with an argument for the nullity of *his* marriage to Her Grace."

Griffiths frowned. "How's that, sir?"

"I believe the courts should dissolve their marriage based on the length of his absence, the legality of his death, and the good faith upon which Her Grace and I finally married—*legally* married."

"But the law in this matter—"

"You yourself said there was little legal precedent, Griffiths. I said, and I'll say it again: We shall create a new one."

"You realize that a nullity by definition means the marriage was void from its beginning. Is that what you're after?"

"Of course not," Tristan snapped. "I wouldn't bastardize their child. No, their marriage is a nullity from the moment the duke was pronounced dead."

Taking a deep breath, Griffiths nodded. "I see. This is . . ." He tapped his fingertips on the glossy table. "Well, sir, it will be a monumental task to—"

"But is it one you are willing to take on?"

Griffiths studied him, his dun-colored eyes holding a definitive gleam. "Yes, my lord. It is."

"Good."

"It is likely we will be forced to appeal, perhaps several times," Griffiths said. "I doubt the lower courts will dare to touch your allegations."

"We will do whatever needs to be done."

Griffiths cleared his throat. "Well then. I have connections with several advocates who are authorities in the laws of marriage. They'll research the legal ramifications of this situation more thoroughly and will plead your case expertly."

"Excellent."

"However, please remember Calton is a duke and a celebrated officer in His Majesty's army, my lord, and you are not. Furthermore, London is aflutter with news of his return—he is considered quite the hero. This puts you in a precarious situation. It is true you are popular, but the duke, I fear, has captured the emotions of the people. No one will forget the truth that the duchess was his wife first."

"But she is my wife now," Tristan said.

Griffiths smiled wryly. "Of course."

"Well. Thank you for your time, Mr. Griffiths. I am sorry to have troubled you to make the drive out here. Yet—" As he rose, he motioned to his bruised face. "—as you can no doubt tell, I can hardly go about publicly in this state. I prefer to avoid causing a stir."

"Of course, my lord. It was no trouble. No trouble at all."

Tristan rose to shake Griffiths's hand, and then he watched the solicitor disappear through the murk as he made his way toward the exit.

Tristan returned to his wobbly chair and drained his ale. Once his face healed, he would stand tall and return to his duties in the government. He would maintain his cool composure, and he would face the scandal with his head held high. Furthermore, he would suffer all their questions and spiteful remarks with assurance and congeniality.

Tristan gathered his coat and exited the gloomy tavern. He had a few more contingencies to cover, but he intended to hurry. He hated leaving his wife alone with Garrett.

Hours later, Tristan shrugged on his robe as he strode to the desk beside the hearth in the Tulip Room, where he'd laid his silver timepiece. He'd missed dinner and hadn't been able to see the children before they were put to bed, but his day had been productive enough. After his meeting with Griffiths, he'd hired a man to keep a discreet eye on Garrett and Fisk on their affairs outside the house. Tonight, Tristan had paid quiet visits to several close friends from the House of Lords to explain the situation to them, and they'd assured him they'd keep him apprised of the talk regarding Garrett's return.

He glanced down at the timepiece and returned it to the sleek surface of the table. It was just after midnight. Sophie would most likely be asleep.

God, he missed her. It wouldn't hurt to check on her. Perhaps he could convince that ridiculous nighttime henchman Garrett insisted on keeping at her door to allow him to say goodnight. Even if she was fast asleep, just one look at her face would bolster him.

Turning the door handle, Tristan eased out, looking one way and then the other. The corridor was dark and quiet. His bare feet silent on the cool wood floor, he walked around the bend in the passage to the opposite wing of the house.

Now that was odd. The chair beside her door was empty. Perhaps her guard had gone to relieve himself.

He didn't hesitate. He strode to her room and pushed open the door.

Through the earth-colored India chintz bed curtains, a bit of her pale leg peeked from the edge of the blankets. Quietly, he closed the door and went to the bed, pushing the fabric aside to see her better.

She had curled on her side, her clasped hands resting beneath her cheek. Her honey-colored hair fanned out from her head, and her lips were parted in slumber. Her eyebrows arched over her wide-set eyes and her skin glowed incandescent in the moonlight seeping through the crack in the curtains.

In the past eight years, her face had matured from the childish innocence it had held before Garrett's disappearance. Her round cheeks had thinned, the slanted cheekbones become more pronounced, and fine lines had appeared at the corners of her lips.

A stray curl had fallen across her cheek, and Tristan reached over to push it aside. She opened her eyes and blinked up at him.

"Tristan," she murmured sleepily.

Smiling, he lowered himself at the edge of the bed. "I missed you, love."

She reached out to place her hand over his. "Me, too."

His chest constricted, and his body grew warm. Being separated from her like this tore him apart. The past days had been hell, starting from the moment Garrett had ripped him off her. "Are you all right?"

"Yes," she murmured.

He trailed the back of his finger down her cheek and leaned down to press his lips to hers. "You're so beautiful to me, Soph."

His touch seemed to rouse her and she rose up onto her elbow, her light brown curls tumbling over her shoulders. She glanced at the door. "How were you able to pass by the man at my door?"

"I didn't. There was no one there."

"That's odd."

Tristan shrugged. "Perhaps it was time for a changing of the guard."

Below the short ruffled sleeves of her nightdress, gooseflesh covered her arms. Tristan swung his legs up onto the narrow bed and drew her against him, running his fingers up and down her chilled skin.

"You're so warm." She snuggled close to his body, slid her arms around him, and squeezed. "How was your meeting with the solicitor?"

Tristan forced a smile. "He said the case will cause quite the stir in Doctors' Commons."

"No doubt," she said wryly. "I'm sure we are the talk of the town, and not only amongst the lawyers."

"Yes, we are."

She nuzzled closer to him. "What did he say about Garrett's suit against our marriage?" she asked in a low voice.

Tristan paused. He hesitated to cause Sophie any additional worry, especially when she lay so comfortably, so trustingly, in his arms. He couldn't tell her that it might be a long, difficult court battle . . . And God knew he didn't want to share his biggest fear—that the judge would fail to delve into the complexities of the law, and taking it only at face value, would nullify their marriage immediately.

"Griffiths will do whatever he can to uphold our marriage," Tristan finally said. "He intends to solicit advocates experienced in marital law who can research precedents for our situation."

She didn't respond, just tucked her head under his chin and fitted her body against him. "You should leave." She gave a low chuckle that reverberated through his chest. "Though I can't imagine the look on that awful guard's face should he see you walking out of here as casual as you please."

"It might almost be worth it." He sighed, stroking her soft, cool flesh. "Ah, Sophie. I don't want to go."

He knew—they both knew—that if Garrett discovered him here, violence would ensue. Still, it was impossible to walk away from her.

"I don't want you to go."

"I want to make love to you." No doubt she could feel the proof of that underneath her hip.

She sighed, and the warmth of her breath washed over his neck. Her fingers slid into his hair and gently combed through it. "But you must leave, darling. I don't want to cause trouble."

Guilt flashed in her expression, and a sudden realization slapped him in the face. The bastard had touched her. Anger rose up from deep inside him, simmering, threatening to boil over. Every muscle in his body tensed in possessive rage.

As if she read his thoughts, her arms tightened around him.

"You're mine, Sophie," he ground out. He bent his head to press his lips into Sophie's hair. "Mine," he whispered as the silken strands brushed over his lips.

She looked up at him, her eyes shining with sadness.

He couldn't bear it. He kissed her. Hard. His fingers caught the bottom of her nightgown and hiked it up her smooth thighs. The touch of her sweet, tender skin set his own flesh on fire.

Groaning softly, she kissed him back, equally on fire. Her hands dove into the front of his robe and upon finding him bare underneath, she murmured "*mmm*" against his mouth. He gasped as her fingertips grazed his nipples.

He dragged his hand up her thigh until he reached her center. Then he gently parted the folds and slid his fingers into her welcoming heat.

She was slick, smooth, ready for him.

A floorboard creaked just outside the door and Sophie jerked away from his embrace. She scurried away from him, and when she reached the foot of the bed, she tossed the hair out of her face to stare at him. Her changeable eyes had darkened with hunger, need . . . fear.

Tristan sat up, clenching handfuls of the blanket to restrain himself from following her to the foot of the bed, pushing her onto her back, and taking her there.

Finally, she spoke in a whisper. "The guard's back."

Tristan didn't care. He stared at her, at the flush of her cheeks, at the taut peaks of her nipples showing through the thin muslin of her nightgown, at the smooth, pale flesh of her thigh.

"Lord," she groaned, casting a terrified glance at the door, "if Garrett should find us—"

He didn't care about that, either. Not now.

She saw the intent in his eyes and gave a little whimper, holding her hand out in a gesture for him to stop. "No, Tristan. Stop. Please. He'll kill you."

He moved closer, like a prowling panther prepared to pounce. The musky scent of her sex swirled around him. His cock was like steel, aching with the desire to be buried inside her softness, throbbing with the need for release.

Her expression was fraught. Her skin was pale, her eyes wide. "No, Tristan."

He froze. Tightening his fists, he reined in his lust.

She sank her face into her hands, her breaths harsh in the room's stillness. "What are we going to do?"

He reached forward and peeled her fingers from her face, studying her. Was she truly so afraid for him? And if so, what did that say of her belief in him, in her confidence he could protect himself and what was his? And why did she care so much about Garrett's reaction?

He had to get the hell out of here. He was a fool. Jealous, apprehensive, in a tangle he couldn't seem to fight his way out of without sacrificing what was most important to him: his family and his honor.

God, what a damn fine mess.

He squeezed her hands. "It's still possible it was no one, but if the man is there, you must distract him while I slip away." He smoothed his thumbs over the pulse points on her wrists. Her heart was beating too rapidly. "Sophie?"

She gulped in a breath. "Yes."

Trembling, she climbed out of the bed. He came to stand beside her as she stared at the doorway.

"It'll be all right," he murmured into her ear. He brushed his lips over her cheek.

Without further hesitation, she took a fortifying breath, moved to the door, turned the knob, and pulled it open.

She stepped out and looked to the left, where the guard usually sat on his chair. Then she glanced in the other direction.

"There's no one," she whispered.

He could stay longer, but it would only cause her further anxiety and him to go mad with wanting her. With a sigh, he walked to the door. "Goodnight, Soph," he murmured. He gave her hand a quick squeeze and strode out of her room.

But he stood in an alcove and watched her door for the remainder of the evening. Nobody came. Apparently Sophie was no longer being guarded at night.

Tristan slipped back inside the Tulip Room, absorbing this information.

Delia slid the final pin in Sophie's hair and then patted the tight chignon she had created. Peering into the foggy old mirror, Sophie sighed. Delia had left soft curls to fall about her face and skim her shoulders, making her appear much younger than her thirty years.

Her day dress, a soft periwinkle blue muslin with darker blue flower buds embroidered around the hem, neckline, and cuffs, added to the impression of youth. For a long moment, she simply stared at herself in the mirror. Other than the dark smudges under her eyes, she looked as she always did, and besides the thinning of her face and the faint lines at the edges of her mouth, she had to concede it was not very different from how she had looked the day Garrett had left for Brussels.

Since then, however, she had borne much, and even if she appeared similar on the outside, inside she was a completely different woman.

"You look lovely, ma'am."

Sophie smiled. Delia said the same thing every day. "Thank you, Delia. You may go."

After the maid left, she sat a few moments longer, taking deep, strengthening breaths. She would go to the nursery to see the children. Maybe read to them awhile. It was important to stay close to both Miranda and Gary—surely they must be feeling the tension between the adults.

Prepared to explain to her disagreeable guard where she was going, she opened the door and stepped into the corridor. But to her surprise, Garrett was sitting in the chair his henchman usually occupied. He looked like a new man this morning—for once he wasn't wearing that awful old coat. Instead he sported striped trousers and a sharp black waistcoat over a fine new linen shirt with a tall collar and a white stock. His clean, combed hair fell in waves down his neck and shone in the dim light. His face was freshly shaved, revealing the tiny cleft in his chin and the broad, masculine lines of his face.

His gaze raked up and down her body, giving her the

distinct impression that he was undressing her in his mind's eye, and a flutter of fear—or was it desire?—brushed through her.

How awful she was, after just having felt a similar desire for Tristan last night.

Yet as much as the feeling was similar, it was different, too. Her need for Tristan was a clawing, relentless, wild longing. She'd wanted to devour him last night. Be devoured. It had nearly killed her to push him away. Only fear for his life had kept her sane.

On the other hand, her desire for Garrett was a warm, clinging ache deep within her. An ache that hadn't disappeared for eight years.

"Sophie," he said gruffly.

"Good morning, Your Grace." She made to walk past him, but rising from the chair, he caught her arm.

"I've come to speak with you."

She stopped and turned slowly to face him. It was no use fighting him. An image of the bulging muscles she'd seen in the bath flashed through her mind. "About what?"

"The guards outside and at your door. I've called them off. You may come and go at your leisure, and they will not be present to upset my sister's delicate sensibilities."

"Thank you, Garrett," she said softly, but even as renewed hope welled within her, his hand tightened around her arm.

"However, I demand you steer clear of Lord Westcliff. Promise me you will obey me in this matter."

She hissed out a breath. Just when she thought he was softening, becoming reasonable, on his way toward forgiveness, he once again turned into a boor.

"Forgive me." She glanced pointedly at his fingers wrapped around her sleeve. "I was on my way to see the children."

He tugged her closer and said in a low voice, "You are my wife. Is it not your primary duty to be by my side, seeing to my needs?"

She stiffened. "First of all, the courts have not yet reached a decision as to whose wife I am."

"They will soon. Within the week, I'm told."

"Second, I've no doubt you can see to your own needs."

He arched a brow and his lips twisted sardonically. "What needs do you imagine I speak of?"

Carnal needs. She remembered the kiss yesterday, how she had almost given over to it, and she clenched her teeth. "I'm sure I have no idea."

He bent down, and when he spoke, his lips brushed her ear. "I need you, Sophie. I've never stopped needing you. You must know that."

She inhaled sharply. "Have you forgotten you discovered me in another man's bed a few days ago? Because *I* haven't, Garrett. In fact, I find it rather difficult to forget."

He dropped her arm as if it were on fire. She brushed past him and headed for the stairs. This time, he let her go.

Chapter Eight

Confound the woman. Garrett could survive battle, memory loss, living in a strange land, and losing everything, all the while keeping his—admittedly tenuous at times—hold on sanity. But Sophie—God. The woman might just drive him over the edge.

It was easy to fall under her spell. Yesterday, as she had bathed him, her focus singularly on him, her hands caressing him, he had almost forgotten Tristan's unfortunate presence in her life. And in her *bed*.

He didn't understand her snappishness after their comparatively civil interaction yesterday. Had his kiss upset her? Perhaps she believed he was rushing her into fleshly relations.

But hell. He couldn't help himself. Her body called to his.

And, goddamn it, she was his *wife*.

Garrett descended the staircase, the heels of his new shoes clicking on the polished planks, and turned toward his study. Since he'd returned to London, the room had rapidly become his only escape from a world that seemed determined to drive him straight to insanity.

He passed a curtsying maid polishing silver in the corridor and entered the study. Now that he was clean and the tailors had delivered the first batch of quickly made clothes he'd paid a small fortune for, he was beginning to feel somewhat at home, but the servants still unnerved him.

The room was peaceful and blessedly empty. He strode to the desk and sat behind it, wearily observing the piles of papers that awaited him. A glass of wine set on a round silver platter stood on the corner of his desk, and he sipped at it as he contemplated what he needed to do, abstractedly tugging at the unfamiliar stiff collar that felt like a board round his neck. Work had already begun to bury him. Problems he'd rather not have to think about or address until the situation with Sophie was resolved. Today, especially, the issues twisted and tangled in his mind until his head throbbed with pain and he couldn't think straight.

The door swung open without warning. With a roar, Garrett surged up, yanked open the top drawer of his desk, withdrew his pistol, and aimed it at the intruder.

The man stumbled backward, his hands raised. "Please, Your Grace—"

Garrett blinked hard. Hell, it was Connor. The damned butler. He lowered the weapon shakily and uttered an oath. "I apologize, Connor."

The man had turned completely white. "Forgive me, Your Grace. I didn't mean to disturb you."

Garrett squeezed the bridge of his nose as he slid the

weapon back into its drawer. Hell, he felt dizzy. "It's all right. Just knock in the future, why don't you?"

"Of course, sir."

Garrett dropped into his chair. "What can I do for you?"

"There are several visitors here for Her Grace. The Countess of Duns—"

"No."

" 'No,' sir?"

"Right. Tell them—" He filed through his memory for the appropriate thing to say. "Tell them the duchess is not at home to visitors."

Connor bowed. "Of course, sir."

As he began to leave, Garrett, said, "Oh, and Connor?"

Connor turned. Garrett couldn't help but to be impressed at the blankness in his expression less than a minute after nearly receiving a bullet in the chest. "Yes, Your Grace?"

"That shall be your standard answer, understand? Until further notice, any visitors to this house are to be informed the person they wish to see isn't at home. Is that clear?"

"Yes, Your Grace."

"Thank you." When Connor didn't move to leave, Garrett added, "You may go."

After Connor shut the door behind him, Garrett sank his face into his hands. Good God, he'd just aimed a loaded weapon at his butler. Had he lost his mind? Rising unsteadily, he took his empty wineglass to the sidebar and, after studying a bottle of brandy for a long moment, decided on plain water. The liquid seemed to clear his muddle, and he drank several glasses before returning to his desk.

Blinking at the pile of work, he began to sift through it, painstakingly organizing it and taking notes. Hours passed, and eventually the headache faded and his mind cleared. Lost in his work, he bolted upright in his chair when someone scratched at the door.

He took a few deep, calming breaths before responding. "Who is it?"

The door opened to reveal his daughter followed by the timid Miss Dalworthy. Garrett's heart began a slow thud as he rose from his chair.

Miss Dalworthy curtsied. "I am so sorry, Your Grace. Lady Miranda has been—" She looked up, her round face flushed and her expression flustered. She was a young girl, probably not too many years out of the nursery herself. "Oh, dear." She wrung her hands as Miranda stepped fully into view, looking like a determined little Sophie but for her eye and hair color, which were more like his own.

She nodded regally at him. "Good morning."

Garrett's lips twisted. He glanced at the governess. "Is it normal for the child to be traipsing freely about the house?"

The governess's mouth moved like a landed fish. She seemed incapable of speech. Christ, was he really so terrifying?

Miranda strode right up to him and stood across from the desk. "I usually stay in the nursery unless I am with Mama. However, today is special."

"Special?"

She nodded pertly, her blonde curls bobbing. "Indeed. You see, you have been home for many days already."

"Yes?"

"And I have not seen you often enough. It is time for us to become better acquainted. I *am* curious about you, you know. You *are* my papa."

Garrett's twisted lips eased into a wry grin. "So I am told."

"Oh, you are," she assured him. "The fact is listed on my baptismal records, as you would find if you were to read them. And just looking at you is proof—when I look into the mirror, I see it, clear as day."

"Exactly what do you see, child?"

She placed her little hands flat on the desk and leaned forward, staring at him.

"Your eyes and mine, for one. They are the same color. But yours are . . . older."

He stood still under the scrutiny of her blue eyes. It was true hers were the same color as his own. But whereas his might be called chilling, hers were light and airy and happy, like a cloudless summer's day. It was as if the girl had never experienced pain.

Something flared within him, some protective, unfamiliar paternal instinct. At all costs, he would protect her from pain. He never wanted to see the jaded look in her eyes that shone in his own.

"What else?" he inquired.

She looked him up and down. "The shape of your jaw. It is just like mine."

He laughed out loud, a sound that surprised him as much as it seemed to surprise Miss Dalworthy, who took a step backward. How could his large, masculine jaw, with its shadow of a beard, compare to her little one?

"Don't laugh, I beg you," she said. "I speak the truth.

Come, I'll show you." She held out her hand. Bemused, he took it and allowed her to lead him to the large gilt-edged mirror set between the two long shelves of books set in the wall.

She slid a look up at him and lifted both her arms. "Carry me, please, Papa. I'm not tall enough to show you what I mean."

Papa. The word resounded through his chest and dove straight into his heart. He picked her up and turned her in his arms until their faces were level in the mirror.

"Very good." She pointed at the glass. "See there. See the curve of our jaws where they reach our ears? They are very, well—" She pondered for a moment. "—they are triangular, I think. And look—" She motioned to his chin, then hers. "You see, we both have little dimples in our chins."

"I do see," he admitted.

She shrugged. "Well then. There's absolute proof that you are indeed my very own papa."

Garrett gently set Miranda down. "Well then." He was at a loss. He cleared his throat. "Now . . . ah, run along, child. I have work to do."

She curtsied to him. "Of course, Papa. I wouldn't want to interfere with your extremely important work. But I shall come back to you tomorrow, yes? Here in the study at noon? It is a good time for me, because that's when Gary lies down for his nap, and I'm *far* too old to be napping, you know."

She didn't wait for him to answer but threw her arms around his waist before dropping another quick curtsy and sweeping out the door, followed by a harried Miss Dalworthy.

He stared after her, spellbound.

Miranda. His own precocious, precious daughter.

As his carriage rattled along the busy roads of Westminster, Tristan mulled over his first visit to his club in several days, as his face had finally healed enough for him to appear in public. Men had surrounded him as soon as he arrived, and he'd spent a good hour patiently and circumspectly answering questions about Garrett's return.

He soon discovered the murmurings were circulating in earnest. The Duke of Calton lived! Mortally wounded on the battlefield of Waterloo, he miraculously recovered! He suffered torture and imprisonment in Belgium before he was able to escape and return to England, his adventures comparable to Odysseus's long journey home from the Trojan War!

But alas, the duke's wife didn't wait as faithfully as Odysseus's Penelope. No, she'd married the duke's heir instead. Whatever would become of them all?

The rumor mill had churned theories at astonishing speed—divorce, separation, a ménage à trois akin to Admiral Nelson's scandalous relationship with Emma Hamilton, or perhaps a duel?—and the best Tristan could do was feed it truth. He explained they were attempting to work out the legal ramifications of Garrett's return, but they had no intention of killing each other, engaging in illegal or illicit behavior, or arousing the enmity of their families or their peers.

Just as the questions became tedious, Tristan had received a message from Jennings, the man he'd hired to follow Fisk and Garrett. Jennings had suggested they meet at the Somerset Coffeehouse in The Strand in an hour's time, and Tristan was more than happy for the excuse to leave his club.

Jennings was a one-time Bow Street officer who had retired from the runners for reasons undisclosed, but according to Tristan's sources, he was honest and discreet, and most important, loyal to his employers.

The older man rose from a table and strode toward Tristan as soon as he opened the coffeehouse's black door. A thin ring of white hair encircled Jennings's otherwise bald scalp, and such deep grooves lined his forehead it was a wonder they didn't trap debris. He took Tristan's hand in a firm grip and shook it. "Shall we walk outside, my lord?"

Tristan nodded his acknowledgment, clapped his hat back on his head, and strode out behind Jennings. Street lamps cast long shadows across the damp pavement, and evening traffic rattled by. Tristan and Jennings headed eastward, toward the spire of St.-Mary-le-Strand Church, with its garish baroque ornamentation and tiered steeple glowing pale in the gas light.

Rain hung in the air, and people hunched over and moved quickly, as if to hurry home before being caught in the downpour. It was a perfect opportunity to speak without being overheard, and Jennings drew close to Tristan as they made their way over the paving stones and avoided oncoming pedestrians.

"Mr. Fisk visited the Covent Garden theater this morning."

Tristan glanced sharply at Jennings's haggard face. "Have you any idea who he saw there?"

"No, my lord. I approached the entrance to the theater just after Mr. Fisk, but it was locked from the inside. I only saw enough to discern that the person who opened the door for Mr. Fisk was male."

"How long was he there?"

"Just a half an hour, my lord."

Just long enough for a quick tryst with an actress, if that was what he fancied. Yet if he met with an actress, why had a man opened the door? And why would they meet at the theater rather than her lodgings?

Or Fisk could simply have an interest in the workings of the theater. Tristan shook his head—he didn't have enough information to speculate. "Where did he go afterward?"

"He went to the solicitor's office, where he remained for two hours' time. Afterward, he returned to the duke's residence."

The solicitor's office. Tristan had spent the greater part of the day conferring with his own lawyers. Their first court date was set for tomorrow, and Tristan wished he could be there, but his counsel had advised against it, not only for the sake of gossip, but for the benefit of their case as a whole. He'd finally agreed, but the anticipation of the result already began to swell within him—a great knot of tension balling in his gut.

"And what about the duke?" he asked as they swerved to avoid a man selling kidney pies and two plump ladies balancing their purchases while they dug in their reticules for coins to pay him.

"Didn't leave the house at all today, my lord."

Tristan clasped the other man's shoulder and squeezed. "Thank you, Jennings. Keep me apprised of anything else you see, won't you? And if Fisk should return to Covent Garden, see if you can learn more."

Jennings nodded his acknowledgment, and they parted ways. Tristan kept an even pace as he continued to stride down The Strand.

Tomorrow, his advocates would argue for him in the Consistory Court of London. It might be easy, but if it was, the news wouldn't be good for him. There was nothing simple about Tristan's countering allegations, and he had no doubt that if the court took his claims seriously, they were in for a long, difficult battle.

Though he'd outwardly displayed nothing but smooth confidence, inwardly he was not so calm. Panic gripped at him, leered at him, taunted him with predictions that stabbed him over and over, like tiny swords piercing his heart. *It's over. They'll nullify your marriage to the woman you love. You'll never touch her again . . .*

He walked until he could banish his fears and thrust away the panic. Finally, when quiet night blanketed the city and the only person he'd seen in several minutes was a watchman wearing an oilskin cape to shelter him from the rain that now fell in a steady sheet, Tristan turned toward home.

Sophie lay on her side staring at the dark puffs denoting the ruffled edges of the bed curtains.

In the morning, the court would hear Garrett's case against the validity of her marriage to Tristan. She had never felt so impotent. This should be her decision to make. Hers and that of the men she loved. Instead, their fates would be in the hands of a court that would only look at the facts presented and then make their decision based on the law. Where were thought, feeling, and emotion—all those things that mattered most—in all this?

Garrett had taken this step without consulting her. A thousand times in the past week she'd wondered how he could do this without talking to her, without hearing her opinion. She simply wasn't accustomed to being treated as if her thoughts didn't matter. Tristan was a powerful man who often made important decisions, but he always listened to her and never failed to take her thoughts into account before reaching a conclusion. Perhaps he had spoiled her.

She shivered. She was cold. Lonely. It reminded her of those first days after Garrett had left for Waterloo and she'd found herself with child and all by herself, terrified that her husband would never return. Only now she was terrified Tristan would never return.

Turning onto her back, she closed her eyes and tried to sleep. She lay there for long minutes, which eventually turned into restless hours tossing and turning, but sleep never came. Finally, she rose, shivering with a chill even the six blankets on her bed couldn't conquer.

She poured herself a glass of wine and drank it. The fire was cold, and she tugged a woolen cloak over her shoulders, intending to go find someone who would stoke it for her. She padded to the door, opened it, and stepped into the dark corridor.

It was very late, and the house was still. No movement, no sound. The cold from the wood planks crept up the backs of her calves.

"Sophie."

She gasped and spun toward the voice. Tristan stepped around the corner, looking dark and delicious. He wore a loose white shirt open at the neck and close-fitted trousers. He'd pushed his damp hair back from his face, but an errant shiny black lock fell over his brow, partially hiding one eye.

He took another step toward her and she smelled him—exotic, spicy, male. He'd been outside in the rain, and a sheen of moisture covered his skin. If he moved another inch, he would be pressed against her from shoulder to foot. But he didn't touch her. The distance between them aroused all her senses.

She breathed him in. "I miss you."

He gazed down at her, and the wicked gleam in his chocolate eyes was impossible to misinterpret. His need rushed over her, encased her in a shell of longing. He wanted her.

Silently, he placed a hand on her shoulder and, with gentle pressure, nudged her toward her bedchamber door.

As soon as they walked through it, he closed it behind them. Then, all pretense of patience abandoned, he spun her around and pinned her against the wall, pushing the cloak from her shoulders. Finally touching her. The contact robbed her of her breath.

"Tristan," she gasped. "Tristan . . ."

But she couldn't say any more, because his lips were on hers. Voracious, insisting. She opened for him, eager, wanting him to be rough. Needing it. Though his clothes were damp, his skin was hot, and its heat seeped through her night rail and danced over her skin. She felt warm for the first time in days.

She pulled his shirttails from his trousers and plunged her hands under his shirt. She pushed her palms over the smooth skin of his torso.

He kissed her lower, down her neck, over the curve of

her shoulder. She leaned into him and murmured, "I want to touch every part of you."

"Then do it, Sophie. Touch me."

She lowered her hands to his waistband and fumbled with his buttons. When they were open, she pushed the trousers down his narrow hips, and he kicked them off. She lifted off his shirt and threw it across the room. Then she tugged up her night rail and pulled it over her head. Making a low sound in his throat, he pressed her against the wall and kissed her again, his erection a rod of hot, silken steel cradled by the soft skin of her stomach.

Being cold was a far distant memory. Her skin had caught on fire with the need, and the only way to douse it was to lose herself in Tristan.

"Hold me, Sophie," he said roughly.

She wrapped her arms around his neck, tangling her fingers in the wisps of soft hair at the base of his skull, and clung to him as his hands slid down the sides of her waist, over the flare of her hips, over her bottom. She shuddered violently when he cupped her buttocks. He moved lower to her thighs and suddenly he lifted her clear off the floor, spreading her thighs wide as he fit his body between them.

"Wrap your legs around me, love."

She locked her ankles behind his waist.

"Now guide me in," he whispered, supporting her against the wall.

She reached between them, grasping his swollen shaft in her fist, nearly moaning at the burn of him against her palm. He sucked in a breath.

"Now, Sophie," he ground out.

She maneuvered in his arms until he hovered at her entrance, but he hesitated, holding her suspended over him, his arms shaking not from her weight but with the effort of keeping from pounding into her without restraint.

"Make love to me, Tristan."

Still, he held her suspended over him, his face a mask of restrained agony.

"Please, Tristan. I need you. Please, please—"

Tristan's control snapped. Digging his fingers into her thighs, he pushed her down, eliciting a soft cry from both of them. And then he pumped into her, pinning her against the wall, his face buried in her hair. His thrusts were hard, desperate, exquisitely jarring. She was completely helpless in the steel of his arms, completely subject to the relentless, ruthless thrust of his hips.

Heat, burning, singeing her inside and out. The small whimpers she couldn't help but make each time he drove into her. He was spearing through her, taking her completely. Deep. Driving into her very soul.

And then it was over. He grew stiff and shattered all around her. She burrowed her hand between them, touching herself in that secret, sensitive spot. The feel of him pulsing within her drew out her own orgasm, and she threw back her head as they pulsed together, moaning with the glory of long-denied release.

He held still, gradually relaxing, but still holding her up as the joint contractions of their sexes continued for several long moments. Then his hands loosened and she slid down his body until her feet touched the floor.

He still held his body against hers, both of them now slick with sweat and their combined release. He wrapped his arms around her and held her up as he pressed his forehead against the wall.

"I'm sorry, love."

She only squeezed him tighter.

"I lost control, Soph. I'm so sorry."

His hand cupped her cheek and she turned her head to kiss his palm. "Shhh. How can you be sorry? We both lost control."

In silence, they clung to each other until Tristan lifted her in his arms and carried her to the bed. There he set her down and made love to her again. This time, he was slow and silent, worshiping her body as only he could, pleasuring her with his mouth, fingers, and sex, before taking his own pleasure deep within her.

Afterward, finally fully sated, she slipped off into a sweet, deep sleep, warm for the first time in many days.

When she awoke, she reached for Tristan, but he was gone.

Chapter Nine

Tristan opened the drawing room door to find Sophie, Fisk, and Garrett drinking tea. At first glance, the atmosphere appeared relaxed and congenial, but it only took a few seconds before he sensed a thick tension in the air.

The tension gripped him full force when he saw Ansley seated in the armchair with his back to the door. Ansley had already returned from court. Damn it— Tristan hadn't received word from Griffiths yet.

He stepped more deeply into the drawing room and paused as Fisk set his porcelain cup upon the silver tea service tray and rose. He was dressed impeccably in a cream-striped waistcoat with gold buttons, a gold watch chain looping over the front pocket, stylish pantaloons, and shiny low boots.

Fisk offered him a congenial smile. "Ah, Lord Westcliff. Good afternoon. Mr. Ansley and I just returned from today's court proceedings."

"Good morning, Fisk. Your Graces. Ansley." Ansley

refrained from meeting his gaze, but Tristan couldn't really blame him. He'd worked side by side for the past eight years with Ansley, and now the solicitor was, by all rights, his enemy.

"Please. Sit down." Fisk gestured at the only empty seat in the room.

Tristan stared at Fisk. The gall of the man—to invite Tristan to sit on a chair that had once belonged to him. He understood Fisk often took the reins for Garrett, who was still learning his way, but he had lived in this house for a large portion of his life and refused to be treated like a guest by any upstart newcomer.

Tristan gave Fisk an apologetic smile. "Of course, Mr. Fisk, but would you mind moving? I'm afraid you've taken my favorite chair."

Tristan didn't miss the quickly masked flash of irritation in the other man's eyes, and it annoyed Tristan even more. Who was Fisk to have proprietary feelings over a chair in the Duke of Calton's drawing room, for God's sake?

"Not at all, my lord." Fisk retrieved his teacup and moved to the only unoccupied seat, a high-backed, uncomfortable chair upholstered in the same palm-print silk as all the other furniture in the room, but set slightly apart.

Pushing aside his annoyance, Tristan flicked back the tails of his coat and lowered himself into the chair abandoned by Fisk. As Sophie rose to pour him a cup of tea, he turned to Ansley. As always, the man looked like a caricature—round as a cricket ball, with greased mousy hair, heavy side whiskers, and round blue eyes sunk behind heavy features. His jowls hung low enough to grab in handfuls. But he always dressed in the height of fashion, in an impeccable stiff black tailcoat that managed to cover his spectacular girth without buttons bursting. Beneath, he sported a spotted black and gray waistcoat over a crisp white shirt and cravat that merged into the pale folds of his chin. His gigantic pantaloons matched the gray of the waistcoat, tapered down his legs and strapped around the arch of his tiny feet. His black shoes were narrow at their tips and just as shiny as if he was wearing them for the first time.

"Would you like some tea, Tristan?"

He smiled at Sophie, who gazed at him with dark amber eyes as she offered him a cup of tea. From the corner of his eye, he saw Garrett scowling at them. She returned to sit beside him on the sofa, but Tristan was gratified to note she kept a foot of space between their bodies.

Fisk cleared his throat. "The court certainly had strong opinions of the matter of your marriage, Your Grace."

Tristan took a sip of his tea and glanced at Garrett to see him studying Fisk with interest, clearly unaware where this was leading.

Fisk continued, "The court reasoned it would be best to nip the speculation in the bud by coming to a quick resolution. The judge also said it was a clear-cut case, as I'm sure you'll all agree."

"I don't," Tristan stated flatly.

"Your agreement isn't necessary," Garrett snarled. "The court has the final say on this matter."

With massive palms engulfing his delicate cup, Ansley studied his tea with great interest. Sophie twisted her hands in her lap and chewed her lower lip. She looked as though she'd rather be anywhere but here.

Tristan leveled a stare at Garrett. "On the contrary, Your Grace, my agreement is necessary, for if the court comes to a conclusion I deem unsatisfactory, I will appeal, and I will continue to appeal until I am satisfied."

Garrett shrugged. "The law is the law, Westcliff. And in this case, I believe the decision is obvious. You're merely blinded by your own petulance."

Tristan ground his teeth.

"Garrett," Sophie reprimanded softly, clasping his arm. "Please."

As always, her touch seemed to calm him. As unwelcome jealousy surged through him, Tristan looked away. He focused once again on Fisk.

But Sophie wasn't finished. "I shall accept no resolution unless it is one all three of us find satisfactory."

Fisk, Ansley, and Garrett all stared at Sophie, mouths agape, but then the other three men didn't know his wife as well as Tristan did. He wasn't surprised in the least.

Ansley was the first to open his mouth, instantly proving he knew Sophie least of all. "Your Grace, your desires will have no effect on the decision of the court. The outcome of this case is a purely legal matter."

He took a sip of his tea as if to wash down a terrible taste in his mouth.

"I don't care a whit about legalities," Sophie said, her voice calm and clear. "I care about my family. I won't have the people I love torn apart by discord."

"Unfortuately," Fisk cut in, his tone apologetic, "I fear that has already begun to happen, Your Grace."

Sophie set her own teacup on the highly polished round marble side table. "Whether or not that is the case,

I insist upon taking steps to solve problems rather than exacerbate them."

"Exactly." Fisk rose and walked to a small table near the door. A sheaf of papers rested on its top, and Fisk collected them. "I do believe that is everyone's wish, Your Grace."

He glanced pointedly at Ansley, who added, "Indeed. That is one of the reasons the courts came to such a rapid decision."

Tristan sat very still as Ansley laboriously rose. "My lord, Your Graces—the court decided this morning that Lord Westcliff's responsive allegation was immaterial to the resolution of this case, and therefore, it was not admitted into court."

Tristan hissed out a breath. *Damn it.* He gripped the arms of his chair and braced himself as Ansley turned to him. "Given the evidence produced, the court has upheld the legality of the marriage of the Duke and Duchess of Calton and further determined that the marriage of Lord Westcliff and Her Grace is illegal. Sir Robert Islington, judge for the Consistory Court of London, has pronounced said marriage null and void."

Over. Their marriage was over.

Sophie gasped. Rage buzzed in Tristan's ears as Ansley went on, motioning to the sheaf of papers in Fisk's hands. "These documents confirm the nullity of the marriage between Tristan James, Viscount Westcliff, and Sophie, the Duchess of Calton."

Fisk's grin spread wide across his face as he gazed raptly at Sophie and Garrett. "You are legally wed once again, Your Graces. Congratulations."

* * *

Curled in a tight ball on the frayed armchair in the duchess's bedchamber, Sophie dragged her heavy lids upward and nodded at Delia, who opened the door to Tristan's insistent knock.

He strode into the room and knelt beside her, his eyes dark with concern. "You look pale, Sophie."

She waved him off. In fact, her mouth was as dry as parchment, but she had no intention of admitting it to him.

Not that it mattered—Tristan knew her too well. "Please fetch Her Grace some claret," he said to Delia. "And something to eat as well."

The maid curtsied and left them alone.

"Sophie."

"Yes?" Her voice sounded small. Defeated.

"I must leave this house."

"No." Her head bent, she fought the bile rising in her throat. Her marriage to Tristan was over. In fact it had never really existed, not according to the law.

"I must. It belongs to the Duke of Calton, and he wishes me gone by tomorrow."

She glanced up at Tristan's handsome face. Would she never hold him in her arms again? Would she never again experience his devotion to her and the children, his companionship, his friendship, the gift of his dominance in bed?

His big hand curled over her knee. "This isn't over, love."

"Isn't it?"

"I plan to appeal to the Court of Arches."

She groaned softly.

"I'll appeal on the grounds of the length of his absence—

of his abandonment. And if that doesn't work . . . believe me, there are other ways." Tristan sighed, and his hand tightened over her knee. "Come, love, you mustn't give up. Where is your optimism?"

She traced his knuckle, then trailed her fingertip down his long, elegant fingers. "I'm afraid, Tristan. It will destroy me to let you go, but I . . ." Her voice lowered to a whisper. "I can't leave Garrett, either. I won't leave him."

"Sophie." He drew in a breath, and his eyes shone with emotion. "I know you care for him. You care for us both."

She swallowed hard at his understanding. "I wish the three of us could be as we once were."

His hand left her knee and he gripped both arms of the chair. "I don't."

"Tristan . . ."

"I knew I wanted you from the beginning. I always knew you'd be mine. I never wanted anyone else."

"Please don't—"

He pressed a finger to her lips. "I have to say this, Soph. In Garrett's last year at Eton, he told me he planned to make you his wife."

She stared at him. "You knew before I did, then."

Tristan nodded. "Yes. I was fifteen years old, and at that moment, I felt as if my life had ended. But I did nothing. I allowed him to take you from me. Instead of challenging him, I gave up. Damn it, Sophie, I let him walk away."

Sophie blinked away the film of tears covering her eyes. She reached to take his hands, and he laced her fingers with his.

"I'm not weak anymore," Tristan said in a low voice.

"I'm not giving you up this time. I'll fight to my dying breath if that's what it takes."

Sophie stood at the top of the stairs leading to the back drive, her fists clenched at her sides.

A hired carriage headed the small procession of vehicles parked on the gravel. Frantic with the task of packing and preparing Tristan's and Gary's personal items, servants bustled about the two carts behind the carriage. Garrett had decreed all of Tristan's possessions be out of the house by noon, and the sun was high in the sky. Sophie had not looked at a clock for hours, but it must be coming upon midday.

Just under two weeks from Garrett's return, Tristan and Gary were leaving them.

The air was still and close, and a thin haze shimmered over the rooftops of the stables and the line of trees beyond. Nevertheless, Sophie was cold—even with a woolen cloak draped over her shoulders, gooseflesh prickled her skin and she had to clench her teeth to keep them from chattering.

Tristan wrangled with his son as he stepped into the carriage. Garrett's imposing presence had no effect on the boy today—Gary clawed at Tristan's shoulder, trying to squirm free of his father's hold. "I want Miranda! Don't make me go, Papa. No!"

Sophie's heart ached for the boy. She'd said good-bye to him earlier, but he was more interested in playing with a toy carriage Mr. Fisk had brought for him, and he'd wriggled out of her embrace. He hadn't understood, but Miranda did, and she was devastated. Sophie pictured her daughter upstairs in the nursery. A row of windows faced the back drive, and she had no doubt Miranda was up there, watching Gary go, a solemn look on her heart-shaped face. Miranda's feelings for the boy ran deep, and Sophie was certain her daughter's heart was tied in nearly as many knots as her own right now.

"Mirandaaaaaa!" Gary screeched.

Holding Gary firmly against his chest, Tristan closed the carriage door. Only then did his gaze meet hers.

The depth of anger and remorse in his expression made her stomach clench. She couldn't fathom what this must feel like for him. Leaving his wife in the arms, and bed, of his cousin and onetime close companion who had risen from the dead. As painful and difficult as this was for her, it must be a thousand times worse for him.

"Tristan," she breathed. She took a step toward the carriage, but Garrett's hand descended on her shoulder, heavy and hard, drawing her to a halt.

She stood tall, unwilling to create a scene before the servants. Holding her gaze, Tristan rapped the roof of the carriage, signaling the driver to leave.

Sophie's heart fluttered in sudden panic as the reality of it crashed down on her. She was losing the rock that had always stood beside her in both good times and bad. Her confidant, her friend and lover. They might never hold each other in bed, talking late into the night. They might never again laugh together, or argue, or smile over their children's heads at something sweet one of them did. She might never feel his lips on her again. His hands exploring her body. The hard flesh of his chest pressed to her breast. Loving her. Stroking deep inside her body. Straining against her as he reached his peak.

Her body surged toward him, but it was no use. Garrett held her anchored in place.

The carriage lurched forward and turned the bend around to the front of the house, wrenching Tristan's gaze from hers.

Sophie swallowed hard, pushed her palms over her eyes, then turned on her heel. She brushed past Garrett and strode into the house.

Tristan sat stiffly on the squabs, one hand relaxed and resting on his knee, the other on the shoulder of his son sleeping beside him. Rather than gazing out the window of the carriage at the elegant Mayfair buildings they passed, he stared across at the seat where his wife should be sitting, all her focus directed at him as she discussed her day or argued politics or household management with him. Now that seat was empty.

Tristan grimaced and rubbed the back of his hand across his prickly jaw, flinching as he realized he'd forgotten to shave this morning. How unlike him.

The carriage came to a jolting halt in front of the townhouse Tristan had selected to be his residence until such time as he could reclaim Sophie. From the corner of his eye, Tristan caught movement, and he turned to look out the window. A servant walked sedately toward the carriage.

The man opened the door and bowed. "Good afternoon, my lord."

Tristan turned to Gary and shook him softly, until the boy's eyes flickered and opened. "Wake up, lad. We're here now."

Rubbing his eyes, Gary sat upright to survey his surroundings. Tristan tried not to fixate on the trail of tears carved down his cheeks. The child had fallen asleep sobbing for Miranda moments after they'd left Garrett's house.

Looking from Tristan to the scene outside the carriage door, Gary frowned. "This isn't home."

His lower lip began to tremble, and panic welled within Tristan—that uncertain desperation his son's tempers instilled in him. Gary had always been prone to fits of emotion. Nothing and nobody had been able to pacify him until they had come to live permanently with Miranda and Sophie. For the last year, the females' constant presence in his life had calmed him considerably.

He pulled his son onto his lap. "This will be an adventure, Gary." He motioned outside. "See that? That's the house where we'll be living for a time." How would Miranda approach this situation? He searched his memory, trying to recall one of the stories he'd heard the little girl telling his son. He found a vague recollection and latched on to it. "I've heard it was once a fairy house."

The boy eyed the place dubiously. Tristan couldn't blame him. The townhouse hardly appeared a fantastical home of fairies, with its white painted stone front and rows of plain diamond-paned windows. It was adjacent to an inn that had a large blue placard nailed beside its door, stating, "The Blue Swan Inn," in black letters with curlicue flourishes.

"Really, Papa?" Gary asked.

Tristan nodded sagely. "Indeed. It is said the fairies used their magic powers upon all the swans in the area, and turned them blue, as that is their favorite color."

Gary frowned. "Miranda says silver is the fairies' favorite color."

"Oh, not these fairies. This . . . this is a special fairy family—distant relatives of the fairies who prefer silver. Perhaps if we search hard, we will find a blue swan on the premises."

Of course there was a marked lack of premises upon which a blue swan might be found. The house abutted the pavement, and there appeared to be no garden. An alleyway bordered one side, but it led to mews, so it did not offer much hope for a blue swan sighting. But it was the best he could do under the circumstances.

Gary looked thoughtful. "Maybe I shall find a fairy inside."

"I doubt that, son, as they lived here long ago. But certainly there will be no harm in trying. Perhaps you will be able to find some treasure they left behind."

Tristan stepped out of the carriage, looking over his shoulder to the cart behind them. He longed for Miss Dalworthy, but he would not have taken her from Sophie and Miranda. He would have to find a new governess for Gary, posthaste.

Tristan didn't wish to linger on the street, for someone might recognize him, and he'd rather not have the gossips making a mockery of the move of all his belongings into a townhouse, not to mention his unshaven appearance. Taking Gary firmly by the hand, he strode to the door and through the small entryway, passing his hat and gloves to the portly butler, who bowed politely. "Welcome home, my lord."

"Thank you, Steadman."

He looked down the dim corridor, its walls decorated

with red fabrics and brown upholstery. This wasn't his home. But where was? Since childhood, he'd always lived in Garrett's family homes. Perhaps, at the advanced age of thirty-one, it was finally time for him to make his own way.

"Come, Gary. Let's look for those fairies."

Sophie was in the nursery reading with Miranda when Garrett found her. His stony expression softened as he knelt beside their daughter to ask how she was. Miranda solemnly kissed him on the cheek, and then held out the thin volume of "The House that Jack Built" for her father's perusal. Garrett gave a small smile.

"I know this book. Were you almost finished with Jack's tale?"

Miranda nodded. "We're at the priest, who's all shaven and shorn."

"Shall I read with you to the end? That is—" He slid a glance at Sophie. "—if your mama won't mind."

"Of course not," Sophie murmured.

Garrett settled in beside Miranda, looking like a giant on the undersized sofa. In a low, steady voice, he began to read. "This is the priest . . ."

Sophie watched as Miranda twisted a curl around her finger and mouthed the words with him, for she'd long since memorized this story. When he was finished, Garrett shut the book and smiled at her. "I need to speak to your mama for a short while, Miranda. Would you excuse us, please?"

She glanced at Sophie, her blue gaze wiser than Sophie would have liked. "Of course, Papa."

Sophie squeezed her daughter's hand and dropped a kiss on her forehead. "I'll be back soon, darling."

Miranda shrugged. "It's all right, Mama. Take as long as you need."

Sighing, Sophie followed Garrett to the door, leaving her daughter in the charge of the governess, who was sitting in her favorite chair—a rocking chair brought back from America by Tristan—sewing one of Miranda's frocks.

Garrett held the door for Sophie, allowing her to exit the nursery first. Maybe he was slowly learning how to be a gentleman.

"To my bedchamber," he growled in her ear after he shut the door.

Instantly revising her opinion of his newfound gentlemanliness, Sophie snapped him a stare, then whirled around with a swish of skirts and led the way down the stairs. With each step, her annoyance with him grew. What now? Would he so quickly demand the reinstatement of his conjugal rights? Would he dare go so far?

When they reached his bedchamber, he nudged her inside, went in after her, and closed the door behind them with a definitive click.

Clasping her wrist, he led her to the bed, then took her by the waist and lifted her to sit on its edge. "Stay there," he ordered.

She slid off the bed instantly, staring daggers at him. "Bullying again, Garrett?" She gestured at the bed. "Why, look, I've disobeyed you. What will you do? Force me back onto your bed?"

"Should I?"

"You might try."

"I merely wanted you to be comfortable."

She made a disbelieving noise. "Please. There are several chairs that could be used for that purpose. In fact there are several less suggestive rooms in this house that could be used for that purpose. You try to mask your threats, but they are clear to me. You're angry with me again for some reason, but your attempts to frighten me into compliance won't work."

"Very well." He gestured to one of the armchairs near the fire. "Would you like to take a seat?"

"I'll stand."

He gave a terse nod. "We've a few matters of business to discuss."

She met his gaze evenly. "Indeed we do."

A long silence stretched between them. They stared at each other, each challenging the other to begin.

Finally he gave a gallant gesture. "Go ahead. Ladies first."

She smiled. "Gentlemen first. I insist."

He huffed a breath. "Very well." After a short pause, he said, "I dislike how you behaved when Westcliff left this house."

She narrowed her eyes at him. "What is your complaint? I was the model of propriety."

"It was clear to all in attendance that you wished him to stay."

"Of course I wished him to stay. Everyone knows that. They'd have to be fools or blind not to. And you should be thankful I restrained myself from doing what I really wanted to do."

Garrett raised a brow. "What was that?"

"Tear myself from your grasp, throw myself into his arms, and go away with him."

Garrett's lips thinned, and he spoke through gritted teeth. "Why did you stop yourself?"

"I don't know."

His blue eyes seemed to pry into her soul as he regarded her. "Oh, but I think you do."

"The law wishes me to stay."

"Surely there's more to it than that."

He held her pinned beneath his gaze, and she couldn't lie to him. She looked away. "Once upon a time, that body held the soul of a man I loved. I want to know if he's still there, or if the swaggering bully has taken his place."

"But you still love Tristan and want to run away with him."

Tristan. It was the first time she'd heard him use Tristan's given name since his return, and it shook her.

"I love him. But run away with him?" She shook her head. "I . . . can't."

He thrust a hand through his disorderly hair and let out a harsh breath. "What do you want from me, woman? No matter what you say or do, I will never calmly stand by as my wife professes to love someone else." His expression darkened. "Westcliff found another woman once before when he fancied himself in love with you. He'll do it again."

"He's older now, Garrett."

Garrett was silent. Then the corner of his mouth lifted. "Yet he walked away from you today. Again."

Some of the tension melted in Sophie, and she very nearly smiled. "He walked away because it was the wisest course of action. Because he knew I didn't want him, or anyone else, hurt."

Sighing, she held her hands out toward him in a gesture of peace. "I don't hate you, Garrett. I am angry, though. Just as you are. Please don't be a boor. I'm not part of your army. I'm not someone you can lead about by the strings."

"You were before."

Her breath stalled in her throat. Had she been? It was true she was so in love with him, she'd have done anything he'd asked. And he'd been gone so often . . . first at Eton, then Cambridge, then Spain and Belgium. Whenever he'd come home, her sole aim had been to please him.

"The years I spent without you forced me to mature. I'm not exactly the woman you left. We cannot rebuild our lives if you persist in the assumption that I'm someone you can order about."

"Rebuild our lives?" He lifted a sardonic eyebrow. "Together? I can hardly believe you think that is a remote possibility."

"I don't know if it can happen," she said honestly. "I don't know who I'm meant to stand beside."

Both of you? She didn't dare say it, but an image of herself standing between them, holding both their hands, flickered through her mind.

"You're meant to stand beside *me*."

"I know that's what you believe. I just don't know if I agree."

"It doesn't matter. You vowed before God to be mine first."

She studied him, long and hard. "You must start treating me like your friend rather than your enemy."

A frustrated sound emerged from Garrett's throat. "Damn it, Sophie, I don't want your enmity." He turned and took several steps away from her, then spun around. "I . . . love you."

Sophie froze. Silence lengthened between them as they stared at each other across the room, the thick burgundy strands of the Aubusson carpet stretching like an eternity between them.

"You've a fine way of showing it," she said softly.

"What would you do if you loved someone who loved someone else?"

"I don't know."

"And what is the solution? I allow you to talk to him, continue to love him? Bed him?"

"I don't know." She raised a hand to her temple to press against the headache building there.

"I won't allow it." He strode forward, and his hands closed around her shoulders. "You're mine. You've always been mine, since we were children. I remember, Sophie. I never gave you up to him. I never would have."

"But you *did* give me up to him."

"I didn't know who I was! If I'd known, I would never have allowed him to touch you." He swiped a hand over his brow. "I expected you to wait," he said dully. "You promised you'd wait."

"I did! I waited for years!" She groaned. "Seven interminable years."

He dropped his arms and stared at her.

"Do you know what it's like to be a woman on her own, Garrett? Do you know what it's like to raise a child alone? To live from day to day ignorant of the fate of the man you love most in the world?" Tears pricked her eyes, but she didn't cry. She wasn't prone to weeping, or any of the emotional outbursts most women of her station affected. "Those events will change a person. They will force a soul to become stronger—more independent. If you can't accept that I've changed, then there is no use in either of us trying to rebuild anything."

"Do you still love me, Sophie? With all those changes you made, did your affection for me simmer away?"

"I never stopped loving you." Her voice was quiet. Calm. "But I love Tristan now, too. I'm sorry, but just as I couldn't stop loving you when you were gone, I can't—I *won't*—simply stop loving him now that you have returned."

He bowed his head, then looked up at her, his eyes shining like a sunlit sea.

"Sophie . . . Sophie." He took her in his arms, but her body was stiff. She couldn't relax against him as she once had. "What can we do?"

She simply shook her head.

"I can't allow you to see each other," he said. "Each time I watch the two of you together—" He stopped speaking abruptly.

"I know." She sighed. It had been so different when they were children.

He pressed his lips to her head. "Let me make love to you, Sophie. Let me show you—"

"No." Her body went still and tight in his arms. Her voice was little more than a whisper. He recoiled as if she'd stung him.

She covered her face with her hands. "How can I touch you? How can I touch either of you now with a clear conscience?"

He pulled away from her. Taking her chin between firm fingers, he tilted her head up so she faced him. "Everything has been resolved. *I* am your husband."

"Was that my choice?"

He stared at her, stark pain flaring in his eyes, and guilt flooded through her. She hated to hurt him.

"No, it wasn't your choice. Nevertheless, you're married to me. It is your duty to stand beside me. To fulfill me in bed and out of it."

After gifting her with a glimpse of the old Garrett, he'd retreated to his bullying tactics. She laughed mirthlessly. "So you will threaten me with coercion."

"It is within my rights as your husband."

She stared at him, searching his face. "Would you do that to me, Garrett? Have you changed so much?"

Again emotion flickered through his eyes, but then they went flat, as if he'd placed the final brick on his wall of defense. "How do you know I've changed? You never refused me before. How do you know I would not have forced myself upon you had you resisted?"

"I know," she said flatly.

He dropped his hand from her chin and narrowed his eyes at her. "Not today, Sophie. Not yet."

"So you won't rape me today, but you might tomorrow."

He rose and stood before her, slowly perusing her with his gaze. She averted her eyes as the warmth of a flush spread over her chest.

"Perhaps," he said.

Chapter Ten

Garrett rolled over. Since the war his sleep was restless, fraught with nightmares, uncomfortable. He dreaded nighttime because it meant he must suffer through the horror all over again.

The sharp cracks of gunfire surrounded him. Men shouted. Christ, they were dropping like flies all around him. Blood sprayed everywhere. In a daze he looked at his hands. Sticky, bright-red blood drenched them.

"Go away," he shouted to the bastards shooting at him. If only they would leave him in peace then he could think of a way to save his men.

But the chaos didn't stop. The Frenchmen merely redoubled their efforts to kill him. But then a soothing feminine voice interfered, wrapping around him like a soft quilt, instantly comforting. Half awake, he settled into the sheets, still trembling, his shaking made worse by the coldness of the bedding dampened by his sweat.

"Joelle?" he whispered, reaching for her soft, lush body.

"No, Garrett. It's Sophie."

His eyes flew open. "Sophie," he croaked. Dressed in a white shift, her blonde-streaked hair flowing freely past her shoulders, Sophie stood beside the bed carrying a candle. The dim light flickered across her face, turning her into a beautiful specter. He yanked the blankets up to cover his naked torso. "What are you doing here?"

She set the candle on the bedside table and mounted the step to sit on the edge of the bed beside him. "I couldn't sleep . . . again . . . so I went downstairs to find a book." She held up a thin volume. "I was returning to my room when I heard you moan. Were you having a nightmare?"

"I . . . Yes." He closed his eyes as the images of battle swarmed through his mind like angry wasps.

God help him, he'd thought she was Joelle. He rubbed his arms briskly to stave off the gooseflesh.

"Will you be all right?"

He nodded, but he wasn't convinced, and she seemed about as convinced as he was. "Would you like a posset? It might help you to sleep more soundly."

"No." He didn't want her to leave him in the dark. Alone. He swallowed, opening his eyes into slits. "Will you stay with me for a while?"

"Of course." Not seeming at all perturbed that he'd called her by another woman's name, or that a few days ago he'd threatened to exercise his marital rights with or without her consent, she placed the candle and the book on a side table, and crawled up beside him. "Would you like me to rub your head?"

"Why?"

She frowned at him. "Do you remember how I used to rub your scalp before we went to bed?"

"Yes." Oh, yes, he remembered. He'd lain in her lap while they discussed the events of the day, and her fingers sifted through the unruly tangle of his hair. "But I wonder why you agree to stay with me after . . . the discussion we had a few days ago."

Her brows rose to pointed arcs. "Do you intend to ravish me tonight?"

He laughed. God, it felt good. Her presence pushed away the demons. They lingered on the fringes now, as if waiting for her to leave so they could come out to assault him again. "No. Not tonight."

She shrugged. "Why not, then? I can't sleep, and you don't want to be alone."

"It seems logical, I suppose."

"It certainly is." She patted her lap. "Lay your head."

Obediently, he lowered his head to rest on her thighs. Her fingers plunged into his hair, and after a few moments, his eyelids drooped and his muscles relaxed.

"It feels so good," he murmured.

"It's always had this effect on you, hasn't it? It was the best way to melt away the difficulties of your day."

"I remember."

For several minutes, he closed his eyes and simply enjoyed the feel of her hands on him. Her fingertips pressed on his scalp, rubbed his temples, even squeezed around the shell of his ear. When she spoke again, he had nearly dozed off.

"Who is Joelle?"

He stiffened, and she huffed out a breath. "It's all right, Garrett. I'm not going to shoot you."

He opened his eyes, staring across the dimly lit room. The candle flame flickered and cast long, eerie shadows across the walls. If he were younger, they'd frighten him.

"She was a woman I knew in Belgium."

"A lover."

"Yes." His throat was dry. He could use that posset about now. Or, even better, a stiff drink.

"Do you love her?"

He paused, then sighed. "I don't know."

Her fingers stilled on his scalp, but then they began to move again, slowly. "I won't lie and say I'm not terribly jealous."

"I'm sorry," he choked out. "If I'd known—"

" 'If' is a word we could repeat forever, isn't it? If I'd known you were alive . . ." Her voice trailed off. "Yes, I am jealous," she said firmly. "Hearing about the woman you bedded pains me. But I understand how it happened. You're not a man inclined to celibacy."

"No." Even now, speaking of Joelle and celibacy and lying in Sophie's lap, breathing in her sweet floral scent, his loose drawers grew tight. He willed his errant body to behave.

"As difficult as it is to hear, I can only conceive how devastating it would be to see," she said quietly.

The image of her tied up in bed—in *this* bed—with Tristan on top of her barreled through his mind, and his shoulders tightened. "It wasn't . . . easy."

"I imagine not."

They lapsed into a long silence. She continued to rub his head, moving down to the back of his neck at his hairline.

Her cool fingers feathered over the hot flesh behind his shoulder. "What were you dreaming about?"

"The war," he murmured.

"Do you have nightmares often?"

"All the time."

"How awful." There was true sympathy in her voice. "You sounded . . . terrified."

"Usually am." He was half asleep, sinking deep into the pleasure of her gentle touch.

Her fingers curled over his shoulder. "If it helps, I'll rub your head. Whenever you need it."

"It helps," he whispered. It helped him more than she might ever know. "Thank you, my love."

Sophie spent the better part of the morning companionably writing letters with Miranda, who'd been uncommonly quiet for the past few days. With painstaking effort, Miranda had written a long missive to her grandmother. Then she'd written to Gary.

Dearest Gary,

I hope by now you have stopped weeping, for as I have told you many times, weeping has no useful effect besides making the person who weeps quite ill. Mama is here and she is well, as am I. And I am certain you are well, too, for Mr. Fisk has told us so. Mama says we will meet again very soon, and there you can tell me about all your adventures in your new home. Mr. Fisk says you live beside an inn claiming to house blue swans, and I am exceedingly

*eager to learn whether you have indeed seen swans
which are blue, for I never have.*

*With much love and greatest affection,
Lady Miranda James*

Sophie's own letter writing had been difficult and rather
frustrating. As she wrote, she became increasingly nervous about Garrett and his reaction to the flurry of femi-
ninity that would overtake his home when Becky and his
aunt arrived. Sophie found it difficult to imagine him idly
sitting by as the ladies chatted about balls and fashion and
gowns and potential beaux for Becky. Tristan would have
taken it all in stride—in fact, he likely would have joined
in the discussions with his opinions. But those matters
wouldn't interest Garrett. They never had.

"Mama?" Miranda was studying her with her corn-
flower-blue eyes.

"Yes, darling?"

"Will you be attending many balls this Season?"

She nodded. "Yes, Miranda. As your Aunt Becky's
chaperone, I shall have to attend a great many, I
imagine."

"And will Papa go with you?"

She paused, then answered honestly. "I don't know."

"I don't think he's ready to go to a ball, Mama." Miranda folded her hands primly in her lap and gazed at
Sophie with utmost solemnity. "He might frighten some
of the more delicate ladies in attendance."

Sophie burst out laughing. Her little girl was truly wise
beyond her years.

Miranda just stared at her, and she sobered quickly.

"Oh, darling. Don't worry. If he does attend any balls, you and I will be certain he is prepared for them. He won't scare anyone, I promise."

Miranda nodded. Then she blinked and looked down at her lap. "Papa is a very sad man."

Sophie swallowed down the emotion that crowded her throat. "I know, Miranda. I know."

Tristan thrust the pamphlet back at Griffiths. "Lies," he stated flatly. "All of it."

Griffiths's raised brows drew thin lines across his smooth forehead. He took the slim volume from Tristan and tucked it into a pocket of his coat. "Are you certain, my lord?"

Tristan clasped his hands behind his back and looked down the packed dirt path to where Gary had scampered ahead, chasing ducks. Afternoon sun warmed his shoulders through his coat—a hint of coming summer. New leaves blanketed the park's trees in green, and birds trilled cheerfully in the distance.

The pamphlet claimed Garrett's wounds at Waterloo had left him mad—prone to uncontrollable violence, irrationality, and frightful visions. Tristan wondered whether Garrett would blame him for these accusations. Only an enemy of Garrett's would publish such a slanderous report, and Tristan didn't know Garrett had any enemies. Besides himself.

Shaking off the melancholy that thought brought with it, he pinned the solicitor with his gaze. "The Duke of Calton is no more insane than I am. He's suffered through an extended ordeal, and it will take him time to relearn his place."

"But can you be certain?" Griffiths persisted. "If there is any truth to the rumor, his madness could be key to our appeal."

"I'm certain." Tristan released a breath. His son had caught a duck. Grinning from ear to ear, he scampered toward them clutching his flapping, panicked prize. "Gary, release the poor creature," he called.

Gary scowled but did as he was told. Looking quite offended, the duck ruffled its feathers and took flight, landing with a splash in the murky waters of the Serpentine several yards away.

Who would do this to Garrett, and why? Tristan would talk to Jennings, see if he could find the source of the rumors. Even if it ultimately had nothing to do with Tristan or with Sophie, this kind of slander disgusted him.

"Word is that not only is the duke succumbing to violence, but he is also using the duchess quite poorly," Griffiths added in a low whisper.

Tristan stiffened. "Where have you heard this?"

"At my club," Griffiths said. "An acquaintance of mine heard his servants whispering. When questioned, they reported they'd heard from a servant at the duke's household."

Tristan narrowed his eyes. All the servants at Garrett's London house behaved with the utmost discretion. Tristan knew—he'd hired most of them. And Connor and Mrs. Krum, their superiors, kept a tight rein on all the staff. At the first signs of gossip, heads would roll.

"Interesting," Tristan murmured.

"Do you believe there's any truth to these whisperings?"

"Certainly not." There was an offended huff in his

voice, but he remembered Garrett's rage-filled eyes on that first night, and discomfort flooded his veins.

If Garrett hurt Sophie in any way . . . Tristan sucked in a breath. *No.* It wasn't possible. He trusted Garrett—always had. And the Garrett he knew would never lay a hand on Sophie.

But Garrett had changed. He wasn't the same man. What if . . . ? Hell, he couldn't believe Garrett would hurt her, but damn it, he had to make sure.

Ahead of them, Gary whooped. He'd discovered a stick and had tossed it into a bank of mud like a javelin. The tip sank in deep, leaving the shaft trembling. Gary sprinted toward them. "Did you see that, Papa? Did you see how I buried that stick into the riverbank?"

"It was a fine throw, my boy." Tristan allowed pride for his son to infuse his voice, for it was true the child possessed athletic potential. He'd likely make a fine cricket player someday.

"Can we make our boats now, Papa? Please?"

"Soon, lad."

With a dimpled smile, Gary scampered off, and Tristan turned to Griffiths. "I'll inquire into the matter of the duke's behavior. But these are malicious rumors, and I'm certain they're unfounded."

Griffiths nodded. His gaze slid away. "Even if they aren't complete truths, they could prove valuable to our case."

Tristan eyed the solicitor, appraising him. "The appeal progresses as planned, I assume?"

"Yes, my lord. Absolutely."

"Then how could false rumors possibly aid our case?"

"If there is any question regarding the duke's sanity,

or if it's widely believed he mistreats his duchess, he will lose favor with the courts, and it will strengthen our argument."

Tristan stared out over the Serpentine, its surface pearlescent in the early afternoon sun. He wanted Sophie back, but he would win her back fairly and honestly. To win her back using unfounded lies as his weapons would be not only dishonorable, but reprehensible. He wouldn't do it.

"No. Absolutely not. I won't besmirch my cousin's character for my own gain."

Griffiths nodded. "Yes, of course. I understand, my lord."

Tristan's gaze sharpened on the shorter man. "Be certain you do, Griffiths. Now I shall take my leave of you. My boy awaits. Good day."

As Griffiths bowed his farewell, Tristan turned away to make paper boats with his son.

"I should like to see my letters."

Garrett looked up at his wife as she approached the desk. Warily, he folded his hands on the top of the shining wood surface. He couldn't remember much of what they'd said as he'd drifted off last night, and he had no idea when she'd left him. He must have been fast asleep.

It seemed so much easier to talk openly with her under the cloak of night. Everything was harsher in the light of day.

"What letters?"

She sighed. "It has been nigh upon two weeks since I've received any letters. You're turning away visitors at the door—a certain cause of scandal in and of itself, you know—and you're keeping my correspondence from me."

Garrett gestured at the high pile of papers cluttering the corner of his desk. "Perhaps your letters are here."

He'd been flooded with letters daily since he'd returned home—most of them welcoming him home, but some were of true importance and pertained to legal and financial matters. Several were from the steward at Calton House, updating him on the condition of the house and grounds, which was, by all accounts, disastrous. He thought Tristan would have done a better job with his properties. All of those letters had mixed together with Sophie's correspondence. He could do nothing but tackle them one at a time.

"Why would you keep them from me?"

"The ladies of the *ton* thrive on scandal. I'd rather avoid their egging you on to betray me."

"That's nonsense. I wouldn't engage in any effort to undermine you, nor would I countenance any such attempt from any of my acquaintances." She sighed. "Garrett, I must have my letters. If they go unanswered, it will only fuel the flames of gossip. I assure you, you will find nothing to disturb you within them."

He gazed broodingly at the pile of correspondence, struggling with the insane desire to keep her completely isolated. What if she escaped from him? Ran off with Tristan? Took his daughter away?

But perhaps he wasn't giving her a chance. Last night had proven she possessed a great deal of compassion. As much as his imagination liked to run wild, he couldn't bring himself to believe she'd deliberately hurt him.

Tristan, on the other hand . . . Given the opportunity, he might try to spirit her away.

"I will go through them today and give you the letters I deem to be innocent."

She blew out a breath between her teeth. "I am certain all of them will be 'innocent.' "

"We'll see."

Her eyes flashed gold sparks at him. She was annoyed again. He couldn't entirely blame her, but she must understand that he was in ultimate control of her destiny.

He opened the desk drawer and collected the stack of calling cards he'd gathered since his return. "If you would like to know who has come calling, here you are."

"Oh, Lord." Taking them, she sank into the rose-embroidered armchair. "Half of London has come by."

"So it seems."

As she sorted through the cards, he returned to the account he'd been working on when she'd arrived, and for a long while they worked in a measure of companionable silence. When he heard Sophie sigh, he looked up.

She'd sorted through all of the cards and piled them on the small round table beside her chair. "I wanted to inform you that I shall be accompanying Miranda and Miss Dalworthy to the park this afternoon."

He frowned at her, fighting against the compulsion to tell her she couldn't go. He'd given her the freedom to leave the house days ago, yet she hadn't taken advantage of that freedom since the day she'd found him in his bedchamber in farmer's rags.

Oddly enough, she seemed about as displeased by the prospect of her outing as he was. He lifted his brows in question. "It doesn't please you to leave the house after all this time?"

"It should, I know. But—" The pale column of her throat moved as she swallowed. "—I admit to being somewhat apprehensive."

"Why?"

She glanced toward the open window, where a stiff breeze lifted the heavy velvet of the curtains.

"Gossip," she said in a low voice. Her amber gaze returned to him. "What shall I tell them, Garrett?"

"The truth," he replied bluntly.

"I know. But the truth is . . . so complicated."

Garrett rubbed his temples. He closed his eyes and an image fluttered through his mind. An eight-year-old Sophie dodging through the high grasses in the field behind Calton House, her hair glinting with gold streaks in the sun. Laughing as he chased after her—she was small and quick as a sprite, and he'd never been able to catch her.

"Be yourself, Sophie. No scandal can touch you," he said in a low voice.

She smiled, and it was a beautiful, wide smile that reached her lovely hazel eyes. "I think that was a compliment. Thank you."

He returned her smile stiffly. "Hyde Park only. And I shall expect you back within two hours' time."

She inclined her head. "Of course."

He nodded as she turned to leave, and then he lowered his attention to the paperwork on his desk, determined to stop himself from calling her back.

Chapter Eleven

Sophie didn't expect to meet Tristan at the park. So when she saw him kneeling beside Gary on the bank of the Serpentine River, her heart raced and her palms grew damp.

They looked so handsome together, one a smaller, plumper version of the other. It was clear to anyone who looked upon them that they were father and son, with their nearly black hair of exactly the same shade, and their piercing brown eyes now focused on each other. Tristan chafed the boy's hands in his own. His lips moved and he frowned at Gary as if they were discussing a matter of great importance.

Gary hadn't inherited much from Nancy, besides her penchant for dramatics. Normally pleasant and easy-going, when Nancy cracked, she did so with flair. Sophie smiled, remembering Tristan's panic the first time he'd experienced one of Nancy's emotional outbursts. Now, no doubt, he'd had to face Gary's tempers every day since

Gary had been separated from Miranda. He looked as if he was managing well.

It was nearly impossible to prevent herself from running up to him and throwing herself into his arms. Aware of the people all around, she kept a sedate pace between Miranda and Miss Dalworthy as they approached.

Miranda squeezed her hand. "I do believe that's Gary and his papa."

In Miranda's grip Sophie sensed the same tension she herself was feeling. But Miranda, ever sensitive of matters of propriety, didn't leap ahead either.

"Indeed it is." Sophie had no chance to say more, for Gary saw them at that moment. With a shriek, he sprinted toward them and launched himself into Miranda's arms. If not for Sophie's grasp on her daughter, both children would have toppled to the ground.

"Whoa now, boy," Tristan said softly, taking his son by the shoulder.

Sophie couldn't look at him. What would she say? It would be impossible to communicate to him as she wanted to in this public place.

"Miranda, darling. Look at you. You've grown two inches in the past few days, I think."

"I've missed you, sir," Miranda said as Tristan enfolded her in a hug.

Gary tugged on Miranda's arm. "Come look. Papa and I are making boats from newspapers!"

Miranda clapped her hands together and beamed in a smile more relaxed and genuine than Sophie had seen since Gary left the house. "Oh, that's lovely. May I help?"

"Of course!" Gary led her down the embankment, and

without so much as a glance at Sophie and Tristan, Miss Dalworthy hurried after them.

"I'm glad to see you," Tristan said in a low voice once they were alone.

"I . . ." The linen ruffle of Sophie's collar tickled her chin as she stared down at her hands and fingered the row of pearls on the back of her glove. ". . . Didn't know you'd be here."

"Look at me."

Struggling to keep her breathing even, she raised her gaze to meet his. His eyes bore into hers—dark and impassioned. A yellow hue, the remnant of Garrett's blows on the night of his return, still marred his handsome jaw, impossible to see unless one searched for it. He was cleanly shaven and smartly dressed. Not that she'd expect Tristan to appear publicly in any other state.

"I wish I could touch you," he murmured. There was an edge to his voice, and it sent a wicked shiver racing through her.

She flicked her gaze to the right and left. It was early enough—Miss Dalworthy always brought the children to the park before the afternoon crush—and only a few people milled about. Nobody focused on them. Yet it was likely someone would see them, and Garrett would hear of their meeting.

"You can't."

Tristan's eyes narrowed. "I know."

"We shouldn't be seen together."

"Of course we should. Let's stroll along the river. Miss Dalworthy will mind the children."

She couldn't keep the panic from her voice. "But . . . what if someone sees us?"

He shook his head. "What if they do, Sophie? We break no laws by being seen in the park together as our children play. Everyone knows how fond Gary and Miranda are of each other."

Everyone knew how fond Tristan and Sophie were of each other as well.

"If Garrett were to find out—"

A muscle ticked in his jaw. "What then? Have you grown afraid of him in so short a time?"

"No—I just . . ." She took a deep breath. "He would feel betrayed."

"There is no harm in a chance meeting at a park." He held out his arm. "Come. Let's walk."

She stared at the sleek line of his proffered arm. The mere thought of twining her arm with his made her blood race. What odd things this distance had done to her. She felt as she had long ago when Garrett had first begun to court her in earnest, as timid and aflutter as a green girl.

She tucked her arm into Tristan's. He felt warm and solid against her skin, even through the heavy wool of her spencer and his coat. His touch traveled through her, leaving her muscles relaxed and languid.

They strolled at a leisurely pace down the trail leading along the bank of the Serpentine. The day had turned brisk and cloudy, another reason the paths weren't crowded. It looked as if it might rain again.

"Tell me how you are. Are you comfortable?" she asked quietly after they'd walked awhile in silence.

"Yes, I can hardly complain." He paused. "What of you, Soph? Tell me what's happening in the house. There are rumors—"

"What are they saying?" She closed her eyes in a long blink. "Lord, I almost don't want to know."

"Gossip about Garrett is circulating far more freely than gossip about the two of us."

"Tell me."

He spoke quietly. "They say Garrett's gone mad. That he's beating you."

She reeled to a halt. "What?"

Tristan released a relieved breath. "Thank God. I knew it wasn't true."

"Of course it's not true! Did you even question it?"

"Not at first. I know he's no madman. But . . . I admit, I was a little worried for you."

"He's changed, Tristan, but not that much."

"I know, Soph."

She shook her head, aghast. "Why would they be circulating such slander? About Garrett, too. He was always so well-loved."

"I agree, it's odd. I'm told the servants began the rumor that you've been ill-treated."

"*Our* servants?"

He shrugged. "That's what I'm told. Makes it all the more strange, don't you think?"

She paused for a long moment. She'd look into the matter, but in truth, of all the people in the household, she couldn't fathom that a single one would spread such lies. Still, people were willing to go to great lengths for a bit of fame. Even further for money. But how could slander about Garrett result in such a gain?

"I'll question the servants."

"Good."

They glanced at each other. "So what can it mean?" Sophie asked.

He frowned. "I don't know. We have no proof that anything is amiss. And yet . . ."

"Something feels wrong," she finished. "The rumors make no sense. Who would do this, and why? It's almost as if someone is out to destroy Garrett."

"Exactly. We must both be vigilant. I don't trust anyone entirely, Sophie, so please be careful."

She nodded. "I will. And I'll return to my social functions. I've kept away too long. Surely when the world sees I'm well, the silly gossip about my 'abuse' will disappear."

Tristan took a deep breath. "I hate the thought of you in danger."

At that, she laughed. "I'm not in danger, Tristan."

"I cannot shake the feeling that you are."

She squeezed his hand. "Well, you're wrong. In any case, Garrett—our Garrett—is there."

It was a mistake to say that. In her and Tristan's shared concern about the awful rumors surrounding Garrett, she'd forgotten their current enmity. Tristan's face darkened.

"Tristan, don't," she murmured. "I hate the thought of the two of you at odds." And what made it so much worse was that she was the cause.

It didn't escape her notice, however, that despite their battle over her, Tristan still cared enough for his cousin to strive to find the source of the gossip and to put a stop to it.

He squeezed her forearm with his free hand. "I know, Soph. It's just—" She saw his Adam's apple move as he swallowed. "—it's difficult. Forced to separate from you, picturing the two of you together in the house. One's imagination . . . runs rampant."

"Don't allow it to," she said fiercely.

"How can I stop? I imagine you with him, lying in bed beside him, making love to him. In our bed . . ." He sucked in a breath. "It nearly kills me."

"But you're wrong."

"What are you saying?" His hands curled into fists. "That you haven't slept with him? God, Sophie. I know you, and I know him. Hell—"

She came to a dead stop in the center of the path. "I—*we*—haven't."

"You've always loved him. You pined for him for years—you were pining for him the very night he returned, and now he's back." He blinked hard, but he wouldn't meet her eyes. "I know how the two of you are—were. If it hasn't happened yet, it will."

"I assure you, nothing has happened between us." She fought down the guilt bubbling up from her gut, but she couldn't tell him about the single kiss she'd shared with Garrett. Why cause him more pain?

"It would be natural. He is your husband, after all. For now." His lips twisted. "Damn it, Sophie, this is killing me."

"It hurts me, too, Tristan. I miss you. So much."

She closed her eyes. He pulled her in one direction, Garrett in another. It would tear her apart.

He reached down suddenly to grasp her hands in his. "Whatever happens, I intend to take you away from him."

Opening her eyes, she looked at him blankly for a long moment.

"We'll take the children and go somewhere far from here, far from London, where we can be together. Where we can be happy."

"What are you saying?"

He squeezed her hands. "I know you love me, Soph. I know you want me. I can make you happy."

She looked away—anywhere but at him—beyond him to the bank where Miranda and Gary were playing. Both were clapping and jumping up and down as the wind caught one of the sails on their little newspaper boat.

"I've told you before I cannot leave him. He needs me."

"*I* need you, Sophie."

But not in the same way Garrett did. How could she make him understand? It was useless—even she didn't fully understand—it was all too complex, too overwhelming.

A gust of wind caught the edge of her straw bonnet, pulling on the pins, and she clapped her hand to her head.

"I love him, too, Tristan. I love you, and I love him. Equally."

"You and your deuced fairness." His voice was raw. "It's not going to work this time, don't you see? It's impossible, damn it." He tore his gaze from hers, then turned away, taking long strides down the path.

Still clasping her bonnet to her head, she gathered her skirts with her free hand and hurried after him. "No, it isn't impossible." She curled her fingers over his arm. "Listen to me. They say a mother finds it in her heart to love all her children. The love for a child surpasses any kind of love a woman will ever experience." She lowered her voice and tilted her head so she could see his expression. "Why, then, can a woman not be capable of loving two men?"

"It is a different kind of love altogether," he said tightly.

"I'll grant you that. Still, it is not impossible. I wish—" She gulped in a breath. She'd never kept her deepest thoughts from Tristan, and she wouldn't start now. "I wish you would both let me love you."

"That's—" His hand flew upward in frustration. "Damn it, that's blasphemous."

Wanton, wicked, debauched. She knew, and she agreed. And yet how could she force herself to stop loving either one of them? *That* was impossible.

A thick wall of clouds suddenly obscured the sun, casting a shadow over both of them as surely as it cast a shadow over her heart.

"I'm sorry. I don't want to hurt you, but it's true." He didn't answer, so she continued. "I've always loved Garrett. You knew it to be true the day you married me. You were willing to share my affections then."

His upper lip curled. "I could share you with a ghost, perhaps. But a live man? I can't."

A group of twittering ladies was approaching followed by their chaperones, and Sophie's heart sank. As they drew nearer, Sophie recognized one of them, the Lady Ella Worthing, one of the daughters of their friends the Earl and Countess of Harpsford. They could not turn and head back toward the children—it would be a direct cut and utterly rude. No, Sophie would be forced to be civil, after Tristan had just told her he could not accept what was in her heart.

The chattering diminished as the girls grew nearer. All four ladies gazed at Tristan and Sophie in open curiosity.

They stopped when they were within the appropriate distance and exchanged bows.

"Good day, Lady Ella," Sophie said, smiling politely.

"Lady Ella," Tristan said. Sophie risked a glance at him. He smiled handsomely at the young women across from him, showing no outward sign of distress.

"Your Graces." Lady Ella smacked her hand to her mouth, and her doleful brown eyes grew wide. "Oh, dear! I am so, so very sorry, Your Grace and my lord."

Tristan laughed, a sound that seemed to put everyone at ease. "Not to worry. Even I am having a difficult time keeping up with my titles of late, my lady."

They exchanged introductions, and, working together, Sophie and Tristan managed to converse about the upcoming social activities in London and Becky's imminent arrival, and then Lady Ella brought up the weather. "Mama said we must take our walk early today, for it is certain to rain."

"Indeed, I believe I do feel a wetness in the air," Sophie said.

"Oh, yes. And to think not ten minutes ago the sun was shining," one of the lady's companions added.

A gust of wind whipped through the group, smattering them with dewdrops from a nearby tree and causing Tristan to grip his hat to keep it from sailing away.

"Perhaps we should all retreat to more agreeable surroundings. Ladies, may I offer my carriage?"

"Oh, no, sir, I have Papa's. Thank you ever so much for the generous offer, Your . . . my lord."

"Think nothing of it," Tristan said gallantly.

They parted from the ladies, who rushed down the lane toward Hyde Park Corner where their carriage awaited.

Sophie smiled at Tristan. "We managed that rather well, I daresay."

He grinned back at her, showing his dimple. "Excellently, I think."

She wanted to kiss the little indentation in his cheek, then slide her lips over to his. She wanted to abandon herself to him as she had a week ago and every day before that for months. It would heal her, body and soul.

If only . . .

She tore her gaze from the heat flaring in his eyes. "We always do work well together."

"Always," he said softly.

"At the very least, that set won't think I've been abused. But they won't forget they saw us together at the park. Ella will tell the countess—"

"—who is a model of discretion, as both you and I well know," Tristan interjected.

Sophie remained silent. He spoke the truth, after all. The Countess of Harpsford was one of her best friends for that very reason.

He sighed. "One of the other ladies in that group will spread the word, no doubt. Either way, it is what we make of it, Soph."

They changed direction to return to the children. The wind gusted randomly now, and the sky grew darker by the minute. In the distance, she could see Miss Dalworthy restraining Gary from retrieving a boat that had drifted into water too deep for it to be recovered.

After a few moments, Tristan continued, "And all I make of it is you telling me in no uncertain terms that you're in love with Garrett and refuse to leave him. I should think Garrett might be rather pleased to hear it." The smile had bled from Tristan's lips and a thin bitterness laced his voice.

"Tristan—" she began in despair.

He laughed hollowly. "Never worry, love. You know I've no plans to give up on you. Perhaps when you are legally returned to me, I shall change your mind."

"I am constant to those I love, Tristan."

He raised his eyebrows. "Why do you say that?"

"I merely wanted to remind you. I speak nothing but the truth with you. I'd never deceive you. Even though you think I am disloyal to you in my heart, someday you will realize I am not. I'll do anything to keep you free from pain."

He shook his head. "That's not true, Soph. Not anything. You won't leave Garrett. You won't come away with me."

She was silent.

"Would you?"

She couldn't answer.

He merely shook his head in frustration. As they came upon the children, she whispered, "I love you," and hoped to God it wasn't the last time she'd have the opportunity to say those words to him.

Two mornings later, Sophie lay on her back and stared at the small, single window in her bedchamber. Pale dawn light seeped beneath the curtains, yet she'd tossed and turned again and hardly had a wink of sleep. She hated this little narrow room, with its low, slanted ceilings and small, hard bed. She'd be able to sleep so much better in her own familiar spacious room, in her own bed.

Garrett would welcome her there. She'd sensed his arousal when she'd comforted him after his nightmare. But what would it be like to lie with him now?

The spring before Waterloo he'd had to leave for a month on business for the army. She'd waited at the front window on the day he'd returned, and when she saw his carriage, she flew out the door straight into his open arms. He'd jumped out of the carriage, spun her around, then, with a rakish gleam in those blue eyes, carried her upstairs. Past the servants, past the questioning gaze of his aunt. When they reached their bedchamber, he laid her on the pillows at the head of their bed. For a long moment he just stared at her, and then he'd said, "I'm the luckiest man in the world."

"I'm the luckiest woman," she'd replied.

They'd undressed each other, stripping the layers of clothes at a leisurely pace, contenting themselves with small touches, brushes of skin against skin. Her fingers grazing his cheek. His palm rounding over the curve of her hip. And then, when all their clothing was gone, they'd stood before each other in the nude, touching, exploring, rousing a simmering heat in each other. And then, he'd once again laid her on the bed, telling her he'd thought of her every second he was gone, counted every minute before he could see her again.

He'd caressed her gently between the legs, and when she was trembling with need, he entered her. Slowly, they'd made love, staring into each other's eyes. Beyond the rough, purely masculine arousal that enthralled her so much, she could see Garrett's love for her, and in that moment, her heart had nearly burst.

Little did she know then that in just over a month, he'd be gone.

Sophie flopped over onto her belly, pressing her face into the pillow. She was such a pathetic creature. Guilt was neither a valid nor a productive emotion, yet it crippled her. She couldn't seem to overcome it. The guilt took root in her mind and spread like a weed, growing faster than her ability to squelch it.

She wanted Garrett.

She missed Tristan.

Lord, she wanted them both. What would it be like? What if Garrett had agreed to their returning to their childhood in terms of companionship and trust, but with the added concession of allowing her to accept them into her bed? Both of them. Both men made her feel loved, cherished, desired. Both of them together . . .

She groaned aloud. She was wicked. Utterly depraved.

In a way, though, she could hardly blame herself. As an adult, such desires naturally resulted from the level of love she felt for them. If only there was a way to make them accept each other.

The thought was preposterous. Absolutely mad. Even if they did eventually accept her love for both of them—and the idea was absurd—Garrett was a duke. She was a duchess, and Tristan was a viscount. They bore a great responsibility to society—to England itself. It would be impossible for them to disappear happily into obscurity. Whatever actions they took were placed under extreme scrutiny.

The truth was that her last night with Tristan a week

ago just might be the last time she joined with either of the men she loved. If that were the case, she'd simply have to keep him—*them*—in her fantasies.

She closed her eyes, thinking of Garrett in the bath, relaxed and asleep, his lips parted as he took deep breaths. Would it be easy to bring him to full arousal? She had little doubt of it. The way he'd kissed her was clear evidence of how much he desired her.

During the early days of their marriage, she'd teased him incessantly, stroking him covertly as they passed each other in crowded rooms or when they were alone, knowing a servant might interrupt any time. She'd torment him until, gritting his teeth, he'd carry her upstairs and bed her thoroughly. And she loved all of it, from the tease to the thrill of capture and the ultimate ecstasy as he lost himself within her.

What might happen now if she stroked his sex as he lay in her lap after a nightmare? He'd be surprised at first. Then he'd lead her from the bed, stand her up, and turn her around. He'd unbutton her nightdress and slip it down over her shoulders, allowing his fingertips to skim the length of her body.

Skin against skin—his big, rough hands stroking down her arms, then up her bare waist . . .

He'd remove his drawers. The fabric would slide down his body, and she'd long to follow its path with her tongue.

He'd lift her and carry her back to the bed. Then he'd spread her legs and position himself at her entrance. Garrett's big torso would loom over her, naked, heat resonating from it. A determined look would shine in his sky blue eyes, and his shaft would jut out, long and hard and heavy.

On her back, she'd stare up at him, in awe of the strength of him, the sheer, powerful masculinity he exuded.

She remembered the last time she and Tristan had made love. His dark eyes glittering at her as he thrust into her, his jaw tight, the muscles in his arms straining.

In her imagination, with Garrett's big body still looming over her, Tristan appeared at the bedside.

Tristan was naked, also ready for her, and her heartbeat thumped against her breastbone at the sight of him, tall and strong and aroused.

"Take me in your mouth, Sophie." He'd tangle his fingers in her hair, turning her face toward his erection.

And she would. Oh, how she loved Tristan's taste, the feel of him in her mouth. But as soon as her lips touched him, Garrett pushed forward, and with one deep thrust, sheathed himself inside her.

Wicked. Wanton. Brazen.

She didn't care. She wanted them both, in her and around her. In the dark recesses of her mind, both men took her, hard and deep, and she gloried in it.

Both men stilled and stiffened, and then they came. Garrett's shaft contracted deep within her womb. Tristan's salty seed pumped into her throat as a great flush of pleasure rolled through her, starting between her legs and spreading in a powerful rush through her body, leaving every muscle quivering and spent in its wake.

Sophie lay still for a long moment, catching her breath, and then she rolled to her side and clasped her knees in her hands.

As lurid and wanton as the fantasy was, as much as she dreamed about it, such dreams would never come to fruition.

Some dark part of her had allowed that idea to enter and take root. It was something she could never tell another human being. Once she thought she'd share even her most intimate secrets with Garrett, and then she thought she'd share them with Tristan. But this fantasy—it was so perverse, so forbidden, she risked both men's hatred if they ever learned of it. They would both consider the mere thought a betrayal of her love for them.

It would be her secret. Tucked into a tiny chest in her heart and locked away forever.

This was England, and she was a duchess. She might as well dream about walking on the moon. The fact was she would never be able to have them both. And she couldn't choose either man over the other, even if she was legally married to one of them.

The only reasonable solution was a life of quiet celibacy. But it didn't mean she'd stop loving either of them.

Or dreaming about loving them.

Chapter Twelve

Miranda fascinated Garrett. She came to him in his study daily to inform him of the events of her life—what she had learned from Miss Dalworthy or her tutor that day, to whom she had written and what, and the overall status of the household. Oftentimes, he simply stopped what he was doing and watched her prattle on, her blonde curls bouncing, her cheeks flushed pink.

One topic she never discussed in great detail was her mama's state of mind. Though more than willing to mention Bitty the scullery maid's infatuation with Connor, or how a chambermaid had chipped a vase but had glued it back together and turned it so nobody would notice, Miranda steered clear of the topic of her mother.

Garrett never questioned her. He just allowed her to talk, and sometimes in the midst of her chatter, he would find his muscles relaxing or a smile curling his lips.

When she had left his study yesterday, he had stared at the door long after she'd passed through it, wondering what about this little girl he found so healing. She was a salve to his soul.

Now, she stared at him over the breakfast table, her blue gaze too wise for her seven years. She ate quietly, but he knew by the intelligent look in her eyes that she paid attention to her surroundings and listened to every word the adults uttered.

She intrigued him, there was no doubt of it. He saw so much of Sophie in her. At times he caught glimpses of himself in her, too, and that gave him a strange, tingling sensation somewhere in the vicinity of his heart.

Sophie was reading her correspondence, which she made a habit of doing at breakfast since he had allowed her access to her letters. She set down her coffee, studying a sheet of stationery with gilded edges. "Lady Torwood has invited Becky, you, and me to share her box at the opera Friday."

"No," Garrett said gruffly, looking away from his daughter and diving into his poached eggs. Why she did this to him was beyond his comprehension. Couldn't she understand he had no interest in the falseness and affectations displayed at public gatherings? Someday he might go to the theater again, but he'd sit in his box with his wife alone at his side, and they'd watch the performances. He refused to put on airs and behave like a duke—he still wasn't quite sure how, exactly, a duke *should* behave—and gossip and natter with others. The thought made his stomach turn sour.

Sophie set the invitation on the table, her expression neutral. "All right. But I will remind you once again that Becky will be expected to make appearances around Town, and I shall have to be by her side."

"My aunt will be by her side as well."

"Aunt Bertrice is growing older, Garrett. She will when she can, I am certain of it, but the greater part of the duty will fall upon you and me."

Garrett sighed and set down his fork.

"I would very much like to attend the theater with you, Your Grace," Fisk said. Garrett glanced up at him, raising a questioning eyebrow. Fisk gave him his *Trust me* look.

Hell, Fisk was the only man in the world Garrett did trust. Shrugging, he returned his focus to his breakfast.

"I know I am not included in the invitation," Fisk continued, "but perhaps another time."

From the corner of his eye, Garrett saw Sophie's frown slowly transform into a smile. *Damnation.* Sophie's smile lit the whole room, even on a dreary morning such as this.

"Thank you, Mr. Fisk. I would enjoy accompanying you to the theater."

Miranda gave her mama a curious look, no doubt questioning her halting tone. Garrett knew Sophie didn't feel comfortable with Fisk and generally avoided his company, but perhaps if they spent more time together she'd become as fond of him as he was.

Fisk beamed. "Indeed, I should enjoy attending with you, madam. Perhaps next week. I've heard there's a new spectacle at Covent Garden called 'The Vision of the Sun'—a 'grand, splendid, melodramatic tale of enchantment,' according to the playbill. Cal can retire to his study with his port the night long whilst we are thoroughly entertained."

"That would be lovely. And we can bring Becky and Aunt Bertrice with us." She gave Garrett an expectant look across the table.

Why would he say no? She would be with Fisk, whom he trusted implicitly.

He raised his fork and waved it in the air. "Of course you may attend the theater with Fisk, whenever you please." He tilted his lips at her in an attempt at a smile. "Better Fisk than me, no doubt."

When she smiled back at him, the affection in her expression warmed him to his toes.

After breakfast, Miranda and Sophie retired. Sophie was teaching Miranda embroidery, and as with everything, the child was a quick learner. Garrett saw Fisk off on one of his prowls about London, then followed the women into the austere drawing room where he sat in the most comfortable of the uncomfortable palm-print armchairs, opened *The Times*, and read the paper as Sophie directed their daughter on the proper way to hold her needle and how to achieve the perfect stitch.

Their feminine voices soothed him, made his mind drift toward pleasant matters. So this was domestic tranquility.

"Papa?"

Garrett didn't respond at first. The word flowed through him like the rest of the females' conversation, smooth as silk.

"Garrett?" Sophie said softly.

He raised his gaze over the top of the paper. "Yes?"

"Miranda wanted to ask you something."

He jerked his gaze to the girl, belatedly realizing the "Papa" had been directed toward him. It always struck him as odd—and endearing—when she referred to him as her papa.

He frowned at his daughter. "What is it, then?"

She frowned back at him, and Sophie chuckled softly behind her hand. They both turned their glares on her.

"May I ask what is so funny?" Garrett said.

She shook her head. "Nothing. Nothing at all. Miranda, dearest, do ask him your question."

Miranda sighed but kept her direct gaze on him. "I decided I wish to know more about how you occupied yourself in Belgium all that time."

"Is that so?" he asked slowly. In the days that had passed since his return, Sophie had tried to pry more out of him about his time in Belgium. She had succeeded to some extent, but he wasn't quite sure how to describe his time there to his daughter.

She nodded soberly. "Yes. I have never been to the Continent. Well, I know I was there as a baby when Mama was searching for you—" Garrett and Sophie exchanged a glance. "—but I don't remember. What is it like?"

"Well." How to explain the many differences between the Continent and England to this child? "The people in Belgium speak Dutch or French, for one." His lips quirked. "I wasn't overly popular amongst them for a long time. Later, once I adjusted to life there, they began to accept me as a Belgian rather than an Englishman."

"You must speak French and Dutch quite well, then."

"French better than Dutch." At her wistful look, he added, "Don't you speak French?"

Sophie laughed. "Garrett! She is only seven."

"I am learning, Papa. Though I fear I am not yet fluent."

He cleared his throat. "Well. I've no doubt you shall be soon." He glanced down at his newspaper, unable to account for how strange this conversation was making him feel. The three of them, sitting together. As if it were . . . natural.

"I'm certain I shall. But you haven't answered my question," the girl said.

He released a deep breath and returned his gaze to hers. "You wish to know what life was like for me in Belgium?"

She nodded.

Garrett looked to Sophie for help, but she smiled placidly at him and folded her hands in her lap. "I should also like to hear what your days were like while you were gone from us, Garrett."

Garrett blew out a whistling breath through his teeth. Sophie and Miranda together—they were a formidable pair, one staring at him with a direct blue gaze, the other with her soft whiskey-colored eyes.

He couldn't refuse them anything.

And why should he care about revealing an average day? This was his family. Though his memories of his life before Belgium still contained holes, the fragments had now formed into cohesiveness. His memory was a block of Swiss cheese rather than a spray of shattered glass. The biggest remaining gap in his memory had to do with the events surrounding the battle of Waterloo.

He shook his head. There were certain aspects of his existence on the Continent best kept to himself, especially in his daughter's presence. But a day from his life—why the hell not?

"Well," he said softly. "I lived in a cottage with four other men. We were the hired laborers on a barley farm owned by Monsieur Lebeck. Lebeck's wife was barren and his tenants dispersed after Waterloo, so for lack of sons and tenants, he required men."

"Papa, were you in trade?"

"No, girl. I was far below a tradesman."

"Really?" Miranda frowned.

"I was sick for a long time," Garrett continued, "but

I suppose Lebeck saw my size and determined I'd be a fine enough worker if I survived. I farmed his fields like a slave, and it was arduous, backbreaking labor. I was outside all day, every day, from dawn till dusk."

Miranda simply stared at him. No doubt she found it difficult to comprehend the enormity of the difference between his life now and his life of a month ago.

A pang of longing for that life struck him full force in the chest. If he were standing, the strength of it would have driven him staggering backward. Catching his breath, he realized for the first time that something about his existence in Belgium appealed to him. Not being under the hand of a petty tyrant, nor the misery of being ordered about and forced to comply with another man's whim. He'd experienced enough of that in the army and far less tolerable treatment from Lebeck. But in a way he missed the tiredness in his muscles after a long, productive day's work. The feeling of accomplishment at the end of harvest. Outdoor labor, under clear skies and cool breezes. In contrast, the life of a duke in London seemed rather bland. Despite the endless barrage of legal, financial, and administrative problems that beset Garrett at every turn, he felt idle.

Finally Miranda spoke, her lips twisted in a frown as if she were still trying to understand. "I should like to be outside every day. But alas, it is not to be. I have my studies, and it's not fashionable to be out at certain times of day, you know. And Miss Dalworthy says if I go outside in the middle of the day, my skin shall become dark as a heathen's."

Garrett cocked a brow at her. "Like mine?"

Miranda studied him, her expression serious. "Perhaps. Although indeed, Papa, you look less of a heathen every day."

At least the child was honest. Garrett smiled wryly. "I suppose I should be grateful for that, if nothing else."

Sophie had retrieved the embroidery and had worked silently through the entire exchange, a bemused look on her face. He could not read her, and that bothered him. She used to say he knew her thoughts before she had them. Not anymore.

Feeling his eyes on her, she glanced up at him and smiled. But there was a sadness to her expression that disturbed him. "Despite the hardship of that life, you speak of it with a certain measure of longing," she said.

"There was something to it—a freedom—that I enjoyed."

"And yet, by your own admission, you were a slave."

He gave her a rueful look. "True enough. Makes no sense, does it?"

"On the contrary. I believe I understand completely." Her expression was shuttered tight, making him want to dive into her mind and pull out the thoughts buried within. For it was clear she was thinking of something specific, relating his admission somehow to her own life.

But her existence, from birth, had been limited in scope. She went from being the daughter of a baron to being the wife of a duke to being the widow of a duke and straight back to being a duke's wife. Never had she strayed from the structured, glittering confines of her privileged environment.

No, he amended. She was wrong. He must have misinterpreted her expression and her body language. She couldn't possibly understand what he meant.

"Sophie, darling." Aunt Bertrice clasped Sophie's shoulders and kissed her cheek before thrusting her away and taking stock of her with shrewd pale blue eyes. "You are exhausted."

"No, Aunt Bertrice, not at all," Sophie said mildly as she turned to Becky. The girl had grown into a woman over the past months. The straight lines of her body had rounded to reveal an abundant bosom and a narrow waist, and Sophie held out her arms. "Look at you, Becky. A woman full grown."

"Oh, Cousin Sophie," Becky protested, sinking into her embrace. "I haven't changed so very much at all. And," she added, in a low whisper in Sophie's ear, "I am terrified. Promise you will stand beside me through this torture."

Sophie couldn't help but laugh. Most girls spent their childhood dreaming about their first Season. She had, even though she'd known before it began that Garrett would be her husband. But poor Becky, blessed with beauty in abundance, would much prefer to sit in a library surrounded by books.

"You'll trump them all, Becks," she whispered back, and she made a mental note to remember to learn enough about Becky's beaux to ascertain they would be tolerant of a bookish wife who had all the makings of a bluestocking. At least half the potential suitors would tumble off the list right away.

Becky pulled back, frowning as she gazed searchingly past Sophie's shoulder. Even her frown was lovely. "Where is my brother?"

"He's been detained, but he'll join us for dinner." Sophie didn't tell them Garrett was hiding in his study, at the last minute deciding he had too much work to do to be bothered with reuniting with his sister and aunt. Sophie knew he was merely troubled by the impending meeting, and she'd let him go without comment. He couldn't avoid them forever.

Becky's gaze alighted on Mr. Fisk, who'd just returned from a walk and stood at the edge of the landing, looking upon the group with a friendly smile.

"Oh, allow me to introduce Mr. Fisk," Sophie said. "Mr. Fisk, this is Lady Rebecca James, His Grace's sister, and his aunt, Lady Bertrice James." She turned to Becky and Aunt Bertrice. "This is Mr. Fisk. He served with Garrett in the army and was the first to discover him alive in Belgium."

The gentleman bowed formally. "A pleasure indeed, Lady Bertrice. Lady Rebecca."

Becky curtsied. "It is an honor to meet my brother's savior."

Mr. Fisk gave a low laugh. "I'm hardly his savior, my lady. I merely happened to be at the right place at the right time."

Becky flushed and lowered her head. "Nevertheless, we shall be forevermore indebted to you, sir, for bringing him home to us."

Garrett dragged himself down to dinner. The only reason he did so was that he knew Sophie would be disappointed if he didn't appear. He didn't want her forced to make excuses for him.

Still, he arrived uncomfortably late. Everyone else had already been seated when he entered the dining room, and they all looked up in surprise as he opened the door.

His gaze fell on Sophie at the foot of the table. She wore a primrose gown that complemented her hair. The gold of the heavy cross hanging from her neck brought out the smooth paleness of her complexion. She gave him a faint, encouraging smile.

He paused, breathless for a moment at her subdued, understated beauty. When a chair squeaked loudly, he realized the moment of silence had gone on too long, and he moved his gaze to the other people seated round the table.

On Sophie's right sat Fisk, impeccably dressed in a blue tailcoat, with a fancy embroidered waistcoat and blue cravat.

Rebecca was at Sophie's left. Garrett frowned at her for a long moment. She wasn't as he remembered. She didn't take after their father like himself and Miranda. Instead, she had the raven hair and blue-gray eyes of her mother. In fact, she didn't look like a relation of his at all. She was petite and dark, except for ivory pale skin, whereas he was a hulking blond brute with skin bronzed by the sun.

A flush crept over her cheeks as he studied her. She looked modestly down at her plate.

"You're late."

Garrett's gaze snapped to the woman to Rebecca's left. Aunt Bertrice—her he remembered well. His father's younger spinster sister, strict and imposing. Her hair was solid gray and pulled back into a stern chignon. When he was a boy, her hair was tawny, much like his own but with streaks of silver.

A memory whipped through him. Aunt Bertrice, coming into his room after his father had beaten him for some misdemeanor. He must've been seven or eight years old. Miranda's age. Aunt Bertrice hadn't spoken a word, just gently rubbed a soothing salve over the welts, her face pinched in disapproval. Distant and inaccessible, she hadn't quite been a substitute for a mother. But between her and Sophie, his sole true source of unconditional affection, he'd managed.

"Aunt Bertrice." He met her gaze straight on and gave a small bow.

"So glad you could finally manage to join us, Garrett, and in the middle of dinner, too."

He managed a shrug. "I've been busy."

"Well, you've been busy for a long, long time, I daresay, but we thank God you've finally come home." A ghost of a smile tilted her lips. "Well, do sit down," she continued brusquely. "I'm hungry, and they're waiting on you."

He obeyed, seating himself at the head of the table, with Aunt Bertrice on his right and a very proper-looking Miranda on his left. She reached over and gave his hand a squeeze. "I missed you, Papa."

He looked at her in surprise as the footmen served the first course. Normally, Miranda was a model of propriety at the dinner table and never spoke unless someone spoke to her first. She gave him a small, secretive smile and folded her hands in her lap. He glanced at Sophie to see her raise a brow at her daughter, but she didn't say a word of reprimand.

Garrett nodded to the footman at his shoulder. As he was served boiled chicken and spinach, he looked up to see Rebecca staring at his scar—her eyes wide. She quickly dropped her gaze, reddening to the tips of her ears. He supposed he had been rude not to acknowledge her.

"I trust all has been to your satisfaction since you arrived, Rebecca?"

Her gaze shot to him. She licked her lips. "Indeed it has, Your Grace. Thank you."

"Garrett, please." He couldn't remember propriety, but

certainly he was allowed to give leave to his sister to call him by his Christian name.

"Becky," she murmured.

"What was that?"

"You always called me Becky . . . before."

"Of course." He tried the odd-sounding word. "Becky." For the life of him, he couldn't recall what appellation he'd used to address her. Nor could he reconcile this young woman to the shy little girl he'd known.

Sophie's quiet smile lit the room, and he glanced at her. He cocked his head in question, but she looked down at her plate to take a forkful of chicken. At least they'd gotten rid of that awful twisted centerpiece so he could see her clearly.

All was silent for a long while. The only sounds were of porcelain and silver clinking together, and polite "pleases" and "thank yous" as items were passed about the table. Recalling the raucous dinners at the inn during his days in Belgium, Garrett shook his head and swallowed down half a glass of wine.

"By all means, talk," he murmured. "Don't allow my presence to dissuade you from it."

Aunt Bertrice released a loud breath from between her lips. "Nonsense, boy. Please trust that your presence has absolutely no effect on my inclination to jabber. However, we've just completed a long, uncomfortable journey and we're tired. I, for one, thought you might like to entertain us with your wit."

He gave her a wry smile. "*My* wit? My dear aunt, have you forgotten? It is well known that I am witless."

Miranda giggled. Garrett glanced at Fisk, who'd been

unnaturally quiet. He returned Garrett's gaze, smiled, then focused on separating his chicken from the bone.

"Perhaps we should discuss Becky's presentation to the king." Sophie smiled at the young woman as Garrett concentrated on releasing his tension. Sophie planned to present his sister at court in a fortnight, and just this morning, after much debate, he finally had agreed to allow Sophie and Rebecca to attend the theater in a few days and the Countess of Keene's ball the night after. He hadn't decided whether he would attend the ball yet, but the thought of their going alone made him feel ill, and Fisk hadn't been invited. He probably would go, just to watch over them.

"It's in just two weeks' time, Becks," Sophie said. "Are you ready?"

Rebecca grimaced. "As ready as I'll ever be, I suppose."

Aunt Bertrice snorted. "Nonsense, the girl is more than ready." She cast Garrett a beseeching glance. "Please marry her off quickly, Garrett. I can scarcely tolerate her mooning about the house a moment longer."

He inclined his head. "I shall do my best."

"I am absolutely in awe of your court dress," Sophie murmured.

Becky shook her head woefully. "No doubt if I sold it, I might feed and clothe a small village for a year."

"Is it so extravagant?" asked Fisk.

"It is, sir," Rebecca confirmed. "It is made from the finest silk, edged with gilt, and there are eight hundred pearls sewn onto the skirt."

"It sounds lovely." Fisk gave Rebecca a thoughtful look.

"The ostrich feathers they plan to place on my head will make me quite tall." She turned to Sophie. "Do you think I shall have to duck through the door? Will that be a very gauche thing to do before the king?"

"Not at all, Becky," Sophie said calmly.

"You're lucky you're not cursed with excessive height," Aunt Bertrice said. "You'll be fine, though I imagine the feathers will add a good two feet. You might have to bend your knees a bit, but just sink down a little, and His Majesty won't even see it."

"When I was a girl, I used to pretend I was a seven-foot-tall giant." Rebecca frowned. "Now I truly shall be a seven-foot-tall giant."

"I daresay you'll be the loveliest seven-foot giant to ever glide into the king's drawing room," Fisk said.

She met his eyes and just as quickly looked away, flustered, making it rampantly clear she was unused to the attentions of the opposite sex.

"Have you decided which gown you will wear to the countess's ball?" Sophie asked.

Becky chewed her lip, and Garrett noticed that Fisk's gaze had fixated on her mouth. Was the man besotted with his little sister?

Would that be so terrible a thing? Perhaps not. His aunt wanted her married off quickly, after all. And Garrett could hardly imagine a better candidate than Fisk. He trusted Fisk with his life, so why not with his sister's?

"Aunt Bertrice says I must wear the blue silk," she said shyly, glancing at Fisk again.

"Wonderful," Sophie said. "We will go shopping tomorrow to find you the perfect fan to complement the color."

The conversation droned on. Its content didn't interest Garrett nearly so much as the people engaged in it. He studied each person in detail—Fisk, his trustworthy friend who for once didn't seem to have the fortitude to lead a conversation. Rebecca's appearance seemed to have thrown him off balance. Then there was Aunt Bertrice, who presided over the proceedings like a queen. And Miranda, who watched with avid curiosity, answering readily whenever anyone posed a question.

But Garrett's attention kept returning to his wife. The gentle slope of her shoulder. The slender line of her collarbones. The oval shape of her jaw. Her passion, evident in her speech, in her every move. She made everyone feel welcome and comfortable. Even him.

He wanted to take her to bed. In truth, he'd wanted her from the moment he'd laid eyes on her, despite Tristan's presence. He remembered everything about the lush body beneath her gown. Had it changed in the years? Had it changed with the birth of their daughter? He thought not, for she looked the same in her dresses as she had eight years ago, despite the changes in fashion.

When she smiled, he was riveted by her straight, white teeth. By her lips stretched wide. How would they feel kissing him again? Not only on his mouth this time, but over his whole body?

He went hard and shifted uncomfortably in his seat. His skin was prickly and sensitive. Only the wine warmed him, but not nearly as much as Sophie's body could.

He'd had enough of this torture. It was time to formulate a plan to lure his wife back into his bed.

*　　*　　*

Sophie couldn't sleep. Loneliness draped her like a shroud.

Trying to push away the relentless ache for Tristan, she'd retrieved *Robinson Crusoe*, a childhood favorite, from Garrett's study. She'd rekindled the fire in her bedchamber and now sat before the flickering flames, curled up in the faded armchair reading by the light of an oil lamp. A soft knock sounded at her door.

She straightened in the chair and set the book on the side table. "Come in."

It was Becky, dressed in a nightgown and a sensible wool robe. "Oh, Sophie, I'm so sorry to come knocking at this hour. But I couldn't sleep, and I hoped you were awake, too."

Sophie smiled. "Come in, dearest. I couldn't sleep either."

Biting her lip, Becky entered and lowered herself into the only other chair in the room—the wooden chair set behind the makeshift writing desk.

"Why can't you sleep? Aren't you comfortable? Perhaps I should call for some warm milk."

Becky waved her hand. "No, no. I'm very comfortable, thank you." She smiled. "It's just—well, there have been *men* hovering, and Aunt Bertrice, and we haven't had time to chat."

"I know."

"It's odd not to have Cousin Tristan here," Becky said softly. "I miss him."

Sophie forcibly kept her expression relaxed. "As do I, Becks."

Becky leaned forward in her chair. "How did you do it, Sophie? How did you choose?" She reared back abruptly, her hand flying to her mouth. "Oh, I'm sorry. That was too forward."

"No, dearest. You and I have always been friends," Sophie said. "I have always been honest with you, and I wish you would include me in your confidences as well."

"Of course. Always."

Sophie could only hope the sincerity in Becky's declaration would last through the Season, but she doubted the girl would end the summer as innocent and open as she began it. Especially as a member of the Duke of Calton's household during this time of scandal and upheaval.

"I didn't choose between Garrett and Tristan, Becks. I couldn't, because I care deeply for both of them, and I wouldn't hurt either of them by choosing one over the other."

"But you are with Garrett now."

"Yes."

"Though . . ." Becky took a deep breath and gamely forged onward. "Forgive me, but I couldn't help but notice the two of you sleep in separate bedchambers. You and Tristan always slept . . . well . . . *together*."

"Garrett has only recently returned. We are all adjusting."

"But where has Cousin Tristan gone? The last I heard before we left Calton House was that he was here, too."

"He had to leave. He has rented a townhome nearby. You see, the courts have decided that my marriage to him was a nullity. Since I married Garrett first, our marriage takes precedence over my marriage to Tristan."

"Oh, poor Tristan," Becky murmured. "He loves you so."

Sophie couldn't respond to that. She lowered her gaze to her lap.

After a long silence, Becky said, "Garrett has changed, hasn't he?" She wrapped her arms around her slender body. "That scar on his forehead . . . it's so *big*."

"Yes, he's changed a little. But at his core he is still the honorable man we all remember." Sophie looked up at her sister-in-law. "You must promise me not to forget that, Becks. He has a harsh appearance and his behavior can be similarly harsh at times, but that is only his uncertainty coming through. He doesn't remember everything, and seems to have the most difficult time with the smallest aspects of life, such as etiquette and managing the trivialities. But for the most part, he is still the same Garrett I fell in love with when I was—rather younger than you are . . ."

Her voice dwindled as she remembered that summer. When she was hardly sixteen, Tristan had left Eton and Garrett had come home from Cambridge for the summer, and almost daily she had escaped from the window of her room at Loughton Manor to run wild with them. They'd recklessly passed the warm nights together, caught by no one.

One night, Garrett had come alone. They'd kissed and touched each other all over, driving each other to a breathless distraction. Finally, they'd lain on their backs on the riverbank, dipping their toes into the cool water. He'd told her of his dreams of the military and his future with her by her side. She'd told him of her dream of raising his children at Calton House and in London. And then he'd asked her to marry him. Trembling with joy, she'd kissed every inch of his face. They agreed to hold the wedding when he returned home after Cambridge.

Nearly two and a half long years passed before they'd

finally married and consummated their love. To Sophie, those two years had felt like forever.

Becky sighed wistfully, jolting her from the memory. "I wish I could fall in love with someone."

"You very well might. Think of all the gentlemen you are to meet this Season."

"Well . . . I've already met one gentleman," Becky said shyly.

"Do you mean Mr. Fisk?" Startled, Sophie straightened in the chair.

"Yes." Becky licked her lips in a no doubt unconscious gesture. "He is quite . . . handsome."

Sophie studied her sister-in-law. Surely the girl was too sensible to engage in an infatuation with a man like Mr. Fisk. Still, she'd have to watch them both, and she'd have to tread carefully. "He is somewhat handsome," she agreed slowly.

"He has such an engaging manner, and his physique—" Becky pressed the back of her hand to her reddening cheek. "Well, it is quite pleasing to the eye."

"Indeed." Sophie leaned toward Becky. "But Becks, you do realize you must look much higher than Mr. Fisk?"

Becky frowned. "Is Mr. Fisk a man of little fortune, Sophie?"

"I believe so, dearest. And he has no title."

"Oh, I don't care about such trivial things," Becky said airily.

Sophie infused the barest edge of a warning into her voice. "But when it comes time to choose a husband for you, your brother will care."

In truth, she didn't think Garrett cared about such things either. Which meant it was completely up to her to make sure that Becky made a good choice. Well, her and Aunt Bertrice, who surely would make her opinion known in the matter.

Becky shuddered. "Do you think he will choose someone awful for me, Sophie?"

Sophie laughed. "Not at all."

"Because I'd rather marry a young, handsome commoner who loves me than an old, decrepit duke who cares for naught other than my ability to provide him with heirs."

"Becky!"

Becky frowned mulishly. "I have heard about such things coming to fruition, Sophie. Some of my school friends have married the most awful men—"

Sophie stood and knelt before the girl. She took her warm cheeks in her hands and made Becky face her. "Your aunt Bertrice, Garrett, and I wouldn't let that happen, dearest. We care for nothing more than your happiness."

"Do you promise?"

Sophie could see the fear and hope in Becky's eyes. She was truly apprehensive of what was to come. "I promise," she said firmly. "If we find nobody who satisfies you, Becks, I promise you won't have to marry any of them. You're only eighteen. There will be more Seasons for you."

Becky threw her arms around Sophie and squeezed tight. "Oh, thank you, Sophie. Thank you."

The door opened and both women jerked their heads up. Becky's arms slid from her body, and Sophie's heart skipped a beat when she saw it was Garrett in a handsome dishabille. His light blond hair stood up at endearingly odd angles, as if he had pushed his hand through it over and over.

"Oh!" Becky exclaimed in surprise.

Garrett's mouth snapped shut, and he began to retreat. "I am so sorry to disturb you, ladies. Forgive me."

"Not at all," Sophie murmured. But she couldn't say more. A giant lump had lodged in her throat and refused to move.

Garrett bowed stiffly. "I just wished to say goodnight. To both of you."

"Goodnight," Becky murmured.

Sophie just stared at him. He met her eyes, then pulled his gaze away.

"Goodnight," she said. But the door had already clicked shut.

She was nervous, anxious, terrified, hopeful. Torn between letting him go in peace, and dismissing Becky and inviting him back into her room.

For there could be only one reason he had come to see her at this hour. And from the way her heart had stuttered and her body flushed at his appearance, she wasn't certain she would have turned him away this time.

Chapter Thirteen

Blackness surrounded him. Oppressive, stifling. He was in a casket, underground . . . He had to get free. He clawed at the earth, shouting for someone to dig him out.

Garrett surged upward, coughing, his eyes flying open to utter darkness. His clammy fingers closed over silk, and logic told him it was a moonless night, the fire had gone cold, and he was merely in his own bed in his bedchamber. Having another goddamn nightmare.

This one was different. No shooting, no blood. Just black nothingness. God, it was almost worse. His shoulders shook as a cold shudder rippled through him.

He needed light. Swinging his legs over the edge of the bed, he climbed down the step and fumbled to the side table, searching for a candle. Then a scuffing sound came from across the room. He jerked his head up.

Only shadows. But the hair prickled on the back of his neck. Someone was in here. Garrett clenched his teeth and curled his fist. Little good that would do—fists were useless against the demons that haunted him.

A shadow separated from the wall across from him and moved toward him. "Cal?"

Garrett expelled a harsh breath, and his muscles went limp. "Fisk? Christ." He pushed a hand through his matted hair.

The shadow moved closer until it paused on the other side of the bed. "Sorry. I . . . I heard you shouting and came to make sure everything was all right."

"Didn't think to bring a light with you?"

"No. Sorry."

Garrett stood still, facing the dark shadow that was Fisk in silence.

"You all right then, Cal? Can I get you something?"

Garrett's lip curled. "A cure for these goddamn nightmares? Even better, why don't you go fetch my memories for me? Can you do that, Fisk?"

Fisk's shadow shifted. "Maybe," he said quietly.

Garrett stilled. "What do you mean?"

"I've met someone who might be able to help you regain your memories. Not sure about the nightmares—"

"Who?" Garrett demanded.

"He's a doctor here in London. I've spoken to him at length about your affliction, and he thinks he can help you."

"For God's sake, why didn't you tell me about him sooner?"

"I wanted to be certain, before—"

"Bring him to me. As soon as possible."

"Of course, Cal. I'll fetch him in the morning."

*　　*　　*

Tristan leaned against the window in the small upstairs parlor of his rented rooms. The days had passed quickly as he'd continued to move forward with his appeal, meeting with the advocates and Griffiths every day to build his case against the decision made by the Consistory Court.

Tristan gazed down at the busy street below. The sun shone brightly after an earlier rain, leaving the scene laid out before him sparkling and clean. Wagons rattled by, carriages, men on horseback. People strode with intent, skirting the edges of traffic. An urchin wearing a jaunty red beret dodged in the small space between two carts, miraculously appearing on the opposite side of the street unscathed, but the meaty driver of the trailing cart pulled his horses short, raised his fist, and cursed at the boy.

Tristan had sent Gary to the park with the new governess and Jennings had come by to relay his most recent report. Jennings hadn't yet pinpointed the origination of the scandalous rumors concerning Garrett. Apparently the printer had closed his shop just after distributing the pamphlet and had conveniently moved to Wales.

Garrett and Fisk, Jennings reported, were going about their business as usual. Garrett seldom left the house, but Fisk visited Ansley daily, which Tristan supposed was normal, given they were still in the process of dividing the assets and transferring ownership back to Garrett.

Fisk had also gone to Covent Garden theater twice more, the second time after just having come from the Bank of London. Jennings hadn't learned the identity of the man who opened the theater door for him, though he did discover that Fisk always came to the theater just after the rehearsals for an upcoming performance of *Henry VIII* had concluded. Jennings surmised that Fisk was covertly meeting with one of the actresses inside the theater, and the man who opened the door for him aided them in their trysts.

Most interestingly, Jennings stated that Fisk had taken a promenade through Hyde Park three days ago—the same day Tristan and Sophie had met there.

Was Fisk following them? Perhaps Garrett had given Fisk watchdog duty over Sophie. If so, Garrett would already know about Tristan and Sophie's encounter in the park. Would Garrett confine her to the house again?

Tristan pressed his forehead against the window casing and ground his teeth, hating his inability to protect her even as he took comfort in the knowledge she was perfectly capable of protecting herself. God, he missed simply *being* with her. The contentment and comfort of sharing his day with her. The unfading thrill of having her stand by his side. The feel of her soft, warm body beside him as he lay in bed, her arms entwined about him . . .

He pushed his hand flat against the diamond-shaped pane, allowing the coolness of the glass to seep into his heated blood.

A movement below caught his eye, and he looked down to see Fisk and Ansley turn the corner, Fisk appearing stately and sleek beside the shorter, rotund solicitor who today was dressed in a most unappealing—yet fashionable— shade of puce. When they reached the front of his house, the two men stopped to face each other. The solicitor handed Fisk a small wrapped packet, which he tucked in his breast pocket, and they shook hands. Ansley turned to lumber back the way they had come, while Fisk turned to gaze at the façade of Tristan's townhouse. For a long moment, he simply stared toward the entryway with a look on his face Tristan had never seen before. His eyes were narrow, his lips twisted, his face dark. It was an expression of open hatred.

Tristan moved behind the curtain and studied the younger man. Each time Tristan had had dealings with Fisk, the man had been solicitous in the extreme. To see such a look on his face made an unsettled feeling swirl in Tristan's gut.

Fisk strode to the entryway, and Tristan turned away from the window, taking a deep breath to prepare himself for an intrusion. He lowered himself into his favorite of the three lumpy damask-covered armchairs, propped his feet on the fender, and snapped open *The Times*.

A few moments later, Steadman entered. "Mr. Fisk is downstairs, my lord."

"Of course. Show him up."

Steadman nodded and closed the door. Tristan set the newspaper down and crossed to the mahogany sidebar to pour a brandy. He looked up when his visitor appeared. Of course Fisk had reestablished his usual friendly, placid expression.

"Afternoon, Fisk. Brandy?"

Fisk bowed and smiled pleasantly. "Good afternoon, my lord. No, nothing to drink, thank you."

Tristan realized he'd never seen Fisk take a drink. No after-dinner port or casual brandy. No wine with his meals. He'd never paid much attention, so concentrated had his focus been on Garrett and Sophie. He arched a questioning brow. "A teetotaler, are you?"

The other man gave an unassuming shrug. "I do try to avoid spirits and intoxicants."

Tristan raised his glass, swirling the amber liquid. "Why is that?"

Fisk looked him directly in the eye, unflinching. "My own father was a sot, and we—meaning my brother and I—found his behavior abhorrent. Particularly his behavior toward my mother."

"Ah." Tristan set the glass down. "Sorry to hear that, Fisk."

Fisk shrugged, and his expression was, as always when he knew someone was studying his reaction, mild. "My sire died before I joined the army. In truth, I can hardly recall him. I only know I don't wish to become like him."

"Of course. Completely understandable." Tristan gestured to the arc of armchairs in the center of the room. "Please make yourself comfortable."

Fisk obligingly lowered himself on one of the chairs and crossed his legs. Tristan left the brandy on the counter—clearly coaxing the man to drunkenness wasn't an option—and walked around to sit on the opposing sofa. "Where does your family hail from, Fisk?"

"Leeds, my lord."

"And your mother still resides there?"

After a slight pause, Fisk responded. "No, sir. My mother perished of consumption several years ago."

Tristan nodded. "I see. And your brother?"

This time the pause was long. Nearly palpable. Finally, Fisk answered, "He was a lieutenant in His Majesty's Army. Died from a gunshot wound inflicted at Waterloo."

"I'm very sorry."

"Thank you, my lord."

"Well." Tristan cleared his throat. "What brings you by on this fine day?"

Beneath the wool of his dark coat Fisk's shoulders lowered minutely. "Well, frankly, I was passing by on my way home—to the duke's residence, that is—and I wished to see how you fared."

Tristan smiled politely. The younger man might excel at maintaining a neutral, pleasant demeanor, but Tristan could do it better. "I am well, thank you. I'm quite pleased today, actually, for I have just hired a most promising governess for my son."

"That's wonderful news." Fisk's smile melted into earnestness. It would be easy to forget the man was twenty-six years old—at times he seemed much younger. "But I rather meant in your separation from the duchess. I know it has been . . . difficult." He raised his hands in silent apology for asking so personal a question. "I merely wanted to see if there was anything I could do, my lord."

"I appreciate your concern." Gritting his teeth, Tristan masked his bristling reaction to Fisk's forwardness. No doubt the man felt entitled after all he'd witnessed between the three of them, but in Tristan's mind, he'd always be an intruder, and an unwelcome one at that. His mind working rapidly, Tristan shrugged and offered a blatant lie. "I feel myself compelled to move onward. I have considered leaving Town."

Fisk's dark brows crept toward his hairline. "Leave London while you're preparing for your appeal?"

"The appeal will take some time. And . . ." He affected a frown. ". . . my lawyers say the chances of the court's decision being overturned are slim to none."

Fisk nodded. "That I believe, my lord. Forgive me, because you know I am Cal's friend, but I certainly do see your perspective as well, and I am sorry."

"Thank you, Fisk."

After a thoughtful pause, Fisk said, "Then you intend to leave London while Parliament is in session?"

"I feel it is the best course of action. I merely think it best I disappear—just for a while. Until the rumors recede."

Fisk nodded somberly, yet he looked oddly disappointed by the news. "I understand, sir. Now that news of your meeting with Her Grace in Hyde Park is being circulated—" He raised his hand in a placating gesture when he saw the dark look on Tristan's face. "Don't fret, my lord. I have no intention of informing Cal of your trysts."

"Trysts?" Tristan narrowed his eyes. "Our single meeting at Hyde Park occurred completely by chance, I assure you."

"Oh, of course. Unfortunate wording on my part." Fisk looked down and flicked a piece of lint from his cuff, but his expression told Tristan he believed otherwise.

Why had Fisk followed Sophie if he didn't plan to tell Garrett what he saw? Tristan tapped his fingertip on the arm of his chair. "I hope you aren't spreading untruths that might tarnish the duchess's reputation."

Fisk's eyes widened to round brown pools as he met Tristan's gaze. "Most definitely not, sir. I only wish to guard Cal's fragile temperament from further . . . disruption. He's been rather overwrought, and things are quite complicated now that his sister and aunt have arrived."

Tristan forced himself to appear relaxed, and he nodded at Fisk as if in approval. "I am continually impressed by your level of compassion and concern for His Grace."

"Thank you, my lord." Fisk glanced aside, then looked back at Tristan with a self-effacing smile. "The duke was a fair and kind colonel. Knew each of us by name, and inspired each of us to be the best soldiers we could be. When I saw him in Belgium . . . Well, I couldn't believe it. It affected me to see him that way. Deeply." As he spoke, Fisk's hand drifted from the arm of the chair to rest over his heart. "The days we spent together as the duke began to regain his memories—well, my lord, I must admit they were the most meaningful days of my life. To suddenly realize that I could help this gentleman, bring him home to the people who cared for him. To England herself, which had glorified him. I realized there was nothing more important I could do with my existence. I am honored that he has made me his friend, and I strive to continue to serve him to the best of my ability for as long as he allows it."

Tristan sat back in his chair, less impressed than Fisk would have liked after such a fine speech. In fact, an odd suspicion niggled at him. It had taken root when he'd seen the expression on Fisk's face outside, and it had grown with every word the man had uttered since. He nodded compassionately. "I understand. I cannot imagine how I'd feel in your place."

"May I tell you something in confidence, my lord?"

"Of course."

"I see His Grace at his worst." Fisk leaned forward, and a flush bloomed in his apple-round cheeks. "In all honesty, I fear he treads the fine edge of sanity."

Tristan kept his fingers relaxed over the armrests. He wouldn't reveal he was already familiar with the gossip regarding Garrett's sanity, although it had spread through Town more quickly than the Fire of London. Why would Fisk bring this up now? Did he want Tristan to fear for

Sophie? Did he wish to keep him close? If so, for what purpose?

What a mystery this man was. Tristan needed to delve further into his background. So far in London his efforts had revealed nothing. Not only had no one he knew ever heard of Fisk, but the secretary at the offices of the adjutant general wasn't able to find any records containing information about him—in fact, all the records for Garrett's regiment for the year 1815 were missing.

Still, Sophie and the other women in Tristan's family came first. If there was any truth to what Fisk said, Tristan would be the first to address it and take action.

"That's terrible news, Fisk," he said after a long pause. "But whatever has he done to rouse such a suspicion in you?"

"He's prone to . . . *fits*, my lord. I try to hide them from everyone—even the servants, but I fear they've seen some."

"What kinds of fits?"

"He rants and raves. He suffers from visions—violent, frightening, spectral visions of the battle of Waterloo."

"When does this happen?"

"In the middle of the night most of the time. I often stay up late, and my bedchamber is close to his, so I can hear it when the shouting begins." Fisk gave a small shudder. "I immediately rush to his room and attempt to soothe him. I'm sorry, my lord. But it's . . . disturbing."

It wasn't difficult for Tristan to affect a façade of deep concern. "Do you believe Garrett is prone to violence?"

Fisk took a deep breath. "I'm not certain. However . . . you're not the only man he has threatened with a gun."

"Is that so?" Tristan shifted uncomfortably in his chair.

He wasn't inclined to trust Fisk, but was he a fool to leave his family at Garrett's mercy? He'd known Garrett to be full of hot air and prone to ranting, but a true danger? It was difficult to fathom, especially after Sophie had so vehemently rejected the idea just a few days ago. "Who else has he threatened?"

"The butler, Connor."

"Why did he threaten Connor?"

Fisk shook his head. Pulling out a gold-trimmed handkerchief embossed with his initials, he dabbed at the sweat beading on his forehead. "I'm not certain, but I believe it had something to do with him interrupting the duke at his work."

Tristan rubbed his hand over his jaw. It was true Garrett seemed to have an aversion to the servants since his return from Belgium. Fortunately, Tristan knew exactly where he might find Connor on his day off—at his sister's house in Cheapside. He'd seek him out.

"Do you believe he might threaten any of the ladies?"

Fisk shook his head. "It's hard to say, my lord. Cal becomes . . . unpredictable when in the throes of one of his tempers. I think Lady Miranda is surely safe—they keep her away from him for the most part. And Lady Bertrice and Lady Rebecca will hardly be at home—I've read their social schedule. But Her Grace—I cannot say."

"Perhaps," Tristan said slowly, "I should delay my trip until I can be more certain of His Grace's sanity."

Fisk's shoulders slumped, and a crestfallen expression creased his face. "I'm so very sorry, my lord. I shouldn't like to be the cause of any distress on your part. Never fear, I am keeping an eye on all the ladies, and should

Cal . . . become unstable, I will certainly do whatever is necessary to protect them."

"Don't underestimate the duchess, Fisk. She's quite capable of looking after herself."

Fisk nodded vigorously. "Oh, yes, I have seen that in her. We've become good friends—in fact, we have planned to attend the theater together in two days' time."

Tristan couldn't conceal the suspicion that clouded his face. He rose abruptly and returned to the sideboard for the untouched glass of brandy.

Fisk continued blithely on. "We are going to see the new melodrama at Covent Garden."

Could this have something to do with Fisk's visits to the theater? Tristan didn't like anything about it, and he'd damn well be there for Sophie should anything go awry.

Tristan took a long draught and savored the burning sensation of the liquid searing a path down his throat. When he spoke, he managed to sound calm, even approving. "Sounds like a capital idea, Fisk. I'm sure Sophie is looking forward to it as much as you are."

"I certainly hope so, my lord."

As suspicion trickled through him, Tristan managed to make himself look grateful, even though a part of him wanted to grab hold of this presumptuous upstart's neck and shake the exuberant innocence out of him. For the first time, it struck him as false, as a cloak for some sinister persona.

Either that, or Tristan was in such denial over the loss of his wife and his life that he had finally succumbed to suspicious fancies.

"I'm glad you came today, Fisk," he pushed out. "And I'm relieved you are keeping an eye on my family. It wasn't necessary, and I understand you have come only out of true concern, and for that I thank you."

"It's true, Lord Westcliff. I was there at the beginning." Fisk coughed into the handkerchief as the image of Sophie tied to their bed speared through Tristan's mind's eye. Hell. He hated, *hated* that this man had witnessed that moment between him and his wife. Fisk continued, "And I understand the upheaval all this has caused to you and your son."

His son. Interesting touch, to add his concern for Gary. Tristan distrusted the man more with every passing second.

"Where did you say you were traveling, my lord?"

"Perhaps north to visit my family in Yorkshire."

Maybe he'd be taking a trip away from London after all. But he rather thought he might journey somewhat to the west of Calton House, to dig up more information about William Fisk in Leeds.

First, though, he needed to see Sophie.

Dr. MacAllister was a small man with frost-colored hair, bright blue eyes, pink cheeks, and a friendly smile, and Sophie disliked him instantly.

At Mr. Fisk's urging, Garrett had employed Dr. MacAllister to help fill in the holes of his memory. The doctor had first come two mornings ago, the day after Becky and Aunt Bertrice arrived. He'd prescribed a potently foul remedy that darkened Garrett's mood and worsened his nightmares. Last night it had taken nearly an hour of Sophie holding Garrett and whispering to him before he'd awakened enough to recognize her. No sooner had he done so than he'd fallen into a deep sleep she couldn't rouse him from. And this morning he hadn't remembered any of it.

Sophie was absolutely certain it had something to do with the tonic Dr. MacAllister had given him. She'd tried to convince Garrett of it, but he'd brushed her worries aside, saying MacAllister was one of the most skilled doctors in the field of mental disorders in London.

At the moment, Sophie stood at the side of the bed watching the doctor bleed Garrett. When she'd asked why he had prescribed this particular treatment, the man had pontificated for ten minutes about ill humors, but his speech didn't make any sense to her at all. She didn't understand what bleeding or ill humors had to do with Garrett's memory.

Garrett lay sprawled on his belly, the heavy burgundy counterpane turned down at his hips. Black leeches covered by small glass containers dotted his naked back, cheerfully sucking his lifeblood and growing fatter by the second. Her stomach roiled, and she looked away.

"Ah, very good, they're starting to come off," Dr. MacAllister pronounced jovially. "You may remove the remaining ones, miss."

Sophie heard trickling noises as the maid dribbled water over the remaining leeches so they'd fall from Garrett's skin.

Garrett groaned softly and then addressed the doctor. "Is there anything you can give me for the nightmares, doctor? My wife says I didn't recognize her last night, I was so deeply in its thrall. I'm afraid I'm frightening her."

Sophie turned to face him, and though his body was blocked from view by the maid scooping the leeches from his back, his pale face wasn't, and he offered her a wry smile, which she returned. By now, he knew well enough he was incapable of frightening her.

The doctor's forehead furrowed as he thought. "Well, Your Grace, this is a common effect of war and battle, you know. The nightmares likely have little to do with your loss of memory."

"Still, is there something that can be done about them?"

"Hmm . . . perhaps. Allow me to consult my books to see if I might find an appropriate prescription. You do understand that whatever I might give you for the nightmares will have to be taken in conjunction with the memory therapy tonic I have given you?"

"Of course." Garrett sat up, but not before Sophie saw the raw red spots on his back. He swayed as he reached for his shirt.

Lord, how much blood had they taken? She ground her teeth. She had to convince him to stop this madness. His memories would return in time, or not, but surely they weren't worth suffering for. And she was certain this doctor was a quack.

Dr. MacAllister emitted a long sigh. "In truth, Your Grace, I fear your health might worsen before it takes a turn for the better."

Garrett narrowed his eyes at the doctor. "How do you mean?"

"The mind is a fragile thing, Your Grace. Think of it as a child's toy—as a collection of blocks, if you will. When you're building a castle with your blocks, in order to create the most spectacular tower, for instance, it is often necessary to collapse a part of what you've created and rebuild. Sometimes this must be done again and again, until the result is as perfect as possible, given the limitations of the sizes and shapes of your blocks. The mind works in a similar way. We might have to tear part of it down in order to rebuild it into a healthy state."

Sophie stared at Dr. MacAllister, and she knew her distaste for him resonated in her expression. He still made no sense. It was illogical to think that Garrett would get worse before he got better. Without the "benefit" of any tonic, Garrett remembered more and grew mentally stronger every day. And now this man proposed he take backward steps?

She wouldn't let it happen.

"A note for you, madam."

Grinding her teeth, Sophie took the piece of stationery from the silver dish the footman held out. The envelope wasn't addressed, which told her without a doubt it was from her irascible husband. She'd spent the better part of the day arguing with Garrett about Dr. MacAllister. Finally, after a tense afternoon tea, he'd shouted to her that she was a shrew who clearly had no desire to see him heal. Too frustrated to express surprise over his testiness—no doubt also triggered by the quack's poisonous tonic—she'd responded that he was an obstinate bully with no respect for her observations or opinions, so why should she bother to speak to him, much less look out for his well-being? At which point he'd stumbled out of the room and locked himself in his study for the remainder of the day.

Of course, now that she was seconds away from leaving for the theater with Mr. Fisk and Becky, he decided to send her a missive when he could have come to speak with her hours ago.

After the footman closed the door, she opened the folded note.

> *Very well. I will refrain from calling upon Dr. MacAllister as long as I continue to improve. And as long as my memory doesn't fail me again.*

He'd underlined each "as long as" several times for emphasis. Sophie sucked in a breath. Why did Garrett have so little faith in his own ability to recover when his recovery was so clear for everyone to see? Such a stubborn man. She looked down to read the final line.

> *I predict I will be recalling him in a week or less.*

She curled her fingers, crumpling the paper in her hand. If it came to it, she'd replace the doctor's noxious tonic with a sleeping potion of her own. A gentle, harmless brew of chamomile, lemon, and spearmint.

That thought calmed her, and by the time Becky came to her door, Sophie was prepared to enjoy the evening. She straightened her pale yellow skirts and checked her bandeau in the mirror before opening the door to her exquisitely costumed sister-in-law. Becky wore a silver net dress over a blush rose silk underdress. Gold cording trimmed the neckline and hem, a gilded ribbon defined her tiny waist, and her maid had entwined a matching golden rope in the strands of her hair. She wore a gold link necklace that had belonged to her mother and tiny diamond teardrop earrings.

"You look beautiful, my dear."

Becky's grin lit her face. "So do you, Sophie. You don't

look nearly as old as you are." Sophie chuckled as Becky added, "And those pearls are exquisite."

"Thank you, Becks." She brushed her fingertips over the sleek strand of oriental pearls round her neck. A wedding gift from Tristan. Smiling, she took Becky's arm in her own. "Shall we?"

"Oooh," Becky murmured as they stepped into the Duke of Calton's box. She glided all the way in to gaze out over the balcony railing. The view was of the entire theater, blazing with gas lights and already filled to brimming with patrons eager to view the highly touted melodrama. It was going to be another of Covent Garden's famous spectacles, more pleasing to the eye than to the mind, but Sophie looked forward to the distraction.

She smiled as Mr. Fisk led her to her seat, and she lowered herself onto the velvet cushioned chair in the center of the front row. From the corner of her eye, she saw groups of people in the audience hush and look up at them curiously, but she kept her focus on Becky. "Beautiful, isn't it?"

Becky turned back to her, her dark blue eyes round. "Beautiful it might be, but I don't doubt it's a fire hazard of the very first order!"

Sophie chuckled. "The lighting is magnificent, isn't it?"

Becky shuddered. "It's almost frightening. So many lights . . . If there was a gas leak, this whole building would be a ball of flames in seconds."

"It does take some getting used to," Mr. Fisk said. "But I assure you, my lady, should a fire start, you shall be the first soul to escape."

Becky raised a brow. "How's that, Mr. Fisk?"

Her tone was almost flirtatious. Sophie brushed the wrinkles from the satin skirt of her gown and sighed. Becky was almost too breathtaking tonight. The flush in her cheeks matched the color of her gown, and her figure was voluptuous but so slender even a man as comparatively small as Mr. Fisk could probably span her waist with his hands. Perhaps it had been a mistake to bring Becky and Mr. Fisk to the theater together.

Mr. Fisk gave a sly smile. "I know a clandestine exit from this level."

His use of the word "clandestine" disturbed Sophie. She gave him a sharp glance, but Becky had completely captured his focus, and he seemed not to notice.

"Do you?" Becky asked in surprise.

Mr. Fisk nodded sagely. "Indeed I do. I've taken it many times, in fact."

"Well," Becky said. "There is some comfort in that, at least."

Sophie patted the seat next to her. "Come, dearest. Sit here."

She watched Becky's eyes slide toward the empty seat beside Mr. Fisk, but she obediently came to sit beside Sophie instead.

Within moments, the curtain rose to a lavishly decorated scene. "Peru," Becky breathed, no doubt in response to the shape of the mountains painted on the backdrop. "Those are the Andes."

Mr. Fisk raised his brows, clearly impressed by her knowledge, but Becky didn't notice, for she was staring in rapt attention as the action began on stage.

They didn't have the opportunity to watch the show for long, because five minutes after the spectacle began, a sharp knock sounded at the door. Mr. Fisk opened it to the Countess of Harpsford and her four daughters, who crowded into the box in a flurry of colorful silk and bows and lace. Sophie made the necessary introductions, and within moments, the girls were chatting like lifelong bosom friends to Becky, who kept glancing longingly at the stage as if she'd prefer to be watching. Mr. Fisk politely bowed and went to the corner of the box to peer down at the audience through tiny golden opera glasses. The countess, who wore a gown of midnight blue and a matching turban over her powdered russet-colored hair, drew Sophie toward the opposite corner.

"My dear, Lady Trelawny is pining to see you, but her gout is troubling her so, she hardly could limp up to her box this evening. Would you mind popping in on her?"

"Of course I wouldn't," Sophie said warmly. She liked both ladies and had seen neither since Garrett's return. It troubled her to hear Lady Trelawny's gout had flared again. She flicked a glance at Mr. Fisk, hesitating.

"Oh, don't worry yourself," Lady Harpsford said in a low voice meant for Sophie's ears alone. "We'll stay till you return."

"Ooh!" squealed one of the girls, pointing at the stage. "Look! The water's made of gold!"

Sophie glanced down at the stage to see that, indeed, a golden lake rippled across the stage. An orange sun shone upon the lake, and a soft mist rose up from the surface. The effect was marvelous, and she chuckled as all five girls gathered at the rail to murmur their amazement.

Sophie looked back at her friend. "They seem content. I'll try to return quickly. Thank you, Sarah."

Lady Harpsford squeezed both her hands. "Lady Trelawny will be absolutely ecstatic to see you. We've all missed you, my dear."

She smiled at the other woman, realizing how much she'd missed her female friends in the last few weeks. "I'll be back shortly."

Lifting her skirts so they wouldn't drag on the floor, she slipped through the door and turned down the carpeted corridor that led to the stairs. Lady Trelawny was in a lower box, so she'd have to descend to the lobby, then ascend the stairs on the other side.

When she reached the bottom of the stairs and turned into the lobby, someone grasped her arm, pulling her to a stop. She let out a small yelp before a hand closed over her mouth.

"It's me, love."

Sophie went from high alert to placid calm in an instant. Tristan's low voice slid through her like the finest wine, sweet and familiar, and so very welcome.

His fingers slipped down to her wrist. "Come with me."

She glanced back at him. Dressed in a dark, close-fitting double-breasted jacket that accented his broad shoulders and formal breeches that highlighted his narrow hips and long legs, he took her breath away. He took a step closer to her, close enough that his arm brushed against her side, sending tingles through her body. Sophie nodded mutely.

He turned and set off in long strides to the end of a deserted passageway that curved around the outside of the orchestra seating, tugging her along behind him. He stopped at a tall, narrow doorway. Papered in the same red and gold wallpaper as the walls, the door was undetectable unless one was searching for it. He opened it and ushered her into a small, dark retiring chamber consisting of one flickering lamp and a low sofa upholstered in green to match the darker green flourishes on the wallpaper.

As soon as he closed and locked the door behind them, he tossed his hat to the ground, jerked her to face toward him, wrapped his gloved fingers behind her neck, and slanted his lips over hers.

Heat, desire, longing. They all swept through her, then spread through her limbs and straight into her blood. She needed him. She reached up and gripped his lapels to pull him closer.

Tristan. Handsome, and commanding. Forbidden. She missed him. She needed him. She *wanted* him. It had been too long.

She slipped her arms around him, her buttery soft kid gloves scraping over the wool of his coat.

Their tongues tangled, hot and smooth. He smelled of spice. Her body had long since equated his essence to desire. Lust rode through her veins, rushing between her legs. She was hot, so hot and achy.

His erection pressed hard against her belly, straining against his breeches. She rubbed wantonly against him, kissing his soft lips, nipping across the slant of his cheekbone, sucking the rough, masculine skin on his neck as the starchy linen of his neckcloth rubbed her jaw.

He held her tightly, his arms strong, like steel bands encircling her. She never felt so safe, so open and free, as she did when locked in Tristan's embrace.

With her next gasping breath, reality slammed into her. *Garrett* . . . She yanked away from Tristan and stumbled backward.

Her cheeks on fire, she glanced up at him. What she saw in his expression made her bury her face in her gloved hands. She couldn't look at him, at any part of him, without wanting to fling herself at him. Or at least beg him to take her away so that they could be together again.

But that wasn't her. The steadfast, loyal Duchess of Calton.

He stepped toward her, gripped her wrists, and pulled her hands away from her face.

As much as she wanted Tristan, she couldn't do this. Garrett was hurting, he was ill. He was the father of her daughter. He needed her.

"You know we cannot," she whispered. "We can't touch each other. We shouldn't even be seeing each other."

His eyes narrowed and he dropped her hands.

Composing herself, she reached up to push a strand of hair off her forehead. "I cannot—I *won't*—betray him."

Tristan lurched backward as if she'd dealt him a blow to the stomach. "You've slept with him."

"No."

"But you will." His voice was low, but so cold it chilled her blood.

She couldn't lie to him. "I'm his wife."

There was a long silence. She stared at the tips of her yellow slippers peeking out from the darker yellow of the beribboned hem of her gown.

In her peripheral vision, she saw him inch closer to her. "You will refuse my touch now? Is that what you're saying?"

"No . . . yes. I don't know." Sophie wanted to pull out her hair by the roots in frustration. She looked helplessly up at him. "It's not for lack of wanting you, Tristan. You know that."

"No, I don't." His lips tightened. "Do you approve of my appealing the court's decision?"

"I . . . yes. I approve. But . . ."

His face looked ghostly with the pale light of the lantern shining behind him like a halo. "But what, Soph?"

"I don't . . . I can't . . . hurt him."

His lips were so thin and tight, they had lost color, too.

"I want you both," she said softly. "I'm sorry." She looked at her feet, the lamp, the sofa, the green walls. Anywhere but at him.

He cupped her chin, tilting her head to force her to face him. She stared into his piercing dark gaze. "Do you see what you're doing?"

Miserable, she shook her head, looking at him with pleading eyes. *Please, Tristan. Please understand why I can't. Please . . .*

"You've chosen him over me."

"No—"

"You've said you can't choose, but you have." He pushed his hand through his dark hair in frustration. "You accept your marriage to him."

She couldn't say no to that. At the time of her marriage to Garrett, she'd never desired anything more in the world.

He reached to the floor to retrieve his hat. Turning the brim in his hands, he gazed down for a long moment. When he looked up again, the anguish had left, leaving his expression flat except for the strain pulling at his eyes. "I apologize for my outburst, Soph. I didn't come to throw accusations at you—I came to speak of other matters."

"I wish I could talk to you all night, Tristan, but Lady

Trelawny is expecting me in her box and Lady Harpsford is chaperoning Becky in ours. I can't be too long."

Tristan's lips curled in the ghost of a smile. "I asked Lady Harpsford for her assistance tonight. Lady Trelawny isn't here. And don't worry—I chose her for a reason."

Relieved, Sophie nodded. Lady Harpsford was a gem, one of the few who didn't thrive on gossip and scandal. She might ask Sophie for details later, but she'd never expose their secret to anyone.

"Please sit down with me for a few moments." Tristan gestured to the sofa.

"All right." She settled onto the soft cushions and he lowered himself beside her.

"How are Becky and Aunt B? Does Garrett continue to improve? Miranda?"

"Miranda is well, as always. She is a sweet therapy for Garrett, and they've grown quite attached, in their way."

Tristan's gaze sharpened. "You say she is spending time with him?"

"Every day."

"Interesting. I was told you keep them separated."

"Who would say such a thing?" she asked in surprise.

"Fisk. He came to see me."

"Why? He's Garrett's friend, not yours."

"I don't know, exactly," Tristan mused. "But go on. How are Becky and Aunt B?"

"Becky has finally made the transition into womanhood, I think. It seems when she left Yorkshire, she abandoned all vestige of the little girl we adored. And Aunt Bertrice—" Sophie released a small laugh. "—is the same as ever."

Tristan looked away, and after a long moment, his expression tightened. "And Garrett?"

She clenched her hands in her lap and her teeth closed down over her lower lip before she answered. "I wouldn't admit it to anyone else, but I worry about him, Tristan. He's hired a quack of a doctor whose medicines seem to exacerbate his nightmares, and—"

"He's having nightmares?" Tristan cut in with a frown.

"Yes." She shuddered. "Awful nightmares. When I hear him, I come into his room to comfort him and help him back to sleep."

"Hm. Fisk said he 'rages' at night. Falls into 'fits.' "

She shook her head. "No, I wouldn't call them rages or fits. Just terrible dreams."

"And is he irrational? Violent?"

"No, neither, but recently it's become more difficult to rouse him." She ground her teeth. "I'm sure it's the dratted medicine from that awful doctor."

"Does Fisk ever go to him when he's experiencing one of these episodes?"

"They're merely nightmares, not 'episodes.' And, no, I've never seen Mr. Fisk tending to him, though he might on the nights I'm not there."

"Sophie." Tristan took her hand, his big palms engulfing hers. "Tell me true. Look at the situation not with your naturally optimistic eyes, but as a realist. Please—it's important." He took a deep breath, as if gathering his strength before voicing the question. "Do you believe he's going mad?"

"No, Tristan, I don't." She looked up at him. "He's less confused, more settled in every day. This doctor has thrown him off balance, but before he came, I promise you, he was well on the road back to becoming the Garrett we both knew and loved. I swear to you I'm telling you the truth. I wouldn't keep my child and Becky near him if I believed otherwise."

Tristan let out a sigh of relief and brought her hand up, pressing it to his lips. "I felt it was so, but I needed you to reassure me. The gossip has been brutal, and even Fisk seems to think Garrett is doomed."

Her lip curled "Ridiculous. He's merely . . . well, he comes off as so rough and harsh, but he was always that way. Remember how people used to fear him, but it used to be our secret what a sensitive, vulnerable man he was? Almost naïve, really."

"Yes." Tristan frowned. "And that's what concerns me. People—like this doctor you mention—might see his extended illness as an opportunity to deceive him."

"I know. But he refuses to listen to reason."

"And what about Fisk?"

She frowned. "What do you mean?"

"Do you feel he is trustworthy?"

Staring down at her lap, she played with a bit of lace on her skirt, its rough texture scraping gently between the pads of her fingers as she considered his words. Then she raised her eyes, feeling almost guilty for what she was about to admit. "No," she said softly. "I've tried to like him. I've tried to trust him, Tristan, because he's been such a loyal friend to Garrett. Even Miranda adores him. But in truth I try to avoid him as much as I can. I've never liked him, not since that first night."

"I've attempted to learn more about him, but he's not from London and no one I know has heard of him. I'm going to have to travel to Leeds if I want to discover anything more."

The thought of Tristan leaving London sent her heart fluttering. "Do you really think that's necessary?"

Tristan shook his head. "I don't know. I'm torn between wanting to stay here—close to my family in the event you need me—and riding to Leeds. It doesn't feel right to have someone we know so little about so intimately entwined with our family."

"Speaking of entwined . . ." She took a deep breath. "Even Becky seems to have developed an affection for him."

Tristan stiffened. "Damn it. Could that be what he's after? Securing Garrett's trust so he can steal his sister's fortune by marrying her? Do you think he's a fortune hunter?"

Sophie shuddered. "I don't know, but if it should come to that, I promise you, I'll do everything in my power to stop Garrett from allowing it. Aunt Bertrice will support me as well."

"All right, then. I'll let you know if I leave London. If I do, rest assured it will only be a few days."

"Where will you leave Gary?"

"With the servants. I've hired him a new governess and they're getting along splendidly."

"Oh, no, Tristan. It is too soon for another change for him—he will be miserable without any of us. If you do go to Leeds, you must bring him home."

Tristan raised a brow. "Would Garrett approve?"

"He wouldn't turn away family."

"Right," Tristan said wryly. "Unless it's me."

"You're a special case," she responded in an equally

wry tone. Then she covered his hand with her own and squeezed. "But Gary is not. He's just a child, and we miss him."

"All right, but I must be certain Garrett approves first. And Sophie . . ."

"Yes?"

"Keep an eye on Fisk, and don't let him near Becky. Promise me you'll be careful, love."

She let her eyes drift shut at the endearment she so loved hearing from him. He cupped her cheeks in his hands and pressed his forehead to hers. For a long moment, she just allowed his spicy essence to wash over her. "I miss you, Tristan," she finally whispered.

She wished she could convince him to return with them to Yorkshire when the Season was over. At Calton House, where they'd spent their childhood, she might find a way to bring her men together again. Placing her hands over Tristan's, she sighed—even if Tristan agreed at this point, Garrett would never allow it.

Releasing her, Tristan stood and reached down to help her up. They stepped out into the corridor to voices behind them, near the door that led backstage. Sophie glanced over her shoulder at the small gathering, and her heart nearly dropped to her toes. For there was a group of costumed actors, clearly actors in the play, but standing in their tight circle was a round little man—none other than the despicable Dr. MacAllister.

Chapter Fourteen

Tristan glanced down at Sophie's fingers curling like bird talons over his forearm. "It's him," she whispered.

"Who?"

"That blasted doctor," she said with a scowl. The look of disgust on her face made it abundantly clear she despised the man.

"Would you like me to speak to him?"

She nodded, tight-lipped. "You'll recognize him right away. He's wearing black pantaloons and a blue jacket. He's the shortest of the group, smaller than any of the women. And Tristan—" Her fingers tightened around his arm. "—will you ask about his credentials? I've asked him several times, and he circumvents the question every time."

"Of course, Soph. Why don't you go back to your box, and I'll send a message to you through Lady Harpsford."

"Thank you."

He curved his hand over her fingers and gave them a soothing pat. "Of course. Now go on."

With a small smile at him, she inclined her head, then stood tall, took her skirt in hand, and began to ascend the stairs back to her box. Tristan smiled and bowed politely at two ladies lingering in the lobby before he slipped back down the curving corridor.

The good doctor sensed his approach and glanced over his shoulder. Before Tristan's eyes, the man blanched. He turned back to his group, murmured a few soft words, then hurried into the shadows and disappeared through the door that led backstage.

"Good evening, sir," said a flirtatious vixen as Tristan approached the group. She was dressed as a fairy, wearing a slip of lace and not much more, and she'd used far too much kohl to line her eyes.

Tristan bowed. "Good evening to all of you. I just wished to say how greatly I've enjoyed the fine entertainments of this evening."

One of the actors thumped him on the back. The man's cheeks were flushed scarlet—no doubt he'd been imbibing. All the better for Tristan. "Thank you, sir. Thank you very much, indeed."

"I am curious—who was that man who scurried off just now?"

"Oh well, that was *Doctor* MacAllister," said the drunken actor. He glanced at the other actors. "That's what he told us, wasn't it?"

"Aye, Ned. Dr. MacAllister," confirmed a thin older woman with white hair and prominent collarbones. Beyond the wall, the audience gave a collective gasp. "Oh, my dears, the golden fruits are blooming in the forest.

That's my cue, loves. Goodnight!" Blowing kisses to her friends, the actress slipped through the black-painted backstage door.

Tristan turned to the others. "I wished to ask the doctor for some medical advice. Do you think I might go after him?"

"Backstage?"

Tristan nodded.

"Oooh, no," said the vixen. "I doubt he's back there, at any rate. He said he was late for a meeting, and he's probably *miles* away by now."

The actors all looked at him expectantly.

"Well, do you know where he resides? Or anywhere I might be able to contact him?"

"He spends the evenings here at the theater, of course, but—" The drunken man's words were cut short as the vixen kicked his shin in plain view.

Odd.

Tristan would return. Not tomorrow night, because the Countess of Keene's ball was tomorrow. But perhaps the night after.

"May I offer you refreshment, my lord?"

Tristan stood awkwardly in the small, shabby front parlor belonging to Connor's sister the next afternoon. Dressed in gentlemanly street clothes, Connor stood across from him, clearly equally uncomfortable. Both men were out of their element.

"No, thank you." Tristan tapped his hat against his thigh. "I am sorry to intrude upon you like this, Connor."

"It's quite all right, sir. I am at your service."

"Thank you." Tristan cleared his throat. "I've come out of concern for the duke's household."

After a short pause, the butler said, "We have been through some upheaval, as you yourself have. But everything is quite well, I assure you."

"I have heard some . . . concerns. Regarding the duke's sanity."

Connor gave a fleeting look of distaste before his face returned to its standard impassivity. "I have heard the rumors, of course."

"Is it true that the gossip was begun by a member of the staff?"

Connor's shoulders squared. "Absolutely not. Mrs. Krum and I have questioned each member of the staff, down to the scullery maids, and so has Her Grace. We are all satisfied that none is responsible for spreading these untruths."

"You believe the accusations are completely untrue?"

"I have no doubt of the duke's sanity, sir. It is true he is facing a difficult adjustment to his way of life, but if you are asking my opinion . . . ?"

"I am, Connor. You have worked in his household since before he left for the Continent. I believe you to be a trustworthy judge of his character."

"In my opinion, he is perfectly sane, my lord. He is prone to periods of frustration, it's true. But—"

"Did he aim a pistol at you?"

The butler's eyes widened in surprise, then his gaze narrowed. "Why, yes, sir, he did. I didn't know anyone but the duke and I were aware of that incident."

"Why did he do it?"

"I surprised him in his study. His reaction when I

walked in the door was instantaneous—almost as if he were reliving the war and believed me to be the enemy."

Tristan released a breath. "Damn it, Connor. What if he had aimed a gun at one of the ladies? What if his finger slipped on the trigger?"

"It was an honest mistake, my lord, in the first days following his arrival home. He meant nothing by it, and he discarded the weapon once he realized who I was. He is much calmer now. He no longer takes his pistol everywhere he goes."

Tristan studied Connor. The man was nothing if not steadfast and trustworthy in the extreme. But at this point could Tristan trust anyone? He let his gaze drift toward the window as rain pelted against the panes.

"You would say the ladies are completely safe, then?"

"Yes, my lord. I truly believe they are safe." In a rare movement contrary to his butleresque stiffness, Connor bent his head so Tristan saw the bald spot. Then he looked back up. "Where His Grace is concerned, that is."

"What do you mean?" Tristan asked sharply.

All the man's stiffness returned, and he gazed at Tristan. "You were asking my opinion, my lord?"

"Yes."

Connor hesitated. "I'm hesitant to break the confidences of the household to which I belong—"

"For God's sake, Connor. You know I wouldn't do anything to put your position at risk. You know I only care for my wife—Her Grace—and Lady Miranda. And the rest of my family."

Connor's eyes flicked away, then came to rest on Tristan. "Yes, sir. I do believe your intentions are honorable."

"Do you require money? How much—"

Connor held up his hand. "Of course not. Please, sir. I would not dream of taking a bribe from you."

Tristan took a step closer to him. "Tell me your concerns."

"They could quite possibly be unfounded."

"Tell me."

"It's Mr. Fisk."

"What about him?"

"I don't trust him, sir."

Tristan forced his gaze to remain neutral. "Why is that?"

"Just a feeling I have. And—" Connor blew out a breath. "—in truth, sir, I fear His Grace has placed too much trust in him. He has managed all the duke's fiscal matters for some time. His Grace has given him the power of attorney."

Tristan sucked in a breath. "I see."

He knew Garrett had given Fisk too much power, but for him to place all his money into Fisk's hands . . . That act gave Fisk power far beyond what his youthful imaginings had probably ever conjured.

God, Garrett was being a damn fool.

"Sir, I don't see how you could have heard about the incident with the duke aiming his pistol at me, unless Mr. Fisk was lurking about somewhere and witnessed the scene. And frankly, sir, if that is so, it makes me uncomfortable that he didn't make himself known."

"Understandable, Connor. It makes me uncomfortable as well."

*   *   *

A massive crystal chandelier hung from the ceiling and gilded wall sconces blazed with candles in Lady Keene's ballroom. Garrett smiled down at Sophie, who tightened her hand over his arm. Though he had remained unfashionably close to her, the evening had gone passably well. He managed dinner without making any faux pas, and he miraculously survived an awkward quadrille with his sister without stepping on any toes. He could thank Miranda for that. In the past week, they'd taken to practicing the dances together, and the steps had eventually come back to him.

Sophie looked up at him, her smile warming him to his toes. "Are you ready for our waltz, Your Grace?"

Determined to counter the gossip of his insanity and her maltreatment, they'd planned to dance the waltz together. Displaying themselves in close proximity would be just the thing to show the *ton* that the Duke and Duchess of Calton were content.

Even if it were not the case. Garrett knew she was suffering. She displayed a good façade, but he saw beyond it. She was pale and drawn, thinner and quieter than the Sophie he'd once known. Lines of strain had formed at the corners of her mouth. Most upsetting of all, the color of her eyes had changed from sparkling whiskey to a deep, sad brown.

Perhaps in part he was responsible for that. She seemed determined to counter him, to argue with him at every turn. She thought he didn't respect her opinions—but it wasn't that at all.

He did respect her . . . but she couldn't understand the extent of his fear. He hated feeling out of control. He hated the damned holes in his memory. He hated how he didn't know how to respond when someone spoke to him. Every day, his frustration with himself grew, and every day it seemed his goal of becoming a normal English gentleman drifted farther from his reach.

Sophie didn't see any of that. In that way, she was like the Sophie of their childhood. She only saw the positives . . . the one step forward for every ten steps back.

He wanted nothing more than to make her happy, but that was yet another elusive aspect of his old life he grasped for so desperately but was never able to cling to. If only he could find a way to make her love him as passionately, as wholly as she once had.

Garrett handed his empty punch glass to a servant and held out his arm. "I'm ready."

He led Sophie out to the center of the dance floor. Aware of all the eyes witnessing the scene, he clasped her small hand in his much larger one. Her fingers twined with his, and he slid his arm around her waist.

From their unobtrusive position on a balcony at one end of the room, the orchestra played the opening strains of the waltz. The music swelled around them, and as Garrett looked into Sophie's eyes, he thought they lightened a little.

They swept into movement. When they were younger, they'd loved to dance together. He remembered waltzing with her once, back when the waltz was a forbidden, sinful dance, on the fields of Calton House. They'd spun round and round together, humming the tune as Tristan had sat nearby, chewing on a strand of grass and watching them. Finally exhausted, they fell to the ground beside him, laughing and sweaty, the hem of Sophie's gown sopping wet from the puddles they'd danced through. Tristan had turned his nose up at them and said he abhorred sweating because it made his clothes dirty. In response, Garrett had jumped on him and they'd wrestled while Sophie cheered them on. By the end, they were all three muddy and wet to the bone. It had earned both Tristan and Garrett a birching when they'd returned to the house.

"Oh, Garrett," she breathed, looking up at him with shining eyes as he whirled her round Lady Keene's ballroom. "Do you remember how we used to waltz together?"

Christ, it was hard not to stop. Not to bend down and kiss her senseless. Right here.

"I remember," he murmured, reveling in the curve of her waist beneath his hand. The feel of her fingers pressed against his own. Even through their gloves, he felt her warmth.

She was a vision in silver silk and sparkling diamonds tonight. She took his breath away when he first saw her in her ball gown. It transformed her into an angel.

His angel.

A surge of optimism welled from somewhere deep within him. This apparition, this angel, belonged to him alone, and he had all the time in the world to win back her love. Maybe someday they would have another child together, as beautiful and precocious as Miranda.

He tightened his hand over her waist and pulled her an inch closer.

"I want you, Sophie," he breathed.

Her expression didn't change, and he thought for a moment that she hadn't heard him. But then she smiled. "I never stopped wanting you."

They neared the edge of the dance floor, deftly avoiding other couples. From the corner of his eye, he saw his sister's twirling powder-blue gown. She was dancing with Fisk for the second time tonight. Garrett hoped Fisk had left more distance between himself and his partner than Garrett had with his.

He pulled Sophie closer still. A curl bounced at her cheek, and he wanted to wrap his fingers in the satin strand. "Let me make love to you, Sophie."

She held him tight but didn't break her gaze away from his. Her warmth swept through his body, leaving him hard. God, he hoped the waltz wouldn't end soon—he'd risk half the *ton* seeing him in this state.

Although, he thought wryly, that might put to rest any doubt about his level of affection for his wife.

Her eyes drifted shut, and he led her in sweeping circles across the floor.

What did it mean? Was she waging some internal battle over resuming marital relations with him? Or did she not want him to see the regret in her expression?

That thought cooled the inferno in his blood. They still drifted effortlessly over the dance floor—how was it she made him feel so weightless?—but the waltz was coming to an end. Slowly, he drew her to a stop.

"Sophie?"

She opened her eyes and gazed at him. They were still the lighter color, but maybe it was due to the blazing light from the chandelier just overhead.

"I want to, Garrett. I want to be yours again . . . in all ways. But . . . I need time."

They had all the time in the world. Unfortunately, his body didn't respond well to logic.

Still, she offered him hope. He'd take it and hold on to it like a precious gem.

Just then Fisk and Rebecca approached, and Fisk pressed glasses of punch into Garrett's and Sophie's hands.

"A lovely waltz, wasn't it?" Rebecca's cheeks flushed pink. Garrett downed his drink, watching his glowing, happy sister over the rim, noting the look of adoration she cast Fisk when he turned away to greet someone.

Sophie's hand curled over his arm, and a warm, contented feeling settled in his stomach. But dark foreboding singed the edges of his contentment, and along with it came the disturbing thought that it wouldn't—couldn't—last.

Standing behind one of the regal Ionic columns that set the main floor of the ballroom apart from the conservatory, Tristan watched them, unease swirling in his gut. He hadn't expected Garrett to be here. Worse, everyone was studying Tristan carefully, to see how he'd manage this more-than-awkward situation. He felt as if they all perused his body with quizzing glasses, searching for a way inside to analyze his soul.

Worst of all was the way his elegant wife had responded to Garrett as they waltzed. Dressed in a shimmering silver that caught the eye of every person in the room, she gazed at Garrett, affection brimming from her eyes. A near-palpable heat swirled between the two of them.

Tristan ground his teeth. This was an impossible, hopeless situation. For the first time, as he watched Sophie speak in low, urgent tones to Garrett, he considered abducting her against her will.

Such an action wasn't in Tristan's style. Perhaps Garrett had rubbed off on him. But God . . . there was nothing to compel him to action like watching the woman he loved with another man.

But it wasn't what she wanted. It would be brutish and dishonorable. If he kept nothing else, damn it, he would keep his honor.

So he kept his face stone still and expressionless as they waltzed, and he didn't allow himself to react as he witnessed the intimacy of their conversation afterward.

As tempting as it was to call Garrett out and end it with pistols at dawn, or toss Sophie over his shoulder and escape from this place, neither would help him to win Sophie back. Or to regain Garrett's trust.

For, as Sophie and Garrett glided toward the refreshment table, Tristan finally admitted to himself that he craved the close camaraderie he'd once shared with Garrett. As much as he wanted to deny it, he wanted Garrett's friendship again. For almost all his life he'd loved Garrett like a brother, and to be at odds with him now felt like he was losing him all over again.

The music began again—a quadrille—and Tristan abruptly looked up as a man slapped him on the shoulder. He spoke congenially for a few moments, hardly paying attention to what his companion was saying. When the man wandered away, Tristan's roaming gaze found Sophie and Garrett, along with Fisk and Becky, near a large potted palm, drinking, talking, and laughing as if everything were perfect in the world.

"Nephew."

He turned to find his Aunt Bertrice looking like a butterball in her jonquil gown, and released a deep breath.

Keeping his composure, he bowed, then took her hand and kissed it. "Aunt B. You're looking well."

She snorted. "Don't lie to me, boy. My joints are on fire. I daresay I won't make it to another one of these routs this year. They're too late in the night for me. These days I prefer to be abed by sunset."

He squeezed her hand before letting go.

She squinted up at him through pale blue eyes. "You look awful, too, nephew. Tall as ever, though."

"I thank you," he said dryly.

Her mouth quirked. "Well, I daresay there's something to thank the Lord for. At least you haven't developed a hunchback."

His gaze wandered back toward where Sophie and Garrett stood. "I thank the Lord for that blessing every day."

Her lips flattened. "Why are you here, Tristan? I rather think it's a bad idea."

With Aunt Bertrice, honesty was always the best policy. "I'm leaving London. I had to see her again before I left."

She sighed. "You boys. Always pining over that one."

He slid her a glance. She'd always been fond of Sophie. "Would you have had it any other way, Aunt?"

"No, Tristan. She took care of you where I could not. I've done better with Rebecca, but she's a girl, after all, and very docile. Unlike the two of you wild urchins. I was never very maternal, you know."

"Yes." Both he and Garrett had struggled without a mother's love. Aunt Bertrice, while always a presence in their lives, offered little in the way of motherly affection.

During their childhood, she had spent about as much time avoiding Garrett's tyrant of a father as they had.

"But I did care for you both. In my small way."

"I know that, Aunt," he said softly.

"Good." She thumped him on the back. "Now what's this about leaving London?"

"I have some business to attend. I won't be gone long."

She released a breath through pursed lips, following his gaze to where Sophie and Garrett stood, their heads bowed together. "It's odd having him back, isn't it?"

What did she mean by that? He merely gave her an expectant look.

She shrugged. "Something about it feels wrong. Off. Who'm I to say, though. I've only been here a few days."

His breath caught in his throat. "Are you saying you feel he's dangerous?"

She waved her hand. "No, no. Not at all. Garrett is a puppy. He has a loud bark, but he doesn't bite like his father did. You, of all people, know that. Don't be a ninny, boy."

She was right. Garrett looked like his father, even sounded like him. But unlike the old duke, he never raised a hand with the intent to truly hurt anyone, even when he threatened to. Tristan cocked a brow. "What do you mean, then?"

"Him and Sophie." She pierced him with her blue eyes, her wrinkled expression unreadable. "They're not the same together. Not like how they once were. *He's* not the same. It's almost—" she fingered her chin thoughtfully. "Well, it's almost as though they've reversed roles. Garrett was always the protector, the leader, but now it is Sophie who plays those parts." Her eyes flickered away, and then lit up. "Oh look, there's Lady Collins, and I haven't seen her in years. Good-bye, nephew. Safe travels, and Rebecca and I will visit you when you return home."

With that, she lumbered off in the direction of a lady of equally advanced years, and they engaged in much kissing and gushing over each other. Tristan nearly smiled. She'd never treated him with such affection. That wasn't to say she didn't care, because he knew she did.

Had she meant to give him hope with her words? Regardless of her intention, she had.

A crash from Sophie's direction drew Tristan's attention. She stood in a wash of glass and punch, her mouth agape. Everyone around her froze, stock still. Only Garrett moved. He stomped to the nearby punchbowl, lifted a second glass, and sent it crashing to the floor.

"Good Lord, George, I told you he was mad as a hatter," muttered a nearby lady to her husband.

"Sophie!" Tristan sprinted toward his wife. As he neared, Garrett's blue gaze speared into him.

"You!" Garrett roared. A glass flew at him, but Tristan ducked, and it hurtled into the wall. Droplets splattered on his neck.

A part of him, the part always attuned to propriety and his reputation, realized that he was being seen by the most influential people in London bounding toward his ex-wife while he dodged missiles thrown by her husband, his cousin. God, they'd make a joke of this moment throughout the kingdom.

Crystal exploded at his feet. He leaped over it and kept running. When he reached Sophie, she grabbed his arm.

"Tristan! Thank God you're here. I don't know what's wrong with—"

Glass glanced off his arm. He thrust Sophie behind him to shield her from flying shards. She grabbed the tails of his coat and held on for dear life.

"Your Grace, cease this immediately!" he shouted. Why was nobody rushing to stop Garrett? The crowd seemed frozen, as if in a painting, agog and waiting to see what would happen.

Garrett raised two glasses, one in each hand, wielding them as weapons. Good God, was he frothing at the mouth? Just moments ago, he'd appeared the perfect gentleman.

He swayed on his feet, collecting glasses one at a time from the serving table and slinging them randomly. A lady dressed in the same shade of gray as Tristan let out a muffled scream and ducked behind her companion as a glass soared past her head to crash somewhere behind her. Garrett spun around, raising a glass at a man nearly Tristan's height.

Garrett dropped his hands, a bewildered look crossing his face. "Christ! He's everywhere, and he won't go away."

Fisk took a step toward Garrett, but Becky grabbed his arm. "Be careful, Mr. Fisk," she whispered. "Please."

Another glass shattered as it struck the wall and rained down the wainscoting in a shower of pink champagne and glittering shards.

Fisk patted Becky's hand. "Never fear, Lady Rebecca. I shall manage your brother."

She hesitantly released him, and he stepped forward

again, holding his hands out in a placating gesture. "Cal, I'm here."

"Fisk?" Garrett's face twisted in confusion. "Fisk, is that you? I can't see, Fisk. It's like . . . it's like it was before . . ." He sucked in a wild breath.

"It's me, Cal. Everything is going to be just fine," Fisk said soothingly.

"Tristan . . . won't go away. He's everywhere." Garrett blinked hard, but his eyes rolled backward in his skull.

"He'll go now, Cal. We'll take you home."

Just as Fisk reached him, Garrett collapsed.

Tristan turned to Sophie, grabbing her shoulders. "Sophie, love. Look at me. Are you all right?"

She blinked. "Tristan? Yes. Yes, I'm fine. Perfectly all right."

The ballroom came to life in a flurry of activity. Gentlemen swarmed over Garrett while ladies crowded around Sophie, pushing Tristan away from her. He watched her struggling to go to Garrett as the crowd overtook her. She didn't have a scratch on her, thank God, but her whiskey-colored eyes were wide with shock. Words were being bandied about. *Mad. Insane. Lost his mind . . .*

Tristan was torn between thrusting aside the women and checking on Sophie, and going to see if Garrett was all right.

Fisk played the hero, with Becky at his elbow staring at him like a fawning pet. Men slapped him on the back and offered him congratulations on his handling of the madman's outburst.

Tristan gritted his teeth. No, this wasn't right at all. The crowd parted momentarily, and Tristan saw the same look of confusion on Sophie's face he was sure reflected on his own.

He needed to talk to her. But he couldn't, not in this crush. What he most wanted to say was, "For God's sake, don't trust Fisk," but he couldn't even do that much.

For now, it had to be enough that Sophie believed Garrett wasn't mad, and that she was just as suspicious of Fisk as he was. Tristan trusted her implicitly, he respected her, and he believed her, even if what he'd just witnessed seemed in direct contradiction to her opinion. And if Sophie was right, it must mean the good Dr. MacAllister had given Garrett something that had altered him.

"Idiots," Aunt Bertrice said in a low voice, coming to stand beside him.

He looked down at the old woman. She seemed to be the only person in the entire room who hadn't lost her wits.

"Look at them. They're like a godforsaken herd of sheep. One mischief-maker shouts 'madman,' and they all fall into the spirit of it."

He found the crowd a little easier to forgive, considering that Garrett *had* just behaved like a raving lunatic. But then Tristan caught a glimpse of his young cousin, who had gone quite pale and had wrapped her arms around herself. Fisk had abandoned Garrett and was leading her to a chair. "Even Becky," he murmured.

"Even Rebecca." Aunt Bertrice frowned. "Fools, the lot of 'em."

"Will you deliver a message of warning to Sophie for me?"

His aunt snorted. "She hardly needs warned, boy. She's

as wound up as a watch, her claws are extended, and she's prepared as ever to do battle for any one of us."

Tristan nodded. "Just tell her to be careful."

"Of course." The old woman waved her hand in the air as if shooing him away. Then her face darkened, her expression reminiscent of Garrett himself. "This must take precedence over all your other business, Tristan. I insist you get to the bottom of this drama, and soon. Sophie is too deeply caught up in all of it, and Garrett—well, he's too damn blind. But something tastes rotten."

Tristan agreed. "I intend to, Aunt. That's why I must leave Town."

Chapter Fifteen

Cal?"

Garrett looked up from his desk. "Oh, Fisk, I'm glad to see you."

"The doctor's returned."

As if to prove Fisk's statement, the jolly man peeked around Fisk's shoulder, though at the moment, he didn't look nearly so cheerful as usual. Garrett stiffened, and his throat went dry. Fisk had called MacAllister to his side once they'd brought him home from the ball, and the doctor had tended to him all night. When Garrett awoke feeling well except for a touch of a headache, MacAllister had said he suspected the cause of Garrett's outburst, but he wanted to mull over the case before pronouncing a definite diagnosis.

"Dr. MacAllister," he said softly. "Come in. Make yourself comfortable."

"Thank you, Your Grace."

Fisk smiled encouragingly at the man. "The doctor

says he has a prognosis for the affliction that overcame you at Lady Keene's ball."

Exactly what Garrett feared.

He felt the sudden urge to call for his wife. With jerky movements, he took the golden bell from his inkstand, rang for a footman, and asked the man to summon her.

Her presence would keep him calm.

Christ. He deluded himself. At the ball, even her solid strength beside him hadn't prevented him from succumbing to madness.

"Are you sure you want the duchess to hear this, Cal?" Fisk said softly. His eyes were soft, full of compassion, and Garrett despised the pity he saw in them.

Garrett moved his head in a brusque nod. "As my wife, she should know."

"Even if the prognosis is less than ideal?"

He gave Fisk a sharp look. "I retain hope for the most ideal outcome."

"Of course." Fisk's voice was mild.

Moments later, Sophie entered, her emerald-green skirts lifted to reveal heeled leather shoes and a bit of white stocking. She looked harried, as if she'd dropped everything and run to the study. Garrett rose, and Fisk and the doctor followed suit.

She released her skirts, smoothed the shimmering fabric, straightened, and inclined her head. "Good afternoon, doctor. Mr. Fisk."

They both bowed and greeted her pleasantly.

Garrett reached his hand to her. "Come stand beside me, Sophie. The doctor is prepared to give his diagnosis, and I want you to hear it."

She slipped her hand in his and squeezed reassuringly.

He was still awed that she didn't cringe away from him in fear after what he had done—he'd seen his sister in the hall earlier, and she'd looked as though she were about to faint. But Sophie said she believed in him, she'd stand beside him, and together they would find the solution. She steadfastly believed his condition was reversible. As misplaced as her confidence in him was, her words kept him from descending into dark panic.

Because after last night, a part of him—a very large part—truly believed he was going mad.

The doctor cleared his throat. "Given the new symptoms you've exhibited, I must revise your diagnosis, Your Grace. I fear you have a rare condition characterized by outbursts of lunacy and caused by severe trauma to the brain. Sometimes after an upsetting experience or injury, the mind continues to return to the trauma even when it occurred long ago. At those times, the victim is unaware of his true surroundings and behaves as if he is reliving the disturbing event. Essentially reliving his memories."

"Are you referring to Waterloo?"

"Yes—that is the most likely event in this case, sir."

"That doesn't make sense. I never had an episode like this when I was living in Belgium." Garrett's brow furrowed. "At least, I don't think I did."

"I believe this corresponds directly to your return to England and your recollection of your memories."

"Will it happen again?"

"Yes, Your Grace. It is very likely."

"Is there a way to control it?"

"No, sir. None that we know."

"You say it is a temporary affliction?"

The doctor's eyes flicked to Fisk, then lowered. "The fits

are known to recur more frequently as the condition progresses, ultimately overcoming its victims permanently."

Permanently? The word hung in the silence like a phantom.

"How sure are you of this diagnosis?"

"Completely, Your Grace."

He was going mad. The doctor had just confirmed it.

He glanced at Sophie, who stood very still, a stoic expression on her face. But her fingers tightened over his.

Then he looked at Fisk. His friend sat frozen, tears shining in his eyes.

Garrett squared his shoulders. He would not crumble before the people who meant the most to him. "How long?"

"Your Grace?"

"How long do I have before the madness controls me?"

The doctor cleared his throat. "It could happen anytime. It truly varies from case to case. You may or may not recover from the next episode."

"I see. Thank you, doctor."

"I intend to analyze this thoroughly and develop a prescription to contain your symptoms for as long as possible."

Garrett slid into his chair and stared dully at the inkpot as Sophie moved to see Fisk and the doctor out. When the door closed behind them, she came to stand on the opposite side of his desk.

She slapped her hands on the polished wood surface. "I don't believe him. I don't believe a word that man says. Don't listen to him, Garrett."

He looked up at her. Her eyes sparkled back at him

with intensity, glowing amber. "I know you don't like him—"

"Don't like him? I despise him! How dare he say such things to you! How dare he frighten you like that!"

"Sometimes the truth *is* frightening," he said in a low voice.

"I can't—I won't believe you're going mad, Garrett. I refuse to believe it. He's wrong."

Garrett heaved a sigh. "He's a doctor, Sophie."

"I don't care if he's the Lord himself come down from Heaven." Again she whacked the desk with her palms. "He's wrong, damn it!"

"How can you explain what happened last night, then?"

"There is an explanation," she said stubbornly. "I don't know what it is, but we'll unearth it. It's not madness, that much I know. Dr. MacAllister is a charlatan. He's trying to upset you—to what end I cannot say."

She walked around the desk with purpose in her stride. Then she took his cheeks in her palms and tilted his head up so he faced her.

"I'm not going to allow you to believe you're mad, Garrett. You're not. You're honorable and sane. Don't ever let anyone say you're mad."

Then she bent down and kissed him on the mouth. Hard. Shocked, he froze for a long moment, but then he came alive. He slipped his arms round her silky emerald bodice and tugged her to his lap.

Her lips were soft, luscious. When they'd kissed before, he'd been completely entranced by the moment, but this time, kissing her felt like coming home. Her delicate floral scent clung to her and wafted over him, along with his memories.

Kissing her under the stars. Behind the stables, in the stables. In every room of Calton House. This house, too.

Her lips clung to his, gentle and tentative yet with an underlying, insistent, powerful strength.

He felt sane when she kissed him. Life flooded into his blood, and desire replaced defeat. He smoothed his hand up the curve of her waist and cupped her breast, soft and supple, even through the many layers of her clothes.

"Your Grace?"

They broke apart. Sophie didn't spare a glance at Fisk, whose voice had come from the door. She kept her warming gaze on Garrett instead.

Annoyed, Garrett turned to the doorway.

"Oh, forgive me," Fisk murmured. "I've just come to assist you with the rents, Your Grace. I'll return later."

"No, please, Mr. Fisk. Do stay." Sophie slid off Garrett's lap. "I was just leaving."

"Lord Westcliff is in the drawing room, Your Grace."

Garrett's head snapped up, and he gaped at the butler. "*What* did you say?"

Even Fisk, sitting across the desk from him, looked surprised. They'd spend the better part of the day untangling Garrett's investments. He seemed to have a hand in every single financial pot in England, and it took a great deal of concentration to organize. Fortunately, he'd not lost money in the years since Waterloo, as so many other men of the aristocracy had. Fisk credited conservative investing, but Garrett knew that Tristan as his trustee had made wise decisions, despite his seeming lack of concern for the maintenance and care of his properties.

"Lord Westcliff is in the drawing room, sir."

"And may I ask who allowed him to enter this house?"

"Lady Bertrice, Your Grace," Connor said stiffly, his beaklike nose quivering at its tip.

"And where is Her Grace?"

"Her Grace is in the drawing room with them."

Garrett heaved out of his chair, and Connor scurried backward. Scowling, Garrett pushed past him and strode toward the staircase, Fisk at his heels.

Please, God, help me keep my sanity.

Fisk laid a hand on his arm as they walked up the stairs. "Are you certain you should go in there?"

Keeping his face stony, Garrett mounted the stairs. One foot in front of the other.

"Surely it was Lord Westcliff's presence at Lady Keene's ball that pulled you over the edge, Cal. What if it happens again?" Desperation edged Fisk's words.

Garrett paused just outside the drawing room door. He was afraid, so afraid, of losing his mind.

"I can speak with him on your behalf," Fisk continued in a low voice.

Garrett stared at the white-painted door panels. Fisk's offer was so damn tempting. But then he heard Sophie's melodic voice coming from inside the room.

"No," he pushed out. "I'll do it." Steeling his jangling nerves, he turned the handle and pushed open the door. Tristan, who'd been sitting on one of the silk armchairs, jumped to his feet, blocking Sophie from view.

Damn the man. Always so utterly protective of her. Wasn't that Garrett's job?

He glared at Tristan. "What are you doing here, Westcliff?"

Tristan took in a deep breath. After he exhaled, he seemed to relax a little, and stepped away from Sophie, who sat calmly, her hands folded in her lap. She gazed at Garrett as if willing her own serenity to transfer to him.

"I've come to ask a favor," Tristan said.

Garrett narrowed his eyes. From the corner of his eye, he could see Aunt Bertrice, whose scowl matched his own, and Rebecca cowering in her chair.

"What might that be?"

"I've come to ask you to take Gary."

That stunned him. He was silent for a long moment before he spoke. "Why?"

"I'm leaving Town, and it will be best for him to be in the company of his family."

Garrett stared hard at his cousin, trying to discern an ulterior motive. "You saw what happened to me last night," he said gruffly. "Why would you want your son near me?"

"I don't fear you. You wouldn't hurt a child."

"At this moment, I wouldn't," Garrett said. "But—"

Tristan took a step toward him, raising his hand. "I would never doubt my son's safety in this house. Are you saying I should?"

Garrett spoke the truth. "I don't know."

"The boy is a creature of habit. It has been difficult for him without Miranda and Miss Dalworthy. I only ask because I know it will be better—even *safer*—for Gary to be here with his family than with his new governess in unfamiliar surroundings."

Garrett paused, stunned by Tristan's show of faith. Did the man merely possess the same confidence in him Sophie had, or was he a damn fool? Garrett's stubborn mind wanted to believe the latter, but something nudged his gut, telling him Tristan truly did believe in his sanity.

Tristan believed in him. After all that had happened between them. For a long moment, Garrett fought to keep steady, to maintain his composure. Finally, he cleared his throat. "Ah . . . when will you return from your . . . travels?"

Tristan shook his head. "I'm not certain. I won't be long, though. Early June, at the latest."

Sophie released a breath through pursed lips. Garrett glanced at her. "I don't see why not," she said softly. "Gary and Miranda complement each other—they draw out each other's best qualities. I also think it will be beneficial for him to spend time with Becky and Aunt Bertrice. They are his family, after all."

Garrett turned to Rebecca. She merely sat with her head down, her hands clenched in her lap. She wouldn't even look at him. Sighing, he focused on Aunt Bertrice. She gave a brisk nod. "There's no harm in taking the child for a while, Garrett."

It was true—Garrett couldn't see any harm in it. The boy was only five years old, after all, and couldn't be a great threat.

Gary was still family. Before Waterloo, Garrett would never have considered turning a family member away.

"Very well. The boy may stay here while you are gone."

Tristan smiled. It was the first time Garrett had seen Tristan smile since he'd returned home. His lips spread wide, and his cheek dimpled, making him look much younger. It reminded Garrett of their boyhood together. Laughing as they played on the moor behind Calton House.

On one of those occasions, Garrett had stumbled, and his head had struck a rock. He remembered the sharp, blinding pain, then opening his eyes to find a very young Tristan leaning over him, his pale face streaked with dirt, sobbing, "Oh, Garrett, you're dead. I'm sorry, I'm sorry," as if it had been his fault.

"Oh, shut up," Garrett mumbled. "I'm quite all right." And he had felt fine except for a terrible ache in his temple.

Through his tears, Tristan had given him the same smile he was now. But then he'd sobered and said, "You've got blood on your shirt. Uncle will beat you for it."

Garrett merely shrugged. "Ah, well, look at the bright side. At least I'm alive."

With a deep sigh of relief, Tristan had reached out and helped Garrett up, and they went home, where Garrett had smiled through his birching.

At least I am alive.

Garrett found his fingers tracing the hairline scar that ran through his eyebrow.

Tristan's smile faltered. "Thank you, Your Grace. I'll bring Gary tomorrow. He'll be ecstatic to see all of you." He bowed at the ladies. "Good-bye."

The women rose. Garrett saw how tightly Sophie had clenched her hands at her sides. Her knuckles had whitened. The blood had drained from her cheeks, leaving her pale and wan.

"Good-bye, Cousin Tristan." Without a glance in Garrett's direction, Rebecca rose and curtsied to him. "I am sorry we couldn't spend more time together before you left."

"Me, too, Becky," Tristan said gravely. He then went to embrace Aunt Bertrice. Finally, he bowed before Sophie, his body so tight, Garrett was surprised it didn't snap in two. "Your Grace."

"My lord," she murmured.

Garrett watched every move they made. Both of them were the epitome of propriety, but they struggled for it, that much was clear. There was only so much a person could hide. Like the glow of unshed tears in Sophie's eyes and the muscle twitching spasmodically in Tristan's jaw.

Tristan eyed her for a long moment, no doubt taking in the fact that she was paler than normal and that she had lost weight. And the lines of sadness etched into the edges of her pretty mouth.

Tristan jerked around to face Garrett. "Thank you again, Your Grace."

Stiffly, Garrett moved aside to allow Tristan to walk past. Just outside, Tristan inclined his head at the man standing behind Garrett. "Fisk."

"Good afternoon, my lord," Fisk replied with a congenial smile.

With a final nod, Tristan strode away, disappearing down the stairs.

After a moment, Garrett followed him, leaving the uncomfortable silence of the drawing room for the solace of his study.

*   *   *

Tristan stared down at the record in his hands. On a whim, he'd gone directly from Garrett's house to the offices of the adjutant general in one final attempt to find information about Fisk.

While the officer lists for Garrett's disbanded regiment were still missing, the record of officers who'd perished in the battle of Waterloo hadn't mysteriously disappeared. The secretary handed over the sheaf of papers, beaming, no doubt because he was finally able to prove that his recordkeeping was at least somewhat dependable.

In a dim hall surrounded by shelves containing piles of military records and rows of clerks sitting at old desks busily scribbling away, Tristan sank into an uncomfortable wooden chair to sift through the papers. Moments later, his hands dropped into his lap. There it was, in plain view on the center of the page surrounded by names of other men who'd lost their lives that day.

Warren Fisk, Lieutenant of the Fourth Coldstream Guards, of Kenilworth, age 18.

It had to be Fisk's brother—he was the only lieutenant listed from Garrett's regiment who also shared Fisk's surname.

So Fisk was not from Leeds after all, but from Kenilworth, a town southeast of Birmingham. What luck Tristan had come this afternoon. If he hadn't, he'd have been heading in the wrong direction tomorrow.

Tristan narrowed his eyes at the document. Warren Fisk had died on the eighteenth of June 1815, at the age of eighteen. If he were living today, he'd be twenty-six. That made him exactly the same age as William.

Twins? Or was Fisk impersonating another man?

Tristan frowned . . . Garrett had never stated whether Fisk had given him his name or whether Garrett had remembered first.

Either way, Tristan was determined to uncover the truth in Kenilworth.

Sophie stood in front of her fireplace. The clock showed a little past midnight, and she was exhausted. Her heart felt cracked and brittle, heavy in her chest. She hated it that Tristan was gone. Even after he'd left the house, she'd taken comfort in the fact that he was close, that he'd be there for her should she need him. And although he'd only be gone for a week or two, it felt as if everything was coming to a head with Garrett, and an unfamiliar sensation of anxiety crawled in her chest.

Once again, she opened the cryptic note Tristan had slipped into her hand in the drawing room on the day before he'd left. His bold hand slanted across the wrinkled sheet of stationery:

> *MacA elusive, so have resolved to leave London seek information on F. Have employed a man to delve into MacA's background. We will know more by the time I return.*
>
> *Trust no one, and be vigilant.*

Always, T.

At the bottom of the note, he'd added a postscript that contained the name and address of a man to contact in the event of an emergency. *Robert Jennings.*

Sophie carefully refolded the worn paper and slipped it into a drawer in her dressing cabinet.

Every day, despite her protestations, Garrett grew more convinced madness was overtaking him. The doctor had prescribed a "treatment" to slow the process, but he persistently claimed insanity was inevitable, and Garrett—gullible man that he was—believed him.

It didn't help that he'd had another nightmare, followed by another episode of "madness," just last night. And it didn't help that she'd replaced Dr. MacAllister's noxious tonic with a harmless one of her own ... and it hadn't made a whit of difference. Garrett's episode had overtaken him swiftly and ruthlessly, much as it had at the Countess of Keene's ball.

Now, between missing Tristan and the constant battle to prove Garrett's sanity while Garrett and everyone else viewed his outbursts as irrefutable evidence he was losing his mind, her nerves had begun to fray.

Instead of breaking down, however, taking to her bed and weeping, or smashing everything breakable she could find against the wall, she began to fixate on Mr. Fisk. His uncanny presence at the most inopportune moments. His unflinchingly polite personality. The subtle ways he was seducing Becky.

Since her conversation with Tristan at the theater, Sophie had allowed her latent distrust of Mr. Fisk to emerge. She watched him carefully and discovered that, as much as he tried to make his actions appear natural, every move he made, every word he uttered, was precise and deliberate.

Mr. Fisk wasn't the right man for her sister-in-law. The

subtle flirting between him and Becky had to stop before it went too far.

She intended to warn Garrett. Tonight, when there would be no risk of Mr. Fisk lurking about and overhearing their conversation.

She strode to her wardrobe and found a light peach silk robe, for the evening wasn't cold. She'd find him in one of his sanctuaries, either in the study or his bedchamber. She hoped it was his bedchamber—there was less chance of encountering Mr. Fisk there, even at this late hour.

Just as she stepped toward the door, someone knocked on it.

"Sophie?" Becky's voice.

She opened the door, and her heart sank. Becky stood there breathless, her cheeks pink and her hair askew.

Sophie knew what this meant, knew it to her core. She reached out to grasp Becky's hand and pull her inside. "Oh, Becks, has something happened? Come in and tell me why you're so flushed."

"Something? Oh, yes." Dreamily, Becky swept over to the armchair and drifted into it, as graceful as a leaf in a gentle autumn breeze.

Sophie pulled the desk chair to sit across from her sister-in-law. "It appears it's time for another of our midnight confidences."

"Do you promise you won't tell a soul? *Promise?*"

"Of course, Becks."

Becky clasped her pale hands together and held them before her chin. "It has happened, Sophie. I can scarcely believe it, but it has happened. I am well and truly in love."

Nooooo! Not Becky, not her bookish, intelligent,

prudent sister-in-law! Surely not so soon after her arrival in London.

Sophie gazed unflinchingly at her. "Truly?"

"Yes." Becky lifted shining blue eyes to Sophie. "It is true. I've never been happier."

It was Mr. Fisk. Sophie knew it had to be him. He had merely smiled at Becky, complimented her, perhaps stolen a touch or two, and—God forbid—a kiss, and now it was clear: His attentions had annihilated Becky's sensible nature.

Sophie took a deep, fortifying breath. "This is very exciting. Now you must confide in me. Who is the recipient of your affection?"

Becky stared at Sophie for a long moment, then said in a whisper, "Do you truly promise, Sophie?"

"I promise."

"It is Mr. Fisk."

Sophie tried to look surprised, but couldn't seem to find the strength.

"Did you know?" Aghast, Becky pressed a hand to her chest.

Sophie tilted her lips in what she feared was a skeletal smile. "Alas, I did suspect it."

The younger woman's eyes widened into deep blue pools. "Have I been so obvious?"

"It's—difficult for anyone to hide strong feeling for another." Sophie nearly cringed, thinking of her own reaction before Tristan had left London.

Becky bowed her head. "Oh, Lord. I have been a besotted fool, haven't I? I tried to hide it from everyone, Sophie, most of all from myself. But now I know there is no sense in hiding it, for I love him. And," she whispered, leaning closer, "he loves me, too."

Sophie bit down hard on the inside of her cheek. What a coup it would be for Mr. Fisk to win Garrett's well-dowered, immensely beautiful sister. It would link him to their family forever.

Sophie would fight this to her last breath. But how to convince this inexperienced dreamer of a girl to fall out of love with the vile, conniving man?

"Has he touched you?"

Becky's flush deepened, and Sophie's heart tapped frenetically against her breast. This was all her fault. She'd been too distracted by her own problems. She'd been too confident in Becky's innate good sense, and she hadn't protected her sister-in-law as she should have.

"You can tell me, Becky."

Becky licked her lips. "He kissed me," she breathed. "And . . . touched me."

Sophie's eyelids sank like lead weights, but she pried them upward. "Oh, Becks. That was a foolish thing to do."

Becky's lips tightened. "I love him, and I wanted him to touch me." She gazed at Sophie as if that fact surprised her. "I wanted him to."

Sophie held out her hand, and the girl reached out and took it. They squeezed each other's hands tightly for a few moments, then Sophie took a deep breath and forged ahead.

"I understand what it's like to want to be touched by a man, dearest."

"I know you do," Becky whispered. "I remember when I was just a small girl, I saw my brother escape the house in the middle of the night so he could be with you. He wouldn't have if you hadn't desired it."

It was true. In anyone's eyes, Sophie had behaved like a young fool. But Garrett hadn't completely compromised her. He was too honorable to take advantage of her in such a way. They'd kissed, they'd touched, and they'd driven each other mad with wanting. But as much as they'd wished to consummate their love for each other, he insisted they wait until marriage. That was why he'd often brought Tristan with him to be their chaperone.

Mr. Fisk wouldn't be so honorable—Sophie knew it to her soul. But how could she convince Becky that Mr. Fisk wasn't honorable, whereas Garrett was? Everything the girl had seen since her arrival in London proved otherwise. Becky was terrified of Garrett, and Mr. Fisk had been the one to provide her solace.

Her only hope was honesty. She squeezed Becky's hand tighter. "I don't know much about Mr. Fisk, and I agree with you, he's very charming indeed. But, Becky, he behaves like that toward everyone. None of us knows who the real Mr. Fisk is."

"He doesn't kiss everyone."

"True," Sophie said, "but dearest, you're not unaware of your fortune. You know that men of lesser scruples would not hesitate to ruin you just for a chance at your inheritance."

"Mr. Fisk would never do that." Smug confidence laced Becky's voice. "He is the sincerest man I know. A man of principle."

Oh, Lord. Sophie inwardly rolled her eyes heavenward. "Can we be certain of that?"

Becky gently pulled her hand away from Sophie's. "I

am. Truly, Sophie, when you feel for someone as deeply as I feel for Mr. Fisk, you simply *know* what's inside his soul. And what I see in Mr. Fisk is a true gentleman. Kind, caring, handsome. What he desires above all is not my fortune, for he already possesses one of his own. All he wants is to make me the happiest woman in the world."

This had gone even farther than she'd thought. "Did he say that to you?"

"Yes, he did. He even loves my interest in reading and philosophy. Do you know we've begun to read Plutarch together?"

"You said he possesses a fortune?" Sophie asked, frowning. That didn't sound right. She'd always imagined Mr. Fisk as one of those impoverished gentlemen who subsisted off the generosity of others.

"Two thousand a year," Becky said proudly. "With my three thousand, we shall have a tidy income." She leaned forward. "In truth, Sophie, I require nothing of the grand living you and my brother enjoy. I only need the simplest of comforts—a roof over my head. A husband who cherishes me."

Two thousand a year? Could it be true? Would he descend so low as to lie to Becky about something like this? "Have you spoken with your brother?"

"Oh, no! You know I wouldn't approach Garrett." She shuddered. "He frightens me so."

"And what about Mr. Fisk?"

"He plans to ask for my hand in marriage soon. He's hoping to do it before the duke fully descends into madness."

Sophie's blood instantly heated to a boil. "I've explained this to you already, Becks. Garrett isn't mad. Nor is he descending into madness. He's perfectly sane, I assure you."

Becky sighed and gave her hands a sympathetic squeeze. "I do understand how you only want to think the best of him. It is natural, considering he is your husband. Nobody wants a husband who is insane, I'm sure. But you must face the fact, because it is true. All of London is aware of his condition. Everyone knows he's on the road to lunacy."

"How do you know this?"

"I have school friends in London, you know. And Mr. Fisk tells me everything."

Tamping down her frustration, Sophie leaned back in her chair, regarding the flushed beauty sitting before her. She changed the subject. "Tell me, Becky. Are you so very sure Mr. Fisk is the one you want?"

"I'm absolutely sure."

"You've hardly given any other eligible gentlemen a chance. The Season has hardly begun."

"Oh, they won't want me now," Becky said matter-of-factly.

"What do you mean?"

"Of course they won't want me." Becky spoke patiently, as if Sophie were a dimwitted child. "Due to my brother's madness. Who wants to take a risk on the sister of the Mad Duke?"

Sophie ground her teeth. "I assume this theory has come from Mr. Fisk?"

"It doesn't matter," the girl announced, her tone serene. "I don't want any of them. I want only Mr. Fisk. *He* knows I am not mad."

Becky was so convinced of Mr. Fisk's undying affection, she was sanctimonious about it. Sophie would have to take stronger steps. Keep Becky and Mr. Fisk separated at all times. Explain the situation to Aunt Bertrice. Warn Garrett of the impending disaster.

She couldn't allow this to continue. But there was no reasoning with Becky. The girl was hopelessly besotted.

"Promise me one thing," she said softly.

"What's that?" Becky asked.

"Don't give yourself to him. Becky, please wait until your wedding night."

Becky smiled and laughed softly. But she didn't promise.

Chapter Sixteen

Relief rushed over Sophie when she saw the light coming from beneath Garrett's bedchamber door. He was still awake, thank God.

She knocked and heard his gruff voice in response. "Come in."

Pushing open the door, she began, "I'm sorry to interrupt—"

She broke off abruptly. Garrett rose from his back to a seated position on the carpet, his face flushed. His shirt was open at the neck, revealing a hint of his broad, bronzed chest. He smiled at her. A real smile, not one of the forced ones he normally gave. It took focus away from the angry scar on his forehead. It was handsome enough to strip away her defenses.

"What on earth are you doing?"

"I . . . ah . . . well, I was exercising." His gaze lowered to his bare feet, and his toes curled into the plush maroon strands. "I find it to be . . . invigorating after the long days of inactivity."

"I understand," she said softly. Tristan had often complained of feelings of lassitude brought about by such inactivity—that was why he'd taken to daily alternating vigorous riding with boxing at Jackson's.

Garrett rose to his feet and took a step toward her. "I'm glad you came."

The look in his eyes said he thought she'd come for an entirely different reason than she had. She'd need to nip that in the bud right away. "There's something very important I need to discuss with you."

Instantly, lines of concern creased across his forehead. "What is it? Has something happened?"

"Yes." He opened his mouth to speak again, but she motioned to an armchair. "May I sit down, Garrett?"

"Please."

She crossed the room and lowered herself on the edge of one of the chairs. It always felt odd to be in this room alone with Garrett, when it elicited such vivid memories of Tristan.

Yet Tristan's essence had vanished from the place. It smelled solely of Garrett now, of his musky, almond scent. And though he hadn't changed the furnishings, they now looked more a part of him than of Tristan.

She took a deep breath and glanced up at Garrett. He had sat opposite her and gazed at her in concern.

"What is it, Sophie?"

"It's about Mr. Fisk."

Garrett seemed to relax a little. "I see."

"Is it true he has two thousand a year?" she blurted.

He looked surprised but quickly recovered. "Yes, he does."

"Where does it come from?"

"An estate outside Leeds, left him by his uncle. But soon he shall have far more than two thousand a year. I intend to add another four thousand to his income."

"What?" she gasped. Perhaps her husband had gone mad after all.

"He deserves it. For liberating me from my reduced circumstances." He cocked an eyebrow at her. "Wouldn't you agree?"

She wasn't so certain. To her, it sounded like highway robbery. On the other hand, a part of her understood Garrett's logic . . . as illogical as it was.

"Does he know of this?"

"Yes, I told him today. That sum takes into account his continued services as well. He'll continue to manage all of my assets, including Calton House."

Sophie swayed in her chair, gasping for breath. She clutched the arms to steady herself. "Garrett, what—how—?"

He shrugged, his face relaxed. "I trust William Fisk implicitly. The work is too much for me to manage alone. I have more pressing problems to worry about." He looked directly at her, piercing her with the icy blue of his eyes.

"Garrett . . ." She tried to stifle the urge to whimper in despair. What had he done? Handed control of his fortune, of everything Tristan had worked so hard to build for him, to a dishonest man who had already compromised his sister?

"He saved my *life*, Sophie," Garrett said in a low voice.

"He gave me my life back. I will forever be indebted to him for that."

Sophie pressed a shaky hand to her forehead.

"What's wrong? I'm not abandoning my fortune, just assigning Fisk to manage it. He will only help me to build it, I promise you."

Sophie rubbed her temple. First Becky and now Garrett. Either they had both lost their minds or she and Tristan had. She thought back, running through her conversations with Tristan, and through all her past encounters with Mr. Fisk.

Truly, she had disliked him from the moment she'd seen him looking at her naked body tied to the bed. Logic told her it wasn't his fault he had witnessed that scene, and she'd tried to forgive him for that, as much as her instincts screamed in protest.

He'd never done anything blatantly wrong. He made her and Tristan wary, but that wasn't enough of a reason to accuse him of the offenses she had already accused him of in her mind.

Perhaps he *was* truly, madly in love with Becky, and perhaps he did respect and ultimately support Garrett as much as he pretended to.

"Becky wants to marry him," she said abruptly.

Garrett smiled. "I thought that might be the case."

"She says it's what Mr. Fisk wants as well."

"Then it sounds like a perfect match to me."

Sophie's chest tightened. She was ready to weep with frustration. "I disapprove," she said stiffly. "I don't think it's a perfect match."

"Who do you see for Rebecca, Sophie? Nobody

will want her now that my inevitable madness is public knowledge."

It seemed Mr. Fisk had gotten to him, too. Sophie jumped to her feet, her anger bubbling over. "You're not mad."

He looked up at her with the same sympathetic gaze Becky had. As if to say, *Poor, deluded Sophie. Thinking there's hope where there isn't any.*

"I am, Sophie. We might as well face the facts. Fisk and I have already started planning for the future."

"No," she gasped, staring at him.

Slowly, he rose, his palms held out to her in a calming gesture. "Yes. I can't control it, and I ultimately can't control myself, and there's no cure. There *will* be a time when I lose all my faculties. Permanently. I need to make sure you and Miranda are well provided for."

Garrett was not mad. He wasn't. He couldn't be. Only one doctor—a doctor she didn't like and trusted even less—had made this ridiculous diagnosis.

"I want you to see another doctor. You must hear a second opinion."

Garrett paused. "Of course. If that is what you wish."

"Thank you."

"But it'll just be a waste of time. Based on your suspicions, I asked Fisk to obtain MacAllister's credentials. He is the most prominent specialist of psychology in this country." His face gentled, and his eyes filled with compassion. "I've accepted the truth, Sophie. Why can't you?"

She turned away from him and covered her ears like a child. "Stop it. Just stop."

He came up behind her. His hard chest pressed into

her back and his warmth spread through her. Slowly, he pried her hands from her ears, then held her pinned in front of him. "Listen to me. If—*when* that day comes, I want you to have me confined. I won't be a burden to you and Miranda. When that happens," he paused for a moment, then finished in a low voice, "I want you to go back to Tristan."

She felt sick.

"Until that day, I want you to promise you will be mine."

No, no, no. Stop it, stop it!

"But we need to take precautions. I don't want to hurt you, and if I should fall into one of my fits while I am alone with you, my pistol is in the oriental cabinet in the dressing room. I want you to—"

"Stop," she groaned.

He pressed a kiss against the top of her head. "Yes. I'll stop. There's no need to dwell on the future. I want to live for the present."

His hands slid up her arms, skimming beneath the sleeves of her robe and nightdress. Still callused from his toils on the farm, his fingertips rasped gently over her skin. He lowered his head farther, and his breath danced over her earlobe.

"Let me make the most of the time I have left. Let me make love to you."

Sophie couldn't bring herself to speak, so she leaned against him, tucking herself deeper into his embrace.

His lips grazed the shell of her ear, and she shuddered.

"Sophie." His voice caressed her, slid under her skin, stroked her soul.

He reached down to untie the sash on her robe, then spread it open and pushed it off her shoulders. It puddled on the floor. Slowly, he raised his hands back to her shoulders and turned her around to face him.

She looked up at him. The scar on his forehead was a lurid reminder of all the pain he'd suffered, but besides the scar and the tiny lines around his eyes and mouth, he looked the same. Strong jaw and masculine, aristocratic nose. Stormy blue eyes. The small cleft in his chin, the burnished gold hair she loved to run her hands through.

She slipped her arms around his torso, clinging tight. For a long moment, they both stood still, and she reveled in the feel of their bodies pressed together. Garrett had been home for over a month, and this was the first time they'd simply held each other.

Sophie breathed deeply of him. He smelled of the almond soap she'd used to clean his hair on the day she'd helped him bathe. It seemed like an age had passed since then.

His hands slid up to cup her cheeks and then he lowered his lips to hers. Softly, he nudged against her until she opened for him, and their mouths began a smooth, sensual glide. Sophie bunched his shirt in her fists.

Still kissing her, he dropped one of his arms and reached behind him, finding her hand and lacing her fingers with his own. Finally, he pulled away and led her to the bed.

The bed she'd shared with Tristan.

Trembling from head to toe, she pushed away the thought. Before Tristan, this bed had belonged to her alone, and before that, to Garrett and her. Miranda had been conceived in it shortly before Garrett had left for Brussels.

He helped her climb up the steps. She slid under the blankets, and he tucked them around her. Looking down at her lovingly, he brushed a knuckle over her cheek. "I'll extinguish the lamp."

She nodded, and he strode toward the table between the two armchairs, his figure casting long shadows across the floor. With his back to her, he pulled his shirt over his head and laid it neatly over the arm of one of the chairs. Then he leaned forward and the light slipped away. Only the embers of the fire kept the room from descending into complete blackness. Sophie watched Garrett's silhouette as he pushed his trousers down his hips. In the shadows, she saw the curve of his buttocks and the flex of muscle as they slid down his legs.

Completely naked, he walked to the other side of the bed and climbed in, settling beneath the covers beside her. For a long moment he lay still, not touching her. Then with a soft moan he turned and gathered her into his body.

She held him close, pressing her cheek against the taut skin of his chest. His growing arousal nudged at her thigh.

"I've imagined this moment for a long time," he murmured.

She stroked his chest, in awe of the power simmering just beneath his skin. He was so big, all muscle and sinew.

His hand moved up and down her back, sliding the cotton nightdress over her skin. Snagging its hem, he hiked it upward, his rough fingers skimming her leg. She shivered.

"Are you cold?"

"No," she breathed.

He tugged the fabric higher, and the heat of his erection, now rock hard, pressed against her thigh, skin to skin. Unable to resist the compulsion, she slid her hand between them and fluttered her fingers over his shaft.

"Sophie . . ." He buried his face in her hair. His body was alive, thrumming against her, on fire. Her fingertips traversed his steely length, adding pressure as she relearned the shape and texture of him.

"Does that feel good?" she murmured.

"Yesss," he hissed into her scalp.

His grip tightened over her hip, then moved lower, and she allowed her thighs to fall open to his questing hand. He stroked the insides of her legs, nearing her center, teasing her by coming close then stroking away as she continued to slide her hand up and down his erection.

She curled her fingers around him, squeezing and pulling in short jerks. He sucked in his breath and finally gave her what she needed. He cupped her mound, adding just enough pressure to make her squirm with desire. His fingers delved between the lips of her sex, sliding easily through the silky fluid of her arousal.

He explored her as if he'd never felt this part of a woman, staring at her, his eyes dark with wonder. His fingers circled her, caressed her, teased her, made all thoughts of anything but the man lying beside her dissipate, then flow out of her mind altogether.

"I want you inside me," she gasped.

In one smooth motion, he moved over her, his big body

wedged between her legs, his torso towering above her. He stared down at her, searching her face, studying her.

"Say it again, Sophie."

She raised her hands to cup his big shoulders, then slid them down to circle his flat nipples with her fingertips. He sucked in a breath.

He lowered his head to feather his lips over her cheek, across her forehead, down the ridge of her nose and finally to her mouth. "Say it again," he whispered in a soft brush of air against her lips.

She curled her legs around his big body, tilting her hips in invitation.

"I want you inside me." She punctuated every word in the silence, and they seemed to hover between them for a long moment before he was able to take them in, understand and believe.

He adjusted his body, and she reached down to guide him to her entrance.

He paused there for an indeterminate amount of time, his body shaking over hers, his breath coming in gasps. She knew he was fighting for control, and a part of her wanted to command him to let it go and lose himself within her, to explain that she could take whatever he could give.

But it was important to him not to lose control. To stay in complete charge of his faculties, to prove to himself that he could retain his humanity.

Finally, he pushed into her, inch by excruciating inch, making all her nerve endings scream with delight each time he made a movement, no matter how slight.

She wrapped her arms around him and murmured, "Yes, yes, yes," at the exquisite invasion. He was so strong, so beautiful, inside and out. She wished he'd see his own perfection rather than constantly thinking the worst.

Finally he was seated all the way inside. He released a long sigh.

Though his body pinned her in place, she squirmed, desperate for him to move.

"God, Sophie." He shook from head to foot with restraint. "Oh, God."

She let out a choked sob. "Please move. Please, Garrett."

He complied, dragging out of her, then thrusting in again, faster this time, the glide of his rigid flesh against her sensitive inner walls making her cry out.

She closed her eyes. Her head lolled back on the pillow as she felt him tense and tighten all around her. In her. She expected him to come, but he didn't. He kept driving into her, driving her upward, pressing against the sensitive area above where their bodies connected, until her peak came. It rushed through her in a shock of sensation, causing her limbs to shudder and her channel to clench hard and ripple around him.

Suspended over her, he froze. Then with a groan he withdrew, turning her over and drawing her up on her hands and knees. He slid into her again, and Sophie gasped. He thrust into her hard, once, twice. Over and over again, Sophie rode the wave of pleasure, cresting and receding with each plunge he took deep inside her. Time meant nothing—it was all red-hot, tingling, exquisite pleasure.

Then his hands tightened around her waist, and he stilled with his shaft lodged deep inside, shaking and groaning as his seed gushed into her in a hot rush. He pressed her down onto her belly, then left her, adjusting into a comfortable position at her side.

She turned over and reached up to tangle her hands in his hair, pulling his head toward hers to give him a soft kiss on the lips.

"Thank you," he whispered.

Silently, she kissed him again, slipped her arms around his torso, and held him close.

Sophie had neglected her little garden for the past few months, but now that summer approached, her rose-bushes had begun to bloom. She liked the stark contrast of red and white, and in her garden there were no pinks or peaches or yellows. Red alternated with white in a checkerboard pattern, and she drifted through the bushes, creating bouquets for the breakfast room and entry hall. Tristan had loved how the smell of roses permeated the house in spring and summer. He always said their fragrance reminded him of her.

Becky and Aunt Bertrice were out making calls in anticipation of Becky's presentation at court tomorrow, and Miranda and Gary were at the park with Miss Dalworthy. After having watched over her sister-in-law's every move for the past few days, Sophie was glad to have some time alone. She almost wished Garrett had kept his henchmen so she could post one at Becky's door at night. It was nighttime she feared the most when it came to Fisk's manipulations, but aside from commanding Becky to sleep beside her, she didn't know what to do.

At any rate, Becky couldn't sleep beside her. Not since she'd moved back to the master's bedchamber to sleep with Garrett.

Smiling at the memory of their gentle lovemaking last night, she knelt beside a plant to cut off a dead stem. Her monthly courses had arrived right on schedule this morning, but for the first time in her married life she didn't suffer a pang of sadness for yet another month of barrenness. If she had found herself with child, she wouldn't have had the first idea who the father was. As much as she longed for another baby, the thought of the further rift that might cause between Tristan and Garrett sent a tremor of panic down her spine.

She was reaching toward another dead stem when the crunch of gravel alerted her someone was approaching.

"Sophie."

She turned, brushing a wisp of hair out of her face, squinting up at the dark figure haloed by the sun. She shielded the rim of her bonnet to see him better, and he held out his hand to help her up.

"My hands are dirty, Garrett. I don't want to soil your gloves."

He chuckled, a low reverberating sound that warmed her body from head to toe. "They'll wash."

She reached out and grasped his hand, allowing him to pull her close to his body. She was dirty, and he was dressed in a handsome striped waistcoat that accentuated his broad, masculine form. His free arm curved around her waist. "Not enough room to waltz," he murmured.

"Mmm," she responded. "I'm too dirty to waltz."

"Later, then."

"All right." Her voice was hardly a whisper. She squeezed her eyes shut, trying not to think about Tristan and how he held her. How different it felt to be in his arms. How empty she felt knowing he was so far away.

Garrett's grasp on her tightened. "I've come to tell you Fisk has formally asked me for Rebecca's hand in marriage."

She wrenched herself away and stepped back so she could see into his face. "What did you say?" she asked breathlessly.

"I gave him my approval."

"Garrett, no!"

Suddenly, the ache she felt for Tristan intensified into a pulsing pain. Tristan would help her fix this problem. He'd listen to her concerns and work with her toward a solution.

Garrett closed the distance between them. "Come, Sophie. I know you're not overfond of Fisk, but you told me yourself that Rebecca is in love with him. And he assures me the feeling is mutual. What better way to bring Fisk into our family than for him to marry my sister?"

"I don't want William Fisk in our family." She sounded petulant. More childish than her own daughter.

"But why? He's responsible for me having my life back. He's responsible for me finding you again. It's not possible to repay him enough."

"No doubt he believes that as well."

He frowned at her. "No, he doesn't. In fact, besides Rebecca's hand, he's asked me for nothing."

Of course he hadn't asked Garrett for anything. He hadn't needed to. He'd slithered his way into Garrett's affections, and once he discovered the duke's honorable, generous nature, had proceeded to take advantage of him. And now he held control of Garrett's fortune and was about to marry his sister.

"You will learn to trust him in time." Garrett's face

darkened, and the scar on his forehead flushed to a deep red. "You aren't being fair to him, Sophie. You didn't meet under the most auspicious circumstances. You can't blame him for that."

Sophie's cheeks heated, but she didn't break her gaze from Garrett's. "I can't," she conceded. "And I don't." She clasped her hands in front of her to prevent them from flying up in frustration. She had nothing—no proof. Only her innate distrust . . . and Tristan's.

Garrett clasped her shoulders, pulled her forward, and pressed his lips to the top of her head. "I have no wish for more dissension between us."

"I don't want that either," she whispered, forcing her hands to drop to her sides.

"Rebecca is very young. She'll need your continued love and support."

"She will have it," Sophie said.

He pulled back, and a ghost of a smile curved his lips. "There's some business I need to attend, but we'll be home by dinnertime. We can discuss the marriage further then. Fisk would like to apply for a special license as soon as possible."

She exhaled, her breath coming out in a wisp of nerves. "Why the haste?"

"Why not? The young people are eager to get it done."

"She's a duke's daughter, Garrett. This will take planning—months, perhaps. We must select the wedding party, and plan for the festivities . . ."

Please, oh, please, she prayed. *Keep them from rushing into this . . .*

"We'll discuss it tonight, my love." He smiled somberly. "My only concern is my own health. I should like to see my sister and friend marry before I—"

She quickly interrupted him. "Is Mr. Fisk going with you this afternoon?"

"Yes, he is."

Sophie forced herself to smile and nod at him like the complacent, accepting wife she'd once been. "I'll see you at dinner, then."

He kissed her, just a brush of lips, and turned away. Sophie watched him as he rounded the corner of the house and disappeared.

Everyone had gone from the house. It was Connor and Delia's day off. For the first time in weeks, she had a few hours completely to herself—a few hours to search for proof that William Fisk wasn't the man he pretended to be.

Chapter Seventeen

It had rained intermittently every day, but Tristan doggedly rode onward, spurred by the information he'd unearthed in London. Arriving at dusk last night, he'd found the King's Arms, an inn on the Warwick road near Kenilworth Castle. He'd spent most of the night in the downstairs tavern, loosening the locals' tongues with whiskey and ale.

They were twins, after all. William and Warren Fisk. Apparently Warren died in battle, and the villagers all believed William had died of infection shortly thereafter.

Restless with the information he'd learned, Tristan tossed and turned on the lumpy mattress for a few hours before awakening to a quick breakfast and a ride in the misty morning a few miles past the castle to the ramshackle manor of the Marquis of Debussey. According to the townsfolk, the marquis had always been reclusive, but since his marchioness died five years ago, he hadn't left the house at all.

In the Tudor style, the house was built of timber, with crossbeams of a dark gray over whitewashed walls. A single plume of smoke curled lazily from one of the three visible chimneys. No servants rushed out to greet Tristan as he dismounted and tethered his horse to a post in the overgrown lawn. Removing his hat, he approached the house. Unpolished brass lions stood on low pedestals flanking the entryway. Tristan mounted the marble steps and stopped at the door. He raised the heavy brass knocker and let it fall onto the dark wood planks. A clap of noise echoed inside.

Nobody answered.

He banged the knocker against the door three more times, but still he was ignored. Sighing, he clapped his hat under his arm and stepped off the landing.

A still, foul-smelling lake bordered one side of the estate, so Tristan rounded the opposite corner and took the overgrown path along the edge of the house. Within moments, his trousers were wet to the knees. He skirted mud puddles, passed windows covered by heavy draperies. When he'd gone about half the length of the building, he came across another door. This one was larger than the other and deep within an arched alcove. And it was open a crack.

For good measure, he knocked again, this time using his knuckles. Again, no one responded. After waiting a few moments, he pushed the door wide to a small, cheerless anteroom branching into a hall. He chose to take the path leading toward the muffled sounds of voices filtering from a room at the end of the stark corridor. As he approached, he smelled baking bread and realized he must be heading toward the kitchens.

Perfect.

He paused for a moment outside, listening to the feminine chatter within. Then he opened the door.

One of the women squealed; another pressed her flour-covered hand to her mouth to stop a scream. A third, the eldest woman in the room, who sat on a chair in the corner mending a pair of trousers, just looked at him with uncannily familiar calm brown eyes. An older, feminine version of William Fisk. The "dead" mother.

"Sorry for the interruption," he said mildly. "There was no response to my knock."

The younger women looked toward the older one, clearly deferring to her. Carefully, she set the trousers aside, taking the time to fold them neatly over the arm of her chair. She finally rose. "We didn't hear you, sir."

He didn't believe that.

"Regardless," she continued, "Lord Debussey isn't at home to visitors."

"Oh, that's quite all right, ma'am," Tristan said smoothly. "I'm not here to see Lord Debussey. I'm here to see you."

After an hour spent searching Garrett's study, Sophie realized it was useless. If Fisk had engaged in nefarious behavior, he didn't keep a record of it under Garrett's nose. Every bill and receipt, and every note of correspondence appeared legitimate.

The only place she hadn't yet explored was the small locked drawer in Garrett's desk, but she only had one guess about where he might keep the key. She pushed a chair over to the window, kicked off her half-boots and, teetering on the velvet cushion, ran her fingertips along the top of the wooden casing.

Her lips softened into a smile when her fingers brushed against metal. Tristan had kept the drawer unlocked, the key in a pouch inside. But this had been Garrett's hiding place before he went to war so long ago.

Grasping the key, she jumped off the chair and hurried over to the desk without bothering to slip on her boots. The lock had been recently oiled and turned easily. She pulled the drawer open.

Its only contents were a sheaf of papers, and she took them out, closing the drawer and setting them on the desk. On the top were her and Garrett's original marriage documents, signed by the clergyman who'd married them in the chapel near Calton House.

Beneath that were the documents pertaining to the court's decision of nullity regarding her marriage to Tristan. Her heart aching, she set those aside.

The remaining papers were letters addressed to her. She withdrew them and flipped quickly through. She didn't have time to read them now, but Garrett must've seen something he considered suspicious—probably just silly gossip or innuendo—to have kept them from her.

Carefully, she set the papers back in the drawer and turned the key in the lock. As she replaced the key on the window casing, she realized there was only one more place to look for condemning information on Fisk. His bedchamber. The mere thought of entering the man's personal domain sent waves of dread coursing through her.

After returning everything to its place in the study, she slipped out the door. The house was quiet—Mrs. Krum was in the kitchen going over the month's menu.

The footmen, free to dally when both Connor and the duke weren't at home, were outside basking in the sun.

Holding her half-boots in her hand so they wouldn't tap against the wood floor, Sophie tiptoed up the stairs in stockinged feet. Fisk's room was just across the corridor and down from the bedchamber she shared with Garrett. After taking a second to fortify herself, she pushed open the door.

She hadn't entered this room since before Fisk and Garrett had arrived in London. Garrett's ancestors had named it the Lavender Room, but in her memory it had never been decorated in purple and bore no traces of a lavender scent. In fact, it smelled faintly of alcohol. She found the source of the smell right away—an open crystal decanter of brandy sat burrowed between piles of documents on the top shelf of the escritoire. Odd, since she knew Fisk never drank the stuff.

She stepped inside and turned slowly, taking in the surroundings. She knew the room well and had decorated it with velvets and silks of deep burgundy just a year ago, but Fisk had placed his own stamp upon the place. It seemed he planned to stay indefinitely, for there was no sign of luggage to indicate he was a mere visitor. He'd re-covered the bed and replaced the draperies with a smart set of striped gray and brown damask with matching bolsters and pillows. There was even a small case full of books beside the escritoire. Moving into the closet, she saw that its shelves were brimming with clothing, most of it crisp and with the appearance of being brand new.

She turned back to the escritoire. Papers were jammed into each of the pigeonhole openings below the shelf. It would take hours of painstaking work to go through all of them and replace them exactly as she had found them. Why on earth did Fisk need so many documents to begin with? It struck her as excessive.

With a sigh, she lowered herself before the escritoire, which, like Garrett's, possessed a locking drawer. Tugging on it, she discovered that it was, of course, locked. She kept one key in the drawer for the use of the room's occupant. But Fisk didn't know she kept a spare in her personal cabinet in Garrett's room in the event this one was lost.

She quietly slipped down the hall and fetched the key, returning to the room just as she heard a creak from the direction of the stairwell. Someone was coming up. Quickly, she shut Fisk's door behind her and leaned against it, her heart pounding. It would be an embarrassment to be caught, even by one of the servants. After a few breathless moments, the footsteps, accompanied by a feminine hum, passed outside. Just one of the chambermaids going about her duties.

When the sounds receded, Sophie rushed to the escritoire. Her hand trembling, she thrust the key into the lock.

Well, Fisk hadn't thought everything through. He hadn't changed the lock. It turned, and she opened the drawer.

Inside was a large stack of bills and receipts. She carefully pulled them out, mindful of keeping them in the proper order. The receipts were for varying large sums and included notations of what they were for.

New doors for Calton House, the previous doors being rotted beyond repair.

New windows for Calton House, the current casings being rotted beyond repair.

Rotting doors and windows at Calton House? The receipts were dated last week. That didn't make sense—Tristan had issued the funds to repair the aging doors and windows just last year.

Recompense to Dr. Labreque of Ligny, for his efforts in saving the life of the Duke of Calton.

The doctor's sum was quite large, Sophie thought. A hundred times more than the amount she'd ever paid any doctor.

Gerard Lebeck for repayment of the debts incurred by Garrett James, Duke of Calton.

Payment to Mr. George Dewitt, Gardener of Calton House, for the purchase of seed due to the extensive damage of grounds from winter storm striking on February 7.

Investment in bank stock.

Payment to Joelle Martin.

Sophie's fingers stilled as she gazed at the receipt. A huge sum to Joelle Martin.

Sophie swallowed, remembering the night he'd thought she was Joelle. Why was Garrett paying her? For what? Her chest tight, she thrust it aside and read on. Some of these couldn't be real. There were several other references to debts she was certain Tristan had already paid. So many receipts for so many things—they must add up to two or three thousand pounds.

Two thousand a year—Fisk's income. Garrett said it came from an estate in Leeds, but what if it was all a lie, and he was embezzling the funds instead?

Sophie's flesh felt cold, but beads of sweat broke out on her forehead. Trying to keep her hands from shaking, she reordered the receipts and stacked them back inside the drawer.

The door creaked.

Sophie swung her head, and her gaze crashed into William Fisk's cool brown eyes, surveying her with her hands in his private papers.

"Good afternoon, Your Grace," he said politely.

When their meeting with Ansley concluded early, Garrett chose not to return home with Fisk in the carriage—instead he strode toward Hyde Park. Maybe there he'd see his daughter—she and Gary weren't due to return home for another hour or so.

He passed Apsley House, the residence of the Duke of Wellington, field marshal at Waterloo. He stared up at the colossal black statue marking the entrance to the park. Achilles holding his shield and looking heavenward after having just defeated Hector. Garrett didn't remember a monument here, and looking closer, he saw why. It was dedicated to Wellington and "his companions in arms" and was made from metal melted from cannon used at various battles, including Waterloo.

Something coursed through him, some residue of pride for his country, for his own regiment that had fought so bravely on the Continent. After a long, silent moment, Garrett tore his eyes from the statue and entered through the gate to Hyde Park.

Immediately, memories slammed into him. The daily walks with Sophie in the days before he left for Belgium. Forbidding her to travel with him to the Continent as so many other officers' wives had. He'd commanded her to stay home, where he knew she'd be safe. He didn't trust her not to run into danger at the least sign he was in any kind of trouble. He hadn't needed the distraction.

She'd agreed to stay without argument, and he was glad for it even now. If she'd gone, the strain of Waterloo might have endangered their daughter.

Would she agree to his demands so docilely now?

Absolutely not. His wife had changed, matured, become more independent. More intractable.

She'd told him that after he'd gone missing in battle, Tristan had wanted her to stay in England while he went to the Continent to look for Garrett. She had agreed, but only until her lying-in was over. When Miranda was an infant, Sophie joined him to continue the search. It seemed unbelievable, but they'd never found a sign of him.

All the while, he'd been right under their noses. It was almost as if someone had been deliberately trying to hide him.

He walked along the path bordering the Serpentine, using his cane like a true gentleman, though it still felt odd. If people recognized him, they didn't approach him. It was likely they worried he might literally bite their heads off. Monster that he was.

The paths were crowded this afternoon due to the fineness of the weather, and it looked as if they were preparing for a festival of some sort, or perhaps a swimming match, for there were buoys topped with flags placed at specific intervals in the water, and several official-looking boats scattered across the river. Seeing no sign of the children, he turned deeper into the park. The path wound, and he turned again, this time down a deserted narrow trail leading into a small copse of trees.

"Well, ain't he a purty 'un?"

Garrett spun round to find two women standing just off the path, both dressed in garish orange and pink, their bosoms overflowing from their bodices.

He wasn't naïve. He knew what they were. He remembered their kind liked to dwell on the less frequently used walkways of Hyde Park, on the prowl for customers.

Embarrassed heat rose through his cheeks, and he gave a short bow. "Good afternoon, ladies. I was just passing through. Excuse me."

He turned to leave, but one of them grabbed his arm, her long, bony fingers curling over the sleeve of his coat. He looked down at his arm, and then at her, hoping he looked disdainfully aristocratic enough to scare her off.

No. He'd never be as good as Tristan at giving that look.

"Now, what's that, guv? You ain't seen whot we've got to offer, now have you?"

He sighed. "I've no interest in what you have to offer. I merely took a wrong turn."

The other one, a plumper, shorter girl with ratty blonde hair, tittered behind her hand. "He's quite the handsome gent, ain't he?" she murmured when she'd stopped laughing, and compassion seeped into her tone. "Where'd you get that awful scar, though, guv?"

He looked at her sharply. The sound of her voice was like velvet, and it reminded him of Joelle. Her smooth words whispering in his ear, flowing through him like warm honey. His body responded instantly, his cock hardening in a blink of an eye.

The whore brushed her hand over the front of his trousers. "Quite the *big* gent, he is, too," she said saucily, batting her eyelashes at him.

He yanked his arm from the unsuspecting woman's grasp and smacked her hand away. "Leave me alone, goddamn it," he growled.

They scattered like frightened rabbits, and he took off his hat and ran a weary hand through his hair. He couldn't blame them for being afraid. Hell, he shouldn't have frightened them. They weren't to blame.

He had simply taken out his disgust with himself on them. God, he despised himself for thinking carnally of another woman when he and Sophie were finally happy together. Or, he amended, back on the road toward happiness. They weren't there yet. Sophie didn't love him as freely as she once had. She smiled and made love to him and tried to cover her sadness, but she still often had a distant, dreamy look in her eyes, and he knew she was far away from him, thinking of Tristan.

A petty part of him wondered why he shouldn't be allowed to fantasize about other women when he knew his own wife was thinking of another man. But that wasn't fair. Tristan couldn't be compared to a whore. Even Joelle, who had been a source of comfort on many of Garrett's darkest nights, wasn't as imprinted into his life as Tristan was in Sophie's.

But the question remained, and it disturbed him to his core. Why were thoughts of Joelle making him hard when he was married to Sophie?

That had never happened before, when they were younger. Back then, she was the only one who could move him.

He looked up at the sky, wishing he had a timepiece with him. It must be nearing dinnertime. Banishing all thoughts of other women from his mind, he relaxed, anticipating a pleasant, quiet evening at home with his family. And Fisk, of course, who would be family soon enough.

Mrs. Fisk led Tristan into the abandoned service hall. The place was dusty from disuse, but she placidly informed him that since there were only four servants in Lord Debussey's household, the chances of them being interrupted were slim to none.

She motioned to a row of chairs lining the wall. "Please have a seat, sir."

He took the one closest to the window, ignoring the dust billowing around him as he sat.

She sat primly on the edge of the chair across from him, and then she simply gazed at him, her expression unreadable.

"Thank you for seeing me, Mrs. Fisk. I am Tristan James, Viscount Westcliff."

She pursed her lips. "You know my name."

"Indeed, ma'am. You bear a strong resemblance to your son."

She didn't move. Then she spoke, very slowly. "I look nothing like Reginald."

"Reginald? No ma'am. I was referring to William."

She stiffened even more. "William is deceased, my lord."

"Oh, but he isn't," Tristan said quietly. "His twin brother Warren perished at Waterloo, but William is still very much alive."

She just stared at him, unmoving, unblinking.

"Does that come as a surprise to you, ma'am?"

She blew out a breath through tight lips. "Sir, I beg you. I've only just recently come to terms with the death of my sons. Why are you doing this?"

All right, then. He took a different tack. "When did you hear of William's death?"

She gave a slight shake of her head.

"Please, ma'am. I believe your son is alive, and if that's the case, I might be able to help you reunite with him."

She gazed down at the black-and-white checkered pattern of the floor tiles. "I received one letter from Willy after the conflict stating the circumstances of Warren's death in very bitter terms. He mentioned the duke's regiment being disbanded, and said he was coming home. Two months later, I received a letter from a doctor and a death certificate stating he died from a pestilence he contracted on the battlefield."

"Your son wanted you to think him dead. Now why might that be, Mrs. Fisk?"

For the first time, her composure cracked. She looked up at him, her eyes glistening with unshed tears. "I—I couldn't say."

Because he was a social climber and didn't want the world to know his mama was the housekeeper of a reclusive bucolic lord, perhaps?

Mrs. Fisk had clearly taught her son well. Her bearing and language were such that she might under different circumstances easily be mistaken as a member of the aristocracy.

"I don't know why either, Mrs. Fisk." He gave her a small smile and tried to cheer her. "I assure you he is well, and living in London."

Unfortunately, he was also probably breaking the law. But how? Embezzling money from Garrett somehow? And Dr. MacAllister—was he involved, too? Were the two men in collusion?

The urge to leave this place, mount his horse, and ride straight back to London nearly overwhelmed him.

"It is . . . so good to hear he's alive." But Mrs. Fisk looked distraught, appalled. As she well might. What kind of son allowed his mother to think he was dead for almost eight years?

"Are you still in possession of that last letter he sent you, ma'am? And the doctor's letter?"

She gazed at him with confused dark eyes. "Why, yes, I am."

"I don't mean to intrude, but might I see them?"

"Of course." She rose abruptly. "I'll return shortly, my lord."

She withdrew, but paused in the corridor outside to speak to someone in low, urgent tones. After a moment, she threw her hands up and strode off, leaving a pale, slender young woman wearing the frilled cap of a chambermaid standing in the doorway.

"Is it true?" she asked in a low voice. "Is Willy alive?"

Tristan rose to greet the newcomer. "And you might be?"

She curtsied awkwardly as if she were unused to the action. "I'm sorry, my lord. My name is Katherine Fisk. I'm Willy's sister."

"I see." He paused. "Yes, Katherine. Your brother lives."

She clapped her hand to her heaving chest, and what little color she had drained from her face. When her mother told her the news, she clearly hadn't believed it, but when he had, the truth seemed to strike her like a lightning bolt.

She swayed, and he reached out to steady her. "Would you like to sit down?"

"Yes, sir," she said breathlessly. "I suppose I would."

He guided her to a chair, and she lowered herself into it, then clenched her hands in her lap. "I can't believe it. Willy's alive."

Tristan studied her. "Are you older or younger than William, Katherine?"

"Younger by five years, my lord."

"What do you remember of your brother?"

"Everything, sir."

"Tell me about him."

"Well, he and Warren were inseparable. Two peas in a pod, they were." She smiled fondly. "They were the stable boys here, back when there were horses. Nobody could tell them apart. They even tricked Mama sometimes."

"And where's your papa?"

"Oh." She frowned. "Well, he abandoned our mama when we were very small. That's why she was ever so grateful to Lord Debussey for taking us all in. Most employers wouldn't care for three little children, you know. But Lord Debussey, he didn't mind us so much. I think because his own wife was barren. And now we all have Reginald—"

Seeming to comprehend that she'd said too much, Katherine clamped her lips shut.

"I see," Tristan said. "So you have prospered with Lord Debussey?"

"Well, Mama's uncle was a baronet, you see, but we don't know them, because her own mama and papa disowned her for marrying our papa. And they were right in warning her off, it seems, weren't they?"

"Indeed," Tristan agreed dryly.

"But," Katherine continued, "though Mama always says the position of a housekeeper is below her breeding, she doesn't mind it so much. We were well-fed and Lord

Debussey and his wife were always very kind, even to the boys, who could be terrible scoundrels. When they were of age, Lord Debussey, who is a great patriot, my lord, gifted them with their commissions."

"That was generous of him." *Too generous.* There was definitely something more to that story.

She smiled. "Aye, it was. He's a generous man. That's why we've stayed on now that he is ill."

"Is he?"

"Yes, sir. They say it's a terrible disease that rots his lungs away. The doctor says he'll be truly blessed to survive the year."

"And what are your plans once Lord Debussey passes on?"

"The estate is to go to a distant cousin we've never seen nor met. But Mama says his lordship's set aside a pension for both of us and an income for Reggie."

"But what about William, Katherine? Do you have any idea why William would lie to you and your mama about his death?"

"No, sir." She shook her head. "But if Warren truly did perish in the war, Willy must've taken it very hard indeed."

"Warren died at Waterloo," Tristan said softly. "I'm sorry. I saw the record myself."

Katherine nodded. "It's a blessing from God, indeed, sir, to learn that one of my brothers is alive after thinking him dead for so long. Tell me, is he a great man of Town? Willy and Warren always used to strut about the grounds with sticks pretending they were the haughtiest dandies to ever walk down the streets of Mayfair." She grinned at him, her smile wide and striking, and at odds with the drab grayness of her attire. "Do tell me, sir. Is Willy a fine gentleman now?"

"Katherine." The sharp voice came from the doorway, and Tristan looked up to see Mrs. Fisk standing at the threshold holding the promised letters and giving her daughter a disapproving stare. Again he rose from his chair.

The young woman's gaze dropped to her feet. "Sorry, Mama."

"Leave us," Mrs. Fisk snapped.

Katherine stood and gave another awkward curtsy. "Pleasure to meet you, sir," she murmured before fleeing, her eyes downcast.

Mrs. Fisk closed the door, then stepped toward him, holding out the letters. "Here they are, my lord."

He took the packet and she returned to the seat across from him, gazing at him with those calm, expectant brown eyes.

"Mrs. Fisk," he said, "is it true your master purchased the commissions for your sons?"

She regarded him steadily. "Yes, sir."

"Quite a benevolent gift, Mrs. Fisk."

"It was."

"Why would a gentleman purchase army commissions for two of his servants?" Tristan tapped his chin in speculation. "Perhaps he was, in actuality, their father?"

She straightened, and her brown eyes bespoke defiance. "No indeed, sir, he was not. My eldest three children were legitimate, all of them."

"Then they must have done him a great, great service to deserve such a gift."

Her brown gaze narrowed. "I want to know more about my son."

"Anything I know, I will tell you."

She stared at him for a long moment before speaking again. "Very well, sir. It was not my sons who did him a great service. It was myself."

"Ah." Tristan paused. So she had sold her body to Lord Debussey for the purchase of her sons' commissions. An interesting exchange, one he'd never heard tell of before. Lord Debussey must have placed an inordinately high value on her "services."

"My father was a gentleman, my lord, and I assure you, my twins did not deserve to be tied to a life of servitude. They were astute, charming, handsome boys, born to be gentlemen. I would have done anything, *anything*, to ensure they had a future."

"I understand, Mrs. Fisk."

"Lord Debussey was in need of an heir. Unfortunately, I wasn't able to provide him with one before Lady Debussey passed on. By that time, he had honored his part of our contract. I am bound to him. For life."

Lowering himself into the chair, Tristan focused on the papers in his hand. Mrs. Fisk watched him silently as he skimmed the top page, which was a quite official-looking death certificate. At the bottom was a scrawl from a doctor adding his condolences. The next sheet was the letter from Fisk to his mother, dated just two days after the battle of Waterloo.

Dearest Mother,

Warren is dead. Shot to death by a man on our own side. We were on the walls of a château called Hougoumont, vulnerable to the enemy's onslaught.

Warren and I doubted the order to scale the wall put forth by our colonel, but as in service, one must always follow one's orders in the army, so we did as we were told. I was hesitant, but as you know, Warren was the less obstinate of the two of us, and he convinced me to follow the order, as madcap a scheme as it was.

My brother was shot in the back. He fell from the wall and died in my arms as the battle raged around us. Many other men in our regiment fell around us in a violent and despicable manner as the French set fire to the château and we cowered in the muddy garden, lambs to the slaughter, sacrifices to Wellington's grand victory.

Mutiny would have been a better choice, no doubt. I am alone in the world because of a vain, spoiled aristocrat who threw us into danger without a care. The colonel himself is missing and likely dead. I hope he is. I hope he burns in the fires of hell for what he has done to Warren and the other men.

The regiment is to be disbanded, and I will be selling my commission. I shall be home within a month's time.

Your Son,
William

Tristan stared at Fisk's angry script. He remembered the burned remains of Hougoumont. Weeks after Waterloo, he'd seen firsthand the château where Garrett had fiercely staved off wave after wave of French troops determined to breach the wall. If they'd succeeded, it would have put them in the perfect location to view Wellington's every move, greatly weakening the allied position.

His heart pounding, Tristan recalled the charred walls of the ruin. The bloodstains everywhere. The overwhelming evidence of death and destruction. At all costs, he'd avoided taking Sophie to the site when she arrived a few months later.

Tristan set the letter in his lap and flexed his stiff fingers. This wasn't the voice of the calm, conciliatory man Tristan had known in London. It was the voice of an angry, vengeful boy.

He glanced up at Fisk's mother. She was like him. Calm and determined. Both would go to any lengths to get what they wanted. And it seemed they wanted the same thing: Fisk's success in the world of men. Because of their distant link to the aristocracy, she had raised him to believe he was entitled to it.

"Please tell me about my son now, my lord." Despite her lack of rank, Mrs. Fisk's clear voice dripped with confidence. It wasn't surprising a man as quietly evil as Fisk had sprung from her womb.

As promised, Tristan told her everything he knew about Fisk. But he could not bring himself to say that after Fisk had spent the funds from his commission, he had become a blackguard and had likely achieved everything through extortion and embezzlement.

As he spoke his concern grew. Sophie could be in danger. The children. And perhaps Garrett himself, blind to Fisk's machinations, was most at risk.

When he had finished, a little towheaded boy ran

into the room and directly into Mrs. Fisk's arms, crying, "Mama, Mama!"

Young Reginald. Lord Debussey's son, no doubt. A bastard gifted him too late after his wife's death to be passed off as a legitimate heir. Tristan wondered if Fisk even knew he had another brother.

Later that afternoon, Tristan was on a horse riding hard for London.

Sophie slowly withdrew her hand from the drawer. She pushed the drawer shut and locked it, willing her hand not to shake, before she responded.

"Mr. Fisk. What a surprise."

"Yes," he said pleasantly. The look on his face was utterly emotionless.

He stepped in and softly shut the door behind him. It was the most menacing action Sophie had ever seen.

She rose unsteadily from the chair. "I was just looking for a document I misplaced. Unfortunately it doesn't seem to be here."

"That's too bad."

She affected a sigh. "Truly it is. I suppose I shall have to try His Grace's study next."

She moved toward the door, but he stepped in front of her, and she jolted to a halt.

"Excuse me, Mr. Fisk." She stared straight ahead at his chin, unable to raise her eyes to his.

"I don't think so, Your Grace."

For the first time, she noticed how large he was. Not as big as Garrett, but he was far wider and taller than her.

She should scream. Surely one of the servants would hear. It would arouse gossip, but if she didn't, she feared something much worse than servants gossiping belowstairs.

She opened her lips, but before any sound emerged, he slammed his hand over her mouth and twisted her body around, clapping the other burly arm across her chest.

Her screams sounded like muffled squeaks, no louder than a frightened mouse. It was hopeless—nobody would hear her.

She couldn't take a breath. His arm clamped tightly around her, constricting her lungs. His hand covered her mouth and nose.

She still held the key to the drawer. Turning it in her fist so the sharper end faced him, she gathered all the strength she possessed and plunged the key into his thigh.

He grunted in pain and released her. Gasping for air, she scurried out of reach. But he was blocking the door. And, faster than she could blink, he leaped on her. They tumbled to the carpeted floor, her head grazing the corner of an end table. The impact of him falling on her jolted through her body, leaving her breathless.

Taking advantage of her momentary daze, he scrambled atop her, pinning her arms beneath his knees. Then he dropped his forearm on her throat. "Bitch." He stared down at her with gleaming eyes. Saliva stretched between his teeth as he sneered at her. "I knew it would be you. You couldn't let well enough alone, could you?"

He was crushing her windpipe. She couldn't breathe, couldn't speak. She could only move her legs, but they flailed uselessly, unable to make contact with his body. She thumped her ankles against the carpet, staring at him in terror.

A knock sounded at the door. "Sir," called a concerned voice from the outside. "May I help you with something?"

It must be the maid Sophie had heard coming up earlier.

"Bloody. Damn. Hell," Fisk gritted out. "No thank you!" he called loudly. But he was out of breath. Surely the girl would have heard.

He looked at Sophie, his eyes gleaming with hatred. In that moment, she knew he wanted her dead. Her terror grew, clawing at her chest, strangling her, helped along by Fisk's strong arm. She choked and gasped, her eyes widening.

Sighing, Fisk reached over and grabbed the crystal lamp sitting on the end table.

Sophie saw the object flying toward her. She could do nothing to stop it. Then the splintering sound of shattering glass, and a sharp, sharp pain spreading over her skull. The smell of lamp oil drowned her senses.

And then . . . nothing.

Fisk was there to meet Garrett at the door as he returned home at dusk. He pressed a glass of brandy into his hand. "Drink up, Cal. You're going to need it."

"Why? What's wrong?" Sudden worry gripped him like a vise, so tight he could scarcely breathe. "Sophie? Miranda?"

"Drink," Fisk said.

Thirsty from his walk, Garrett tilted his head and threw back the brandy in one gulp. It tasted awful, bitter, as if the maids had left a soap residue in the glass. He shoved the glass at Fisk. "Tell me what's wrong, damn it."

"It's Her Grace. No one can find her."

He frowned. "That's impossible. Perhaps she has gone to make a call."

Fisk looked doubtful. "At this hour? It is possible, I suppose."

"Have you searched the house?"

Fisk nodded. "She's not here. Nor has she taken any of the servants. She said she'd be home when Lady Rebecca and Lady Bertrice returned, but nobody has seen her in over an hour."

"Have you questioned the staff?"

"Not yet—we only just discovered she was miss—"

But Garrett was striding away, taking the path around the house to the back flower garden. It was where he'd left her. Perhaps she was still there. But no, the garden was empty. He strode through it—perhaps she had fainted from the heat. But there was no sign of her pale skin or the cinnamon-colored fabric of the dress she'd been wearing.

He stormed into the house through the back entrance, ignoring the servants who cowered from him. Perhaps she was upstairs in the nursery with the children, and they had neglected to look for her there. She had to be here. This didn't make sense. Where would she have gone by herself?

He nearly ran headlong into Rebecca as she was coming down the stairs. She recoiled from him as if he were a poisonous snake. Goddamn it. He had to do something about his sister's reaction to him.

Or maybe not. He was destined for madness. Perhaps it was best she feared him.

Raking a frustrated hand through his hair, he gazed up at his sister, who looked ready to collapse from fright. "Have you seen Sophie?"

He tried to sound gentle, but his voice came out as a growl. God, he needed his wife. She wouldn't have left him. But she never left the house without a servant or a companion.

Maybe she *had* left him.

"No," his sister whispered.

He continued up the stairs. Rebecca pressed her body flat against the wall as he passed.

Damn it, he couldn't think. He came to the landing at the nursery and took a deep breath. *Please let her be inside.* But when he opened the door, the children were on the floor playing, and Miss Dalworthy was sitting on the rocking chair in the corner, sewing. They all stared at him.

"Forgive me," he muttered, and closed the door.

One by one, he searched the bedchambers. By the time he'd finished, his muscles felt like pudding. He could scarcely stumble down the stairs. Then he saw her, at the end of the hallway. "Oh, Sophie, thank God it's you."

"Your Grace?"

He blinked hard at the figure. It was a servant—a tall, dark chambermaid. He'd mistaken a chambermaid for Sophie?

"Sophie, where are you?" he called. Then louder, "Sophie!"

Fisk came beside him. "Perhaps we should retire to your study, Cal."

He wrenched his arm away from Fisk. "Are you mad? We must find her! Something's wrong. She wouldn't go— she wouldn't leave me."

There were people all around, all of them Sophie. No, none of them were Sophie.

Oh, hell. It was happening again. He looked down at his feet, but he couldn't feel them. "Goddamn it," he muttered. He had failed them. He'd failed everyone.

Making one last effort to claw out of the madness, he focused on Fisk's sympathetic face swimming before him. "Take me to my study, Fisk. For Christ's sake, take me somewhere so they're safe from me."

And then the darkness overtook him.

Chapter Eighteen

Her eyelids were weighted by iron. Mustering all the power she possessed, Sophie pried them open.

Where was she?

She blinked against the dim light coming in from the window, and, groaning, she rolled to her back. The action caused pain to shoot through her head, and she cried out, but the sound was low and scratchy, as if it had come from someone else.

"Praise be," murmured a soft voice. "Her Grace is awake."

Sophie squinted and saw that she lay on the narrow bed in the duchess's bedchamber. Slowly, the pale faces wavering over her came into focus. Aunt Bertrice and Mrs. Krum, the housekeeper. Both women looked exhausted.

"What happened?" Sophie managed to whisper. Her throat felt as if it was coated with glass, and then she remembered. There had been glass. Shattering everywhere, all around her.

"You were attacked." Worry flared brightly in Aunt Bertrice's blue eyes. "We are certain it was Mr. Fisk."

"How—?"

Aunt Bertrice blew out a breath. "Praise the Lord you are alive, Sophie. We've no doubt that if the chambermaid hadn't interrupted him, he would have finished the deed."

"Where is he?" Sophie struggled to sit up, but Mrs. Krum's firm hand on her shoulder held her down.

"Best stay in a reclining position if you desire to remain conscious, Your Grace."

"He's gone, my dear," Aunt Bertrice said. "Disappeared."

"Where?"

"We don't know."

"Did you call the watch?"

Aunt Bertrice shuddered. "And have the scandal spread through the country like so much horse dung? Absolutely not."

Sophie breathed a weak sigh of relief.

"Come, madam, take some of my healing broth now," Mrs. Krum said. Propping her head, Mrs. Krum offered her the cool, salty liquid, in which Sophie tasted the distinct tang of wine. The concoction scraped against her throat, and she was glad when Mrs. Krum took it away and settled her back onto the pillow.

She relaxed, closing her eyes. "Where's Tristan?"

"Tristan?" Aunt Bertrice said. "My dear, Tristan has been gone from London over a week."

"Oh, yes." Sophie wished he were here. She longed for the comfort of his arms. But . . . her heart gave an alarmed lurch in her chest. She opened her eyes. "Garrett?"

Aunt Bertrice's lips thinned. "He had another of his

attacks and was dosed with laudanum. He's still sleeping. The doctor said it will be some time before he wakes, and when he does, he might still be altered."

"Oh, no," Sophie moaned. Again she tried to rise, but feminine hands kept her pressed against the pillows.

Tristan wasn't here. Fisk had run off. Garrett was unconscious, and two old women wouldn't allow her out of bed. Clenching her teeth tightly together, she closed her eyes. She tried to remember—had Garrett come home with Fisk? Could Fisk have done something to him?

"Dr. MacAllister said he fell into the fit because he was overwrought that you were missing. You see, it was after midnight by the time we found you crammed in Mr. Fisk's closet, and by then, Garrett had fallen into a stupor and the doctor was gone. I had no desire to call him back on your behalf."

"Why is that?" Pain thrummed through Sophie's head, muddling her thoughts.

"He gave Garrett far too strong a dose, in my opinion." Aunt Bertrice gestured at the matronly housekeeper. "I'd rather depend on Mrs. Krum's excellent hand at healing."

Sophie agreed. She trusted Mrs. Krum far more than she trusted the doctor. She smiled faintly at the housekeeper. "What time is it?"

"It is nearly dawn."

"I slept all night?" She looked between the two women in dismay.

"Yes, madam," the housekeeper murmured. "It's a little before six now."

Reaching up weakly, she fingered a bandage over her eyebrow. "I was cut?"

"A shard of glass sliced through your eyebrow," said Aunt Bertrice darkly.

"It shouldn't scar too badly, madam," Mrs. Krum added. "It's a shallow cut."

"You will have a mark to match Garrett's, I imagine," Aunt Bertrice said. "I mean the smaller hairline scar, of course, not that gigantic purple knot."

Sophie struggled up again, bracing herself against the swirling dizziness. "I must see him."

Heaving a sigh, Aunt Bertrice nodded in capitulation. As Sophie hauled her heavy legs to the side of the bed, Mrs. Krum came around to support her on one side while Aunt Bertrice stood on the other. She waved them off. "I'm all right. Truly."

She rose to her feet, balancing precariously on shaking legs, noticing for the first time that they had managed to divest her of her dress, petticoats, and stays, and she was only wearing her chemise. All of her clothes had been removed to Garrett's room in the past few days, but there was a robe draped over the armchair. Gripping the chair back so she wouldn't crumple to the floor, she pulled on the robe with Mrs. Krum's help.

They left the room and Sophie shuffled down the hall to the master's bedchamber, the two older women following close behind. Garrett lay on the large, high bed unmoving, his arms spread wide as if in benediction.

"He's finally sleeping soundly," Aunt Bertrice murmured. "He's been up and down all night—one moment asleep like the dead and the next wide awake and spewing nonsense." She shuddered. "Most disconcerting."

Like an old woman, Sophie hobbled to his side, mounted the step, and sat on the edge of the mattress.

She stroked the backs of her fingers down his cheek, rough with the stubble of a new beard. His skin was pale and clammy, damp to the touch, and his breaths came in short, jerky gasps.

"What's wrong with him?" she whispered. She thought that his affliction was only in his mind, but now it seemed it had progressed to his body as well.

Mrs. Krum spoke from the other side of the bed. "I am certain it's the laudanum, Your Grace. The doctor gave him too large a dose."

Sophie frowned down at Garrett, trying to piece together her fractured sensibilities.

All of a sudden, fear pierced her chest. She looked up at Aunt Bertrice, who stood at the foot of the bed, frowning.

"Where's Becky?"

"Asleep in her room, I should imagine. She was fast asleep when I checked on her, and I decided not to wake her when we found you—it would only upset her more. And her presentation at court—"

Sophie focused on Mrs. Krum. "Go check on her please, Mrs. Krum."

"Yes, madam." The older woman left, and Sophie tucked her hand below the blanket to fold her fingers over Garrett's. Closing her eyes, she muttered a prayer.

Lord, please give him strength. Please give him the knowledge of his sanity.

She merely sat, willing her own strength and her mental capacity to return. All was quiet for a few long moments. The only sound in the room was of Garrett's labored breathing. And then Mrs. Krum burst into the room. "Oh, Your Grace. Lady Rebecca is gone!"

"What?" Aunt Bertrice gasped.

Garrett stirred but did not wake, but he drew his arms close to his body, shuddering. Sophie tucked the blankets tightly around him.

She looked up at Mrs. Krum. The housekeeper's white cap was askew, her silver-black hair hanging in limp tendrils around it. Her round face was flushed with distress.

Was she really surprised Becky was gone? Sophie wasn't. Not at all.

Mrs. Krum held up a folded sheet of stationery in a shaking hand. "This was on the counterpane, Your Grace. It's addressed to you."

Sophie bent to kiss Garrett's pale cheek, then she rose and reached for the letter.

My Dearest Sophie,

Thank you for helping me to learn what love is, for it has only confirmed what I know to be true: The love that I feel for Mr. Fisk supersedes anything I have ever felt for another living soul. My love is taking me away. We shall first fly to Scotland so we can be married, and then sail to the Continent, where we can live the grand adventure we both crave. Thank you, sweet Sophie, for helping me become wise and brave enough to make my dreams come to fruition.

And now we must go. I shall miss you, dearest sister. Please give my regards to Aunt Bertrice, and Cousin Tristan, too.

With love, your sister-in-law,
Becky

The girl hadn't bothered to mention Garrett. William Fisk had turned her completely from her brother.

Silently, Sophie handed the letter to Aunt Bertrice. She felt nothing. All emotion had been wiped from her mind. She was a perfect blank.

And perfectly rational.

Fisk wasn't so naïve as to believe nobody would eventually try to stop them, which meant he'd hire a carriage to transport himself and Becky quickly to Gretna Green, to be married and done with it before they could be caught. To travel north in the most expedient fashion, they'd take the post road. Which was what Sophie would do. She'd change horses often and forego sleep in order to either intercept them along the way or arrive at Gretna first and lie in wait. She could only hope Fisk wouldn't anticipate she'd recover from her blow so quickly and chase after them on her own. If he thought her either dead, missing, or comatose, and Garrett overdosed with laudanum, he'd probably allow himself some leeway and take occasional rest stops along the way. Still, in order for her plan to work, she must move quickly.

She focused on Mrs. Krum. "Rouse the household. I want every footman, groom, and maid to meet me in the drawing room in fifteen minutes' time. Have Cook send an early breakfast to us there."

Clutching Becky's letter to her breast, Aunt Bertrice sank weakly onto the bench at the end of the bed.

"Don't faint, Aunt Bertrice," Sophie said. "I need you."

"I won't," Aunt Bertrice whispered, but all color had drained from her face, and her hand trembled as she pressed it to her temple. "I've failed her," she whispered.

"She was my only hope, my only true chance for success. I failed with Tristan and Garrett—the only reason they are honorable gentlemen is you, Sophie. But Rebecca, I thought if I gave her the attention I failed to give the boys, she would bloom. She's so bright and lovely, had so much potential. But again, I've failed. I've failed her completely."

Sophie knelt before the older woman. "I need you to be strong, Aunt. I need you here for Garrett and the children."

Aunt Bertrice looked at Sophie with glazed eyes. Becky's letter had sanded away the sharp edges of her disposition, and Sophie had never seen her so distraught. "Why, Sophie? Where did I lead her astray?"

Sophie took the soft, wrinkled cheeks in her hands. "Listen to me. Don't blame yourself. If there is anyone to blame, it is me. Becky used my own brazen behavior as her example."

"I tried, Sophie. I tried so hard to teach her modesty and sensibility, and . . . and . . ." Aunt Bertrice's lower lip quivered.

Sophie drew her into her arms. "Oh, Aunt. We'll have her back, I promise. It's not over. Don't give up."

When Sophie pulled away, Aunt Bertrice's eyes were glassy with tears. Sophie's heart constricted—she'd never seen the older woman cry before.

"Are you going after them?" Aunt Bertrice whispered.

"I see no alternative."

Aunt Bertrice shook her head. "Mr. Fisk is dangerous, Sophie. You are no match for him."

Sophie cast a glance at Garrett, whose skin was sallow and sheened with a fine layer of sweat. In all the activity, he hadn't budged. Her heart thumped dully in her chest. If he died, it would be her fault for not impressing her concerns about Dr. MacAllister and Fisk more strongly upon anyone who might listen.

She turned back to Aunt Bertrice. "There is no one to do it for me. I don't trust the authorities to be discreet. Garrett is ill and we still haven't determined what's wrong with him. Tristan isn't here. I can't allow anyone else to go—if I do, Becky's disgrace will be exposed to the world. She'll be ruined."

Aunt Bertrice shook her head and closed her eyes in defeat. "Rebecca's already ruined, child."

Sophie squeezed the other woman's hands. "I won't believe that."

"Believe it." Aunt Bertrice sighed heavily. "It is too late for her."

"No," Sophie whispered. "I can't accept it." Not sweet, beautiful Becky, not the young, innocent girl she'd always adored. Becky might think she was happy now, but Fisk would make her suffer. He would hurt her, as he'd hurt Garrett.

She'd allowed Becks to be duped by a blackguard. It was Sophie's fault, and now only she could make things right.

"I will bring Becky home."

"And what if Mr. Fisk should decide to attempt to murder you again?"

Sophie stared at Aunt Bertrice for a long moment, then she rose and crossed the room, opening a small cabinet Tristan had brought from his visit to the Orient.

"I know how to use a gun." Kneeling, she retrieved

Garrett's pistol. Grasping it by the barrel, she heaved it up for Aunt Bertrice to see. "I'm taking this."

The old lady's eyes widened. "No, Sophie."

"I'm a good shot. Once better than both Tristan and Garrett."

"Shooting a man is different from shooting grouse. You're no longer the hoyden of Calton House."

"I know," Sophie said. "And I'm no longer a child, either. I will protect my family at all costs. If they're able to find Tristan and bring him home, you must tell him where I've gone. He'll come to my aid."

"And if Garrett wakes?"

"*When* Garrett wakes, tell him where I have gone. But promise me you won't let him out of this bed until he's well enough to do so, understand?"

Aunt Bertrice nodded in agreement, but her expression was terrified.

"There's much to be done, Aunt, and if I am to have any chance of intercepting them before they reach Scotland, I must hurry. Will you help me?"

"Yes, Sophie. Though I suspect Garrett will shoot me himself once he learns I encouraged this madness."

"I have no doubt of your ability to protect yourself against him," Sophie said dryly. Then she dropped her gaze to the gun still resting in her hands. "I'll see you in the drawing room."

As Aunt Bertrice left the room, Sophie's lady's maid arrived. "Traveling clothes, Delia. Quickly."

"Yes, ma'am."

Sophie rose and entered the wardrobe, slipping the pistol in a deep pocket of her heaviest wool cloak.

Delia was always efficient, but seemed to understand

the haste and had Sophie dressed and her hair up in a quarter of the time it normally took, even with the additional time required to use powder to mask the colorful bruises blooming across her throat. As soon as the last pin was in her hair, Sophie sent the maid to pack the necessities for the journey. She rose from the dressing table and walked into the bedroom to kiss Garrett's cold cheek. Anger swept under her skin, and the need for vengeance burned in her blood. She wouldn't let William Fisk get away with this. She couldn't.

Sophie gently placed her hand on Garrett's broad chest as he took a struggling, raspy breath. Fisk was responsible for Garrett's illness. She knew it as certainly as she knew her own role in this disaster.

Sophie wouldn't let the man harm her family and walk away with the prize. Better Becky remain a spinster in disgrace than be shackled for life to a man like William Fisk.

"I'll be back with Becky, Garrett," she whispered. Sliding her hand under the blanket, she laced her fingers with his damp ones and squeezed. "And you will be angry with me for doing such a foolhardy thing on my own."

In a way, she was glad he was unconscious. If he were awake, he'd never allow her to leave the house. Nevertheless, every bone in her body wanted to stay by his side, to nurse him through whatever had overcome him. But Miranda and Aunt Bertrice could do that. She needed to find the man who was responsible. Her eyes stinging, she left him and went to the drawing room.

A footman came in first, and Sophie sent him to fetch Dr. Adams, the learned physician Tristan trusted with all their ailments. If anyone could, he'd be the one to accurately diagnose Garrett. She sent another footman to summon Robert Jennings, the man whose address Tristan had written on his note to call on in case of an emergency. Then she gave the chambermaids and scullery maids the duty of searching Fisk's bedchamber and bringing to her anything that looked the least bit suspicious.

Sophie tasked two stable boys to leave on horseback to find Tristan and bring him home as quickly as possible. She sent a boy to fetch Connor, who was not due back at the house until noon today. Another boy ran off to fetch Tom, the burly groomsman, who was supposed to have the morning off. Miss Dalworthy was ordered to rouse the children and to send Miranda down once she'd had her breakfast.

Though it tasted like paste, Sophie diligently forced down the toast, eggs, and coffee offered to her on a tray.

Tom was the first to arrive. "Your Grace?"

"Good morning, Tom. Please ready our traveling carriage. We will be leaving London in precisely one hour. Bring . . ." She took a moment to consider, then decided on the youngest, smallest boys on staff. They were brothers, orphans of a family from Garrett's lands in the north, and she knew them well enough to know that despite their youth, they were accomplished hunters experienced with firearms. "We shall bring Pip and Sam Johnson with us. All three of you must prepare to be gone for several days. Understand?"

Unruffled, Tom bowed again. "Yes, Your Grace."

"Good. Come fetch me in one hour's time."

When Tom left, Aunt Bertrice turned to her. "You cannot leave London in the company of three men, Sophie.

Whether they're your trusted servants or not, you will have need of a companion."

"I need the men for protection and to alternate driving the team. Another body will slow our travel."

Aunt Bertrice's blue eyes turned as hard and cold as steel, reminding Sophie of Garrett at his most uncompromising. "No. I will not allow it. Enough scandal has been brought down on this family, and I won't tolerate any more. What if someone glimpses you leaving London alone? The scandal wouldn't die for years. No, Sophie. If you choose this route, then I withdraw my support."

Sophie heaved a sigh. "Very well, then, I shall take Delia. And we'll leave Sam Johnson."

By opting to leave Sam, the elder of the Johnson boys, she was essentially valuing her reputation over her safety. *Foolish*, a voice within her said. But by the look in Aunt Bertrice's eyes, she wouldn't budge. And she had the feeling that if she had refused, Bertrice would wake Garrett, and no matter how ill he was, he'd prevent her from leaving. She rubbed her fingertips over her temples. Pain still sliced through her skull, unrelenting.

A soft knock on the door heralded the entrance of Dr. Adams, a balding, reed-thin man with a polite, caring manner. Sophie and Aunt Bertrice led him to the bedchamber, and he quickly assessed Garrett, taking his pulse, feeling his skin, and checking his eyes. Garrett didn't wake—he hardly even moved, and Sophie watched in silence, chewing her lip as her heart thumped nervously. As soon as he finished taking Garrett's vital signs, Dr. Adams turned back to Sophie and said, "Your Grace, I have seen this several times before. I believe it is a clear-cut case of opium poisoning."

"Will he live?" Aunt Bertrice asked bluntly.

"Yes—I have little doubt of that. His pupils are contracted to points but they respond to light, and he appears to have a strong constitution. Though his pulse is rapid, it is quite strong."

"Is the poisoning due to the laudanum the other doctor gave?" Sophie asked.

"How much was he given, madam?"

Sophie turned to Aunt Bertrice. "Looked like nearly an ounce," the older woman said.

"Not enough for this strong a reaction, my lady, at least not for a man of his size. And you said he was dazed and lethargic prior to being given the laudanum?"

"Yes indeed, sir. First he was quite insensible and experiencing rather fantastical spectral illusions, which of course we attributed to his madness."

"His madness?"

"Yes," Sophie said. "He's experienced similar episodes, and the other doctor said his symptoms were proof he is degenerating into madness."

"You say he experienced the exact same symptoms then?"

"Nearly," said Aunt Bertrice. "This time he descended into apathy much more rapidly. And he stayed awake rather longer, though he went to sleep shortly after taking the laudanum. He's been in and out of a conscious state all night."

"And when he wakes?"

"His eyes pop open as if he's been awake all the time and just teasing us. Then he mutters nonsense and drops off to sleep equally abruptly."

"Yes, as I said, a clear-cut case." Dr. Adams frowned. "What is the name of the other doctor?"

"Dr. MacAllister," Sophie said.

Dr. Adams shook his head. "I've never heard of him. And I'm rather well connected in London's medical community, Your Grace."

"Nonetheless, the duke was convinced his diagnosis of oncoming madness was correct."

"I doubt that, madam. His symptoms are classic for opium poisoning and I'd be hard-pressed to diagnose anything else, least of all impending insanity."

Sophie closed her eyes. "Thank God."

The doctor rolled up his sleeves. "I shall require several buckets of cold water, please. And two sturdy men. I must rouse him."

Sophie raised her eyebrows. Garrett already seemed cold, so throwing cold water on him sounded rather brutal. "Is that necessary?"

"Yes. I must awaken him to assess his state of mind and level of intoxication."

"Of course, doctor. I'll send everything you require."

With the doctor looking on, she only had the opportunity to squeeze Garrett lightly on the shoulder before she left the room, nodding to Aunt Bertrice to follow her. When they were just outside the door, she murmured, "Be certain he doesn't rouse Garrett before I leave. And keep my departure from Garrett for as long as possible, whether he is lucid or not. I shall let you be the one to judge whether he is well enough to follow me."

Aunt Bertrice nodded, and Sophie led her to Fisk's room. The room was in disarray—glass still strewn across the carpet, and the neat piles of paper now scattered over the escritoire as if a strong wind had blown them askew. Some of them had fluttered to the floor. The previously locked drawer was halfway open and empty. As she quickly skimmed the remaining documents—all of which appeared legitimate—Sophie described the suspicious receipts to Aunt Bertrice and explained her theory that Fisk hadn't been paying debts as Garrett intended, but rather using Garrett's payments to fatten his own purse. Aunt Bertrice listened in silence, nodding every so often to show her understanding.

"If Tristan's friend Mr. Jennings arrives after I leave, you must tell him everything, Aunt," Sophie instructed. "He will be discreet, and I am certain he will help us. The first order of business must be to have that murderous blackguard Dr. MacAllister arrested."

"I understand, Sophie." Aunt Bertrice was still pale, but Sophie trusted she'd be all right once she had a chance to take a breath. The woman had always been strong as steel.

A gasp came from the direction of the closet, where a scullery maid was searching for evidence on hands and knees. Sophie and Aunt Bertrice hurried to see what was the matter.

The girl rose. "Oh, mum, forgive me, but I do believe I may've found something!"

"What is it?"

The girl held out her hand. Sitting on the red, callused palm was a small, stoppered bottle. Sophie took it and read the label out loud. "Pure grains of opium, of the finest and most potent quality, imported from the Orient." The bottle was empty. She looked from Aunt Bertrice's blue eyes, dilated with shock, to the girl's earth-colored ones.

"Thank you. Please continue searching. I won't be here, but bring anything you might find to Lady Bertrice."

"Yes, Your Grace."

"It was Mr. Fisk all along," Aunt Bertrice breathed. "The despicable man was poisoning Garrett." She gestured at the strewn documents. "And misleading us all."

"Yes," murmured Sophie. It explained the open decanter of brandy on the escritoire shelf—Fisk had mixed the opium with the brandy before offering it to Garrett.

Relief swept through her like sweet wine, leaving her breathless and weak-kneed. This was final proof that Garrett wasn't going mad. That he would be all right.

"Mama?"

Sophie turned to see Miranda rounding the corner from the staircase. The child's eyes widened when she saw the room's disarray. Sophie held out her hand to her daughter. "Come, Miranda. I need to speak with you about something very important."

"Yes, Mama."

When they reached the drawing room, Sophie settled on one of the palm-print sofas and patted the cushion beside her. "Come, dearest."

Miranda obeyed, but her blue eyes were wary. Though Sophie had instructed Miss Dalworthy to stay quiet about the goings-on, Sophie wasn't surprised Miranda had felt the energy pulsing through the household.

"I'll be going on a short journey." When Miranda didn't say anything, she added, "I will be gone for a few days. You will remain under Aunt Bertrice's and Miss Dalworthy's care while I am gone."

"What about Papa?" Miranda asked.

"Your papa isn't feeling well, Miranda. I wish I didn't

have to leave him, but I do. I'm glad you'll be here, though, because I know I can trust you will be beside him in my stead."

Miranda nodded gravely. "Is Papa so very ill?"

"No," Sophie said softly. "In fact, he is less sick than he believes." She reached forward and took her daughter's small hands in her own.

Big blue eyes studied her solemnly. "Will he recover?"

"Absolutely."

Miranda sighed in relief, then frowned. "Mama, is it true that Papa has gone mad?"

Sophie froze, then forced words through tight lips. "Where did you hear that, darling?"

Miranda paled, and her small hands fisted in her lap. "Oh. I promised I would not say."

"Was it Mr. Fisk?"

Tears formed in the little girl's eyes as she gazed down at the tight balls of her hands. "I—I promised."

Aunt Bertrice's sharp voice came from behind them. "Your mother's wishes supersede any and all promises you ever make, child."

Sophie asked again. "Miranda, darling, who told you your father has gone mad?"

"It *was* Mr. Fisk," Miranda said breathlessly. "He told me and Gary a few days ago when we were waiting outside for Miss Dalworthy to fetch her umbrella. He said he had a secret to tell us but we must promise never to repeat it to anyone. He said Papa was going mad and we might never see him again. But he said he'd make sure we were taken care of." She looked up at Sophie with shining eyes. "Is it true? I don't want to lose my papa. Not again."

"It is not true," Sophie said firmly. "Your papa is ill

right now, but he is perfectly sane. Mr. Fisk is a terrible man, and he lied to you, Miranda."

"Oh." Miranda's blue eyes flooded with relief. "Oh, thank goodness."

"Now, will you take care of your father for me while I am gone?"

"Yes, Mama, of course I will. But—" She broke off, frowning again.

"What is it, dearest?"

"Will I go to hell for lying to Mr. Fisk? I promised him I wouldn't tell a soul. I *promised*."

"Don't be daft," Aunt Bertrice snapped. "The Lord understands. And you see, you being honest with your mother helped you learn the truth about your papa, when you were so worried about him. Aren't you happy to know the truth?"

"Yes," Miranda said softly.

Sophie kissed her daughter's hand. "It was right and good for you to tell me, Miranda. And it was very bad for Mr. Fisk to force you to make him such a promise to begin with."

Miranda nodded. "Thank you, Mama."

"And if anyone ever accuses your father of being mad, you will defend him vigorously, do you understand?"

"Yes, Mama." Miranda straightened. "I will defend him to my very last breath."

"Good. Now give me a hug, dearest. I'll miss you."

As she drew her daughter into her arms, she saw Tom waiting at the threshold. He was ready.

It was time to go.

Chapter Nineteen

Tristan was tired. He was covered in mud, and his horse was nearly dead with exhaustion. He came to a stop in front of the Duke of Calton's Mayfair home in the late afternoon, and when nobody ran out to greet him or take his horse, tension rippled through him. He simply left the horse, who was too spent to move, and strode to the front door and opened it.

"Hullo?" he called, stepping through the entry hall.

Mrs. Krum emerged from the doorway leading to the service hall. When she saw him, a relieved smile spread across her round face. "Oh, Lord Westcliff. Thank the Lord. I knew you'd come, I just knew it."

"What is it? What's happened?"

She frowned. "You don't know? The men didn't find you?"

"What men? Where's Her Grace?"

Mrs. Krum shook her head. "Lady Bertrice is in the drawing room with Lady Miranda and Master Gary."

Tristan was already on his way, and Mrs. Krum didn't try to stop him. He called back to the housekeeper to have someone look after his horse, then he took the stairs two at a time.

"Papa!" Gary screamed when he burst through the door. The boy flew into his arms, and he knelt to gather him close, looking over his shoulder at Aunt Bertrice.

"Tristan," the old woman said, her eyes glowing. "Good Lord, you're filthy, but I'm so glad you're home."

"What the hell has happened?" he gasped.

She shook her head, looking pointedly at Miranda, who sat beside her. "Children, leave us now. Gary, I must speak with your papa. Miranda, please take him to the nursery."

"Yes, Aunt." Miranda hopped off her chair and approached them. She looked up at him with her big blue eyes. "Thank you for coming home to us, sir." Then she took Gary by the hand and tugged him away. His son seemed happy enough to follow, dancing along behind her, jabbering about how very dirty his papa was and wasn't it simply wonderful that he'd finally come home?

Home, Tristan thought. Would this place ever be home to him again?

"Sit down, Tristan," said Aunt Bertrice. "And do take off your gloves and hat. I'll order you some food."

"Where's Sophie?"

Aunt Bertrice waved her hand. "First things first, boy. Something has happened, but I don't want you back on a horse until you've had some rest. You look like something's dragged you through the pits of Hades."

Tristan yanked off his gloves. "Please tell me this doesn't have anything to do with William Fisk."

"Oh, it does," Aunt Bertrice said softly. "Unfortunately, it has everything to do with him."

Tristan stared at her, trying to control his temper. "Tell. Me," he said from between gritted teeth.

"Rebecca has eloped with Mr. Fisk. Sophie has gone after them."

What little air he'd been holding escaped from his lungs. "Alone?"

"Yes. Well, she took three servants with her."

"Where the hell is Garrett?"

"He's been very ill, Tristan. Mr. Fisk was poisoning him with opium."

"Was that why—?"

"Yes, it was the opium that caused the outburst at Lady Keene's ball."

"Good God," Tristan muttered. He pushed himself off the sideboard and looked accusingly at his aunt. "You let her go?"

"Yes," she said simply.

"Damn it!" He took several deep breaths to regain his composure. "Forgive me for cursing, Aunt, but you don't know what you've done. William Fisk is an angry man. He's dangerous."

"I know that, Tristan. Sophie knew it when she left in pursuit of them. He . . ." She licked her lips. "He assaulted her."

"What?" He stared at his aunt in disbelief.

"He tried to strangle her, and he hit her with a crystal lamp. He would have killed her, but one of the chambermaids interrupted the deed, so he merely left her unconscious in a closet. Sophie was cut and bruised, but otherwise all right."

"And she still tried to follow him?" he gasped. Foolish, suicidal woman!

"She is Rebecca's only hope, Tristan."

"God." Tristan paced the long length of the drawing room. Fools, all of them. Would Sophie really take such a risk to save something so trivial as Becky's honor?

Of course she would.

He spun to face his aunt. "When?"

"She left this morning. Just before noon."

That gave them almost a five-hour lead. But she was in a carriage and they'd be on horseback. "Where is Garrett now?"

"He's sleeping. The doctor finally determined he was past all danger and decided to let him rest."

"Does he know about any of this?"

Aunt Bertrice shook her head. "I told him Sophie was asleep. As disoriented as he has been, he didn't question it."

"Well, it's time for him to wake up and hear what has happened. His wife needs him."

As he turned to leave the room, Aunt Bertrice grabbed his sleeve. "Be gentle with him, Tristan. The opium is still affecting him."

Tristan looked down at his aunt. True concern clouded her blue gaze, and he put his hand over hers. "I will, Aunt. But we're both going after Sophie and Becky. Together."

"Good," she whispered.

Connor scratched on the door to announce that a Mr. Jennings was waiting downstairs. Aunt Bertrice told the butler to show him up.

Tristan turned to her. "What is Jennings doing here?"

"I don't rightly know," Aunt Bertrice said. "Sophie

seemed to believe he was a friend of yours and he'd help us."

"Well, she was right to call him." Tristan moved to the door to greet Jennings, his mind whirling.

The older man looked surprised to see him. "My lord! I thought you were in Leeds."

"Kenilworth, actually. I was, but I just returned moments ago. Please sit down, Jennings."

Jennings sat, and as Aunt Bertrice fussed over him and brought him tea, Tristan explained all that had happened. Jennings nodded in response, but didn't appear overly surprised.

"I've discovered the identity of 'Dr. MacAllister,' my lord. He is an actor, currently appearing in the minor role of Doctor Butts in Covent Garden's production of *Henry VIII.*"

Tristan sucked in a breath. So when Fisk had visited the theater, it was not for a tryst with an actress, but to collude with the "doctor." How much had Fisk promised to pay him for his deception?

It didn't matter. Now he would hang. "Find him," Tristan ground out. "Have him arrested."

"I will, my lord."

"Also . . ." Tristan cast a glance at Aunt Bertrice. "I believe there might be cause to question the duke's solicitor, Ansley."

"Oh, not Mr. Ansley, too," Aunt Bertrice gasped. "But he has worked for our family for so long . . ." She rubbed her temples as if willing it all away.

Tristan understood her feeling of betrayal. He'd known the man almost all his life, had worked with him, had depended on him. "I'm not certain, Aunt, but he and Fisk were speaking daily, and Ansley's no fool. By now, he should have alerted Garrett that something was amiss. The mere fact that he hasn't raises my suspicions. Furthermore, I'm not certain Fisk could have been so successful in all he has done without Ansley's help."

"I agree, my lord," Jennings said. "I will look into the matter while you are gone."

"Thank you, Jennings."

Tristan showed Jennings out and then he went back upstairs. It was time to wake the Duke of Calton.

Garrett felt as if he'd been eaten by a dragon, chewed, and spat out. He could hardly drag his eyelids upward. He saw everything in double. He squinted at the dark figure hovering over him, then growled out loud when he finally discerned who it was.

Tristan.

"Oh, do calm yourself," Aunt Bertrice snapped from behind Tristan's shoulder. "There's no time for your childish games today, boy."

"What's he doing here?" he rasped.

"I've come to help you," Tristan said.

"I don't need help." Garrett made to turn over and fall back to sleep, but a steely grip on his shoulder kept him in place.

"You must wake up, Garrett," Tristan said firmly. "And you must gather your wits."

"You're going to need them," Aunt Bertrice added.

He blinked until the wavering faces of his cousin and aunt came into focus. "Why?" he demanded in a cracking voice. "Has something happened?"

Where was Sophie? He couldn't remember seeing her

since he'd woken up to cold water being poured over his head by the strange doctor—a most barbaric, painful, and despicable prescription, but the doctor had seemed satisfied it had roused him. As soon as the servants had warmed his chilled extremities, he'd fallen back into bed surrounded by heated bricks. He wondered how much time had passed since then. He'd woken once or twice in the interim. Each time, Miranda had been by his side. The first time she'd read to him in her crisp, sparkling voice from *Gulliver's Travels* until he'd fallen asleep again, and the second time she'd held his hand and chattered on sweetly about nothing.

"Yes, something has happened." Tristan's arms encircled him and pulled him into a seated position.

Garrett's mind was a garble of confusion. But then he remembered—he'd been searching for Sophie in the rose garden . . . and then . . . God. The madness had overtaken him yet again.

He groaned in pain and covered his eyes when Tristan opened the window and sunlight invaded the room like scraping glass against the inside of his skull.

And then Aunt Bertrice explained what had happened. As she spoke, Garrett dragged his legs over the side of the bed so he sat on its edge.

Fisk. The word resonated through him with each heavy beat of his heart.

Fisk had assaulted Sophie. He'd tried to kill her. He'd eloped with Rebecca. He'd lied about his family and about the inheritance he'd said came from his uncle. He'd embezzled from Garrett. He'd eavesdropped on all of them. He'd hired an actor to diagnose Garrett with madness. He'd propagated the rumors regarding Garrett's sanity, and he'd made Garrett doubt himself, all the while poisoning him with opiates.

"No," he whispered. "Fisk is my friend. This is impossible. I cannot believe it."

"You'd best believe it, boy. Fisk has taken Becky to Scotland. Sophie is battered and bruised, with a gash on her head."

"But why would he—?"

"Revenge," Tristan said tiredly. Garrett's gaze shot to his cousin, who'd curled his tall body into one of the armchairs beside the fire and was rubbing the bridge of his nose between his fingertips.

"Why?"

"His twin brother died at Waterloo, and Fisk blames you."

"Why would he blame me for such a tragedy?" Garrett couldn't recall the events of that day, but he knew he'd have done nothing less than follow the orders that came down from the field marshal.

"He believes you placed them in danger deliberately. 'Lambs to the slaughter,' I believe were his exact words."

"God." Garrett raised his heavy arm to push his hand forcefully through his hair. "I don't remember. As much as I remember about everything else, I can't remember anything about Waterloo."

"He hates you, Garrett. He believes you deserve any unhappiness or dishonor that might come your way, so he has taken every opportunity to manipulate your life into a shambles, all the while becoming rich from his efforts and making himself appear to be the hero."

"Not to Sophie," Garrett murmured. She hadn't trusted

Fisk. Why hadn't he listened to her? He was a damn fool and a brute.

Tristan continued. "Fisk is distantly related to a baronet, and he feels entitled to the life of an aristocrat. It explains why he was stealing from you and so fervently pursuing Becky. When he realized Sophie knew of his embezzlement, he still thought he could get his filthy hands on Becky's money by marrying her. That's why he's taking her to Scotland."

All of it made strange, twisted sense. He should have seen it—he was a fool not to have done so.

"Where is Sophie?" he asked gruffly.

"She's gone after him," Tristan said, his face tight with tension.

Garrett stared at the other man, uncomprehending. "Gone after him? I don't understand."

"She took two grooms and a maid and went in pursuit of them."

"Why the hell didn't she call for help?"

"There was no time. Furthermore, she couldn't trust anyone not to spread news of Becky's disgrace all over England." Aunt Bertrice looked pointedly at both men. "The two people she depends on most were unavailable, so she's ventured on her own to make one last attempt to salvage Rebecca's reputation."

"By confronting a man who has attempted to murder us both?" Garrett asked in rising anger.

"She has no intention of confronting him," Aunt Bertrice said. "She merely intends to convince Becky to come home."

Garrett stood, forcing his protesting legs not to wobble. "I must go after them."

"No," Tristan said. "Sophie needs us both. We'll both go."

After a moment, Garrett nodded. Commanding his beleaguered body to move, he strode over to his wardrobe and opened it, yanking out the first articles of clothing he could find. Aunt Bertrice excused herself, leaving the two men alone.

Maintaining a firm grip on his relative calm, Garrett pulled his stockings up his legs. It hardly seemed real that his trusted friend was in actuality the enemy. If it were only Tristan come in to tell him everything the man had done, he'd never have believed him. But Aunt Bertrice was there, too. He had no choice but to accept all this, though a part of him insisted he was still in the depths of his madness, and that must be why nothing made sense.

"We'll change horses as often as possible," Tristan said. "I've already been riding for days, but we'll ride through the night. I imagine you and I will both collapse from exhaustion if we don't stop at some point, but we'll do the best we can. Fisk has most likely hired a post chaise and Sophie's in the traveling carriage. Knowing Sophie, she'll change teams and ride through the night. She's likely to catch them first."

"We'll try not to let that happen." Garrett's gut clenched at the thought of Fisk hurting Sophie. And it was his fault. He'd welcomed Fisk in their home, given him his trust . . .

A memory slammed into him, and he paused with his riding breeches dangling from his fingers. "I have a sensitivity to opiates."

A line appeared between Tristan's eyebrows as he frowned. "What?"

Garrett closed his eyes. The battle. His men had been on the fringes of it, unlike at Waterloo. He'd taken a blow to the arm. The skin hadn't been broken, but it had swollen, and the doctor had given him laudanum to soothe it. "At the battle of Quatre Bras, I suffered a minor injury. I was told afterward the doctor gave me laudanum for the pain. The next morning I couldn't remember any of it, but Sir Thomas said I had behaved in quite a distressing manner, throwing things and raging. By the following afternoon I was able to resume my duties."

Tristan nodded. "Fisk must've witnessed that incident. He intended to have his vengeance on you by allowing the world to watch you decline into madness."

"And in the meantime, stealing my fortune and my sister." The weight of Garrett's arms was suddenly too heavy to bear. He let his hands drop to his sides, defeated. The breeches slipped from his fingers. Christ. He was an idiot. If Fisk had indeed done all they'd accused him of, then he wouldn't hesitate to kill Sophie or Rebecca. If anything happened to Sophie or his sister, he would never forgive himself.

With renewed energy, he retrieved the breeches and yanked them on, then pulled on a shirt and a waistcoat. Then he knelt to retrieve his gun from the oriental cabinet.

"Damn it!" he spat.

"What is it?" Tristan unfolded his body from the chair and came to investigate.

Garrett looked at him over his shoulder. "She took my pistol."

A muscle twitched in Tristan's jaw. "There are more

guns in the gun cabinet," he noted. "But we must leave. Now."

"Yes." Garrett closed his eyes, and a vision of his daughter, his bright blonde little angel, swam in his mind's eye. "But first I have to say good-bye to Miranda."

Miranda looked up from her book when Garrett walked into the nursery. "Papa! You're up!"

He nodded. "Yes, I am, Miranda." He glanced at Miss Dalworthy. "I should like to be alone with my daughter for a few minutes, please."

The governess curtsied. "Of course, Your Grace." She bustled Gary out of the room, and Garrett moved to kneel across from his daughter. He took her soft little hands in his own and squeezed gently.

"I must leave you, Miranda."

"Are you going after Mama?"

He couldn't help but smile. She was too observant. He'd never imagined experiencing any emotion as strong and sweet as what he felt for this intelligent little girl.

"Yes."

"Will you come back?"

The question shot at him like a dart in the chest, and the smile slipped from his face.

He couldn't say he'd be back. He couldn't predict what might happen, but he intended to kill William Fisk if Fisk didn't get to him first. A feeling of dread had settled like a stone in his gut, and her question made it sink even deeper.

He wouldn't lie to his daughter, so he gazed into her little heart-shaped face and told her the truth. "I don't know, darling."

She sucked in a breath. "Mama loves you, too, you know."

She loves you *too*. Not just him. Not anymore. Sophie would never sacrifice that piece of her heart she'd given to Tristan. He knew that now.

"I know," he said softly.

He gathered her in his arms and held her, rocking gently for several long moments.

"I love you, Papa," she said, her voice muffled by his coat.

"I love you, darling." He kissed the top of her head. "I love you, Miranda."

Before he left to join Tristan at the stables, he stopped by his study, where he kept a miniature he'd found of his daughter in one of the desk drawers. It was a good likeness, showing the expressiveness of her eyes, the pink flush of her cheeks, her blonde curls.

He slipped the little portrait into his coat pocket. No matter what happened, she'd stay close to his heart.

Chapter Twenty

Tristan pulled up beside Garrett, who'd slowed his mount, a dull brown chestnut, to a trot. Both horses were tired, though probably not as tired as the men riding them. They'd pushed hard, driving through the night until they couldn't stay seated, then up at dawn after a few fitful hours. It was hell knowing Sophie and Becky were in danger. Tristan just wanted to eat the miles between them and spit them out. He didn't care how tired he was—he couldn't stand the thought of Sophie hurt by that bastard.

"We'll catch them tonight," Garrett murmured. Dark circles ringed his eyes, red rimmed his lids, and he slumped in the saddle. As tired as Tristan was, he knew Garrett was even more exhausted. He still battled the lingering effects of the opium, but he never complained.

Tristan nodded and glanced at the sky. The sun already dipped low, edging from behind a thick cloud cover. The people in the last village they'd passed through had said Fisk and Becky's carriage had stopped there at noon, and

Sophie's had driven through three hours after that. If Garrett and Tristan pushed hard and rode through dinner, they should arrive at the village of Brough just behind Sophie. If Fisk chose to stop there for the night, that was where this drama would play out.

"I remembered something else," Garrett said.

Tristan gazed at his cousin. His mouth was set in a flat line, his fists clenched the reins. "What's that?" Tristan asked.

Garrett slid a glance at him then stared ahead. "The battle. For the first time, I remembered what happened. I remembered—I *think* I remember—Lieutenant Fisk. My first and only encounter with him as a soldier in my regiment."

"Tell me."

"I'd suffered a cut to the head." He reached up and ran his finger over the knot on his forehead. "I'd been shot. I was down, gasping for breath. My mouth was full of dirt and blood, I think . . . God."

He reached into his jacket to pull out a flask, from which he took a long draught. Tristan remained silent, watching him. When he'd capped the flask and slid it back into his pocket, Garrett continued. "I thought I was dead. It was complete chaos—madness all around, men falling everywhere, fire. I didn't know where any of my aides had gone. Blood streamed into my eyes, and I couldn't see. But I could hear. Screaming, shouting, the clash of weapons, the guns and cannon. The sounds were deafening. I felt as if I was drowning in them. And then someone turned me over and wiped the blood out of my eyes, and I saw a wild youth, mad with bloodlust."

"Fisk," Tristan said.

"Yes." Garrett frowned. "I think so . . . yes, I'm sure it was him. He didn't look nearly as . . . *civilized* as he does now." He shook his head. "But I am certain it was Fisk."

"What happened?"

"At first, by the expression on his face, I thought he was the enemy, and he was going to put me out of my misery. But then he dropped to his knees beside me, and when I saw his red coat, I knew he was one of mine. He said, 'You've been injured, colonel.' I couldn't answer him—my tongue wouldn't work, and I could only stare up at him. He said, 'Let's get you somewhere safe.' He took me by the armpits and dragged me to this place, an underground cellar, I think it was." Garrett's brow furrowed. "I can't remember how he got me there—I imagine I was unconscious most of the way. But then I opened my eyes to find myself curled in a ball on my side on a hard dirt floor. The only light was from the door . . ."

Garrett's voice trailed off, his eyebrows drawn together as he stared at a spot in the road just ahead. But Tristan knew he wasn't seeing the road. He was seeing for the first time the scene that had been locked inside his head for eight years. "Or perhaps the light came from a window. I don't know. But Fisk, he crouched on his haunches, looking at me calmly, chewing on a blade of grass. I could still hear the sounds of the battle outside. I didn't know what he was doing—he was just watching me. Not trying to stanch my wounds. Not going for help. Just watching me, chewing and chewing. It was . . . disconcerting. I was more afraid then than when I was shot.

"When he saw me looking at him, he smiled at me. Then he said, 'I suppose I should get some help.' I tried to nod, but wasn't very successful. I was forcing myself to stay awake by sheer force of will, but he kept fading in and out of my sight. He rose to his feet, and even though Fisk isn't a large man, he seemed massive to me at that moment. I saw his bayonet. It seemed to come at me in slow motion, aimed for my head."

Garrett pulled out his flask and took another drink. "It's all I remember."

"He tried to kill you," Tristan said flatly.

"I think so. If it was him." A crease appeared between Garrett's brows. "I'm certain it was him. But why would he stay near me, risk my remembering?"

"Perhaps he believes he was a different man that day. You said yourself he looked different. Perhaps he thinks you'll never recall those moments before he tried to kill you, or perhaps he didn't intend to give you the chance." Tristan shrugged. "Who knows? The man is delusional to think he could get away with any of the things he's done to us. If he were sane he would've taken the money and run weeks ago."

Tristan's throat was dry as a desert. He reached for Garrett's flask, and Garrett passed it to him. He took a deep swallow of whiskey and handed it back. "He knew where you were after Waterloo, and when we looked for you, he didn't say a word."

"He made sure I was hidden. Probably paid Lebeck to keep me out of sight."

"Bastard."

Goddamned Fisk knew exactly where he was the entire time. While Tristan and Sophie had desperately searched for Garrett, Fisk had kept him from being found.

Garrett stared ahead, unflinching. "I have been a fool. I

let the man into my house. I placed myself and my family in danger."

"He will pay for his misdeeds," Tristan said softly.

Garrett raised a cynical eyebrow. "Do you think so?"

"Yes. Sophie, you, and I . . . we have always been fearsome to behold together. Nobody could conquer the three of us. Not your father, not the servants, not even Aunt Bertrice. One at a time, perhaps, but the three of us together? Never."

Garrett sighed—a sound of sheer, bone-deep exhaustion. "True."

"Let's go, then." Tristan gathered his reins.

Garrett raised his hand, and Tristan paused as Garrett turned to him, his eyes a cloudy, anguished blue. "I love her, you know."

Tristan nodded. "I know."

He did know. He understood exactly what it was to love the Duchess of Calton when another man loved her, too.

He urged his mount into a canter.

Her breaths shallow, Sophie slipped the key into the lock and turned it. The door clicked open, and she pushed it wider, thankful it didn't squeal on its hinges.

She'd spent a fortune to bribe the innkeeper for the key to "Mr. and Mrs. Fishman's room." She'd only succeeded because she'd told him most of the truth. That Becky was her sister-in-law and not really married to Mr. "Fishman" but on her way, without her guardian's consent, to Scotland to elope.

The innkeeper found the story highly entertaining, and when his pockets had been weighted down with enough guineas, he'd finally given her the key.

Becky and Fisk were asleep. Though she'd known they'd be sharing a bed, Sophie's heart lurched to see the truth of it. Becky was on the side closest to her, and turned toward the door, her cheeks flushed and a soft smile curling her lips. Fisk faced the far wall, and Sophie's hopes rose. It would be ideal if she could steal the girl away without having to confront Fisk at all.

Keeping the pistol firmly in her grasp, she held it behind her back as she padded to the bed. She bent down and gently shook Becky's shoulder.

Becky's eyes fluttered then opened. "Sophie?"

"Shh." Sophie glanced at Fisk, but he didn't budge. She knelt lower to whisper in Becky's ear. "Becky, dearest, come outside with me. I want to speak with you."

Becky yawned. "Why are you—?"

"Shh. I'll explain everything outside. I don't want to wake . . . him."

"Oh." Becky shifted and crawled out of bed, wrapping her arms around her naked, pale body when she stepped onto the bare wood of the floor. "Goodness, it's cold."

Sophie wasn't prone to violence, but the sight of Becky's bare form made her hand shake with the urge to point the weapon at Fisk's relaxed form and shoot him dead.

Keeping the gun carefully concealed in the folds of her skirt, Sophie turned away from Fisk and hurriedly found a robe to toss over Becky's shoulders. She slipped her hand in the younger woman's, tugging her out the door. Then she closed it, not bothering to lock it. If she took the time, it wouldn't slow Fisk down much.

She glanced down the corridor, meeting Tom's eyes at the opposite end, where he stood, ready for trouble. Poor Tom was exhausted. She'd offered to hire on someone else and leave him after forcing him to drive the team all night last night, but he'd refused to leave her. Now they were in the village of Brough, and it was nearly midnight on the second night. Pip Johnson had been asleep sitting up when they'd arrived, but she'd left him in the yard while she and Tom had gone to fetch Becky. She'd ordered him to keep the reins in his hand, with a steaming cup of dark coffee on one side of him and on the other Delia, who had orders to do whatever was necessary to keep him conscious.

"What's wrong with your head?" Becky asked, frowning at her.

"I was hit with a table lamp," Sophie said grimly. She tightened her hand over Becky's.

"Have you followed us, Sophie?" Becky extricated her hand from Sophie's and pulled the edges of her robe together, crossing her arms over her chest.

Sophie glanced back at the door to Becky and Fisk's room. Fisk could be on them in a second. If it happened, she'd be ready. So would Tom.

"Why did you follow us?" Petulance laced Becky's voice.

"I'll explain everything later."

"I should get back to William soon." Fisk's Christian name rolled off Becky's tongue meaningfully. "If he wakes and I'm not there, he'll worry."

With Tom following at a discreet distance, Sophie led Becky down the two flights of stairs to the ground floor. As soon as they began to descend the final flight, Becky paused. "There are no rooms down there."

"I thought we could talk . . . in a common room," Sophie said, thinking quickly.

Becky's eyes widened. "I can't go into a common room in this state!"

Sophie turned back to Becky. Looking up at her, two steps above, she rounded her hands over Becky's arms. "I'm taking you home."

"What? No!" Becky whispered. She wrenched away, but Sophie grasped her wrist.

"Listen to me, Becks. William Fisk is not what he seems."

"Stop it."

"I speak the truth. Fisk is an evil man. He's marrying you solely for your money—"

Outrage tightened Becky's face. "What are you saying? Are you trying to turn me against him? It's too late for that, Sophie. I'm to be his wife." She smiled and straightened, practically glowed with the truth of it. "I've had carnal relations with him. There's no turning back now."

Sophie resisted the urge to shake the girl. "Look at me," she said in a low, urgent voice. "Do you see my head? He did this to me."

Becky flicked a glance at the scabbed-over wound on Sophie's eyebrow. "I don't believe you. William wouldn't hurt a fly."

"It's true, Becky. You must believe me. He has been manipulating all of us, trying to hurt Garrett. We have all been pawns in his twisted scheme."

"You're a liar!" Becky's lips curled downward. She pulled her hands back, but Sophie held on tighter. "Let me go!"

"How do you think this happened to me? Mr. Fisk discovered that I knew he was a blackguard, and he tried to stop me. Becky, he tried to kill me."

"No." Becky's lower lip quivered. "No, no, no. You're lying."

"I'm not lying."

"Then you're mad. Just like Garrett. Both of you have gone mad!" With force Sophie didn't know she possessed, the girl wrenched away from her and sprinted back up the stairs. Sophie yanked up her skirts and pursued her at a run. Just as Becky reached the door of the room she shared with Fisk, Sophie grabbed her shoulder.

But it was too late. Becky flung open the door, and Fisk, who was standing at the window, turned toward them. Sophie dropped Becky's shoulder as if it had scalded her and buried the gun in her skirts.

"Becky. There you are." Only Fisk's flushed cheeks belied his calm. He was wearing an exquisitely embroidered red silk robe, but he looked young, and so innocent.

It struck her that she hadn't seen Tom at all in her pursuit of Becky back up the stairs. If he'd been near, surely he would have helped her. Good Lord, Fisk must've done something to him. She hadn't even heard a scuffle.

Becky ran to Fisk and clutched at the lapels of his robe. Fisk curled a possessive hand on her shoulder. He tilted his head inquisitively at Sophie, his gaze lingering on the cut on her forehead. "Your Grace. What a surprise."

The sheer blandness of his voice sent cold terror rolling down Sophie's spine. She gathered her wits and matched his neutral tone. "I've come to stop you two from this nonsense of eloping and to beg you to return to London where you can be married properly."

His eyes widened minutely. "Is that so?"

"Yes, Mr. Fisk. Becky's family loves her, and we won't stand for her to be taken from us. Not like this."

Becky burrowed her head in Fisk's shoulder. "She's accused you of things, William. Terrible, terrible things."

Fisk raised an eyebrow. "Really?"

Sophie focused on Becky. Fisk was too terrifying. She wasn't sure she could look at him and think of all the things he'd done and keep her composure. "Come home with me, Becky," she said calmly. "I beg you. You know how we all care for you."

"I can't believe you," Becky whispered. "Not after the hurtful, awful things you just said to me."

Sophie's breath froze in her throat. Despair welled in her chest. Where had they all gone so far astray with this girl?

"Becky . . . please. You will regret this, I promise you. At least give it more time, think things through first."

Why hadn't she thought to bring proof of Fisk's evil-doings? On second thought, she didn't have any. An empty opium bottle wouldn't mean anything to Becky.

Becky shook her head. "There is no need to think of anything. I already know what is in my heart."

Fisk reached up to pat Becky on the shoulder. "You look tired, my dear. Perhaps you should return to bed. We will see the duchess again in the morning, and you can say good-bye to her then."

Sophie knew Fisk wouldn't keep Becky close to her for that long. This was her last chance. "Becky," she pleaded. "Please spend the rest of the night with me in my room."

"Honestly, Sophie." The girl looked exasperated. "Are you trying to guard my virtue? You must know it's too late for that."

"Please, Becky."

"I'll see you in the morning," Becky said imperiously.

"Perhaps after some rest you will see how utterly irrationally you are behaving." She turned away in dismissal.

"No."

Slowly, Sophie raised the pistol, pointing it at Fisk. Lord knew she couldn't shoot him, not now. Becky was too close.

Becky whipped around to face her, her expression dark with annoyance. When she saw the weapon, her eyes widened. "Oh, Sophie! What are you doing?"

"I can't allow you to go with him. He's . . . he's a very dangerous man. Too dangerous."

Becky stared at the pistol, her lips parted in shock.

"He attempted to kill me," Sophie continued. "He was poisoning Garrett with opium, trying to make the world believe he's mad."

"Madam, please." Disgust infused Fisk's voice, and she narrowed her gaze at him.

"You have been trying to ruin our lives. Taking Becky for her money, stealing her inheritance—"

"Sophie, stop it!" Becky sidled behind Fisk, grasping his arm, and Sophie thought back to what Garrett had said when he'd aimed this pistol at Tristan. *The bullet in this weapon is capable of tearing a hole through three men . . .*

"He's been manipulating us from the beginning, Becky. All of us."

"Please calm yourself, Your Grace," Fisk said harshly.

"*You're* trying to manipulate *me*," Becky added in a shrill voice. "Into going home with you. I'm no innocent, Sophie. I'm not a child. I know what you're doing."

Sophie held the pistol in two hands, aiming directly at Fisk. It was heavy. She didn't know how long she could maintain this position—her arms were already starting to tremble.

"Just leave, Mr. Fisk. Go away, somewhere we won't ever have to look at you again. But Becky is ours. We won't let you take her."

Fisk flicked his gaze carelessly around the room. "We?"

"Me, Garrett, and Tristan."

"I don't see either of them here. Your Grace."

"They are indisposed." *Because of you.* "But you're the one who's mad if you believe they'll let you get away with this. I offer you a compromise. Give me Becky, and I'll let you go in peace. Garrett and Tristan won't follow you."

"And if she chooses to come with me?"

"It's no longer her choice. She's unable to think rationally."

Becky's white knuckles contrasted harshly against the blood red of Fisk's sleeve. "You've gone mad," she whispered, her blue eyes wide. "Mad, mad, mad."

"No, Becks. You must see the truth. He's been stealing from us, lying to us, poisoning your brother, hurting us all."

Fisk's eyes darkened, but he didn't break his gaze from Sophie's. "I will take care of this, Rebecca. I want you to go with Mr. Hayes. He'll keep you safe, my darling."

Sophie risked a quick glance at the door and saw a hulking shadow standing at the threshold. She recognized the man as one of the henchmen Garrett had employed to guard her door when he'd first come home.

"All right," Becky murmured.

Yes. Go. Then Sophie would have a better shot at Fisk.

Fisk sidestepped toward the door, blocking Becky's body as she exited.

"You know I wouldn't shoot her," Sophie said softly.

"Do I?" Fisk asked. "Your behavior is quite irregular, madam. I can't be certain what you might or might not do."

She hissed at him through her teeth. She kept her aim steady, but her hands shook now, and she was certain he could see the jerky movements. Could she do it? Could she shoot him?

Hayes took Becky's arm and ushered her down the corridor, and Sophie heard the soft pad of retreating footsteps and the fading sounds of her whimpering sobs.

She remembered Garrett lying unconscious in bed, pale and cold to the touch. She thought of Tom out in the passageway. Probably injured. Maybe dead. Yes. She could do it. She could shoot William Fisk. Her hand tightened over the trigger.

"Well, Your Grace," Fisk said in a low voice. "It's just you and me." Fisk glanced to the pistol, then up at her face. "You're not a murderer, duchess. You won't shoot me."

"Won't I?" Her voice came out clear, softly confident, unlike the rioting panic coursing through her veins.

He shook his head. "Of course not. What gently bred lady such as yourself would shoot a man? None that I know."

"It is obvious you don't know many," Sophie said humorlessly.

He took a small step forward, and Sophie stepped back. "Don't move."

He raised his hands in a conciliatory gesture. "Forgive me."

She couldn't do it. She had her chance. Now, right now. But she couldn't squeeze the trigger. She couldn't kill him, even though she knew he would gladly kill her. Lord, she was a coward. A fool.

A lump formed in her throat, but still she faced him, her hands vibrating as they aimed the gun at his chest.

"Don't take Becky," she whispered, and she nearly cringed. The quiet authority in her voice had taken on a pleading quality.

"Rebecca loves me." A corner of his mouth lifted. "Silly twit that she is."

"Don't take her," Sophie repeated, more strongly. "I will shoot you."

"No. You won't." He paused, and then lowered his chin as if to drill his gaze into her very soul. "Now, my pretty duchess. I need you to go away. I need you to leave me and my little bride in peace."

She shook her head sadly. It would never work. Even if she agreed, Garrett and Tristan, once they discovered everything Fisk had done, never would.

She should shoot him now. Why couldn't she? She sent up a quick prayer for strength.

"No?" Fisk *tsked*. "Now that is a pity."

"It is," she breathed.

He took another small step forward. Sophie's breath whooshed from her chest, and she stilled her trembling hands. Her muscles screamed in protest at maintaining the position. The pistol felt as if it weighed a thousand pounds.

Fisk's upper lip curled. "I just want you to know one

thing, duchess. For the past eight years, I was the one with the power to bring the Duke of Calton home. I knew exactly where he was, who he was with. I went to Belgium every year, watched him from afar, and gloated at his poverty and hopelessness." Fisk smiled faintly. "It was the most beautiful revenge I could ever hope for. It was really too bad he finally saw me and recognized me." His smile widened, and his teeth, glistening white, appeared from behind his pale, thin lips. "Don't blame yourself, Your Grace. Even if you had tried to shoot, I would've been faster."

With a flick of his wrist, he reached into a pocket of his robe and drew out a tiny silver pistol. Sophie whimpered as the barrel rose toward her chest, but she still couldn't squeeze her own trigger. Her legs collapsed beneath her as some instinct compelled her to dive to the floor.

But it was too late. The retort of the pistol shook the walls of the small room, and red, fiery pain consumed her.

The boom of a gunshot echoed through the night, startling Tristan's horse, who leaped into a gallop. Even as he tried to calm the animal, Tristan focused on the light shining from the open, second-story window above him and swung his leg over the horse's back to dismount. He left the animal to languish in the street, or run. It didn't matter. He knew Sophie was up there, and she was in danger.

Please, God. Please. Don't let her be hurt.

Garrett was on his heels as he bounded up the stairs, heedless of the wide-eyed people in their nightclothes peeking at him from behind partially opened doors.

In seconds, they reached the top of the second flight of

stairs. He spun to the right, seeing a lone open door and light spilling from a room at the end of the corridor.

"Sophie!" he shouted, sprinting for the doorway.

The loud crack of a pistol sounded from behind him, and then, almost instantly, another. Tristan flung a look back toward the stairs. Garrett had turned, and though a bullet had torn a ragged hole in his thigh and blood seeped down the sides of his buff breeches, he wasn't down. Garrett's shot had apparently gone wild, because the man who had attacked from behind was racing for him, fists upraised. Garrett threw his pistol down and lunged at him.

Tristan spun back toward the door just as a dark figure slammed into him, dragging him to the floor and knocking the gun out of his hand. The weapon skittered across the wood planks and came to rest at the opposite wall.

Tristan moved his focus from his gun, now out of arm's reach, to the man above him.

William Fisk.

His lips were bared into a snarl behind the fist aiming for Tristan's mouth. Tristan whipped his head to the side just in time, and the blow glanced off his jaw. Pain jolted through his skull.

He pounded at Fisk's sides, but didn't have the leverage to toss him off. Fisk pinned Tristan's arms beneath his legs and leveled punch after punch at his face.

Tristan bucked, trying to throw Fisk off, but the man clung to him like a parasite. And then Fisk's gleaming brown eyes caught sight of the pistol just above Tristan's head. Tristan felt the other man's muscles tense as he prepared to leap for it. The instant he began to move, Tristan jerked his arms free, grasped Fisk's shoulders, and thrust him backward. Off balance, Fisk landed hard on his backside, then scrambled to his feet. Tristan was closer to the gun now, though. He turned over and lunged for it. He grabbed it and flipped his body, raising himself on his elbows to aim at Fisk.

Just beyond Fisk, Sophie stood in the doorway holding Garrett's pistol.

God. Blood stained her white bodice and sleeve in a bright, garish wash of red. She swayed on her feet, her face pale as death.

She didn't even cast a glance at Tristan; she focused solely on Fisk. She narrowed her eyes, aiming, then the loud crack of gunfire echoed down the hall.

The recoil sent her stumbling backward, and she crumpled to the ground. Fisk dropped to his knees, red blooming on his shoulder.

Tristan didn't give a damn about Fisk.

"Sophie!" His heart beating like a drum in his ears, he scrambled through the doorway. Still holding the pistol, he gathered Sophie's still form to him, rocking her in his arms. She was warm, but there was blood everywhere, seeping onto his coat. Her chest rose and fell with light, rapid breaths.

"Sophie." Garrett sank to his knees across from Tristan, his blue eyes wild.

"Fetch a doctor," Tristan shouted to anyone, everyone. He held her closer, cupping her beautiful, warm cheek in his hands.

There was movement outside the door, but Tristan didn't bother to look. It was Fisk escaping. He just didn't give a damn.

He wouldn't give Sophie up, not to Garrett or anyone.

"Let me see her chest," Garrett said softly.

Tristan's instinct was to pull her even deeper into his embrace, but Garrett set his hand over his forearm. "Lay her down," he said gently. "We must see where the bullet hit her. We must stop the bleeding."

Trying to control his wild panic, Tristan nodded. Carefully, he returned Sophie to the floor. There was blood everywhere. He was drenched in it.

Garrett pulled a dagger from his coat. "We'll have to cut her dress off."

"I'll do it."

Garrett stared at him for a moment, then gave a short jerk of a nod and offered him the blade hilt-first.

Garrett's leg wound still oozed, and raw, red flesh showed through his torn breeches. The injury didn't seem to stop him from rattling off orders to the people surrounding them. Hot water, torn cloths, blankets. Someone to go after Fisk, to find Becky. All the activity faded to a drone as Tristan sliced Sophie's bodice down the front, exposing her pale chest. Her skin was damp and growing clammy to the touch, but he couldn't find the source of the blood.

Please, God. Please let her be all right.

"Don't die, love," he whispered. Her chest barely moved now, her breaths were so shallow. He searched more frantically for the source of the blood, tearing her gown, petticoats, and stays to her waist.

"Try her arm," Garrett said.

Tristan nodded. Her sleeve was drenched with blood. Then he saw the tear in the fabric. With shaking hands, he used the dagger to extend the opening up and down the length of her arm.

"That's it."

"Goddamn," Tristan breathed as he revealed the hole in the underside of her arm between her armpit and elbow. Red liquid spurted sluggishly from it with every beat of her heart. "She's bleeding to death."

"We'll stop it," Garrett said, his voice grim. "Hold her arm out."

Tristan carefully raised her hand, letting her sleeve fall away. Garrett wrapped a strip of cloth tightly around her arm, tying its ends together as Tristan mopped away the excess blood.

"The bullet went clean through her flesh," Garrett said. "It must've opened an artery."

Sophie took a deep, gasping breath, and her eyelids fluttered.

"That's right, love," Tristan whispered. "Breathe. Breathe deep. Don't leave me— " He glanced at Garrett, who was applying pressure to her injury. "Don't leave *us*, Sophie. We love you. Miranda and Gary love you."

He hoped some part of her could hear him, could hear the desperation in his voice, could understand.

He bent over her, pulling the jagged edges of her bodice together for modesty's sake, whispering words of love and hope into her ear. He didn't know how long he stayed there, kissing her, talking to her, giving comfort to her the only way he knew how. At one point, Garrett murmured, "I think the bleeding has stopped."

Tristan prayed she hadn't lost too much blood. "Where's the doctor?" he asked without looking up from her pallid face.

"Someone's gone to fetch 'im."

Tristan didn't acknowledge the unfamiliar voice. "Did you hear that, Soph? Doctor's on his way."

In a few more moments, the doctor arrived, and Tristan and Garrett grudgingly gave up their places at her side. Tristan stood, and Garrett stumbled up beside him, favoring his injured leg. Together, they scanned the crowd gathered round. All strangers, with concerned expressions on their faces. No sign of Fisk or the henchman. They'd probably escaped. Nobody had brought Becky, either.

Another stranger appeared at the threshold. "We've found another injured 'un out 'ere, doctor. Says 'is name's Tom," he said in a thick Yorkshire drawl.

Tristan and Garrett exchanged a glance.

"Is he breathing?"

"Aye, sir."

"Strong pulse?"

"Aye, sir. Looks like someone hit 'im over and again with a cricket bat. He's complaining loud as can be, so I'd wager he ain't too bad off."

"I'll be there in a moment." After a rapid assessment of Sophie's limp form, the doctor looked up. "Who wrapped her arm?"

Garrett placed a heavy hand on Tristan's shoulder. "We did."

The man nodded, then took her pulse a second time. "She's lost a lot of blood, but if you hadn't wrapped it as tightly as you did, she'd have bled to death. You saved her life."

"She'll live?" Garrett asked.

"She'll need several days of rest, to regain her strength. But yes, if the wound heals properly, she'll live."

Garrett gave Tristan's shoulder a squeeze.

"Thank God," Tristan said breathlessly.

Sophie's eyes fluttered. "Tristan?"

Tristan sank to his knees beside her and gathered her into his arms. "Yes, love. I'm here."

He bowed his head, blinking back tears of relief.

Chapter Twenty-one

"Good morning." Sophie smiled up at Tristan and stretched her body, pointing her toes toward the foot of the bed but keeping her left arm unmoving at her side.

They'd remained at the inn in Brough since they'd clashed with Fisk five nights ago. Her wound was healing well, but it was still sore and she tended to favor it.

She felt strong, now, though. Ready to go home.

Even though it wouldn't be with Becky. Sophie had injured Fisk, but her shaking hands had gotten the best of her, and she hadn't killed him. He'd managed to slink away while Garrett and Tristan had worked to save her, and he'd taken Becky with him.

"Good morning, love." Tristan stood over her, dressed in gray trousers and a loose shirt. The bruises on his jaw from his fight with Fisk were healing rapidly thanks to an ointment prescribed by the doctor. She reached for him, and he tangled his fingers with hers.

Lord, she loved the feel of his hands. She tugged on his fingers, drawing him to sit on the edge of the bed.

Sophie had taken to sleeping late the past few days, and Tristan came to wake her so they could spend some time alone before they joined Garrett for breakfast.

"I missed you." She looked up at him from beneath her lashes. She infused everything she meant into the inflection of her words. She missed being beside him, talking to him, knowing he'd come home to her at the end of the day. She missed touching him, kissing him. She missed his tall body curled up against hers in bed. She missed his companionship, his ready smile, his possessive, loving nature.

She missed him. All of him.

And she needed him beside her.

Looking down at her with his intense dark eyes, he stroked a knuckle over her cheek, then touched the white scar above her left eye. The wound Fisk had inflicted with the lamp had healed, but it had left her with a twin of Garrett's scar. The doctor had told her it would never completely vanish.

She took a deep breath. "Please, Tristan . . . lie beside me."

After staring at her for a long, assessing moment, he nodded. He kicked off his shoes and stretched his long body next to hers. She lay on her back, unable to roll to her side because of her arm, but still she reveled in his sheer masculine strength pressed to her side.

"How's Tom?"

Tristan smiled. "Better. His fever stayed down all night."

She breathed a deep sigh of relief. The day after the fight, Tom had developed an infection in one of his wounds, and his fever had run dangerously high. But the fever broke early in the day yesterday, and they had been optimistic. "Thank the Lord. He tried so hard to protect me."

"Yes. He is a good man."

"Why, Tristan?" She snuggled deeper against him. "Why would someone try so hard to ruin all of our lives? Hurt an innocent bystander like Tom?"

"Fisk hated Garrett. And by association, he hated everyone who was close to him."

"But surely he must've known the ruse couldn't go on forever."

Tristan shrugged. "I don't know. Perhaps he planned to run off with Becky from the beginning."

Sophie released a shallow breath. The mention of Becky still sent sharp pain slicing through her.

His fingers traveled from her cheek down to her nightgown, and a single digit rounded the lacy edge of her neckline, caressing the delicate flesh of her collarbone.

She turned her head to watch him. The single-minded intensity of his gaze sent tremors running beneath her skin.

His fingers slipped down the front of her linen nightgown, between her breasts and toward her bellybutton, a light, fluttering touch that made her think of the dichotomy of Tristan, at once the gentle lover and the hard, commanding master of her body. The easy, unassuming man everyone loved, and the determined pursuer of what he most desired.

Her.

"I've missed you, too, Soph."

Emotion rolled through her, but she couldn't get the words out. She gazed at his handsome face.

He smoothed his free hand over her hair, and the calm

expression on his face faltered. "You are so precious to me, love."

His fingers traveled over her hip and down the outside of her thigh. "When you aren't with me, I feel like a part of me is missing. When I'm beside you, I feel like I might overflow—" He shook his head ruefully. "I don't know. All these feelings well up within me. Love, affection, happiness. They fill me completely. You—you make me feel *worthwhile*."

"You are worthwhile to so many people, Tristan," she murmured. Then she looked him in the eye. "Most of all to me."

He released a long, slow breath. His fingers caught the hem of her nightgown and inched it upward.

"I want you, Sophie."

"Garrett will be expecting us soon."

She closed her eyes as his palm flattened over her thigh. His warmth traveled through her leg and poured like honey through her, settling warm and smooth in her core.

One corner of Tristan's mouth crooked upward in a smile. "He's been a bear, hasn't he?"

"He's worried about his sister. And he hates being trapped in that bed." His leg was healing, but the bullet had taken a large chunk of flesh with it, and the doctor had forbidden him from leaving the bed until he decreed otherwise. Sophie hoped, for all of their sanity, that would happen today.

Tristan squeezed her thigh gently. "Yes. He'll be up and about soon, and his temper will improve."

She relaxed completely, content beside the man she loved. *The* man she loved.

She never felt so comfortable with anyone. Not even with Garrett.

As much as she'd struggled against it in the past weeks, she'd chosen between them. The truth settled in her heart, and instead of tearing her apart as she thought it would, it healed her.

She opened her eyes, watching Tristan as she spoke. "I—I have to tell you something, Tristan."

"What is it, love?"

"Perhaps it will make you hate me. But I have to tell you. I have to know—" She broke off, unable to finish the sentence.

He met her gaze. "You can tell me anything. You know that, Soph."

Yes, but this?

"Before you left London, I had a thought. An imagining. It came from the deepest, most secret part of me."

She stared at him, knowing he would remember those nights they shared fantasies in the dark, knowing he would understand the carnal nature of her imagining. He went very still. "What was it, Soph?"

"I need to tell you, because I've never kept anything from you, and I don't want to start now. But this . . . this was wicked. I fear you will hate me."

His lips curled into a soft smile. "Nothing could make me hate you."

She took a deep breath and told him her secret, cringing inside with every word. "I imagined you and Garrett and I sharing a bed. Both of you—" She gulped in another breath. "—making love to me at the same time."

Sophie squeezed her eyes shut. Tristan was silent for a long moment. Emotion clogged her throat. They had always been honest with each other, but this—this sur-passed the bounds of acceptability.

She had finally disgusted him. Now he would reject her.

Finally, he spoke. "Is that all?"

She opened her eyes. "What?"

His dark eyebrows had drawn together, and his gaze was questioning. "There's nothing more?"

She shook her head. "No. That—that was all."

His smile returned. "God, Sophie. The way you were talking. Hell, I thought it was something terrible."

"But . . . isn't that terrible? Don't I betray you both by thinking such things?"

"It's not a betrayal, Soph. I understand you love him, too. I know you wanted him—wanted us both."

"You don't despise me for it?"

"God, no." He paused, and then he spoke softly. Sadly. "It will never happen. You know that, don't you?"

She nodded. He cupped her chin, angling her head so she faced him.

"I'd do anything for you." His smile deepened until his dimple appeared. She raised her hand, stroking a fingertip over the tiny cleft. "Anything but that."

"I would never ask such a thing of you, Tristan. It was my fantasy, not yours."

Sweet relief coursed through her. She hadn't trusted him enough. He understood the dark workings of her mind—he always had. She remembered how he'd tied her to the bed, how much she'd needed it that night, more than she'd known until it happened. Sometimes he under-stood her own desires better than she did.

A simmering heat glowed faintly in his eyes. "Our fan-tasies have coincided on so many other levels, I'm certain

I could keep you satisfied in our bed without having to enact that particular one."

She smiled. "I know you could."

Could. Not *will*. He was speaking as if he didn't really expect her to be in his bed. But she wasn't sure what he and Garrett wanted now. The three of them had been cordial to one another for the past few days. Busy recovering from their ordeal, none of them had broached the topic of the future.

All she knew was that she didn't want Tristan to leave her again. She wanted him beside her. Always.

She knew now which of the men she wanted to be with, live with, sleep with. She loved them both, but it was Tristan who understood her, who made her happy. Who completed her.

She allowed her smile to transform as his hand traveled farther up her thigh. He knew her well enough to interpret the subtle messages she gave in the tilt of her lips, and he correctly interpreted this one as acquiescence.

His touch skittered over her belly, then his palm cupped her between her legs. He stilled for a long moment, the only sound his harsh breathing in her ear. He towered over her, and she looked up at him. It was a warm day, and sunlight shone in through the curtains and splashed across his face, highlighting the planes and angles and making him look like a golden angel haloed by his shiny curling black hair.

And then there it was in full force. Tristan's wicked smile and dancing eyes. The look that made her melt from her core to her skin like a wax candle heated from the inside out.

He lowered his mouth to hers, pressing kisses to her

lips with a building strength and desperation that she returned in kind, crushing him to her with her good hand. Her blood came alive, prickling under her skin everywhere he touched, then rushing between her thighs, heating her with a need that left her unable to remain still. She squirmed against him, reaching, straining for what she knew he could give.

He was so hot, so dominating. Every touch of his lips was a command. And, eager and willing, she surrendered.

Frowning, Garrett thrust the key into the lock on Sophie's door. It was late—closer to luncheon than breakfast—and he was famished. Though Sophie was probably still dressing, he intended to prod her maid a little so they could go downstairs and fill their bellies.

The door creaked as he pushed it open.

And there it was.

Tristan and Sophie. Together. Lying on the bed, kissing as if to inhale each other. With a thousand times more need and passion than had ever occurred between himself and his wife.

They jumped apart at the sound of the opening door. Tristan rolled off her, tugging her nightgown over her thighs, and both of them stared up at him. They flushed, both faces bearing horrified expressions that he'd found them in such a state.

Emotions raged through him. First blind anger, just like that first night when he'd found Sophie tied to the bed. But that quickly faded into confusion, embarrassment, sadness. Finally . . . acceptance.

He'd been fighting against it for so hard and so long. He'd tried to force a renewal of a love that simply wasn't meant to be. They'd both changed, and all along, the truth of it had stared him in the face. They loved each other.

Garrett couldn't tear them apart. More surprising, he didn't want to, not anymore. He loved them both, and above all, he wanted to see them happy. And they'd been happy before he'd come to wreak havoc on their lives. They'd been a family.

He'd expected crippling pain, but it didn't come. Garrett realized with only a small pang of loss that he'd already let her go. He'd let her go long ago, but he'd refused to admit it to anyone, least of all himself.

Garrett bowed stiffly. "Forgive me."

In a military gesture, he swiveled around and limped out. The door clicked shut behind him.

Sophie found him at the edge of town, walking north, toward Scotland. He wore simple buckskin breeches, black hessians, and a crisp white shirt. He hadn't bothered with coat or cravat. The morning was warm and still, quiet except for the chirp and trill of songbirds, and the sky was draped overhead like a blanket of soft blue cotton. Just beyond the farmhouse they passed, carpets of late-blooming bluebells spread from either side of the road, a shade darker than the sky and drooping delicately in the increasing heat.

Garrett walked slowly but deliberately, leaning heavily on his walking stick. Sophie hurried to catch up to him, and when he heard the crunch of her feet on the gravel as she approached, he paused to wait for her.

"Garrett," she said breathlessly, drawing up beside him. She set her hand on his arm. He flinched but didn't draw away.

They resumed walking in silence. Insects droned, and

the smell of bluebells, of powder and spice and herbs, wafted around them.

Finally, Sophie found her voice. "You shouldn't be walking."

"The doctor came early. He said it would be all right to walk a little. And ride." His voice was flat; he stared straight ahead.

She squeezed his arm gently. "I'm sorry."

"I know, Sophie."

Sophie was quiet as they topped a small rise. Clusters of sheep loitered in the fields ahead, sunning themselves.

What now? she wanted to ask. But she didn't, coward that she was. It hurt her to hurt him, and it hurt her to hurt Tristan, but no matter what she did, it was inevitable. Her dream of making them both happy was an impossibility.

"I'm going to go after Fisk."

Her heart skipped a beat, but she wasn't surprised.

"I want Rebecca safe."

Aunt Bertrice would say it was too late for Becky, but Sophie agreed with Garrett. It didn't matter that she was ruined. Better ruined and with her family who loved her than staying with an evil man who would undoubtedly cause her horrible pain in the end.

"I want her safe, too."

"Once I've killed Fisk—" He broke off and took a deep breath.

"You needn't kill Fisk, Garrett. Becky should be kept safe from him. That's all."

He turned to her, his eyes as dark as the bluebells behind him. "I will kill him."

Sophie pressed her lips together and nodded.

"I was a fool to come home." Burying his walking stick into a patch of soft mud, he resumed walking.

The words were like a fist in her belly, and she stumbled to catch up to him. "No," she choked out. "No. I thank God every day that you came back to us."

He slanted a look at her, but shook his head. "I've only brought all of you pain. And suffering. Because of me, my sister is ruined, and you—you were almost killed."

"It's not your fault."

His eyebrows snapped together. "So you'll say forever, Sophie. You were never one to place blame. But I am, and I know who is responsible."

"What about Miranda?"

There was a slight falter in his next step. "What about her?"

"You've made her happy. She always thought her papa was dead, but you came back to her, and she loves you for it."

He glanced downward, and Sophie realized he carried a tiny portrait of Miranda in his free hand and was gazing at it, rubbing his thumb softly over their daughter's likeness. After a short silence, he said, "I'll miss her."

Sophie swallowed the lump that had formed in her throat. "You will come home with Becky, won't you?"

Slowly, deliberately, he shook his head and slipped the portrait into his breeches pocket. "I will bring Rebecca home, and I will settle the legal arrangements regarding our marriage, but I won't stay." He glanced at her, then back to the road. "You've made your choice."

This was the moment she'd avoided for nearly two months. She could agree, tell him she had chosen Tristan. Or she could lie.

It was time. She licked her lips and plunged forward.

"Do you remember that day when Miranda and I were sitting in the drawing room, and you told us that you missed Belgium in a way, because there was a freedom in that life?"

"Yes." His voice was wary.

"That is how I feel when I am with Tristan," she said softly. "He makes me feel free."

She closed her eyes, taking the next few steps blindly. He limped silently beside her.

She had to continue, tell him the truth. As much as she knew it would hurt him. Hurt them both.

"Yes. I have made my choice." It came out as a near moan. A great pain twisted in her chest, unbearable. Only by sheer force of will did she stay upright. "I want to be with Tristan, Garrett."

"I won't interfere."

Tears seeped from the corners of her eyes. "I still love you."

"I know."

A breeze ruffled Sophie's hair, whispering Garrett's unspoken words to her. *But not like you love Tristan.*

The tears, great glistening droplets, rolled down her cheeks and clung to her jawline, and two more slipped from her eyes.

"I don't want you to leave us."

"I must," he said stiffly.

"We—*I*—need you."

He stopped, turned, and grasped her shoulder, forcing her to face him. Reaching up, he smoothed the rough pad of his thumb over the tracks of her tears.

"No, Sophie," he said. "You don't. You proved that

while I was gone. You proved it again when I was sick from the opium."

"But M-Miranda . . . she needs you." Sophie's nose was running, and her breath came jerkily between the words.

"I will never leave my daughter. I will visit her, write to her. I want to spend time with her, watch her grow. She must always know I'm close."

Sophie closed her eyes, sending two more streams of hot liquid down her cheeks.

"First I need to catch Fisk, bring Rebecca home, work out the legal matters, regain control over my assets. I won't oppose Tristan's appeal to the dissolution of your marriage, nor will I oppose his attempt to nullify ours. Afterward—well, I might return to the Continent. I have some loose ends to tie there."

Joelle Martin, Sophie thought with a pang in her chest. One of her tears splashed to the ground, and she watched the tiny wet spot bloom in the dirt.

Dropping his walking stick, he cupped her cheeks in his big hands, nudging her face upward. She looked into his blue, blue eyes.

"I'm letting you go, Sophie. You have to let me go, too."

"I—I can't."

"You can. You know you can. You're the strongest woman I know."

"It will be too hard."

His lips, warm and soft, pressed against her forehead. "One thing I've learned from this life is that one can't always have everything."

"I don't want everything," she whispered. "Only Tristan. And you. All of my family."

"It's too much."

She slipped her arms around him, ignoring the twinge of her injury, and burrowed her face in his chest. Grief sliced through her, sharp as a dagger flaying her open. The pain was more than she could bear. It was just like the moment Sir Thomas had told her Garrett was gone.

"I love you," she sobbed. "I love you."

He stroked her hair, her back, as she wept, soaking his shirt with her tears. He comforted her, when it was she who had hurt him, she who had betrayed him.

"Listen to me, Sophie. Listen." His strong fingers forced her chin up. She looked at him through blurry, watery eyes and eyelashes clumped with her tears.

"If it had to be any other man, I'm glad you chose Tristan. He's an honorable man. Loyal. He'll move heaven and earth for you. He loves you, Sophie, and I know you'll be safe with him."

Unable to stop the flood of tears, she sank back against his solid chest, and he held her, muttering soothing nonsense into her hair. They stood that way for a long time, on the edge of the quiet road with only the bluebells to witness their painful good-bye.

When her sobs subsided into hiccups, he eased away. "I'll be leaving today. I'm certain they're already married, but I might be able to catch them before he gets her with child."

Sophie closed her eyes, feeling her shoulders slump, remembering Becky climbing naked from the bed she'd shared with Fisk. She could only pray Becky wasn't already pregnant.

"Your leg?" she whispered.

"My leg is well enough." His lips twisted. "I've suffered worse."

He withdrew a handkerchief from his pocket and dabbed at her tears. "Tristan will take you home, Sophie. Calton House is only a day's ride from here."

"The children are in London."

He nodded. "Yes. Go home to London then."

"And . . . will we hear from you?"

"Whenever I can, I will write you."

She clung to him, fisting her hands in his shirt. "Do you promise? Garrett, promise me you will keep us informed of your whereabouts. I don't think I can bear to live without knowing where you are, that you are well."

He gazed down at her. "I wouldn't do that to you again, Sophie. You, Miranda, and Tristan will know where to find me. I want to know, too, if you should need me for anything. I will come on a moment's notice. For anything."

"I know."

Garrett glanced at the sky. "Let's go back. I want to ride out before noon."

Swallowing down another sob, Sophie turned with him. Arm in arm, they made their way back into the village. From there Sophie would head south and Garrett would head north. And this time, their separation would be forever.

Chapter Twenty-two

Tristan paced the small room, pausing each time he passed the window facing the street. After Garrett had found them in bed together—again—Sophie had leaped out of bed, with no regard for her arm, and called for her maid, commanding the girl to dress her as quickly as possible. Then, scarcely casting a glance in Tristan's direction, she'd hurried out the door.

Tristan stopped at the window again, gripping the sill, staring out into the street. A few people strolled purposefully across it, and a dusty carriage rattled by, but there was no sign of Sophie or Garrett.

He retrieved his coat, strode out the door and down the stairs. With a nod to the innkeeper, he pushed the door open and was met by a warm, fragrant breeze carrying the scent of flowers. Not roses to remind him of home, but something else, something containing the essence of herbs. He stepped outside and gazed down the street.

People strolled by, dull in drab-colored nankeen and

wool. Sweat streamed down their faces. Carriages and carts rattled past, the horses breathing heavily, the mules steadfast and determined. The sun shifted in the sky, beating down on him, the air thick with the moisture of coming rain.

When they rounded the bend, he knew it was them immediately. A lightness seemed to descend upon the street. Sophie, in all her glory. Her beauty, her unconsciously elegant presence instantly overwhelmed everyone else. People took notice of Sophie—they stood aside in respect when she entered a room. Sophie herself seemed not to notice how imposing she truly was. Small but commanding, even dressed as she was in modest white muslin. He remembered her standing in all her furious glory, with blood soaking into her bodice and the pistol pointed at Fisk. Her coolness as she pulled the trigger.

She was the most powerful force he'd ever known. And she gave him everything. He never felt so blessed as when she offered him the gift of herself.

Beside her stood Garrett, tawny and big as a lion, dressed in shirtsleeves like a common laborer. Imposing in his own right. Light where she was dark. Bronze where she was pale. Ragged where she was smooth. Just looking at them was enough to entice anyone to stop whatever they were doing and simply stand and gawk.

She had her arm wrapped around him. Her head rested against his arm.

Fight for her. Don't let her go again. Tristan stepped forward, but they didn't see him. Still several yards away, they turned toward each other. And then they kissed. In full public view.

Pain speared through Tristan. He had to grab the pillar

to keep himself from lunging at Garrett. He knew they'd slept together in the weeks they'd lived as husband and wife, but seeing the tenderness of their kiss was an entirely different matter. It brought a killing rage tearing from his chest, a wholly new emotion, one he could hardly control.

Was this how Garrett had felt when he'd walked in on them making love? If so, it was a miracle they were all still alive.

He clenched the pillar as he watched them pull apart. They spoke urgently for a moment longer, their hands clasped. Tristan couldn't hear anything besides the roar in his ears. Dropping one final kiss on Garrett's cheek, Sophie hurried down the path that led behind the inn to the stables, and Garrett turned toward him.

Garrett saw him right away, but his step didn't falter. Tristan reached up to rub his brittle jaw, clenched so tight he wasn't sure he could pry it open again.

When Garrett stopped before him, Tristan stared at him, and all he could see was the sadness etched deep in his blue eyes.

Suddenly, Garrett reached out and pulled Tristan roughly into his arms. Just as quickly, he let him go and stepped back. "She went to sit by the river for a while," he said gruffly. "She has no companion. You'd best go to her."

Garrett went to the inn's door and opened it. But then he turned back, meeting Tristan's confused gaze. "She needs you, Tristan."

With that, he stepped inside, Tristan staring after him.

Moments later, he found her sitting on the bank of the river running behind the inn's stables, a ways upstream from where the stable boys were watering the horses.

When she looked up at his approach, his heart stuttered. She'd been crying. Dried tear streaks marred her pretty face.

He'd only seen her cry once before—long ago, when Sir Thomas had first told her Garrett was missing.

"Sophie?"

Her lips wobbled into a tentative smile. "Tristan."

"May I sit?" He motioned to a spot beside her on the grass.

"Of course." Her voice was ragged, like a piece of silk frayed by the angry claws of a cat.

He lowered himself beside her and turned toward the water. The crystalline current slipped over the stones in the creek bed, sparkling like millions of tiny diamonds in the sun.

"I'm not leaving," he said softly. His voice held just the slightest inflection of challenge. "Not this time, Sophie. Never again."

Her hand, curled tight in her lap, unfurled like a flower. Holding it open, she reached out for him.

"No, you're not leaving." She looked up at him, her whiskey-colored eyes welling again with tears. "Garrett is. He's riding after Fisk and Becky. And he's not coming back."

It took a moment for Tristan to assimilate what she'd said. Then he took her hand in his. "Is that what you want?"

Tears gathered on her lower lashes. "Yes." She let out a low whimper as two big drops streaked down her face. "But . . . I do love him. I still do."

He reached out and pulled her onto his lap, careful of her wounded arm. She fit perfectly against his body. He stroked her hair, her face, and he kissed her tears away. They were salty, but they held Sophie's essence, and they were beautiful. As she was.

She loved Garrett, but she loved him, too. He could accept that. He always had.

"I know, love. I know you love him," he murmured, rocking her. "I love him, too."

"I'll miss him."

"I'll miss him, too, Soph."

Her good arm twined about his waist. "But, Tristan, it's you I want. I love you. So much, I can hardly bear it. I don't want to live without you anymore."

"Does Garrett know this?"

Wisps of hair framed her face, brushing over her high cheekbones and red lips. Her lashes slanted over her eyes, arched to perfection, contrasting beautifully against her pale skin. "Yes. That was why I had to follow him. To . . . to say good-bye."

He gathered her closer. Her rounded bottom rubbed against him, and he grew hard. He stroked the outside of her arm, just beside her wound. The wound she'd risked out of love and loyalty to her family, to those she loved.

She softened against him. "I have been unfair to you. I didn't want to hurt you, but I pushed you away because I was confused and torn. I didn't want to hurt him, either. I love you both, but . . ." Her voice dwindled.

"But what, Soph?" he asked in a firm tone. He had to hear it. Just once. Just today, and then he'd never make her say it again.

"You . . . you are the other half of my soul. You fulfill me. You complete me in a way nobody else ever has.

It's you I'm meant to stand beside for the rest of my life, Tristan. Not Garrett."

Another tear slipped down her face, and he kissed it away, then swiped his tongue over his lips to taste the salty droplet.

She pushed the back of her hand over her eyes and curved her body more deeply into his. "I'm happiest with you, Tristan. It's you I want, you I need."

"I need you, too, Sophie," he murmured against the top of her head. "You are the other half of my soul, the only person who has ever made me whole."

He held her, thinking of the four of them—him, Sophie, Gary, and Miranda. A family once again. A few months ago, they'd been content together. It would be better now, because Garrett wasn't dead. His cousin was alive. Gary's namesake, Miranda's papa, Sophie's beloved. They could all rejoice in that knowledge. They would be happy again. Happier than ever.

He nuzzled her hair with his mouth, moving lower to her forehead and nibbling over her skin until his lips met hers in a sweet kiss. She was eager and wanting and utterly submissive in his arms, under his hands and mouth.

"I want to take you, right here," he murmured.

Their hands met at the hem of her dress, and they both pulled it up past her garters and over her knees. He laid her on the grass growing from the steep bank of the stream. They were well hidden from the inn and stables by trees and the outcroppings beside the water, but they could still be caught. He didn't give a damn. By the way she rucked up her dress, he knew she didn't give a damn either.

Her hands reached for the falls of his trousers, and she unbuttoned them, then pushed the waistband over his hips.

His unruly cock sprang out from its nest of black curls, and she gazed at it, licking her lips as if it was the most enticing confection she'd ever seen. He groaned softly.

Staring at him, her eyes like whiskey swirling in a glass, she propped one foot on a nearby rock. He let his gaze rake up from her green half-boot to her stockings and her garter. A bit of pale thigh showed just under her raised hem.

He slipped his hand beneath her skirts, finding the seat of her pleasure right away. He stroked her slick folds, and she threw her head back, moaning softly.

He could make her come this way. He'd done it before. But not today. He wanted to feel her orgasm while he was inside her. He wanted to feel her come apart around him. He wanted to be holding her when it happened.

He found the little nub that made her wild and stroked slick little circles around it, ramping her pleasure until a mottled flush crawled up from the white lace of the fichu tucked into her neckline.

He slid one finger inside her, then two, and she arched up off the grass, gasping. "Tristan!"

"You're so wet, love. So ready for me."

"Take me then." Her voice was a whisper. A promise.

He withdrew his fingers, and then as she opened her eyes, he threaded his hand in hers, pushing it against the springy grass of the bank. And with one powerful thrust, he was inside.

They were locked together. Two as one, and Tristan would never let her go.

She tilted her hips to meet every stroke, each one bringing him higher, sending vibrations of pleasure traveling through his body.

She let her left arm lie useless, but she ran her right arm over the dips and curves of his bunched muscles, up his cords of his neck and finally plunging into his hair. He gazed down at her to see her eyes wild with passion and intensity.

"I want you, Sophie. God, how I want you." He punctuated his words with deep thrusts, each one drawing a short gasp from her throat.

"I want *you*, Tristan," she whispered. "Please."

"What do you want?" He lowered his head, grazing his teeth along her jaw. She shuddered against him, clinging to his shoulder, pulling him tight to her.

"You. Just you."

He supported himself on one arm, and brought his hand to her breast, tightening his fingers over her bodice and running his thumb over the jeweled tip he could feel despite the several layers of fabric separating her skin from his. She strained toward him.

"I—" She gasped as he stroked over the spot again. "I need you!"

He growled low in his throat, a feral sound of possession, and his hand closed fully over her breast. "I'm never going to let you go."

She clenched him powerfully, rippling up and down his shaft, and already he felt the tightness at the base of his spine.

"I'm not going to last," he shouted out.

She whimpered. "I'm not—oh, Tristan—I'm not either."

He slipped his free hand between them, rubbing her furiously as he ground his cock into her, deep. Hot. Hard.

His restraint snapped. He yanked himself out of her,

until the head of his shaft rimmed her entrance, and then thrust in, wedged against her womb. Then he did it again, and again. Over and over, he pummeled into her until he could feel nothing but her. Taking him, accepting him, over and over. Rippling around him in spasms that sent deep pulses of pleasure coursing through his body. And she grew even tighter around him, tauter, like a bowstring quivering under a master archer's hand.

Every muscle in her body tensed, flexed to its limit. And then exploded. Her body bowed up into him as release thrummed through it, rippling through her limbs and leaving her shaking helplessly, whimpering his name over and over.

"Sophie," he murmured. "I need you, Sophie. God, I need you."

Her orgasm grabbed onto him. Clinging to each other, they shuddered and moaned together as his seed poured into her body as if each drop was dragged from his heart, through his body, and finally offered to her—a gift born of himself. Her heartbeat seemed to thud right through him, into his veins, until he couldn't separate her heartbeat from his own. They pulsed together, as one, riding the wave of bliss together.

She held on to him with her good arm as his cock continued to clench inside her and her channel rippled in the aftermath of her release.

The last pulse of his release flooded into her, and he was suddenly boneless, his arms shaking with the effort of keeping his weight from crushing her. She looked up at him, her eyes shining. She reached up and pressed her palm over his heart. "What I want," she whispered. "What I need."

He lowered himself as gently as he could beside her, and he rolled to his back in such bliss he might've dozed off. Sometime later, she shifted beside him. "He's gone," she whispered.

His eyes fluttered open, and he stared up at a puffy cloud drifting lazily across the sky. "Did you hear him at the stables?" he murmured.

Yet they were too far from the stables and too close to the river to hear much of anything besides the low drone of insects and the trickling flow of the water.

"No," she said. "I felt him go."

He reached over to stroke her cheek. There were no tears now, just her silky skin beneath his fingertips.

He rolled to his side to face her. "London?"

Turning to him, she smiled and nodded, her eyes shining with happiness and contentment. "Yes. London. Home. To the children. To our family."

"Home," he repeated. "With you."

He stared at the slope of her forehead, the tip of her nose, the shape of her chin. Her soft skin, the satin of her hair. The muss of her clothes, and the shape of her body he knew so well beneath them.

Home with Sophie. Nothing could be sweeter.

Turn the page

for a sneak peak at

A Touch of Scandal

Chapter One

An annoying heat crept into Kate's cheeks as she hurried through the narrow passageway. If only she could learn how to hide her thoughts.

Taking a deep breath, she forcibly slowed her step, squared her shoulders, and lowered her eyes. She was just a servant, finished with her duties for the day, ready to make the three-mile trek home. Not a flustered woman rushing out to a secret, secluded spot to watch a strange man—no, a *god,* more like—bathe in the nude.

Kate paused at the threshold of the front parlor. "Pardon me, my lady?"

She bobbed a curtsy as her mistress looked up from the novel she was reading. Lady Rebecca always kept her head firmly tucked in a book, and a pang of sympathy shot into Kate's heart when the younger woman's haunted blue eyes met hers.

"Yes?" Lady Rebecca lowered the thick volume to her lap.

Lady Rebecca was the sister of a duke, and her breeding showed in her expression, in her bearing, in her mannerisms. Today she wore a plain white muslin gown with a gauze fichu tucked into its rounded neckline, but neither the simplicity of her dress nor her relaxed position on the sofa diminished the evidence of her nobility. She'd kicked her shoes off and settled on the plum-colored velvet, her legs tucked beneath her. With her slender figure, her coal-black hair, and her midnight-blue eyes, Lady Rebecca was one of the most beautiful women Kate had ever laid eyes on, but there was a sweetness about her, a vulnerability, that drew Kate, that made her want to protect her, even to share secrets.

No, Kate reprimanded herself. A shiver skittered down her spine. Some secrets were best left unspoken. *Forever.*

Had the circumstances been different, she and Lady Rebecca might have been friends. But Kate was merely a servant, albeit an unconventional one, considering the fact that she slept apart from the rest of the household. Still, she'd rather have the freedom to sit beside Lady Rebecca and engage in a lively discussion about whatever it was she read with such passion.

"What is it, Kate?" Lady Rebecca gazed upon her without really seeing her, but Kate was used to it. It was how the upper orders always looked at her—as an object rather than a human. She couldn't blame them, for they didn't know any better. It infuriated Mama, though.

"Might I be dismissed, ma'am? I've prepared your bed, brought up fresh water, and set out your nightclothes for Anne." Kate's smile wobbled. The knowledge that she might see *him* again had butterfly wings tickling her insides. She fought not to squirm, but the mere thought of the handsome stranger made her skin prickle.

Lady Rebecca waved her hand. "Of course, Kate. Please do go—I know you've a distance to walk, and—" She squinted at the drab chintz curtain covering the single square window in the parlor. "—it's near dark isn't it?"

"I . . . think so." *Oh, please, Lord, let him be there today. Let me not be too late.*

"Yes, well . . ." Lady Rebecca glanced across the room at the door that led downstairs. The hope in her eyes was unmistakable. "The master should be home soon."

Yes, he should. *He'd better.* But Kate knew all too well he liked her to be gone before he arrived. Keeping her cheerful expression locked firmly in place, Kate inwardly grimaced. How could Willy leave his beautiful new wife so alone and lonely—a virtual prisoner in their home—day in and day out?

Lady Rebecca turned back to Kate. "Of course you may go."

"Thank you, ma'am. I'll be here when you wake in the morning." Kate dipped into another curtsy and tried not to break into a run as she crossed the room to the opposite door. Even so, the clack of her shoe heels on the wood floor announced her hasty departure, and from the corner of her eye, she saw Lady Rebecca's brow tilt in bemusement as she watched her go.

The cottage was elegant and expensive, but tiny, and certainly neither as elegant nor as expensive as a duke's sister was accustomed to. Willy employed only four servants—Kate, the cook, the maid-of-all-work, and the manservant, John. The other female servants lived in the small room in the attic and John slept in a loft above the stable, but Kate walked back and forth to Debussey Manor daily.

All in all, it was surely far less help than someone of Lady Rebecca's breeding expected. Yet although she was a very young, privileged woman, she never complained. Kate admired her for that.

Her cheeks still flaming despite all her efforts to douse the fire in them, Kate descended the last step and emerged into the drawing room. Glancing up, she stopped in her tracks, stiffening. John lay on the tasseled chaise longue, his stockinged feet crossed atop the cream-colored silk and his arm flung over his forehead.

He cracked one lid open to gaze at her with a pale green eye, and Kate pursed her lips in distaste.

"Leaving?" he asked.

"Yes," she answered curtly. Untying her apron, she spun round and strode to the closet behind the stairwell containing her cloak, though she doubted she'd need it. It had been a hot day. Feeling John's eye on her, she pulled off her apron, hung it on its peg, and decided to leave her cloak here overnight. It wouldn't be too cold to walk without it in the morning, and it would be a nuisance to carry both ways.

"You look pretty today, Kitty. That color becomes you."

She cast a look down at her dull, pale brown work dress. How pleasant to know that brown was her color. "Thank you," she replied.

He chuckled but Kate didn't look in his direction. John was negligent, arrogant, lazy, and, with his greased hair and pointed beak nose, unappealing. Whenever Willy was near, John's manner was obsequious to the point of inducing nausea, but when Willy wasn't home, he strutted about the place as if he owned it, even going so far as to be disrespectful to Lady Rebecca. Nothing raised Kate's ire more than to see that man's disdainful attitude toward her mistress.

She turned from the closet and strode to the front door. Opening it, she stepped into the pleasant late-summer evening. As she closed the door, John's voice drifted lazily out. "Tomorrow, then, pretty Kitty."

Her lips twisted, and when the door met its frame, she shoved it hard. The tiny slam brought her a small measure of satisfaction.

If John thought to seduce her with lies, he ought to think again. No man had seduced her yet, though a few had tried, and one had come close. Nevertheless, she'd promised herself long ago to never go down that particular perilous road. And with a man like John . . . not a chance.

Still, it was best to stay away from him and make certain to avoid being alone with him. He didn't strike her as the kind of man who'd take her rejection to heart.

Kate paused on the tiny landing and took a deep breath. Was she a hypocrite? She shook her head, thinking not. *Watching* was a wholly different animal than *doing*, after all. And John the skinny, lazy butler was a wholly different creature from the bronze god at the pool.

Kenilworth's gently curving High Street was deserted for the moment. The setting sun cast a hazy orange glow across the rooftops, and the houses and shops abutting the road shimmered in the haze.

She turned and strode down the street with purpose, her shoes scraping against the hard-packed dirt. Ahead, a woman dressed in black with a dark shawl draped over her shoulders emerged from the front door of one of the pretty neighboring cottages. Kate bobbed and murmured a polite greeting as they passed each other. The woman smiled and wished her a good evening as the clatter of wheels and the sound of hooves heralded a coach and four coming from behind. Kate glanced over her shoulder to see the carriage, a closed, lacquered black beast, approaching, tossing up a billow of dirt in its wake.

She picked up her skirts and hurried across the street in front of it, slipping through a broken slat in the old wooden gate onto a narrow path on the field beyond just in time to avoid a choking spray of dust.

Through the trees just beginning to turn gold in preparation for autumn loomed the tall, jagged, ivy-covered ruins of Kenilworth castle. Keeping the castle to her right, Kate followed the overgrown trail that led along the bank of the brook. She skirted fallen branches and dead leaves, and before long grime caked her shoes and dampness seeped through her stockings.

Her heart thudded in a dull cadence, heavy in her chest. Excitement flushed her skin under the coarse wool of her dress. Would he be there today? He wasn't yesterday, but she'd seen him twice in the past week, swimming in the small lake created by the ruin of a dam that had once formed the castle moat.

The air grew warmer and close. Branches cracked under her feet, and leaves rustled. The faint drone of insects hummed in the air as twilight approached. She'd taken the long way, and it'd be full dark by the time she arrived home, but she cared about that just about as much as she cared about her wet feet and mud-soaked hem. Not a whit.

She slowed as the creek turned northward, and with her lower lip trapped between her teeth, she focused on placing her footfalls so her steps would be quiet.

A splash sounded in the distance, and Kate halted and looked up. Beyond a thick copse of greenery just ahead, the pool glimmered in the gathering dusk, its surface rippling.

Someone had just dived in. *He* had just dived in.

Kate swallowed hard and crept forward, crouching so he wouldn't see her behind the cluster of brambles and bushes.

She ducked behind a particularly dense bush at the water's edge and peeked around it.

Just as the waves on the pool's surface began to settle, he emerged from the depths with his back to her. He rose until the water lapped eagerly at his narrow waist. For the tiniest fraction of a second, she wished she could be that water.

His thick shoulder rippled with muscle as he reached up to thrust a hand through glistening blond hair.

Surely this man couldn't be human. He was perfectly built—like one of the gods she'd learned about when she spied on Mama reading to her brothers. Tall, muscular, his skin bronzed from the sun, as hard and beautiful and intimidating as Apollo himself. He shook his head, sending blond shoulder-length curls flying and a cascade of golden drops showering into the water. Then he dove again, his taut—and quite shockingly bare—backside emerging from the water before his entire body disappeared beneath the surface.

The god-man swam like a fish. Perhaps he wasn't Apollo at all, though he rather looked like she'd always imagined Apollo. Perhaps he was Poseidon—a young, clean-shaven Poseidon. Perhaps this time when he emerged, he'd be carrying his golden trident. She held her breath, waiting, frozen.

Kate had been born at Kenilworth and raised at

Debussey Manor, and she knew without a doubt this man didn't hail from these parts. What was he doing here? And why did he come here—this place that had been her secret spot for so many years—to bathe? The sight of him, and his very strong, very *naked* body, was so far removed from her realm of reality that it didn't seem all too far-fetched to think that a lightning bolt had deposited him straight from Olympus.

He rose from the water again, this time farther away but facing her. She stared in fascination at the jagged scar near his waist, and when her gaze traveled up his solid torso and over his rugged face, she saw the second scar, a terrible knot glaring red just above his left eyebrow.

The scars, the imperfections on his otherwise perfect form, shot home the fact that this was not a god, but a very human man indeed. A man who'd seen, experienced, and ultimately survived terrible things.

He rubbed the water out of his eyes and opened them. The sky blue orbs settled directly on her.

She jerked her head behind the bush, gulping back a gasp. Her heart thumped in her ears. A bead of sweat trickled down the side of her face. Controlling her breaths, she froze in her crouched position and squeezed her eyes shut. She couldn't move, because now he'd surely hear her. Her best option was to remain quiet, hidden behind the bush, and pray he hadn't seen her.

She should fear this giant, intimidating man, but that wasn't why she prayed he hadn't seen her. No, she prayed he hadn't seen her because if he had, she wouldn't be able to watch his sculpted nude body anymore.

She let out a long, silent sigh through pursed lips. It was the undeniable truth. As much as she'd fought against it, she was hopelessly and thoroughly debauched. If not in body, at least in thought. The man could be a murderer or a lunatic, and all she cared about was spying on him naked.

Not only was she debauched, she was an idiot.

Perhaps he hadn't seen her. He had just opened his eyes after being submerged in water, and surely it would take a second or two for him to focus on something as far away as her. And with her brown hair and brown dress, she blended into the landscape like a chameleon.

She'd stay hidden for a few moments, then make a hasty, as-quiet-as-possible retreat.

Keeping her eyes closed, she hugged her knees to her chest and counted to a hundred. All was silent for a while, but when she reached sixty, splashing resumed from the direction of the pond. Clearly he'd resumed his sport.

Ninety-nine. One hundred.

She released a relieved breath and raised her lids.

Impossibly, the man, now dressed in a loose white shirt and leather breeches, sat on his haunches an arm's length away. She blinked several times in disbelief, trying to clear her vision as he gazed at her with narrowed blue eyes, a frown creasing his handsome face. Rivulets of water streamed from his golden hair and plastered his shirt to his broad, imposing shoulders.

He'd been watching her. Spying on her in silence— probably throwing pebbles into the water to mislead her.

With a squeal of fright, Kate stumbled to her feet. Her legs caught in her skirts, but she kicked them free. Brambles clawed at her dress, ripping the fabric as she lunged away.

She'd gone no farther than two steps when he clapped an arm around her waist and yanked her back. She stumbled and would have fallen had his hard body not ensnared her like a net.

Kate trembled all over. Small, pathetic whimpers bubbled from her throat as she futilely tried to twist away.

His warm, damp torso pressed against her back. He smelled fresh and clean, like hay drying in the sunlight, with some underlying male musk she instinctually recognized as purely his. His arm crossed over the front of her chest, pinning her against him. The lock of his embrace rendered her utterly helpless.

"Who are you?" he demanded. He bent his head, and the trace of beard on his jaw scraped against the shell of her ear. "And why were you watching me?"

His voice, low and rough, stroked over her body like a coarse towel, causing every inch of Kate's skin to explode into flame.

Panic wouldn't help her now. She must stave it off, be as brave as a knight battling a rampaging dragon. For several moments, trapped in the steel of the stranger's arms, she worked to control her gasping breaths and to stop her limbs from shaking like autumn leaves in a gale.

When she finally had reined in her foolish feminine impulses, she sucked in a lungful of air. Staring straight over the pool, now glowing purple in the twilight, she said, "My name is Katherine, sir. I'm very glad to meet you. Lovely evening, isn't it?"

THE DISH

Where authors give you the inside scoop!

♥ ♥ ♥ ♥ ♥ ♥ ♥ ♥ ♥ ♥ ♥ ♥ ♥ ♥ ♥

From the desk of Jennifer Haymore

Dear Reader,

When Sophie, the heroine of A HINT OF WICKED (on sale now), first came to me describing her problem— that she happened to be married to two men at once, both of whom she loved unconditionally—I rubbed my hands together in glee. What a juicy, wicked dilemma! Yes, of course, I told her, I would be thrilled beyond measure to pen this tale.

"But how on earth will you resolve my problem?" she asked me.

"Easy," said I, proud of my fantabulous solution, and doubly proud of how quickly it had come to me. "You love them both, right?"

"Tremendously!" she declared, nodding vigorously.

"Then you'll live happily ever after with *both* your husbands," I decreed, leaning back in my chair and awaiting her exuberant and everlasting thanks.

Thus ensued a long, uncomfortable silence. Finally, Sophie looked up at me with somber, golden-brown eyes. "Forgive me, but that won't work. Neither of my husbands will accept such a solution."

"Huh. Are you saying they're the possessive caveman type?"

"Exactly." She leaned forward a bit and lowered her

voice so that no one outside my office could hear her. "In fact, I'm certain if either one saw me so much as touch the other, murder might ensue. It's already come close to that. Thank heavens nobody has been shot." She gave me a significant look. "Yet."

"Hmmm," I said. "I could work on them . . ."

Sophie broke me off in mid-thought. "You could 'work on them' for eternity, but you see, there is another problem. One that might negate any possibility of future happiness for all three of us: I am a duchess. In England. In 1823."

"Ah. I see," I said. But alas, I didn't, not really. I figured, okay, if Sophie doesn't want both her husbands, I'll pick one, and we'll go with that. Cocky writer that I am, I thought maybe I could flip a coin. *Ha!*

Soon afterward, Sophie took me on her journey, and . . . *oh my!* It wasn't easy. Given two powerful, honorable, drop-dead gorgeous men, Sophie had to choose the one she wanted to stand beside for the rest of her days. Moreover, in doing so, she had to break the heart of the other man—a man she also still loved.

And I won't even begin to get into the quagmire of 1823 marriage laws! To work everything out without turning Sophie into a criminal, making her child illegitimate, or having her become a pariah or the laughing-stock of society? Just about impossible!

Eventually, though, Sophie found her way. By the time I finished writing, I was so glad she let me be the one to share her tale with the world.

I truly hope you enjoy reading Sophie's story. Please feel free to stop by my Web site, www.jenniferhaymore.com, where you can share your thoughts about the book, learn some bizarre and fascinating historical facts, and read more about the person who has most recently barged into my office demanding I write *his* story . . .

Sincerely,

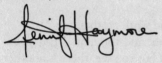

♥ ♥ ♥ ♥ ♥ ♥ ♥ ♥ ♥ ♥ ♥ ♥ ♥ ♥ ♥ ♥

From the desk of Carolyn Jewel

Dear Reader,

People. Really. I tried to warn you with my first book, MY WICKED ENEMY, but I don't think you were paying attention. I'll try again with MY FORBIDDEN DESIRE, my second book (on sale now!). Will you all finally listen up? I certainly hope so. The world is a dangerous place, and not just in the obvious ways. True statement: Things around you aren't always what they seem. Same for people, too. Yeah, I know what you're thinking. How obvious can you get, Carolyn? But really, take a long, hard look at your boss. Is she (or he) really human? How do you know for sure?

Our capacity to deceive others is far exceeded by our capacity to deceive ourselves. Keep that in mind (but not before bed, wouldn't want to keep you up!).

Suppose, for the sake of argument, there really are monsters among us.

Not the human kind—I think, without further discussion, we can all agree *they* exist. I'm talking about something else. What if there really are creatures like demons or, oh, say, fiends? And "people" who can do magic. Why the quotes, you ask? Well, they wouldn't be regular folks like you and me, now would they?

Who would they be? Mages and witches, of course. They rose to prominence in the Dark Ages when they were busy protecting us from demons and the like. Demons, including fiends, were looking for a bigger place in the world then. But thanks to the mages, that didn't work so well. (Thank you, mages!) Over the years, though, some mages went from being the good guys to the not-so-good guys, and now the demons are fighting for their lives. They're sick and tired of being murdered and enslaved.

That's the backdrop of my books: an all-out war between demons and fiends and mages and witches. But what if we take that one step further? What if a demon or a fiend fell in love with a witch or a mage? And now we've got my latest book, MY FORBIDDEN DESIRE.

Xia is a fiend. Alexandrine Marit is a witch. He hates witches for some very, very good reasons. Alexandrine isn't sure demons exist and, well, as witches go, she's not much of one . . . until she gets her hands on a talisman. Now Xia has to protect her from some very nasty people. And Alexandrine's view of the world pretty much explodes. What happens after that? You'll have to read it to find out.

Enjoy!

Carolyn Jewel

♥ ▪ ▪ ▪ ♥   ♥ ♥

From the desk of Robin Wells

Dear Reader,

Have you ever been in one of those slumps when everything in your life is going wrong? Well, the heroine of my
latest romantic comedy, HOW TO SCORE (on sale
now), is in just such a situation, and she decides to hire a
telephone life coach to help her straighten things out.
Only problem is, the man Sammi is baring her soul to
isn't a life coach at all; he's an FBI agent filling in for his
brother—and the man Sammi is falling for.

The idea for this book came to me while writing
BETWEEN THE SHEETS. The heroine of that story,
Emma, needed to change her image after being involved in
a terrible scandal, and I originally intended to have her
hire a life coach to help her. Emma had other ideas, however, and the story went in another direction.

The concept of writing a book about a life coach continued to simmer in my subconscious. The topic intrigued
me, probably because I'm a sucker for self-improvement
plans. I devour magazine articles with titles such as *"Organize Your House; Look like Angelina Jolie; Behave like
Mother Theresa; Become the Perfect Parent; Stay Serene as a
Monk; Clear Up Your Skin;* and *Scorch Your Sheets in Seven
Easy Steps."* (The advice never works, but hope springs
eternal.)

What kind of woman, I wondered, would go beyond
self-help books and actually hire a life coach? Probably a
woman with problems on all fronts—problems with her

job, problems with her living arrangements, problems with her family, and, most important, problems with her love life. Or lack there of. The wheels started spinning in my mind. Maybe my heroine's romantic problem could be of her own making. Maybe she had a painful secret that made her inadvertently drive away potential partners. The wheels started spinning faster. Yes! I was onto something!

I then turned my attention to the hero. What kind of man would make the most interesting life coach? Hmmm. He had to be tall, dark, and sexy as sin—that was a given. What if he wasn't a life coach at all? What if he was a highly structured pragmatist who thought everything could and should be solved through logic, careful planning, hard work, and self-discipline—the kind of man who thinks he has all the answers, who believes that if people would just follow his advice, their problems would all be solved? (My husband wants me to point out here that I, personally, have never known, much less married, a man like that.)

What if the hero also had a painful past that made him crave order, organization, and control? (Anyone who has seen my husband's sock drawer will know beyond a doubt that I really, truly did not base this hero on him.)

Once the characters came to life, the story took off. I set the book in Tulsa because I used to live in Oklahoma and know that the city is renowned for its art deco architecture. The museum, neighborhood, and restaurants in my book are fictional, but the issues facing "recent history" preservationists in Tulsa and other cities are all too real.

The secondary romance between the two older characters in the book came as a surprise to me; I originally planned for Sammi's blue-haired artist sister, Chloe, to have a love interest. Instead, Sammi's landlord and boss fell in love as they helped each other deal with past regrets, find self-forgiveness, and learn that it's never too late for new beginnings.

I hope you enjoy reading HOW TO SCORE as much as I enjoyed writing it. I invite you to drop by my Web site, www.robinwells.com, to share your thoughts, read an excerpt from my next novel, or just say hi!

All my best,

Robin Wells